Rush

Tori Minard

Rush

Copyright 2013 © Tori Minard

Cover art by Tori Minard from photo by © Efe Can Altuncu

Enchanted Lyre Books

Chapter 1

Caroline: This party wasn't exactly foreign territory, but I felt a little like an alien anyway. Someone like me, someone who doesn't drink, well, we sometimes feel out of place at frat parties, especially when they're crowded wall to wall with people we mostly don't know.

I hesitated in the doorway of the cramped apartment, although my boyfriend, Trent, was already shouldering his way into the room. The hosts were buddies of his, frat brothers, and you'd think I would know most of their guests, but I didn't. They were a cold sea of indifferent faces...indifferent to me, at least.

The noise level almost deafened me. Music blared from someone's iPod, and everyone in the room seemed to be talking at once. A thick haze of cigarette smoke hung in the air. I tugged on Trent's sleeve, causing him to pause and look down at me.

"It's too crowded!" I yelled above the din. "There's no room for us!"

He grinned down at me. "Sure there is."

I looked around uneasily, hating that he'd sprung this thing on me at the last minute. When he'd picked me up at my dorm, I'd still thought we were going out to dinner. If I'd known we were going to a party, I would have dressed for it. I would have done something with my impossible hair.

The room was filled with perfectly fashionable, trendy girls who reminded me of my sorority sisters. All of them were dressed in the latest styles, except the ones wearing sexy Halloween costumes bought at the local discount store. Honestly, I sometimes wondered how I'd managed to be accepted by a sorority in the first place. I wasn't skinny, I hated wearing heels and revealing clothes, and my super-curly hair refused, absolutely refused, to submit to flat-ironing. I was hopeless in the looks department.

"We won't be here long," Trent yelled. "I just have to pick up something from Talbot."

His friend Greg Talbot was one of the party hosts. I got up on my tiptoes and craned my neck, looking for him, but saw no sign of him.

"Maybe the kitchen," Trent said, leading me deeper into the apartment.

Girls gave him openly admiring glances as we passed. He had that all-American look, blond and blue-eyed with a great body, and girls were always eyeing him. I couldn't make up my mind whether I was proud of him for being so hot or jealous over the way other women threw themselves at him. Right now, I was going with jealous.

Still, I contained my urge to glare at each girl in the room. We reached the kitchen, which was just as crowded as the living room. A guy I didn't know stood by the fridge, passing out canned beer and red plastic cups of some kind of mixed drink. A girl with wide blond streaks in her perfectly straight brown hair leaned against the worn laminate counter. I smiled hesitantly at her, but her gaze drifted across my face and past me without an instant's hesitation, as if I were invisible.

All righty, then. Guess we weren't going to be BFFs. I looked around for Talbot, hoping we could find him and get out of here ASAP.

"I'm going to try the bedrooms," Trent said in my ear.

He hauled me out of the kitchen and into a tiny side hall that had three doors leading off it. The first door stood open, revealing the bathroom. Trent entered the second room without knocking.

I flinched. Jeez, you never knew what people were doing in the bedrooms at parties like this, and he just walks in? We could be interrupting something really personal.

Smoke hung in the air here, too. Illegal smoke. Four guys sat on the stained Berber carpet at the foot of a queen-size bed, passing around a bong. I'd only smelled pot smoke a few times before, but I'd never forget that unique odor, and I recognized it now.

Two of the guys were people I recognized but didn't know well. One was Talbot, his dishwater blond hair perfectly styled as always. The fourth, a black-haired guy with a vaguely bohemian look, I'd never seen before.

Trent barged into the room and stopped cold, staring at the group on the floor. "Max. What the fuck are you doing here?"

The fourth guy, the one I'd never seen before, looked up with an unsurprised expression on his face. "Smoking weed. What does it look like?"

"What are you doing at Central Willamette?"

Max smiled lazily. "Same thing all the other students are doing. Why? You have a problem with me being here?"

Trent's grasp on my hand tightened so much it started to hurt. "You don't belong here. You need to leave."

"Trent!" I tugged on his hand. He was being an ass, an incredibly rude ass.

He ignored me. "I don't know what you're up to, but you'd better get the hell out of this town."

Max's black brows rose mockingly. "I didn't know you owned it." His gaze slid to me and then down my body in a leisurely examination. "Who's the girl?"

"This is my *girlfriend,* Caroline."

"Ah. Girlfriend. Guess I'm behind on the family gossip."

Family? This guy was part of Trent's family? I glanced, baffled, at my boyfriend's angry profile. Who was Max, anyway, and how was he related to Trent? I'd never heard a word about him, even though Trent and I'd been dating nine months already. A year if you counted summer vacay.

"There's a reason for that," Trent said.

"Aren't you going to introduce me?" Max continued to stare at me.

"No."

"Trent, don't be rude." I stepped forward, holding out my free hand. "I'm Caroline Winters."

"Max Kincaid." His hand clasped mine, his skin warm and slightly callused.

A strange jolt of energy seemed to travel from his flesh into mine. I stifled a gasp and pulled my hand back to rub it surreptitiously on my jeans.

"I'm Trent's stepbrother," Max said.

I fixed Trent with a glower. "You have a stepbrother you never told me about?"

"It's okay." Max gave me that lazy smile. "I'm the dirty family secret."

Trent turned pointedly away from his stepbrother. "Talbot, you got that thing for me?"

"Yeah, just a sec." Talbot set the bong on the carpet and got up.

Max picked up the bong and took a long hit, holding his breath and then blowing the smoke out in a slow stream. He held the bong up in my direction. "Caro, you want a hit?"

No-one ever called me Caro. And I didn't do drugs, or even smoke tobacco. "Uh...no, thanks."

"She doesn't do drugs, asshole," Trent growled.

Max shrugged and passed the bong to the next guy. "Whatever, bro."

"You knew I was going here. You had to know. So why are you really here? What do you want?"

Max laughed. "I want to take some classes. Believe it or not, I don't make all my decisions with you in mind."

The other guys in the room were starting to look uncomfortable at the thick tension. Talbot rummaged around in a dresser drawer and pulled out a sheet of paper, which he gave to Trent. "It's due on Friday."

"Cool, man. I'll have it to you Thursday morning."

I sighed. He was doing papers for other students again, taking money for it no doubt, even though he didn't need the cash. I'd asked him to stop, and he'd said he would.

Max was still giving me the eye. He caught my gaze and smiled, his eyes going sort of half-lidded and sleepy. Damn, he was beautiful. He had an angular jaw scruffy with dark stubble, straight nose, high cheekbones and long, wavy black hair that fell in his eyes. Spectacular eyes, in some dark color I couldn't make out in the dimly lit bedroom but large and beautifully shaped, clearly framed by heavy black lashes.

I shouldn't be staring at him. I was taken and truly happy with my boyfriend. So why couldn't I stop looking at Max?

He wore some kind of beaded necklace with a silver pendant on it that just peeked out of the neckline of his charcoal button shirt. I couldn't see the design of the pendant, just that it was silver. There were a couple of slender leather cords wrapped around his right wrist. Trent would never wear that kind of jewelry—I mean, beads?—or let his hair get that long. It was weird, to be honest, and normally I wouldn't be attracted to a guy who dressed the way Max did. I forced myself to look at something else. Anything.

Trent pointed at Max. "You need to get out of this town."

"Ain't gonna happen."

"Listen here, you—"

I took a deep breath and opened my mouth to tell Trent to cool it. Unfortunately, that breath was laden with pot smoke and I started coughing uncontrollably.

"C'mon, let's get out of here." Trent took me by the elbow and hustled me out of the room.

"Bye, Caro," Max said.

I gave him a half-hearted wave as Trent dragged me through the doorway and into the micro-hall.

The party was even more crowded now, something I wouldn't have thought physically possible. People stood shoulder to shoulder, many of them not talking to each other, just staring into space as they sipped from their plastic cups. Was this really supposed to be fun? I didn't get it.

Talbot's apartment let directly onto a covered outdoor hallway. Outside, the air smelled sweet and clean. I took another deep breath to rid myself of the lingering smoke in my lungs. It was a cool October evening, but I could feel a greater chill in the air that heralded the coming winter. It had been a dry fall, but soon the rain would begin. It rained a lot in Western Oregon winters.

"You said you weren't going to do papers anymore," I said as we walked side by side down the stairs to the ground level of the apartment complex. We didn't hold hands or put our arms around each other's waists. Trent didn't like public touching.

"I know," he said. "But Talbot begged me. He's really worried about this one."

"It's not even the middle of the term. Is he going to come running to you every time he has an assignment?"

Trent looked annoyed. "I don't know."

He was helping people cheat, and I couldn't understand why he'd do that. But I didn't want to argue with him about it tonight. We'd been apart for most of three months, with only texting and occasional phone calls to keep us in touch and we'd only been back together for a few weeks. Let the drama wait.

"My stepbrother is bad news," he said. "You should stay away from him."

So much for letting the drama wait.

"How is it you never told me about him?"

"I hate his guts," Trent said matter-of-factly. "I never talk about him unless I have to."

"Yeah, but we've been dating for a while now. I told you all about my family."

"Your family probably doesn't have anyone like Max in it."

We reached the bottom of the stairs and started across the central courtyard of the complex. The ground was only beginning to lose its summer-dry texture of cured concrete. A scattered handful of brown leaves dotted the grass.

"Every family has a Max," I said, thinking of my Aunt Jo.

Trent snorted. "No, they don't."

"I have an alcoholic aunt who lives on the street and does drugs."

He glanced down at me. "Interesting, but it still doesn't compare to Max."

"What did he do that's so bad?"

Trent shook his head. "I don't want to talk about it."

"But—"

"No, Caroline. Max is off limits."

I stopped in the middle of the walkway. "Trent, I'm your girlfriend. I need to know what kind of family you come from."

He gave a tremendous sigh. "Look, we don't talk about him much. He did some really bad shit and ran away when he was sixteen. It's a seriously touchy subject."

"So touchy you all pretend he doesn't exist?"

"Yeah. That's about it."

5

"That's awful."

He glowered at me. "What do you care, anyway? Do you like him?"

"No."

"You seemed to. You couldn't stop staring at him."

Oh, God. Had it been that obvious?

"I was curious. He gave me the creeps, though. I don't like him, honest."

"Good. His own dad hates him, so that should tell you something."

I stared up at him, both appalled and fascinated. What kind of family would exile one of its own children? What had Max done to justify such treatment? I wanted to know more, but I could see that Trent wasn't going to budge and if I pushed him it would probably result in that fight I was trying to avoid.

"Okay," I said. "Fine. We won't talk about him."

"Thank you." His voice was full of relief. "Let's get dinner."

We ended up at Primo's, a little Italian place with great pizza and lasagna. It was packed, as usual for a Friday night. Students loved it, partly for its cheap prices, so it was always busy even though it really lacked in the decor. The place was like a time-warp with its dark walls and floor and the fake black leather on its banquettes. It even had plastic greenery in "planters" between each booth.

After the waitress had seated us and taken our orders, Trent pulled a small, black velvet box from his jeans pocket and handed it to me across the table top. I took it with some hesitation. It looked an awful lot like a ring box.

"An anniversary present," he said. We'd been together for one year now.

"What is it?" Could it be an engagement ring? Probably not. We hadn't known each other long enough for that...or maybe we had. The idea of marriage made me uneasy, though.

"Open it and find out."

I opened the lid as carefully as if some creature waited inside to bite me. This was shaping up to be the weirdest college term ever, even surpassing my first. So far, nothing had gone as I'd expected.

A set of pearl and garnet earrings winked up at me from the black velvet. I gaped at the jewelry.

"They're the real thing," he said.

"They're gorgeous."

"You like?"

"I—yeah, of course. I love them. But, Trent, they must be so expensive."

He waved a negligent hand. "Don't worry about that. I can afford it."

Maybe he could, but I couldn't afford to reciprocate. My parents made pretty good money, but nowhere near what his parents did.

"I have a present for you, too," I said, hoping he wouldn't be disappointed in the book I'd bought for him.

"You can give it to me when I take you home."

The waitress returned with our lasagna. I dug in my fork as the savory smell of garlic, meat sauce and cheese filled my nostrils. The earrings were lovely. I just wished I could give him something equally expensive.

"About Max," he said.

"We don't have to talk about that if you don't want to."

"I just want you to know he's dangerous, Caroline."

I raised my eyebrows skeptically. "Dangerous? He looked like a regular guy to me."

"Well, he's not. He's a manipulator and a liar, and he hates me. He'll go after you, too, if you let him. So stay away from him."

"You realize you've just made me more curious, don't you?"

"I'm not kidding." He looked so sober that I couldn't continue teasing him.

"Okay, fine. I wasn't planning to hook up with him or anything."

"Like I said, he's a manipulator. He'll probably try to get to you now that he knows about you."

He sounded like a cartoon villain, or one of those evil alternative universe characters who always seemed to show up on TV sci-fi series. "Does he have a good twin in an alternate universe? One with less facial hair, perhaps?"

He blinked at me, apparently baffled. "What?"

"Never mind." Note to self: Trent doesn't get my sci-fi references. Most of my sorority sisters didn't, either. "But you've got to know you can't kick him out of town. You don't have that kind of power."

"Maybe if I make him miserable enough, he'll leave." Trent's eyes glittered in the low light.

I thought about Max, unloved by his own father, apparently alone in the world. What had he done that was so terrible? Drugs? Well, yeah, there was the weed, but that didn't seem like enough reason to hate on him. Aunt Jo was a drug addict, and although we didn't talk to her anymore, we didn't despise her.

Mom and Dad kicked her out of our house. They moved and changed their phone number so she couldn't contact us anymore. Maybe we—they—did despise her. I'd never stopped loving her, but I didn't tell my parents that.

Still, I didn't think drugs would be enough reason for Max's father to hate him. Violence? Had he killed someone?

Trent's lurid hints had aroused my curiosity and now I wouldn't be able to let it go until I found out the truth.

After Primo's, Trent took me back to my dorm. On my floor, people were running in and out of their rooms, shouting in the hall, slamming doors and generally making a huge amount of noise as they moved in. We had some second and third year students, like me, so some of us knew each other. The rest were freshmen.

Out of the corner of my eye, I could see a skinny brunette giving Trent a look up and down as we passed her, like I wasn't even there. We were holding hands and everything. You'd think she'd have better taste than to mack on my boyfriend right in front of me. I glared at her and she turned red.

My room wasn't much of a haven from the noise. The walls in the dorms seemed to be made of cardboard because sound went right through them. But at least no-one was staring at us.

Trent flopped down on my bed and put his hands behind his head, grinning at me. "Come here."

"In a second. I want to give you your present."

I crouched down to pull the wrapped book from under the bed. He sat up as I handed it to him. We hadn't seen each other all summer. He'd gone home to his parents' house in Montana and I'd gone back to Portland. It had been a long three months with only texting and phone calls to keep us in touch.

He ripped the paper from the coffee table book of football's greatest...everything. "Wow. This is awesome. Thanks, baby."

I smiled, relieved that he seemed to like it. My gift didn't compare to real, precious jewelry. "You're welcome."

He set the book on my tiny nightstand before reaching out and snagging my arm. "Now come here. I can't wait anymore."

I let him pull me down to the bed. He rolled me beneath him as he captured my mouth in a hard kiss. His hands were all over me, yanking at my clothes and squeezing me everywhere he could reach. He must have missed me a lot more than I'd realized.

I went along with it with my usual good cheer. It felt nice to have his warmth against me again, to have his arms around me, even if I couldn't get as enthused about it as he was.

Sex had never been a high priority for me. To be honest, I could have lived without it. But it was important to Trent, and I didn't mind it, so when he reached inside my panties I gave a sigh of pleasure.

He toyed with me until I was wet enough for him. Then he lifted himself over me and fit his cock inside me. It slid in without much resistance.

He groaned as he moved in me, an expression of rapture on his face. I put my arms around him, savoring the pleasure I could bring him. It was over soon anyway, when he shuddered and moaned through his orgasm.

My mind wandered back to Max. That was so wrong. The last thing I should be thinking of during sex with my boyfriend was another guy. I couldn't get that lazy, almost mocking smile of his out of my head, though. It had the simultaneous effect of making me want to smack him and wrap my arms and legs around him. Make him want me.

Why—how—did he do this to me? I'd only been around him for a few minutes, and I was already fantasizing about him. I hoped I'd never see him again, so this attraction I had for him would fade.

My foolish heart ached at the thought. As Trent disengaged from me, I mourned the loss of a man I didn't know. Didn't even want to know. Max was, for all the reasons Trent knew and a few he didn't, someone I needed to avoid.

Chapter 2

Max: I stared at my stepbrother's retreating back as he dragged his *girlfriend* behind him like he thought I was the devil's minion and I might pull them both down to hell with me. Okay, actually, I stared at her ass. She had a seriously fine ass on her, tight and round and just the way I liked them. Her hair, too, with its wild curls...it made me want to bury my fingers in it. Preferably while I fucked her until she screamed.

My stepbro, it seemed, was the classic college boy, all clean-cut and Boy Scout. Except for the part where he did other people's classwork for them. Wonder how he justified that? Not that I gave a damn.

Miss Caroline Winters fit right in with Trent's boy-next-door persona, with her prissy cardigan sweater and tasteful flat shoes, her natural make-up, her look of innocence. Not my type at all. My type was the black-haired witch I'd left behind in Seattle. Selene and I had been pretty hot together, but she wasn't big on commitment.

Trent was probably about to warn his *girlfriend* what a degenerate, brother-murdering piece of shit I was. When we'd been in high school—before I dropped out and ran away, that is—he'd made a hobby out of scuttling any relationship I tried to establish with a girl. I'd lost at least three potential girlfriends that way. Not to mention all the other bullying he'd inflicted on me. Asshole.

"Dude, you didn't tell me you and Trent were related," Talbot said, sitting down next to me again.

"I didn't know you two were friends."

"Seriously?"

If I had, I wouldn't have shown up at this shindig. My stepbrother had never brought anything but pain and contempt into my life. Take tonight, for example—standing there ordering me to leave town, like he thought he was fucking king of Avery's Crossing or some shit. Someone needed to take him down.

"Seriously," I replied. "You never said anything."

He shrugged. "You have different last names. I never even thought—"

"It's no big deal."

"Long as you don't fight at my parties," he said, picking up the bong.

"We didn't fight." Much. No blows had been exchanged, at least.

"He hates you." Talbot blew out a stream of smoke and handed me the bong.

"Yep."

"How come?"

Jealousy. Resentment. Murder. "Lots of things."

"You gonna leave town?"

"Hell, no."

He grinned. "This year should be interesting."

"Uh huh." I took a long drag on the weed.

"Saw you staring at Caroline. You like her?"

Now it was my turn to shrug. "Don't know her. Nice ass, though."

Talbot choked out a laugh. "I know, right? I'd fuck her if I had half a chance."

I shot him a glare. "She's taken."

Talbot's eyes went round. Then he laughed. "Yeah, by your stepbrother. Not you."

"Whatever."

What was wrong with me? I never got possessive over a female, especially one who would never kiss me.

On the other hand, who said she wouldn't? What better way to get under Trent's skin, to drive him abso-fucking-lutely nuts, than to take his girlfriend away from him. I smiled to myself. Payback is, in fact, a bitch.

The weather was already chilly at night, but I could sense a more severe chill coming as I left Talbot's apartment complex. The trees rustled their leaves and whispered above me. I could almost hear what they were saying. The spirits were active tonight, watching me, calling my name just at the edge of my hearing.

It could be only the usual extra-intense Halloween spookiness. Besides, I was too high to listen. The weed and the beer I'd had would interfere with whatever message they were trying to send, so there was no point in paying attention to their mutterings. Maybe tomorrow night we'd have our chat.

* * *

The old Dutch Colonial style house where I rented a one-bedroom apartment was absolutely silent, which was a little weird considering it was Halloween. No-one had even put out a jack o'lantern. Guess we weren't getting any trick-or-treaters.

I opened my apartment door. Frederick was standing in the middle of my living room. I jumped and banged my elbow on the doorjamb.

"Jesus, Fred. You could give a guy some warning."

"My apologies. I didn't mean to startle you."

I took off my jacket and hung it on the nail some former tenant had left in the plaster next to the door. "Is everything all right?"

"I just wanted to check in with you."

He wore the same dark-brown sack suit and derby hat as usual. The handlebar moustache that graced his upper lip always made me think of this old-fashioned ice-cream parlor my parents had taken me to once, when my mom was still alive. He looked like one of the line drawings on their menu, come to life. Or afterlife, as it were.

"The annual Halloween visit?" I said.

He smiled wryly. "How are you doing, Max? It's been a while."

"I'm fine. Settling in."

"Do you like Avery's Crossing?"

"Sure. It's okay." I'd liked it a lot better before I'd run into Trent.

Fred pulled out my desk chair—my only chair—and took a seat. I never understood why he did that. It's not like he had a real, physical body that needed rest. He was a ghost, for crying out loud.

I shrugged and dropped to the bare wood floor, crossing my legs tailor-style. "What's going on?"

Fred steepled his hands. "Perhaps you might tell me."

"Don't play word games with me tonight. I'm too tired and too high to follow." I scrubbed my hands over my face. "Dude, I just happened to run into my stepbrother and his girlfriend. This at a party thrown by a guy I never met until today, who happens to be a buddy of Trent's. You know anything about that?"

He regarded me thoughtfully. "Not really, no. Just that you came here to be near him."

"Wrong."

"You could have gone to school anywhere. But you chose this place." His dark eyes crinkled at the corners when he smiled, just like he was a live person. "Did you really think it was coincidence?"

"No. But I didn't come here to see him. I came because it's a good school and because Brad and Marie are here."

Fred laughed. "Does it make you feel better to tell yourself that?"

"Yes."

"You're a smart fellow, Max. I don't think you're fooling yourself as well as you think you are."

Whatever the hell that meant.

"You like your stepbrother's girlfriend."

I sat down cross-legged on the bare wooden floor. "She's hot, but I wouldn't say I like her. I don't even know her. I like Selene."

"But you find Caroline attractive."

"Yes. I do. What's your point?"

He cocked his head. "I'm not sure."

Right. Fred never did anything without a reason. "Anyway, it doesn't matter. She's his girl, not mine."

"You're an honorable man."

I snorted. "No, I'm not."

"I think you don't give yourself enough credit." Fred smiled. "I know you quite well, after all."

He could think what he liked. He didn't know my plans regarding Caroline, although he'd figure it out soon enough.

"Caroline isn't the kind of woman I usually go for," I said. "She's too much like Trent."

"I thought you said you didn't know her."

"I don't. But if she's dating him, she must be the type I can't stand."

"I see."

"It's weird, though, about the party. What are the odds I'd run into a friend of Trent's and get invited to his party? You have anything to do with that?"

"Nothing at all. Pure coincidence."

"Uh huh."

"Truly." He looked sincere. Could I believe him? "I wouldn't manipulate you like that."

"I don't believe in coincidence. Something is going on."

Fred nodded. "Spirits are stirring, gathering around you."

That went right along with all the murmuring I'd heard on the way home. My blood was sluggish with alcohol and pot, but I sat up a little straighter as some of the dreamy relaxation left me.

"Why?" I frowned. "What do they want?"

"I'm not sure. Perhaps you should talk to your circle about it."

"I'll think about that." My circle was a group of people with whom I performed occult work—rituals, divinations, that kind of thing. I wasn't sure I wanted them in on the matter, given my plan to seduce Caroline. They wouldn't approve.

"Did you ever wonder," Fred remarked, "why Brad and Marie chose to move down here, knowing your stepbrother was enrolled at Central Willamette State?"

"Nope," I said flatly. "Marie inherited some property. That's why they came here."

"Is it? She could have sold the farm. Could have made a great deal of money on it, in fact, given the way property values are going back up around here."

"You into real estate, Fred? That's a funny hobby for a ghost."

"Any hobby is a funny hobby for a ghost. I'm merely pointing out the fact that Marie wasn't required to move here."

"Okay." I shifted my weight on the hard floor, looking for a position where my ankle bones weren't grinding against the wood. "She always liked it here; always wanted to live on her grandparents' farm. She said so. That's why they didn't sell."

"But you didn't have to follow them."

I narrowed my eyes at him. "Brad and Marie are the closest thing I have to a family. No, I didn't have to follow, but the fact I did has nothing to do with Trent. Pure coincidence."

"I thought you didn't believe in coincidence."

I groaned. "Give it a rest, Fred. I didn't come here for Trent. Got it?"

"Sure, Max." He smiled knowingly at me.

The problem with having a ghost for a friend is they often think they know better than you do. They've passed on to the Great Beyond, and that supposedly makes them wiser. Unfortunately, it seems to make some of them busybodies who think it's their job to monkey around in the lives of those of us who are still mortal.

I loved Brad and Marie. They'd taken me in at a time when I was perched on the edge of disaster, a runaway living on the streets in Seattle, ready to spiral down into hard drugs and God knows what else, maybe even sex for hire. People do desperate things when they're cold and starving.

They'd saved me, gotten me off the streets and into a GED program. They'd taken me into their home, treated me like a son. When they'd decided to move to Avery's Crossing, Trent's presence there was the last thing on my mind. I wanted to be with my family, and the graphic design business I'd started could be run anywhere since most of it took place on-line. Moving here had been a no-brainer. The business program at Central Willamette was a bonus.

"I passed through this town once, back in 1853," he said meditatively. "I was on my way to Montana."

"Why go through Oregon?"

"Because I started out in California, obviously."

Oh. Right.

"The place has changed quite a bit since I was here last," he said. "Quite a bit."

"The women wear shorter skirts."

He laughed. "That they do."

"Is it fun for you to watch them go by, dressed the way they do?"

Fred smiled, but instead of answering, he countered with his own question. "So what are you going to do about Caroline?"

"Do? I'm not going to do anything."

He still gazed at me like he could read my thoughts. I was pretty sure he couldn't, but not absolutely positive. Christ, I hoped he couldn't.

He was enough of a pain in the ass with his know-it-all advice; if he could read my mind, he'd never stop telling me what to do.

"She has feelings, too, you know," he said.

"Alert the media. They'll want to hear about that for sure."

Fred sighed. "I can see you don't want my perspective."

"Not right now."

"All right. I'll be on my way, then." He stood up and offered me his hand. "Good night, Max."

We shook. His skin felt warm and alive, and his fingers pressed into mine just like we were exchanging a real handshake. A slick illusion, making him seem completely real. Like he wasn't a ghost at all.

"Night, Fred." I smiled at him and he vanished.

I stretched out on my back and stared up at the ceiling. He was right, of course. Caroline had feelings, too, even if she looked like every girl who'd ever snubbed me, every girl who'd ever been too good for a juvenile delinquent like me, and I'd be a jerk to use her just to get at Trent. But that wouldn't stop me.

Chapter 3

Caroline: I had a girl date with my best friend, Paige, and I was going to be late again. I'd never hear the end of it if I kept her waiting, so I grabbed my bag and ran out the door of my dorm room. In my head I could hear her telling me that if I'd moved into the sorority house with her, like she'd wanted me to, then I wouldn't be late at all. We'd be walking over to the cafe together.

Lateness was a chronic problem with me. In that way, I took after Aunt Jo. She'd always been late, too, but she used to say it was better to stop and notice the small and beautiful details of life than to be in such a rush that you're always on time.

I charged down the ugly tan and brown hallway, passing knots of staring freshman girls on the way. No time to talk. I didn't know any of them yet anyway.

Luckily, the student union was only about a block away from my dorm and I made it in record time. I ran up the steps and into the building, then up the broad, sweeping marble stairs that led to the second floor and the huge lounge that always reminded me of a castle's great hall. The cafe was right across from the lounge.

"Caroline." The male voice greeting me echoed slightly in the hard, cold stairwell.

I skidded to a stop and turned. Oh, no. Max. He wore a pair of faded jeans and a white t-shirt so tight it showed every muscle in his torso. There were a lot of muscles. My mouth went dry.

Why had he called my name? He knew Trent wanted him to stay away from us.

I watched him stalk up the stairs toward me, something vaguely predatory in the graceful motion of his body. The beaded necklace still hung around his neck, and I still couldn't see what the pendant on it looked like because it was hidden beneath his t-shirt.

"Um...hi, Max," I said lamely.

"It's nice to see someone I recognize around here." He smiled with a hint of bashfulness.

"Is it?" God, I sounded like an idiot.

"Yeah. I don't know anyone on campus, really."

"I thought you knew Talbot," I said.

"Not well."

He didn't know me well, either.

"Um, well, it was nice seeing you." I edged up one stair step.

"Where are you headed?"

"I'm on my way to meet a friend for coffee."

He rubbed the back of his neck, looking even more sheepish. "Is it all right if I join you?"

"Uh..." How did I get out of this one? There was no polite way to say no to him. "Sure."

He smiled. "Thanks. That's really nice of you."

Yeah, sure it was. I hadn't been able to think of a way to get out of it, and he knew it.

"Well, we're right up here." I pointed up the stairs.

"Are you a junior like Trent?" he said as we started climbing again. "Yes."

He leaned closer to me. His proximity made my heart race and my palms start to sweat. I could almost feel his body heat, he was so near.

"He probably told you to stay away from me," Max said in a low voice.

My face heated and I knew I was turning pink. "Yeah, he did."

"I'm surprised you're talking to me."

I glanced sidelong at him. "I like to make up my own mind about a person." Also, I was too polite for my own good.

He aimed one of those lazy smiles at me. "I'm glad to hear it." His smile broadened into a grin, which brought out dimples in his cheeks. Damn it. He had to have dimples, too? "Everything he told you about me is probably true."

I stared at him openly. "Huh? Why would you say that?"

He shrugged. "I'm a terrible person. You should stay away from me. Far away."

"I expected you to tell me how wrong he is about you."

"What would be the fun in that?"

I shook my head. "You're very strange."

"That's what they tell me."

We reached the cafe. It had little bistro tables at the edge of the long, wide second-floor hall with its rows of international flags. Ever since I'd started at Central Willamette, I'd wondered why we had a hall filled with those flags.

I stood at one of the tables and scanned for Paige, but couldn't see her. "I guess my friend isn't here yet," I said.

"Get a table and I'll pick up your drink for you. What do you want?"

"I'll have a sixteen ounce mocha." I opened my bag and started digging around for my wallet.

"Don't worry about the money. I've got it."

17

He walked off before I could protest. I really didn't want him buying me anything, even a coffee. However, I also didn't want to run after him and argue about it in front of all the other patrons. I sat down at the table to wait. When he came back, we'd discuss the money.

Paige still hadn't arrived when Max returned with the drinks. He set mine in front of me and took the other chair. I had the money ready and I pushed a five dollar bill across the table at him.

He jerked his head back slightly, as if affronted. "I told you I've got it."

"I can't let you buy me a drink."

He slid the bill back toward me. "I'm not buying you a drink. It's just coffee."

"You know what I mean. I need to pay my way."

"I'm not taking your money, Caro. Put it away."

"No. I need to pay for my drink."

"If you won't put it away, it's going to stay on the table. I'm serious." He narrowed his eyes at me.

Was he really offended that I wouldn't let him pay? I sighed and took back the fiver.

"Okay, fine. You can pay."

"Thank you." He leaned back in his chair. "Now, what would you like to know about me?"

Why does your dad hate you? But I couldn't ask him that. "Did you really run away when you were sixteen?"

"Yep."

"Where'd you go?" Trent's family was from Billings, Montana.

"I hitchhiked to Seattle."

"That's dangerous."

"No shit." He gave a careless shrug. "I came through okay, though."

"I'm glad."

"Are you?" His gaze sharpened.

"Yeah. I hate thinking of kids living on the streets. Runaways...it's scary, that's all."

He held my gaze a lot longer than was comfortable. I flushed, but for some reason I couldn't understand, I didn't look away. His eyes were blue. Dark, deep-ocean blue. There was pain in them...but then it disappeared, so quickly I wasn't sure it had ever been there.

"It's nice of you to care," he said dryly.

"Well, I do."

Awkward silence. I took a sip of my mocha. He drank whatever it was he'd gotten. I glanced around, looking for Paige. *Rescue me, best friend.* But she wasn't in sight. I was on my own with this strange, intense man I wasn't supposed to like.

"So, what's your major?" he said.

Ah, the quintessential college ice-breaker. "French."

"Really, French? That's different."

"Yeah. Not too practical." My parents and Trent were always bugging me to change it to something "normal," like education. But I didn't want to be a teacher like my mom. I didn't know what I wanted to be.

"What's yours?" I said.

"Business."

My brows rose. "Business, huh? I never would have tagged you as a business major."

"I own a business. I thought it might help my career to spend a few years in college."

"Wow." My brows rose even higher. "You have your own business?"

So not what I'd expected from him.

"Yeah. I'm a graphic designer."

Again with the surprises. I'm not sure what I thought he'd major in or do for a living, just that owning his own graphic design business was not it. Did Trent know about this?

"That sounds really interesting," I said.

"Don't get me started, or I'll talk your ear off." He gave me a self-deprecating smile.

"You'd have to start from the beginning, because I don't know anything about either graphic design or business."

"What do you plan to do with that French degree?"

"I have no idea."

He grinned at me. "Good plan."

"I like to think so."

I shouldn't be sitting here with him. My stomach was full of hysterically panicking butterflies, and the rest of me ached in weird places. Intimate places. He made me feel things that, honestly, I'd never felt for any guy before. Not even Trent. I'd never had such a powerful reaction to anyone else.

His hand moved a few inches toward mine where it rested on the table. Was he going to touch me? I wanted him to, and I felt bad for wanting it. This was not me. I'd never cheated on any of the guys I'd dated. I was a committed serial monogamist.

Max's hand stopped, then retreated back into his own space. I lifted my coffee to my lips, pretending I hadn't seen. Maybe I'd imagined him reaching out to me. Part of me hoped I had and the rest of me wished he'd kept going so I could feel his skin against mine again.

I glanced up, trying to ease the sudden tension, and saw Paige coming toward us, looking like an Asian-American fashion model, as always, with her long, slender legs and ultra-chic dress. She had a big smile on her face and I wasn't sure what that meant. She wasn't the most discreet person in the world, and now that she'd seen me with Max, the news would probably be all over our sorority house by this evening.

"Paige, this is Max, Trent's stepbrother," I said by way of greeting.

Her dark, almond eyes widened. "Trent's stepbrother? Wow. I didn't know he had any brothers at all."

"Max, this is my best friend, Paige Lin."

He offered her a hand. "Nice to meet you."

"And you." She shook hands with him.

I watched her closely, to see if she had any kind of unusual reaction I could detect. As far as I could tell, he didn't affect her at all. Not the way he did me, at any rate.

Paige dragged an extra chair to the table. "Did Trent introduce you two?"

"Not exactly," I said.

Max just smiled blandly.

"Well." Paige looked from me to him and back again. "I'm just...really surprised."

This was going to get icky fast unless I changed the subject. Paige could be obnoxiously inquisitive and she didn't care who knew. She wouldn't hesitate trying to pry Max's family history out of him.

"Max is a business major," I said in my perkiest tone. "He owns his own graphic design business."

Her eyes widened even more. "Do you? I'm a design major myself."

Oh, boy, here we go. I'd made a bad choice of subject change. They'd be off in design land now, talking in their special language no-one else could understand. I got this from Paige all the time.

But Max only said, "do you two share an apartment?" Apparently, I wasn't the only one looking for another topic.

"I live in the sorority house," Paige said. "And Caroline, for reasons no-one understands, still lives in the dorms."

I rolled my eyes. "I like the dorms."

"No-one actually *likes* the dorms, Caroline," she said. "You've been brainwashed or something."

"Whatever."

"Hey, dorms can have some advantages," Max said.

"Oh, yeah?" Paige turned to him skeptically. "Like what?"

"Uh...hmmm...she's very close to all her classes," he said. "That's convenient. And the library, also convenient."

Paige just looked at him, her face blank, as if he were speaking in a foreign language. "She's away from all the action."

"I never miss a party at the library," I said.

She snickered and after a second's pause, I joined her. Max was looking at me and smiling, and the warmth in his eyes startled me. It made me hot all over.

Why was he looking at me like that? Why was he even here? Maybe Trent was right about him and he was trying to get close to me just to mess with his stepbrother. That seemed so unlikely, though. I mean, who did that?

* * *

Explosions were going off right in the hallway of my dorm. I groaned and pried my eyes open. In the thin light of early morning, a girl stood by the side of my bed, staring down at me. She had long, perfectly straight blond hair and wore a white tunic-like top with blue embroidery around the neckline. Her face, bare of make-up, seemed contemplative, as if she was studying me.

The explosions resolved into the sound of someone banging on my door. I blinked and the girl in white vanished. For an instant, I lay there frowning at the place where she'd been, while the pounding continued even more loudly than before.

I must have been dreaming. I glanced at the clock to see it was only five-thirty. Whoever was on the other side of my door had some explaining to do, and the explanation had better be that the building was on fire.

With another groan, I crawled out of bed and hobbled to the door. Opening it, I found Paige in the hallway, looking offensively bright and chipper. She had full make-up on her face, for pity's sake. And she carried one of those enormous flat doughnut boxes from a supermarket, with a tray of coffee cups balanced on top.

"What do you think you're doing?" I croaked. "Where's the fire?"

She brandished the treats at me. "I brought buttermilk old-fashioned. Your favorite. And coffee."

"Do you know what time it is?"

"Five-thirty." She had the nerve to smile at me.

I opened the door to let her enter. "I'm in pain right now, Paige."

She pranced into my room like she'd done something wonderful. "I couldn't sleep this morning, so I thought I might as well get up and get us some breakfast."

Why? Rubbing my eyes, I fought down the urge to glare at her. She meant well, after all. "My first class isn't until nine. Which I scheduled on purpose, just so I wouldn't have to get up at five-freaking-thirty."

"Oops." She sent me an apologetic glance. "Sorry. I thought you had a seven o'clock like usual."

"Just get me some of that coffee, quick. But what's with all the cups?"

"They were running a special. I figured we couldn't have too much coffee this early in the morning."

"You got that right."

Paige set the doughnuts and coffee on the tiny built-in desk that would have belonged to my roommate, if I'd had one. I'd lucked out this year and gotten a room to myself. I opened the doughnut box and grabbed one, sniffing its sugary aroma before taking a bite.

"How come Trent never mentioned Max?" she said.

I shrugged, trying to seem casual. "They don't get along."

"That's some pretty serious not-getting-along, if he won't even talk about him."

"Tell me about it."

"And he's so freaking hot. I thought I was seeing things when I walked up to you two at the cafe."

"Yeah, he is good-looking." No way was I going to admit how much I lusted after him. I took another bite of doughnut. Nope, no inappropriate hankering going on here.

"You like him, don't you?" Paige said.

"No, I don't. He's weird. He kind of gives me the creeps."

"Really?" Her delicate dark brows climbed. "Why? He seemed nice to me."

"I'm not sure. Maybe it's the way he looks at me." I set down my doughnut. "You can't tell anyone you saw us together. Have you told anyone yet?"

"No." Her eyes were wide and serious. I hoped she was telling me the truth, because I really didn't want any gossip about this.

"I can't have it getting back to Trent. He'll have a fit."

"You guys were in public. Other people besides me probably saw you."

"Yeah, but they didn't know who Max is."

"You don't know that," she said. "One of Trent's frat brothers might have been hanging around and we didn't see him."

"That's true." I rubbed my eyes again. "What if he wanted to be seen with me?"

"What do you mean?"

"Trent claims he's a major manipulator and that he has it in for him. What if he's getting all cozy with me just to irritate Trent?"

"That's twisted." She bit thoughtfully into a maple bar. "Do you suppose he's really that bad? Maybe Trent is exaggerating."

"I don't know. What really bugs me is he wouldn't say why he hates Max so much. He just said he was a wild kid and ran away when he was sixteen."

"Sounds like you need to do some detective work."

"Do I? Maybe I just need to mind my own business." Besides, I hadn't got a single clue how to be a detective.

Chapter 4

Max: The next time I saw Caroline, it was several days after our cafe meeting. She was walking along the sidewalk next to the chem hall, wearing a huge backpack slung over one shoulder. She had on shorts that exposed the bottom half of her legs and a hoodie to keep her warm in the morning chill.

Those were some incredible legs. Tight with muscle, a sexy curve in her calves, tiny ankles. I swallowed hard as I watched her stroll down the street ahead of me, unaware of my presence. She didn't have Selene's overt sexuality, yet I couldn't stop looking at her.

Our prior conversation had revealed a different person than the one I'd expected. She wasn't quite the empty-headed party girl I'd thought she'd be, but she still looked like Miss Sweet Girl Next Door with her long shorts...you know, the kind that go all the way down to the knee. Prissy. And she was still Trent's girlfriend, so although she might be friendly on the surface, she had to be like him underneath. Where it counted.

I quickened my pace to catch up with her. My heart started its usual frantic pounding whenever I saw her, which was totally due to the fact I was ruthlessly using her to get back at Trent. Treating women badly wasn't normal behavior for me and I didn't much like it. But I wouldn't really hurt her; I'd only go far enough to drive my stepbrother crazy and then I'd back off.

"Hey, Caroline," I said as I came shoulder to shoulder with her.

She jerked her head around and stared at me like I'd really scared her. "Um...hi."

Was she afraid of me? Maybe Trent had already told her what I'd done. My pounding heart seemed to shrivel up inside my chest at the thought that Caroline saw me as a murderer.

I forced a smile. "How are you?"

"I'm good. You?"

"I'm fine." Yeah. A scintillating conversationalist, too. "So...are you headed to class?"

"Um..." She glanced around as if looking for someone to bail her out of a bad situation. "No. I have an hour until my next one."

"What a coincidence. So do I."

"Oh." She smiled weakly. Trent had definitely scared her.

A good guy would back off at this point and let her go her way. But I wasn't a particularly good guy, and I wanted to shake up my stepbrother badly enough that it didn't matter to me if I made Caroline nervous.

Okay, yeah, it bothered me. A lot. But I wasn't going to let that get in my way.

"I was just on my way to get some coffee. Come with me, keep me company."

She ducked her head. "Oh, no. I couldn't."

"Aw, come on. I promise I won't bite."

Her lips pressed together like she was trying not to smile. "How do I know you'll keep your promise?"

"I always keep my promises."

Caroline glanced furtively around at the other people going to and from classes. "No. Really. Trent might find out."

"You're that worried about him?" Good.

"Yes. He told me to stay away from you."

"Hmm." I tilted my head, watching her as we continued down the sidewalk. "I thought you liked to make up your own mind."

"I do. But I don't want to make him jealous, either."

"Jealous?" I laughed a little. "Over coffee? I think he's way too controlling if you can't even go out for coffee with a friend."

That must have been the right button to push, because she lifted her head with a determined frown. "You're right. Okay, let's go."

"Great. You want to hit the same place as last time?"

"No. I know a place downtown."

"Won't that make you late for your next class?"

She glanced at me with a sheepish-looking smile. "I sort of lied. I don't have another class until this afternoon."

I'd hit the jackpot. I could have her to myself for a couple of hours, maybe. That would give me plenty of time to work on getting her defenses down.

Another point: maybe she hadn't heard about my crimes from Trent, because if she had she probably wouldn't want to have anything to do with me. In my experience, people who kill their little brothers have a hard time making friends. Especially with Miss Sweet Girl Next Door.

We didn't talk much on the way to her coffee house. The thought that she would eventually find out what I'd done made me less talkative than I'd otherwise be. And Caroline kept looking over her shoulder. She was really worried that Trent would find out we'd been hanging out.

An ugly idea occurred to me. Maybe his controlling went beyond warnings and into physical violence. The thought made my heart hammer in my chest and my throat go so tight it started to hurt. It was strange for me to get so angry, considering I really didn't know Caroline very well. While I hated the idea of any woman being subjected to violence, I didn't normally get so worked up about it unless the woman was a true friend of mine.

"Will you be okay?" I said as we approached Avery's Crossing's tiny downtown. My voice was hard with the tension I felt.

"Okay? What do you mean?"

"If Trent finds out. Will you be safe?"

Her mouth opened but no sound came out. She closed it, then opened it again. "Of course I'll be safe."

"Good. I just wanted to be sure."

She put a hand on my arm. The heat of her touch pierced right through the sleeve of my denim jacket. "He doesn't hit me, if that's what you're thinking."

I wanted to put my hand on top of hers, but I didn't. "I just don't want to put you in danger. But I like you. I liked talking to you the other day."

That was true, even though I'd initiated the conversation with revenge in mind. In fact, I'd enjoyed her company a little too much, but I could keep it together long enough to make things difficult for Trent.

Her face turned an adorable shade of pink. "I liked talking to you, too."

Now we were making progress. I stifled a grin. "If you ever feel unsafe, you'll let me know, right?"

"Um...sure. But he's not like that. Really, he isn't."

"Okay."

"We turn here." She took a sharp right and I followed.

Avery's Crossing had that all-American small town feeling, especially downtown. Old buildings from the late nineteenth and early twentieth centuries, a sprinkling of big shade trees and old-timey storefronts gave it a charm you usually only see in movies. I hadn't made up my mind how I felt about it yet. Sometimes I just wanted to run back to Seattle and the hurry-hurry of a big city.

Things felt awfully slow here.

The coffee house was on the edge of the downtown core and from the minute I walked in, I could see it was another student hang-out. There seemed to be older people here, too, though. Maybe Caroline thought it was less likely we'd be seen in this place.

Finally, we had our drinks and snacks, and had claimed a table in a back corner where we could be incognito. Caroline leaned across the table with an earnest expression.

"Why did you think Trent would hit me?"

"I didn't. It was just a random thought, that's all."

"Oh." She had the longest blond eyelashes I'd ever seen. "Why does he hate you so much?"

Well. She didn't waste any time, did she? I leaned back in my seat to cover my discomfort. "It's a long story. Goes back to when my dad married his mom."

"Yeah, you said that to Paige."

I shrugged. "It's the truth." Part of it, anyway.

"So that's all there is to it?"

"No, of course not. We have years of childhood fighting behind us."

"Are you older or younger?"

"Younger by six months." I gave a humorless laugh. "Our parents thought it was a good thing we were so close in age. They thought we'd be great buddies or something."

Her eyes—chocolate brown and unusually dark for a blonde—softened in sympathy. "I'm sorry. That must have been hard."

"You have no idea."

"Couldn't you have gone to live with your mom?"

"She died when I was five," I said, with as little expression as I could manage.

"Oh, no." She put her hand over her mouth. "I'm so sorry; I didn't know."

"Obviously."

"I didn't mean to upset you."

"You didn't." I waved off her concern with a shake of my head. "It happened a long time ago. I hardly remember her." Except for that trip to the ice-cream parlor. For some reason, that one memory stood out after all these years.

"Still. I just assumed your parents got a divorce."

"Don't worry about it, Caroline. I don't." I forced another smile. "So tell me about your family. Are your parents still together?"

"Yes, they are." She took a bite of the carrot cake on her plate.

"Any sisters or brothers?"

"I have one of each. Lily and Landon. They're twins, ten years old."

I smiled, more out of politeness than anything. "Your family sounds...nice."

"They are. My mom is a high school teacher and my dad works for the Bonneville Power Administration. What does your dad do?"

I shrugged. "Who knows?"

"Really? You're that out of touch with him?"

I truly didn't want to talk about him. "It's been a while. He owns a construction business in Billings."

"Oh. Duh. I already know that. Because of Trent."

The expression on her face was one of guilt. Was she worried about hurting my feelings? It seemed like every time I talked to her, she surprised me by being someone so different from the person I'd expected. Maybe she wasn't the stuck up rich girl I'd seen the night of the party. She wasn't a flaky party girl, either, and I wasn't sure anymore about the prissy good girl. The fact was, I didn't know what kind of girl she was, but I was starting to genuinely like her.

That wasn't going to stop me from taking her away from Trent, though.

That asshole had been asking for a take-down from me for so many years I'd lost count and I wasn't going to pass up an opportunity as golden as this one.

"Hey," I said, glancing around the room. "Want to get out of here? We could walk along the river bank. It's only a block away from here, right?"

"That's right. Sure, sounds good."

We put away our dishes in the bussing station and left the coffee house. The sun outside was so bright it almost hurt my eyes after the dim lighting of the restaurant. I squinted into the glare. Everyone had told me it rained down here almost as much as it did in Seattle, but we were just on the cusp of the wet, still coming out of the dry time of the year, when the sky seemed perpetually blue. Rain was coming, though. There was no such thing as a dry winter in the Pacific Northwest.

We ambled down to the river, not saying much along the way. I can't claim it was a comfortable silence. I think we were both too aware of each other...or maybe that was just me. I couldn't think of much else besides the way her body moved, the swing of her curvy hips, the way her hair was made up of every imaginable shade of gold and amber.

What was she thinking about? I have no idea. She didn't seem to be afraid of me, though, and that was a good thing. If she'd been afraid of me, it would make my plan a lot more difficult to carry out.

The river bank was mostly unimproved, although there was a narrow footpath we followed along the edge of the water. This was the Willamette, and the crossing for which the town was named was somewhere along here. According to my Internet research—I'd read a couple of Wikipedia articles before moving here—Avery's Crossing was named after a local farmer, one of the original settlers of the town, who'd also operated a crude ferry right in this area.

Out of the corner of my left eye, as if on cue, a shadowy shape moved out across the water. It was flat, like a large raft, with a human figure on top. Unlike a raft, it moved perpendicular to the current. I moved my head to get a better look and it was gone.

"What is it?" Caroline said.

"Did you see it, too?"

"See what?"

I glanced at her. She looked puzzled, but I wasn't prepared to discuss my occult activities with her, or the fact that I sometimes saw things, shadows of the past. "Never mind. I just thought I saw a bird. A heron or something."

"Yeah, we see them around here sometimes."

Besides, the ferry ghost might have been a trick of the light or some other illusion. Even when you have the second sight, not everything you notice is really a spirit.

Caroline leaned her back against the trunk of an oak tree, turning her head to smile at me. "It's beautiful here."

"Yeah. It is." I was thinking of the woman beside me, though, not the natural scenery.

She flushed, as if she knew what I was thinking. "I love the river."

"I love rivers, too." That was actually true.

"They make me think of all the places they pass through," she said, staring at the water. "I like to imagine drifting along with the current, just seeing what comes next."

"There was a ferry crossing near here," I said.

"That must be why it's called Avery's Crossing."

I sang a couple of lines from The Decemberists' song "Avery." It was just a random impulse, because the song title matched the name of the town. Caroline turned and stared at me with an open mouth. She was actually gaping at me, she was so surprised.

"You know The Decemberists?" she said.

"Their last album is one of my favorites. You like them?"

"The King Is Dead. I love every song on there. Most of my friends don't even know who they are."

I winked at her. "We have something in common."

She stared at me for another moment and then pushed off from the oak's trunk. "Yeah."

It was taking every bit of my concentration to not reach for her hand. This walk we were taking together felt more like a date than just friends hanging out, and I wanted to touch her. But she wouldn't welcome it. Not yet.

"So," she said brightly. "How long have you been doing graphic design?"

"I've loved to draw all my life. I got into graphics in high school, started my business not long after I got my GED."

"Ah." She sent a sidelong glance my way, and I pretended not to notice.

Was this—the fact I hadn't graduated but had to get my GED—the little detail that would turn her off? Make her avoid me for real? I couldn't tell yet, since she was putting a good face on everything.

"I think it's great you have such strong direction," she said. "I wish I did. I still don't know what I want to do when I grow up."

"You'll figure it out." Probably marry Trent and have a herd of beautiful blond kids who'd have the world handed to them on a platter.

She tripped over an exposed root and tumbled forward, toward the water. I jumped to catch her before she landed in the river. She barreled into me with surprising force, considering her slight frame, and her momentum carried us both down to the hard-packed ground.

"Oof," I said as she landed on top of me.

She gazed down at me with wide, brown eyes, her breath coming in startled pants, hair tumbling around her face in a golden cloud. My arms slipped around her taut waist, holding her to me so I could feel every curve on her delectable body. My cock began to throb and ache.

Her full, Cupid's-bow lips parted. She looked like she wanted to kiss me, which was exactly what I wanted, too. I lifted my head, bringing our faces closer together.

"Oh, God, I'm so sorry." She scrambled to get off me.

I let her go. The bulge in my jeans was getting painful and I didn't want her to see it, so I sat up and bent one leg at the knee to hide myself.

She was still so temptingly close. I lifted my hand to her face and brushed a tendril of hair from her eyes. She jerked backward.

"I-I'm sorry. I can't."

"Yeah." I dropped my hand. "I shouldn't have—sorry about that."

"It's okay." She gave me a brilliant, fake smile as she clambered to her feet.

"Are you okay? You didn't get hurt, did you?"

"I'm fine."

My butt was feeling a little sore because I'd landed on a rock, but I wasn't going to admit it to her. I brushed off my backside.

"I was afraid you were going to end up in the river," I said.

She flicked a glance at me, then looked away. "Thank you for catching me."

"No problem."

"Well...um...I should probably get back to my dorm. I need to get ready for my afternoon class."

"Okay. I'll walk you back."

She ran her fingers through her curls. "You don't need to do that. I'll be fine on my own."

"I want to. I'd like to make sure you get there all right."

Her lips flattened into a straight line. "Max," she said in a strange tone that seemed to hold both pity and regret. "I can't. Honestly. It's better if I go by myself."

Damn it. I didn't want or need her pity. Anyone's pity. Words refused to come as I watched her turn around and climb back up the embankment toward the street. Christ. She felt sorry for me.

* * *

It was a handgun. A pistol of some kind. I didn't know much about guns, but I saw them on TV. It seemed huge and felt surprisingly heavy in my hands, the dark gray metal cold.

My brothers were in the hallway outside my bedroom, playing. I could hear their voices, Trent's high and childish and Carter's even higher, with a baby's lisp. Carter's little feet made rhythmic thumping sounds as he ran back and forth down the hall. I didn't know what game they were playing but I wished they'd shut up. They were so loud and I couldn't concentrate.

I turned the gun over in my hands, looking at it from different angles. Not down the barrel, though. Even I knew better than that.

Except it didn't have any bullets in it. Didn't that make it safe?

So I could look down that barrel if I wanted to, only I didn't want to. It was just a tube made out of metal. What was there to see?

A noise made me look over at my door. Carter stood in the doorway of my room, giggling at something. He did that a lot. Half the time I didn't know what he was laughing at or why it was supposed to be funny. I frowned at him, annoyed. Wasn't it enough for them to make noise in the hallway?

"What are you doing?" I snapped.

Carter just laughed.

"Go away. I'm busy right now."

He looked back over his shoulder at something I couldn't see, something in the upstairs hallway. Trent, maybe. Whatever it was made him laugh even harder. I glared at him, willing him to go away and quit bothering me. Couldn't he see I was busy with something off limits for little kids like him?

I lifted the gun, experimentally pointing at the blank nighttime darkness of my window, my finger hovering over the trigger. No way did I want to fire this thing, even if it wasn't loaded. But I could point it and imagine what it would be like to face down the bad guys.

Bam, I thought. Got ya.

Carter darted into my room, laughing hysterically. I swung my upper body around to glare at him and order him out. My hand tightened on the gun.

31

The explosion almost deafened me. Carter pinwheeled backward and tumbled to the floor, his chest nothing but a red ruin. He made no sound. Just fell to the floor.

I stared at him, my mind blank and uncomprehending. Then I looked at the gun. My ears rang with the blast of its firing. It was the only sound I could hear. I had fired the gun.

Carter! I threw the weapon onto my bed and ran to my brother. He lay on his back. His eyes were open and staring.

My hands started to shake. I gathered him up and lifted him into my lap. His little head lolled to the side, his whole body limp and unresponsive. Blood gushed from the wound, the terrible wound. It flowed all over my shirt, my jeans, the carpet.

No. No. No!

"Carter," I said. "Carter."

As if my words, the sound of his name, could pull him back from the arms of death. It was too late for that. He was already gone.

Brad and Marie's farm lay on the western edge of town. It was pretty small, with a little apple orchard and some cow pasture. They kept chickens and goats and grew a market garden, which they were planning to expand so they could get into CSA—community supported agriculture. That's where people basically subscribe to receive a weekly allotment of vegetables, herbs, fruit, eggs and whatever else a farm produces.

I drove up the long, rutted dirt road that led to their vintage nineteen-thirties farmhouse and parked in the shade of a huge old tree still covered in feathery-looking golden leaves. A long drift of the same leaves lay at the foot of the tree. Brad's beat-up relic of a pick-up truck was parked over by the barn and Marie's sedan sat next to the house. They were home, then.

She came to the door as I walked up the front steps. Her graying brown hair was tied back in a ponytail and she had a kitchen towel slung over one shoulder. She pushed the screen door open with a grin.

"Max!" She held out her arms.

I moved into the hug gladly. "Marie." She felt tiny in my embrace.

"How have you been? You should come by more often."

"I've been busy. Work and school, you know."

"That's no excuse. Get your butt in here and tell me all about it."

I followed her into the little house, which looked like it hadn't been upgraded or changed since at least the sixties. Maybe not even then. The kitchen was still almost original and smelled, deliciously, of cinnamon.

"You're in luck," she said. "I just happened to bake an apple pie today. I'm practicing for Thanksgiving."

"No wonder it smells so good in here."

She opened her ancient fridge and pulled out two cans of soda, handing one to me. "Brad is in the barn, but he should be back soon. So tell me about school. How is it, after being gone so long?"

"It's not like high school, so I'm doing fine with it." I sat down at the diner-style kitchen table. "Lots of classwork."

"I'll bet. Have you found yourself a girlfriend yet?"

"No." I tried to hide my flaming face by lifting my soda can and taking a long swallow.

"But you met someone."

Marie always saw too much.

"Maybe," I said.

"Who is she? What's her name?"

I set the can down and gave a careless tilt of my head. "She's just someone I ran across at a party. Not a big deal."

"No? You're blushing."

"That's because you're pestering me."

Marie laughed. "No, it's not. It's because you really like this girl. I can tell."

Maybe I shouldn't have come to visit. I tapped my fingers against the side of the soda can, wishing I'd just called. She wasn't as intuitive over the phone.

"I'm still attached to Selene."

"Oh, that." She waved her hand dismissively. "That wasn't ever going to go anywhere."

"You don't know that."

"Sure I do. You and Selene are too much alike."

What the hell was that supposed to mean? "How do you like farm life?" I said by way of changing the subject.

"It's great. A lot of work, though, especially for Brad."

He had a regular job in addition to everything he did here on the farm. It must be difficult, putting in full-time hours just to come home and work a hard physical job.

"I hope it works out for you."

"Oh, I'm sure it will." She gave me a knowing look. "Now, about this girl."

"I really don't want to talk about her."

Marie sighed. "You're no fun."

"I ran into Trent the other day."

She stared at me over the top of her soda. "You did, huh?"

"At a party. I didn't know he was going to be there or I would have stayed away."

"How did it go?"

"He ordered me to leave town."

She pulled her head back in a disbelieving gesture. "Was he serious?"

"Seemed like it."

"That's ridiculous. You're not going to do it."

"Of course not. He doesn't get to tell me where to live."

Marie sighed, shaking her head. "I just don't understand his hostility."

I cocked an eyebrow. "You don't?"

"This garbage started long before Carter was even born, so it's not because of the accident."

She always referred to my shooting of my little half-brother as "the accident," as if I were somehow not responsible. I knew the truth, though. I was the only one to blame.

"I'm pretty sure he'd be a lot less hateful if I hadn't killed Carter."

"Maybe," she said. "Maybe not."

Whether he would or wouldn't was immaterial. I'd shot our brother and Trent would never forgive me. Therefore, he spent a lot of time trying to pay me back for what I'd done. When we were kids, he'd had a lot of opportunity, since we'd lived in the same house. After I ran away, he must have been frustrated as hell with his target gone.

The strange thing was, he'd never asked me how I felt about killing Carter. He'd seemed to assume I meant to do it. Even my own father thought I'd done it on purpose. And no matter what I said, they wouldn't change their minds.

My plan to seduce Caroline was pushing on me, trying to get me to confess to Marie. I didn't want her to know. She'd only argue with me and put a big guilt trip on me and I didn't need that. So I kept my mouth shut. I was going forward with the plan. No matter what.

Chapter 5

Caroline: I had several sorority functions that weekend. Rush—when all the girls who wanted to belong to a house went from one function to the next, wearing the approved clothes and sporting the approved attitude, hoping to be accepted—was over and most of the accepted candidates had pledged a house. I remembered how nervous I'd been during my own rush week, terrified no-one would like me and I'd end up as a reject, otherwise known as an independent. By some miracle, one of the more prestigious houses had accepted me.

Yet I still lived in the dorms. Why was that? Maybe I was more of an independent than I thought.

Tonight, my house was having a dinner with the pledges—they lived in the dorms by necessity and could only visit the house—and I had to be there. As I welcomed the freshman girls to our house, I wondered what Max would think of all this. I could picture the wry lift of his mouth as he watched all of them, dressed in outfits so similar they almost looked like a uniform, filing into the house. The idea he might find us amusing made me want to squirm.

Well, what did he know? A high school dropout who'd run away from home, who spent his spare time smoking weed. By belonging to a sorority, we were developing our social skills and our network of contacts, things that would serve us well later in life. Sorority women were much more successful than independents and if Max couldn't appreciate that, well, his opinion hardly mattered.

Yet the words and tune of the song he'd sung by the river started running over and over in my mind, distracting me from the evening's activities. "Avery" was about a runaway. Was that why Max had chosen that song to sing?

Or maybe he was only referring to the name of the town—Avery's Crossing.

We crowded into the dining room and chose our seats, Paige and I taking chairs next to each other. Tiffani, the chapter president, was her usual glossy brunette self, complete with cat-eye makeup and nails lacquered in navy blue. I could smell her perfume from my seat halfway down the table from her. She presided over all our house meals as if she were queen instead of a sorority house president.

"You're awfully quiet tonight," Paige said.

I nodded. "I've got some things on my mind."

She leaned closer to me. "Would one of those things start with the letter M?" she said in an undertone.

"You know I can't talk about that."

Her eyes sparkled as she smiled at me. She loved having secrets, even if she couldn't keep one worth a damn. I wondered how many people she'd told so far. Maybe I'd gotten lucky and she hadn't spilled the beans yet.

"Have you dealt with the big M lately?" she said, continuing the stage whisper.

"No." Yes. Was I blushing? I hoped not.

"What are you two whispering about over there?" Tiffani leaned over the table. "Don't keep secrets."

"Oh, Paige is just teasing me about my class load," I said.

Tiffani wrinkled her nose. "I know we say our education is the most important thing, but let's not talk about classes tonight. 'Kay?"

"Sure, Tiffani."

Paige kicked me under the table. She was probably planning to corner me as soon as possible and wring every bit of intel regarding Max out of me. Since I didn't want word getting out, I'd just have to slip out of the house and sneak back to the dorms before she could get me alone.

On Monday, the first class I had was in essay-writing. I didn't actually need the class to graduate with a French degree, but it seemed like the kind of thing that might come in useful later. I took a seat in the middle of the room, just out of the reach of a broad bar of early morning sunlight streaming through the old double-hung windows.

A big male body slid into the desk next to mine. I glanced over as I set my laptop on the desk and did a double-take. Max. Max?

"What are you doing here?" I whispered.

"I'm in this class." He smiled smugly at me as he stretched his long legs to the side of his desk.

"No, you're not." I returned his smile with the fiercest glare I could muster. "You're following me."

"That's so not true. I'm really in this class. Ask the prof."

I glanced at the man standing by the lectern. "But I thought this was your first year. This is an upper division class."

He smirked. "I'm just that good."

I still didn't believe him. Shaking my head, I turned back to my laptop and started setting up a file for my notes. I would not look at him or notice the utter fineness of his body, nor would I think about the way his black hair slipped forward over his eyes in that irresistible way that made me want to touch it.

"How are you?" he said in a low tone that seemed to get inside me and make my whole body vibrate.

"Fine," I said, still not looking at him.

"No delayed reaction from that fall?"

I glanced at him sideways. "You're the one who took the most damage. Are you okay?"

"Never better."

I ran out of busywork. My file was set up and the lecture hadn't begun yet. I could continue avoiding his gaze, but what would be the point? The longer I refused to look at him, the ruder my behavior would be. Still, I couldn't encourage him. Trent might hurt him if he found out Max was flirting with me.

I turned to Max. "You'd better be careful. Trent sometimes meets me after this class."

"He does, huh? That's too bad."

His lingering gaze seemed to imply he wanted to be more than friends. That was hard to believe, given my shortcomings, but the long looks continued and I didn't know how else to interpret them. Could Max really want me?

He wasn't going to get me, of course. I'd never cheat on Trent. Still, I couldn't get the thought of Max's hands on my body out of my mind.

How would he taste? How would his hair, his bare skin feel under my hands? This room was awfully hot. I fidgeted with the neckline of my sweater and wished I'd worn something cooler.

"It's hot in here," he murmured.

"Yeah." I frowned at him. "I still think you're following me. You keep showing up, and this is a big campus. It can't just be coincidence."

"Maybe you're following me."

"What? Why would I do that?"

Another smirk. I wanted to wipe that superior expression off his face. "Because you can't stay away from me, obviously."

"Oh, of course." I sent him a smirk of my own. "Thank you for clearing that up for me."

"You're welcome."

He winked at me and I couldn't help it. I laughed.

The silver pendant he always wore peeped out of his shirt collar again. All I could see was the very edge of it, which looked circular. I pointed to it.

"What's that?"

He put his hand over it. "Just something a friend of mine gave me."

"Can I see it?"

The professor cleared his throat and Max straightened out and faced front. I couldn't figure him out. He seemed like a truly nice guy, other than the outrageous flirting, and that was harmless, really. The dangerous schemer Trent had described was someone I'd never seen.

Maybe Trent had misjudged him. Maybe he'd let their past—whatever it was—warp his perception of the person Max was now. If I could just get the two of them together to talk, they might be able to stop hating each other.

A coffee date, just the three of us. It would be a start, anyway.

* * *

"No way in hell," Trent said when I suggested it to him.

"Why not? It's just coffee." I sat down on my pale aqua bedspread and crossed my arms.

"I don't want to see him."

"Trent, he's your stepbrother."

He fixed me with a hard-eyed stare. "Believe me, I wish I could forget that fact."

"I just don't understand why you're not willing to try to work things out."

His hand slashed down through the air. "It's none of your business. Drop it, okay?"

I made an impatient sound. "You're making no sense."

"I hate him; he hates me. End of story."

"But if you got together and talked things out, maybe you could mend fences."

He shook his head. "Our fences are fine the way they are."

"But—"

"Trust me, Caroline, Max would tell you the same thing. We don't want to talk."

I jumped up from the bed and started to pace my room. There wasn't a lot of space for it, but I made do with the three or four pace distance I had. Trent backed up a step and leaned against my door, giving me a tiny bit more room.

"He has no family. That isn't right," I said.

"First of all, it's his own damn fault. Second, why do you care? Have you been seeing him behind my back?"

"No!" Liar. If I'd had pants, they would have burst into flame. Luckily for me, I was wearing a skirt. "It just makes me sad."

"Don't be. There are things you don't know."

I whirled to face him. "Yeah. So enlighten me. Tell me about it."

Trent leaned his head against my door and closed his eyes. "I can't."

"Sure you can."

"Well, then, I don't want to."

"Oh, for pity's sake, Trent. I'm your girlfriend. I have a right to know."

He opened his eyes and watched me pace for a couple of turns, his jaw working back and forth.

"Can't you just take my word for it that he's dangerous?" he said.

"No. Why should I? You need to be a lot more specific than that."

"All right." He pushed off from the door and stalked toward me, his square jaw tense and angry-looking. "Stop pacing."

I stopped. We stood at the foot of my bed and stared at each other like opponents in a boxing match.

"So tell me," I said.

Trent drew in a huge breath. "He killed our little brother."

"What?" I stared open-mouthed at him. That couldn't be right. No.

"I said he killed our half-brother. The son of his dad and my mom."

"But...why? Why would Max do something like that?"

"I don't know." Trent raked his fingers through his pale hair, making it stand on end. "He always claimed it was an accident, but I didn't believe that."

"Why not?"

"He never seemed to have much remorse."

"But...he seems so normal." More or less. "I can't imagine him wanting to kill someone."

Trent's eyes narrowed into cruel slits. "You have been seeing him."

"No, I haven't. I just ran into him on campus once."

"I'm not sure I should believe you."

"You can believe whatever you want. I'm not seeing him."

Trent loomed over me. "You'd better not be."

I lifted my chin. There was no way I'd back off from this one. "Are you threatening me?"

"No. I'm warning you."

"Don't even think you can tell me who I can and can't see," I said, beginning to pace again. "How did it happen?"

"He shot him with my stepdad's gun."

I halted to close my eyes. "Oh, my God."

"It was bad, Caroline. Real bad."

"Was he playing with the gun?"

"Yeah. He claimed he thought it was unloaded. It went off by accident."

"But you didn't believe him."

"No. And I still don't."

I put my hands to my forehead and blew out my breath. "This is so not what I thought you'd say."

"What were you expecting?"

"I don't know. Joyriding. Breaking and entering or something. Maybe robbing a gas station, at the worst. Not murder." I looked over at him, knowing my expression was as bleak as it could get. "How old was he?"

"Max or Carter?"

"Both."

He reached into his back pocket and pulled out his wallet, flipping through the pictures he kept there until he got to the right one. Then he handed the wallet to me, displaying a snapshot of a smiling, blond toddler. The kid was preciously cute, with big blue eyes and a dimpled grin. He'd kept a picture of Carter in his wallet and yet somehow I'd never known it was there or that he'd had a little brother. "Max was ten. Carter three."

I blinked. Ten? Ten years old? "He was just a little kid himself, Trent," I said with a frown.

"Some kids are just evil. You've seen news stories of murdering psycho kids."

"Are you saying Max is a bad seed? A psycho?"

"He killed Carter in cold blood. For no reason, except maybe it was his idea of fun." Trent's blue eyes were hard and cold. Like glacier ice. He really despised Max.

"I'm just so shocked. I can't believe it." How could I have liked someone so horrible? How could Max have done those things? I couldn't wrap my mind around the notion that the Max I thought I knew had deliberately murdered a little boy, his own half-brother.

"You should. And you should be careful. Stay away from him. You see now why I warned you?"

I nodded slowly. I felt like I had a big chunk of concrete attached to my heart and it was dragging me down into deep water. "Yeah. I do."

"Good. Let's go eat. I'm starved."

I, on the other hand, had lost my appetite.

* * *

"Don't you love fall weather here?" Paige said, kicking at a pile of leaves on the sidewalk as we walked together to the campus gym.

The air was full of the musty scent of fallen leaves, the air was bright blue against the gold and red and orange of the leaves still on the trees, and everything looked as beautiful as I could imagine. We'd had some wet days; today was a sun break. Soon the rain would start in earnest and it would all turn gray, but for now it was in autumn Technicolor.

Max was a murderer.

I couldn't get that thought out of my mind. I didn't even know why it bothered me so much, why it made me feel like something inside me was collapsing. As if the knowledge broke my heart. I hardly knew the guy. There was no reason for it to matter so much to me.

There was Trent. But somehow his pain didn't seem as real to me as the searing disappointment I felt over Max.

"What's up?" Paige said as we took a left along the main street of campus.

"Nothing. Why?"

"You've been kind of down lately."

Should I tell her? But Trent had been so secretive, I assumed he didn't want anyone outside the family to know.

"It's nothing. I'm just tired."

"Maybe a good workout will perk you up."

"Yeah, I'm sure it will."

I glanced across the intersection toward the student union and saw her. The blonde who'd been in my room the morning Paige had brought over the doughnuts. She stood at the bottom of the steps leading into the commons. She wore the same white tunic with blue embroidery over bell-bottom jeans. Her hair was so long it came all the way down to her butt. And she was looking at me. Staring.

I grabbed Paige's wrist. "I've seen her before."

"Who?"

"That blonde standing under the light-post."

Paige wrinkled her brow. "What blonde?"

"Can't you see her? She's right there." I pointed.

"There's no-one by the lamp-post, Caroline."

"Yeah, there is. Right there." I pointed again.

The blonde spun on her platform heel and dashed up the steps into the student union commons. I bolted after her, scattering pedestrians and bicyclists in the street. People hollered at me and I ignored them.

I yanked open the commons doors and ran right into a wall of man. A warm, muscular, male-scented wall that instantly made me tremble and ache. Which was weird and completely out of character.

"Hey, are you all right?" It was a familiar voice. It explained my reaction, too.

I looked up into Max's concerned eyes. "I'm fine. Did you see her?"

"See who?"

"A blond girl. She just came this way." I leaned around him, trying to see if I could pick her out in the commons.

She seemed to have disappeared. It was the middle of the afternoon, and the dining area was only sparsely occupied. The blonde seemed to be nowhere in the room. Where had she gone?

"I didn't see anyone," Max said.

"God, that's so weird," I muttered. "She was right here."

"Caro, are you all right?"

I looked up at him. Max. My conversation with Trent came back to me and chills broke out all over my body. This was the murderer I'd almost kissed. And I still reacted to him, still got all breathless and filled with idiotic butterflies who didn't know they were fluttering over a guy who'd killed his own brother.

"Fine," I said, taking a step away from him. "I'm fine."

"Who were you chasing?"

"Just some chick I thought I knew."

"Hi, Max," Paige said behind us. "Caroline, what were you trying to do there?"

"I wanted to talk to her."

Max looked over my shoulder at my friend. "Do you know what girl she's talking about?"

"I didn't see her," Paige said.

"She was the same girl who was in my room," I muttered to myself.

"What girl? In your room? What are you talking about?" Paige's eyes were wide and startled; she was starting to sound agitated.

"Come and sit down," Max said. "We'll figure it out together."

I couldn't meet his eyes. Could he tell I knew his secret?

"No, I can't. We don't have time," I said. "Paige and I were on our way to the gym."

"You seem pretty upset. I think you should tell me what happened."

"Yeah," Paige said. "I want to figure this out, because you're starting to scare me."

I looked back at her, then at Max. They both looked worried. Did they think I was losing it? Did I care that a murderer thought I was losing it? No, not really. But if I was scaring Paige, it would be worth sitting down with *him* in order to reassure her.

"Okay. Fine. But just for a couple of minutes."

We chose a nearby table. Somehow, I'm not sure how it happened, I ended up sitting next to Max instead of Paige. He turned to me with a serious expression on his face, the kind I imagined a psychiatrist might use. Which was pretty funny, coming from someone like him.

"Tell me what you saw."

I made a vague wave gesture. "Just a girl. Dressed in seventies clothes. She was standing by the lamp-post at the bottom of the stairs outside there."

"But you said you saw her in your room," Paige said.

"Yeah, I did. When you were pounding on my door that morning. I opened my eyes and there she was, standing by my bed and looking at me. When I blinked, she was gone. I thought it was just a dream. And then I saw her here, and I didn't know what to think." Now I thought about it, the blonde was so much like a ghost it gave me a case of the chills all over again. But I didn't believe in ghosts. I refused to believe. There was no way I was going down the Aunt Jo Highway to Hell. That was not an option.

"God, that's bizarre," Paige said in hushed tones.

"Sounds like a ghost to me," Max said.

I looked at him warily. "A ghost? I don't believe in that crap." And I never would. Unlike Jo, I didn't want to. All that woo-woo stuff was just too silly for me.

"I'm not saying it's for sure or anything," he said evenly. "But it does sound like a classic ghost encounter. How else would you explain it?"

Paige leaned across the table, seemingly fascinated. I just raised my eyebrows.

"Coincidence," I said. "She just happened to look like the girl in my dream. I had no idea you believed in ghosts."

"I believe in all kinds of things," he said.

Very evasive. Did he believe in murder?

"I've never seen a ghost." Paige sounded jealous.

"It wasn't a ghost," I said. "Come on, guys. It had to be a coincidence."

"Then why did you run after her that way?" Paige said. "If you really thought it was just coincidence, you wouldn't have tried so hard to catch up with her."

I shrugged. "It was just a momentary impulse. It didn't mean anything."

The only person I'd ever met—until Max—who really believed in ghosts was Jo, and she wasn't a person I wanted to emulate in any way. She lived in some hazy, drug-addled underworld where her imagination mixed freely with reality and gave her visions, not just of ghosts, but of angels and demons and who knew what else. I didn't want to go where Aunt Jo lived. Ever.

I rubbed my arms, trying to calm the shivers that had inexplicably taken over my body. "I'm not going to worry about this. It doesn't mean anything."

"You might be right," Max said.

I raised my brows at him. "Why do you say that? I thought you believed."

"Ghosts aren't normally hostile. Most of them are just hanging around. She might not want anything with you in particular. Maybe she's just going through some kind of routine."

"Really? How do you know all that?" Not that I was giving his nonsense any credence.

He shrugged, looking modest. "I've done a lot of study on the subject."

"You're just full of surprises." There was too much bitterness in my voice. "I never expected you to be a ghost hunter."

"Oh, I don't hunt them. I let them come to me."

Paige laughed. I merely looked at him. Maybe he could tell that I knew what he'd done; I wasn't doing enough to hide my anger and confusion from him if I didn't want him to guess.

Max met my gaze steadily for a moment before looking to Paige. He knew. He had that look in his eyes, as if he knew exactly what was going on in my head. I dropped my gaze and stared at the table top, hoping he'd decide he was wrong. I should have smiled or said something lighthearted. That would have cast more doubt than me being unable to even look at him. By acting uptight around him, I was only confirming his suspicions.

Why did I even care whether or not he realized I knew? He was the guilty party, not me. There was absolutely nothing for me to be ashamed of, yet here I was, trying to hide my thoughts from him. It made no sense, even to me.

He turned back to me, his jaw tense. "You know, don't you?"

I met his gaze head-on instead of flinching away like I wanted to. "Yes."

It seemed to be his turn to look down, to avoid contact. "So."

"Is it true?"

"Every word." His voice had a flippant tone that made me want to smack him.

Paige was looking back and forth from me to him. I could see in her expression that she knew something was going on but she couldn't guess what it was.

"Do you mind cluing me in?" she said.

"I can't," I said. "It has to do with Trent."

"Oh." She looked back and forth between us again. "Okay, then."

"Sorry," I said. "We didn't mean to be rude. I'd much rather talk about ghosts anyway." Right now, a root canal sounded better than yet more elliptical conversation about Max's past misdeeds.

"Okay, then what if the ghost comes back?" Paige said. "What should she do then?"

"Like I said, they usually don't mean any harm," Max said, carrying on as if he hadn't just confessed to murder. "But if she does anything that seems threatening, Caro, don't hesitate to call me. I'll be happy to help."

I refrained, just barely, from rolling my eyes. "How would you do that?"

"There are a number of things I could do. I can try to communicate with her and find out what she wants; I can banish her and I can put a protective seal on your dorm room to keep her from coming back. It all depends on the circumstances and what you want."

"I want to forget all about it." I picked up my gym bag. "Come on, Paige. We should get to the gym before it gets crowded."

He frowned slightly, watching me as I stood. I could see that he was trying to figure me out, trying to make sense of my curt behavior. It should be obvious to him. I'd found out about him and I couldn't stand to be near him anymore. There was nothing ambiguous about it.

I made myself smile at him. "Thanks for the advice, Max. We'll see you around, okay?"

"Sure. Have a good time at the gym."

"Will do," Paige said with a broad smile.

I turned and stalked toward the door. I was being rude and bitchy and I knew it, but at the moment I didn't care. Ever since Trent had told me what Max had done, I couldn't look at or think of him the same way.

He'd only been ten years old when it happened. Maybe I should have had more compassion for him. It was the no-remorse part of it that bothered me the most. Accidents happen, sometimes tragic accidents, but to have no remorse and no sense of responsibility, that was unforgivable.

"Are you mad at me?" Paige said as we left the commons for the sunshine of the outdoors.

"No. Why?"

"You seem mad."

"I told you; I'm tired today. It's making me cranky."

She sent me a wide-eyed, disbelieving glance and started down the stairs. "If you say so."

I couldn't tell her about Max and Carter. I just couldn't. Trent would be furious with me if I did. He'd had a difficult enough time trusting me with the information in the first place; if I betrayed his trust, he'd never tell me anything again.

Still, it would be good to get an outside perspective on the situation.

"You were kinda rude to Max in there," she said.

"I know."

"Is he the one you're mad at?"

"Paige, I'm just tired. That's all it is."

"Sure."

I sighed. "There's some stuff going on with Trent. I can't talk about it."

"I knew it! I knew you weren't just tired. So tell me all about it."

"I told you; I can't. He'd be pissed if he found out I told you."

She stopped me with a hand on my forearm. "You're not pregnant, are you?"

I almost laughed. "No. Not pregnant."

"Whew. Good."

"It has to do with his family. It's not something he wants to get out."

"Ooh. Mysterious. Now I have to know."

"I'm not telling," I said in an overly dramatic tone. "Nothing you can do will make me betray my secrets."

She put her hands on her narrow hips and gave me a menacing glare. "I have ways of making you talk."

"No! I'll never talk."

We both laughed as we broke into a run for the gym.

Chapter 6

Max: I had only a few seconds to contemplate Caroline's hostile behavior before Fred showed up. He took the seat across from me and clasped his hands on the table, smiling like I should be glad to greet him in the middle of a very public place. Which I was not. Since I was the only one who could see him, I'd look like a loon sitting here and talking to him. I didn't mind being unconventional, but carrying on a public convo with my invisible friend was something else again.

I bent my head and muttered at the table top. "What are you doing here?"

"Talking to you. What does it look like?"

"I'd rather not look like a nutcase in public, thank you."

"No-one is paying any attention to us."

I glanced around. The commons was nearly empty and, at the moment, his statement was true. But who knew when someone would walk past my table, probably at the worst possible moment?

"You couldn't wait until I was alone at home?" I said in an undertone.

"No, I couldn't."

"Okay, what's so damned important, then?"

"There's a spirit attempting to contact you."

I raised my brows at him. "So? I thought we'd already established that."

"Before, all I knew was there were spirits gathering around you. Now, I'm aware there is one in particular who wishes to speak with you."

"Who?"

He spread his hands. "I don't know yet."

I shook my head. "When you find out, let me know. Until then, stop trying to embarrass me."

"You know I'd never deliberately embarrass you, Max."

"Do I? Sometimes I think you spirit types forget what it was like to be alive. You forget how freaked out people get when they see anything the least bit unusual."

He gave a short nod. "Perhaps we do."

"Try to remember that we mortals do care about the opinions of other mortals."

"Even you?" His dark-blue eyes crinkled at the corners. "I thought you were above all that."

"Not me."

"There was a time when you claimed you didn't give a damn what anyone else thought of you."

"Yeah, and I was about fifteen at the time. I didn't know any better."

"So you've decided to turn over a new leaf and become entirely conventional?"

"Of course not." I tapped my fingers on the table. "Just because I care a little about how others see me doesn't mean I'm going to turn normal."

"So you care, just not very much."

I grinned. "That's it in five seconds."

"I could materialize, and then anyone passing by would see me as an ordinary person."

Yeah, except for the fact that he was dressed in nineteenth-century clothing. What was with the sack suit, anyhow? It was kind of ugly, if you asked me—not that he ever had. But he could change his appearance at will, so maybe it would work out, except for the minor detail that it could make the room as cold as the inside of an industrial fridge.

"Wouldn't that take an awful lot of energy?"

He shrugged. "Yes. But it might be worth it. I don't want to embarrass you, after all."

I decided to ignore that. "Did you hear Caroline's story?"

"About the ghost?" he said, raising his brows.

"What do you make of it?"

"I'm not sure who her ghost is, but I am sure she's connected to yours."

My breath left me in a rush. "That's what I was afraid of."

"Why afraid?"

"Let's just say it's damned inconvenient. How can I help her or find out how her spirit is connected with mine with Trent hanging around? Plus, I think she's mad at me."

"You want your brother's girl," he said with a knowing look.

I sighed. "What's your point?"

"Trent could make a lot of trouble for you. Give him any excuse and he'll be after you."

"Thanks. I didn't know that."

Fred tilted his head slightly to the side. "Are you trying to provoke a confrontation?"

"I've got nothing to hide. You know that. What could he do to me that he hasn't already done?"

"You're breaking the law, Max."

"Not at the moment," I said with a shrug.

He smiled wryly. "Quit smoking marijuana. I don't want to see you go to jail. After all, I'd have to visit you there and I've seen enough of prison to last me for eternity."

Fred had gone to jail for a few years in his youth for an unspecified crime. Unspecified to me, that was.

"Why would you have to visit me there?" I said. "Not that I don't appreciate the offer, understand."

"You're my descendant. It's my job to look out for you."

I stared openly at him, forgetting all about the other people in the room. "You're what?"

"I'm your great-great-something or other grandfather on your mother's side. Didn't you know?"

"I had no idea." In all the years I'd known him, I'd never guessed he was my ancestor. No wonder he looked so familiar. We were relatives.

"It's why I came to you in the first place."

He'd appeared to me when I was eleven, still so torn up over Carter's death I could barely function. I'm not sure I would have survived if it hadn't been for Frederick. He talked to me in a way my dad couldn't—or wouldn't—and helped me understand that the accident was just that. An accident. Not that I fully believed him—I had been playing with a gun, something I'd had no business even touching.

"Your mother was gone," he said. "And your dad didn't seem to care about you anymore. In fact, I was starting to think he was going to murder you during one of his rages. I had to do something."

"Thank you," I said through a tight throat.

Here I'd thought no-one gave a shit about me and all along Fred had been looking out for me. Even if he couldn't physically interfere with my dad, he'd kept me sane and whole in my mind. He'd made it possible for me to survive long enough to grow up. If we hadn't been in a public place, I might have given him a hug, something I rarely did with anyone. There were too many potential witnesses here, though.

Let's face it, talking to your invisible friend isn't nearly as bizarre as hugging that friend.

"You know, you don't need Caroline's cooperation to deal with any of this," Fred commented.

"I realize that."

The problem was I wanted it. I wanted an excuse to spend more time with her and I wanted to protect her from whatever spirit entity was trying to intrude on her. Not that I thought Caroline was in danger, but I didn't like the idea of her being made uncomfortable or afraid.

She claimed not to believe in ghosts. I'd seen fear in her eyes, though, when she'd described the blonde to me. Part of her believed, even if she hated to admit it. And she was no witch, like Selene; she'd have no tools or experience to fall back on in this situation.

Damn it. What was I doing? The only reason I was friendly toward Caroline was to take her from my stepbrother. I wasn't supposed to care about her or get emotionally involved with her. I needed to get hold of myself before I blew the whole project.

A disturbing thought wormed its way into my brain. Was it truly so important that I hurt Trent? Did I really want to use Caroline that way?

I pushed out my breath without looking at Fred. Yeah, it was and I did. The gods knew he deserved some kind of consequences for everything he'd done to me over the years.

She'd seemed so upset, though, and the ghost-girl wasn't the only reason. Trent had told her about my past. He'd put the worst spin on it that he could, probably embellishing with all kinds of bogus details.

My gut went cold at the thought that Caroline knew what I'd done. She hated me now. She judged me—I'd seen it all over her face. I'd never be able to get close to her now she knew the truth about me.

My face flushed as a wave of shame washed over me. My prick of a stepbrother would never let me get past what I'd done to Carter, no matter how many years went by. That hideous deed would follow me everywhere I went, haunting me until the day I died.

Caroline's good opinion meant nothing to me except for the fact I wouldn't be able to use her as a weapon against Trent if she kept avoiding me. I had to find out exactly how much she knew. Maybe I could explain myself, get her to understand.

Ah, hell, who was I kidding? Nothing could explain away the shooting death of my three-year-old brother. Nothing.

Chapter 7

Caroline: Mid-November days in the Willamette Valley tended to be rainy and cold, but the Wednesday before Thanksgiving was an exception. We had a rare blue sky and I took advantage by taking my studies outdoors to a bench outside the student union. Unfortunately, the bench was wet, something I didn't think of until after I'd already sat down.

I hadn't seen Max since Monday. He hadn't even been in class this morning. He must be avoiding me.

That was sensible of him. Neither of us needed any extra drama in our lives and Trent would never tolerate me being friendly with his stepbrother, even if nothing ever happened between us. The ridiculous thing was, I couldn't get Max out of my head. I'd thought about him every day since I'd met him, and the thoughts always came with generous sides of lust and butterflies in the stomach, even after finding out what he'd done.

I should have been catching up on my reading. But instead of pulling out my books, I took out my phone and called my mom.

"Looking forward to Thanksgiving?" she said cheerfully as soon as greetings had been exchanged.

"Yeah." I guess. "Trent and I are leaving as soon as we're done with our afternoon classes."

"I hope you drive carefully, especially if you hit any ice."

"We will."

"You sound kind of down. You don't want to go?"

It was always annoying when my mom saw through me so easily. She had mom superpowers, including mind reading and eyes in the back of her head.

"It's kind of weird," I said.

"How come? Trent's a great kid."

He wasn't a kid at all, but I let that one pass. I guess to someone my mom's age, we college students were all kids.

"I'm just not sure where this relationship is going."

"Oh. I thought things were good between you."

How much should I tell her? "They're okay, I guess."

Only they weren't okay. I was daydreaming constantly about another guy. My feelings for Trent had gone from fantasies about marriage proposals to resentment and boredom. This wasn't going to end well.

"He's got a lot of potential, Caroline. And he's so good looking."

"Yes, he is."

I couldn't tell her I didn't feel any passion for him. I mean, she's my mom. That would be, like, the most awkward conversation in the history of all mother-daughter conversations.

"Well, I think you should go. Sometimes you have to put some work into a relationship."

"Yeah, I know. And anyway, it's too late to back out."

"It's never too late if you're that uncomfortable. You can stay in the dorms, can't you?"

"Yeah, mine is open for the holiday. But I don't want to do that to him."

The conversation lagged. I watched clumps of students pass me as they crossed the quad separating the student union from huge, old Merriweather Hall. Everyone seemed happy, looking forward to their holiday.

"How are studies going?"

"They're fine," I said.

"It's not too late to pick up a minor in education, you know."

"Yeah, I know. I don't want to teach."

There was a long pause. Mom was probably trying to pull herself together on the other end. She got so worked up over the fact I didn't have a solid career plan.

"And Paige?" she said, with a bit of strain in her voice.

"She's great, Mom. We see each other almost every day."

"I'm so glad you have such a good friend. Is she going home for the holiday?"

"Yeah." Paige's family lived down in Medford, so she'd be traveling in the opposite direction from me.

"I think it's great that you're getting to meet Trent's family. He's been to see us, so now it's your turn to meet his folks."

I hesitated, wondering how much I should confess to my mother. "The thing is, I found out something about him, Mom." And that discovery had irrevocably changed the way I felt.

"Oh?"

"He has a stepbrother named Max. He never told me about him. I found out by accident."

"Why didn't he tell you?"

"Because Max's family hates him. I met him on campus. He seems like a nice guy. I don't understand why they hate him so much."

Actually, I knew exactly why, but I didn't want to say that to her, or go into any details about his odd involvement in magic. I didn't want to prejudice her against Max, just in case.

In case what?

Yeah. I didn't want to go there, not even with myself.

"That's too bad," my mom said. "I had no idea there was anything like that in Trent's family."

"Neither did I. How do you date someone for a whole year and not know something like this?"

"Maybe you'll find out more over the holiday."

Maybe I would. The thought of spending over three days with those people made my stomach feel like I had swallowed a really big rock, though.

"Yeah. I don't think they'll talk to me about him," I said. "They hate him."

Oops. I so did not want to explain Max's history to my mom.

"Really," she said. "Why is that?"

"I'm not sure."

"Well, you accepted Trent's invitation already, so go up to Montana with him and do your best. You should probably avoid talking about Max. And if it doesn't work out, at least you'll have important information about his family."

"Such as that I can't get along with them?"

"Exactly."

We both laughed. I loved my mom, even if she did push me in the direction of a life I wasn't sure I wanted. What would she think of Max and his unorthodox beliefs?

My parents were the kind of people who thought that if you couldn't see it, touch it, taste or hear it, then it didn't exist. The idea of spirits and the unseen were ridiculed when I was growing up. I mean, look at Aunt Jo. She was a shining example of what could happen to people who messed around with that stuff. If I said anything about Max, or my recent experiences with Retro-girl, I'd get an earful. Or maybe just pained silence, which might be even worse.

* * *

It takes about fourteen hours to drive from Avery's Crossing to Billings, and that's if you don't stop for lunch, snacks, and pee breaks. Of course, it's also if you don't drive eighty miles an hour, like Trent. Either way, we had to stop overnight in a motel somewhere in Idaho.

I wished I'd brought something beefier to wear than my pea coat. It was made of wool but relatively thin. The mountain wind drove right through it and every time I got out of the car, I was shivering nonstop.

We made Billings at four o'clock on Thanksgiving Day. Compared to Avery's Crossing, it's a big town but compared to Portland, not so much. At least, that was the impression I had as we drove through the outskirts and into Trent's subdivision, one of those developments where both the lots and the houses are enormous.

A thin layer of snow covered the ground. We went past a parade of gigantic houses in all kinds of styles until he finally turned into the driveway of the biggest one of all. It looked like a lodge hotel or something, it was so huge, and all made of logs. A log castle. There was a giant bank of windows in the front and through them you could see a palatial living room glowing with lamplight from the gigantic Western-style chandelier hanging from its cathedral ceiling.

"Wow," I said.

"Yeah. Wait until you see the inside." He pulled up in front of a separate, five-car garage and parked.

"Is this where you grew up?"

"Mostly. My stepdad built it not too long after they got married. I was six, I think. Carter was a baby."

And Max didn't even get a mention. Not that I could blame Trent, considering what his stepbrother had done.

I stared up at the beautiful monstrosity in front of me and tried to imagine him living here. The Max I knew didn't seem to fit in a place like this. Of course, no-one I knew would really fit here, except maybe Trent. The house I'd grown up in was a featureless little ranch from the seventies that my dad had bought right after Aunt Jo moved out. My parents were so busy working that they'd never really updated the place and now all that seventies stuff was cool again.

But this house...this house had seen a murder. Was it haunted? Did a little boy ghost run through its rooms?

That was such an Aunt Jo train of thought that I shut myself down before I could follow it any further.

We pulled our bags from the car and scrunched through the snow to the front door, which was one of those giant double doors made to intimidate visitors with how grand they are. These were in a rustic style with wrought-iron hardware. Each door sported a wreath made of Indian corn and wheat.

One of them opened to a slim blonde of indeterminate age with a huge smile on her face. She wore an apron, but her hair was up in a French twist. She looked so much like Trent that I knew she must be his mother.

"Hi, sweetie," she said, putting her arms around Trent. "It's so good to see you finally."

"Hi, Mom." His voice was muffled against her hair.

She released him and turned her blinding smile on me. "And you must be Caroline. We're so glad you could come for Thanksgiving. We've heard a lot about you."

"Thanks, Mrs. Kincaid. I'm glad to be here." A little polite lie wouldn't hurt anything, would it?

"Come on in and put your bags away. Dinner is ready."

We made our way into the foyer, which rose at least two stories above us. Somewhere in the stratosphere, another Western chandelier like the one in the living room dangled above our heads. A sweeping staircase with a wrought-iron banister led upward. The floor was covered in slate tiles and a mountain landscape painting hung on one wall. They were really working the Western theme here.

"I've put Caroline in the blue guest room," Mrs. Kincaid said. "Go get your stuff put away and come to the kitchen." She almost bounced with eagerness.

I gave her another polite smile as Trent led the way to the second story. I was hungry and the house smelled delicious, like roasting turkey along with something oniony and a hint of sweet spices. But I was also incredibly tired after such a long drive and what I wanted more than anything was to soak in a very big tub of really hot water.

"Sorry about the guest room," Trent said when we reached the second floor landing. "My mom doesn't want us sleeping together."

"That's all right." I didn't mind at all.

The landing was more like a grand hall. It was so broad there was room for a bench on one wall and some potted plants, plus more landscape paintings and a table with a bronze sculpture of a horse. I looked at the procession of doors along its length and wondered which one had been Carter's, which one Max's.

Trent led me to a generous room decorated in blue toile, thus breaking the strict Western theme. There was a floral rug on the floor in blue and cream, and curvy French-looking chairs in the reading nook. It even had a crystal chandelier, very ooh-la-la.

"This is a beautiful house," I said as I set my bag on the floor at the foot of the bed.

"Thanks. My mom hired a decorator."

"I've never even been in such a nice place."

He grinned at me. "I'll tell her you like it."

"No, I'll tell her. It'll score me a couple of points." I winked at him, although I wasn't really feeling it.

The truth was, I couldn't get Max out of my head. He'd grown up here, too. Had he run up and down that gigantic upstairs hallway when he was a kid? I would have.

Had they replaced the flooring after the shooting? My skin crawled as I thought about what had really happened here twelve years before.

"Let's go eat," Trent said, taking my arm.

The kitchen was super-sized, just like the rest of the house. It had black granite counters, Shaker-style cabinets in some kind of pale wood, and more Western-style light fixtures. A long, farmhouse-style table covered in platters of food took up the breakfast nook. A low arrangement of green and white hydrangeas marched down its center like a floral stripe.

"I hope you don't mind that we're doing this so casually," Mrs. Kincaid said to me. "We decided to make it family only this year, so we're eating in the kitchen."

This was casual? My family ate in the kitchen every year because we didn't have a formal dining room. And we never had floral arrangements on our table.

"This is great. You have a beautiful home," I said.

She beamed at me.

A man emerged from some back room of the house and I almost gave a visible start. He looked exactly like Max, except older. He was tall, with the same nearly-black hair and dark-blue eyes, the same straight nose and faint dimple in his chin. He gave me a welcoming smile, and more dimples appeared in his cheeks. He was like a picture of how Max would appear in twenty years or so.

"Hi, Caroline. I'm Peter Kincaid," he said, extending a hand.

We shook, but I didn't feel anything like the energy I'd experienced coming from his son. "Hi, Mr. Kincaid."

"We're glad to have you join us," he said.

"Me, too." I felt my face heating. Did he know I was acquainted with his lost son? Did he know how much Max resembled him?

"Now, let's eat," he said.

We sat down to one of the best Thanksgiving feasts I'd ever tasted. The conversation, though, lagged. There was so much I wanted to say but couldn't. Max sat invisibly in one of the empty chairs, like the proverbial elephant in the room, and I felt like we were going out of our way not to mention him.

It probably wasn't true. They were used to pretending he didn't exist. The elephant was really in my head, because I kept trying to imagine Max here at this table, eating with them. With us. It was hard to wrap my mind around the picture. Add in Carter in a booster seat and my brain just froze.

"So what are you planning to do when you graduate?" Mr. Kincaid said, interrupting my gloomy thoughts.

"I'm not sure yet."

"I hear you're a French major."

"That's right." I glanced at Trent, whose face was carefully neutral.

"There's probably not a lot you can do with that," Mr. Kincaid said.

"You'll figure it out eventually," his wife offered. She smiled at me. "And there's always the wife and mother path."

"Yes, there is that." I took a large bite of turkey and started to chew. They couldn't expect me to talk with food in my mouth.

They seemed to like me. His mom even seemed to think Trent and I might get more serious, like engaged serious. I wasn't ready for that step.

Until I'd discovered he'd been hiding the fact of his stepbrother's existence, I'd been looking forward to maybe getting more serious. I'd even had a few fantasies of marriage proposals. Now, the idea made me squirm. We'd dated for a year and he'd never mentioned Max. Not once.

How could I marry him? What else was he keeping from me?

Finally the long dinner was over. I complimented Mrs. Kincaid on her cooking and claimed exhaustion. They were so understanding as Trent and I left the room that it crossed my mind they might have been uncomfortable too. Maybe he didn't bring many girls home with him. I was one of a privileged few. Why didn't that make me feel any better?

Trent came into my room with me. As soon as he'd closed and locked the door, he started taking my clothes off. I let him do it. I wasn't in the mood, but then when was I ever?

Afterward, I stumbled into the shower and got cleaned up before dragging on my nightshirt and falling into bed. Trent had gone into his own room and I was alone. I fell asleep so fast I wasn't even aware of pulling the covers over myself.

* * *

Mom and Dad were arguing again. They'd been doing a lot of that lately. Our rented house was small and cheap, with thin walls, and even in my bedroom with the door shut I could hear them. It scared me when they yelled at each other. Usually my parents were so quiet and soft-spoken that yelling seemed foreign and startling.

My dad yelled something that ended in "Jo." They were talking about my aunt again. Lately, it seemed like she was all they talked about. Could Jo hear them? They'd hurt her feelings, yelling like that.

I sat up in my pink princess bed. I had my own room because I was so much older than the twins, who slept with my mom and dad. Moving slowly so as not to make my bedsprings squeak, I crept out of my ruffled floral nest and went to my door to listen.

"She'd never hurt the kids," my mom said, her tone defensive.

"Maybe not intentionally, but you have to admit she's a bad influence," my dad retorted.

"She's not that bad."

"I overheard her talking to her invisible friends today."

My mom sighed so loud I could hear it even in my room. "Oh, no."

"And yesterday, Caroline was talking to someone I couldn't see. She insisted there was a little girl in our kitchen with her." My dad sounded so angry.

I hadn't meant to make him angry, and I'd tried to introduce him to my friend Patsy, but he claimed she wasn't there. She was. I saw her and even touched her hand. She wore a pink dress with a ruffled, white pinafore over it and old-fashioned black patent shoes with straps across the top. Her socks were plain white. I saw her. But now my dad was angry about it. Had I done something wrong?

"I'm sure Caroline was only playing," Mom said. "She's very imaginative."

"I don't think so. She seemed to really believe this little girl was there. She even had a name for her. Patty or something like that."

Not Patty. Patsy. Hadn't he been listening?

"I'll talk to Jo about it."

"I don't want her living here anymore, Heather. She won't get treatment and she won't stop acting like a lunatic. She has to go."

No! He couldn't make Jo leave. I loved her. Who would play with me and tell me fairy tales at night if Jo left? Mom and Dad never wanted to tell me fairy tales, and when I managed to pester them into it, their stories weren't as good as Jo's.

"Where will she go?" my mom said. "She doesn't even have a job."

"That's not our problem anymore. We've been more than patient. We've tried to help her get it together, but nothing seems to work. We have to think of the kids."

"Caroline loves her."

"I know. That's half the problem."

It was my fault. They were going to get rid of my aunt and it was all my fault because I loved her too much.

* * *

In the morning, there was a cardboard box sitting at the foot of my bed. It was the kind that copy or computer paper comes in, sturdy and white, with handles built in. Written on the side, in somewhat messy black felt-tip marker, were the words "Max's stuff."

I sat up, frowning. Max's stuff? Who'd put that on my bed? And why? Had Trent come in this morning and done it as a joke?

I didn't really see the humor in it.

Sitting up, I tugged the box closer. It made a sloshing sound as whatever was inside it slid around and hit the sides of the box. Whoever had put it on my bed must have meant for me to look inside it, or they wouldn't have left it for me. The top had been folded shut but not taped, so I opened it, my heart beginning to pound. I was about to see pieces of a murderer's childhood.

There was a loose pile of old photos at the top of the contents. I pulled them out. They all featured Max at various ages beginning from infancy, including school pictures, casual snapshots, and a couple of family portraits. There were quite a few of them, especially the baby pics.

Had they thrown every picture they had of him in this box?

I held up each one in turn. He'd looked happy as a baby, all smiles. Innocent. I wondered briefly what he'd think if he knew I was looking at his baby pictures and grinned. If he was like most guys, he wouldn't be too pleased. He'd been a cutie, though, all black hair and huge blue eyes, adorable dimples in his cheeks.

Did I have a crush on him? The thought stopped me for a minute, made me put down the pictures. I shouldn't be having these thoughts about him. He'd killed his own brother, for pity's sake. Plus I was still attached to Trent. Sitting in Trent's house.

But I couldn't help how I felt, and Max had been a beautiful baby. Also, a beautiful toddler, preschooler, and grade school kid. It hurt to think of this innocent child becoming slowly warped until he turned into a killer.

You could see the change in him, though, in the pictures. His face went from happy to sad sometime in preschool, and the pictures became fewer. Then, in grade school, he started to look like a different person. Sullen. Angry. And there were hardly any photos of him from this period.

After that, it was like no-one wanted to notice him or look at him. I only found a handful of him in his teens. Not surprising, considering what he'd done.

Or maybe they were stored somewhere else. Maybe these were just extras and they had the others in regular photo albums with the rest of the family pictures. I set the photos aside and dug deeper into the box. There was a copy of one of Robert Jordan's Wheel of Time books and a concert t-shirt from a metal band I remembered being popular when I was in middle school. Beneath that were several sketchbooks.

I pulled those out and opened the first one. It was filled with drawings of typical boy stuff...dragons, motorcycles, swords, cars, skulls. Lots of skulls. They were remarkably detailed, though. I could see the talent and skill in them.

Leafing through the book, I found the drawings increasing in sophistication as his skills grew. The second book was darker, and the drawings more complex, more like complete compositions. Their subject matter was often violent, although mostly fantasy stuff with armored knights and castles. I could feel the anger coming off them, see it in the dark, slashing lines of his drawings.

Flipping through pictures of knights slaying dragons, demons abducting beautiful women, and dancing skeletons, I was in reluctant awe of his artistic abilities. He was really, really good. I didn't want to admire him for anything, but it would have been impossible not to acknowledge his gift.

Then I turned the page to a picture of a fist breaking glass, finely rendered shards spraying across the paper. An openly violent image, with no fantastic elements at all. It looked completely realistic. Under it, Max had written "he broke my ribs today."

I stopped and stared at the words, my stomach turning. Someone had hurt Max. Hurt him badly. Who? Was it Trent or someone else?

Until now, I'd imagined Max as the villain, the aggressor. Maybe he hadn't meant to kill Carter, but he had been playing with a gun. But this...he'd been a victim too. A weight seemed to settle deep inside me as I thought of him getting beaten so badly his ribs had broken.

Should I sympathize with him? He'd killed someone, after all, and Trent believed he'd done it on purpose. But Max was human, too, and he'd been a vulnerable child once. Someone whose ribs had been broken by another person. I wondered if anyone else, anyone other than Max and me, had seen this picture.

The door opened. I started and knocked some of the photos onto the floor. Trent barged into the room, a smile on his face, stopping short when he noticed the box.

His smile disappeared as his eyes went round and his mouth fell open. "What are you doing?"

"Looking at this stuff someone left for me."

"Where did you get that? His crap is all in the basement." He advanced on me, his eyes narrow now and angry-looking. "Were you snooping around looking for Max's shit?"

"No! I told you; someone left it for me."

He crossed his arms over his chest and scowled down at me. "That's bullshit and you know it. Who would give you that box?"

"How would I know? I thought you did it."

Maybe there really was a ghost and he was trying to communicate with me. No. Nope, not going to Jo-ville.

"Don't lie to me, Caroline."

I scowled back at him. "I'm not lying. I woke up and this box was sitting on my bed. I thought someone wanted me to see what was in it, so I opened it. That's all."

He gave me a disbelieving look. "What are you saying? A ghost put it here?"

"No. I'm saying I don't know who did."

Trent picked up the first sketchbook and leafed through it, then tossed it in the box with a snort of disgust. "He was always doodling this crap."

"He's really good."

"Oh? You like him? Is that why you're going through his things?"

I held up the picture of the fist. "Who broke his ribs, Trent?"

He shrugged. "I don't know."

"Really? You don't know? Are you sure you didn't do it?"

Trent's mouth fell open again. "What kind of question is that? No, I didn't do it."

"And you have no idea who did?"

He looked down, avoiding my gaze. "No idea. Anyway, he was always getting beat up. Nobody liked him."

I shook my head. "That's sad."

"So you do like him." He glared at me accusingly.

"I just think it's sad. That's all. Don't you have any compassion?"

"Not for him, no."

I stared at him for a moment and he dropped his gaze again, almost as if he felt ashamed. I didn't believe that. Maybe he was covering up some other emotion. I was becoming highly suspicious of everything Trent did and it seemed like an ominous trend.

Trent shifted his weight from one foot to the other. He sighed. "I came in here to ask if you were ready for breakfast and find out if you wanted to go on a little hike today," he said in a grudging tone.

What I really wanted was to get away from him and his messed up family. "A hike sounds good, but I need to get dressed first."

"Yeah, I can see that."

I put the things back in Max's box. "Trent, I don't want to fight over this. Honestly, I have no idea how the box got here. I don't like Max."

He glanced at me. "Are you sure?"

No. "Absolutely."

The rest of Friday was spent carefully avoiding the subject of Trent's stepbrother. I never mentioned him to their parents. We hiked, had lunch in a local cafe, ate Thanksgiving leftovers for dinner. On

Saturday morning, Trent and I started the drive back to Avery's Crossing.

I was never so happy to come home as when we re-entered town on Sunday afternoon.

✱ ✱ ✱

On Saturday morning, I woke up hungry and decided to go downstairs and forage in the kitchen for something to eat. I hoped the Kincaids didn't mind. They seemed to like me, so it should be okay, but no-one had said I was free to raid the fridge.

Downstairs, the only sound I could hear was the ticking of an old-fashioned clock in the living room. I padded into the kitchen in my stocking feet. The air was fragrant with the smell of coffee brewing; someone must have the coffee maker on a timer. Now that I was here, I felt a little nervous looking for food on my own. I hated imposing on people.

My stomach growled so loudly it hurt. On a sigh, I opened the refrigerator door. There was still half an apple pie left over from Thanksgiving, so I pulled it out and began the hunt for a plate. Unfortunately, this involved opening cupboard doors, which for some reason made me even more uncomfortable than getting in the fridge.

I persevered.

I'd just cut myself a slice of the pie when Mr. Kincaid walked in, looking sleepy and rumpled as if he'd just gotten out of bed. He wore sweats and a t-shirt under a loose cotton bathrobe and his salt and pepper hair stuck up in seven different directions.

I gave a guilty start. "Good morning. I hope you don't mind that I got myself something to eat."

"Of course not. Help yourself." He walked stiffly to the coffee maker, opened the cupboard above it, and pulled out a mug. "Want some coffee?"

"Yes, please."

I glanced at him covertly as he took down a second mug and was struck all over again with his resemblance to Max. He was a good-looking man, his looks tempered rather than diminished by age. I was alone with him, with no Trent to interfere or be embarrassed if I brought up the other son.

"I—um—I thought you might want to know—" I said hesitantly.

He glanced at me with little curiosity. "Yes?"

"I—um—met your son. Max. He's—uh—he's going to Central Willamette State this year."

Mr. Kincaid's face took on a fixed aspect that said I was treading on dangerous ground. "I have no son named Max."

"Okay. Well, I met Trent's former stepbrother, then. He looks just like you."

Mr. Kincaid sent me a chilly look. "Did he tell you what he did?"

"Trent told me."

"Then I'm not sure why we're having this conversation." He poured coffee into the two mugs.

"I'm not sure either," I said with a nervous laugh. "It just seems so weird to visit here and not even mention him."

"It's not weird at all. He committed a terrible crime and this family no longer has a place for him." His voice sounded so reasonable, so calm and assured, that I almost believed him.

But there was that drawing. *He broke my ribs today.*

"He told me—um—that someone broke his ribs once," I said, watching Mr. Kincaid's face.

His jaw tensed. "He did, did he? You must know Max pretty well."

"Not really. We were just talking about growing up, you know?" Again with the lies.

Mr. Kincaid handed one of the mugs of coffee to me and leaned back against the edge of the granite counter. "Max wasn't a popular kid. I'm sure you can imagine why. He got beaten up so many times we lost track of all the fights he was in."

I frowned, unable to stop myself from saying "did anyone try to help him?"

He looked me right in the eye. "No."

"But...why not?"

"Because Max lost his right to protection when he murdered his little brother."

His eyes looked as cold and hard as the granite against which he leaned. There was hatred in them. Hatred for Max. I couldn't keep looking into his face, so I glanced down at his hands where they clasped the coffee mug. He held the cup so tightly his fingernails were bleached almost white. A huge gold signet ring on his right hand flashed the letter K at me from a black background.

"I'm sorry," I said. "I shouldn't have brought it up."

"Caroline, I'm sure you mean well," he continued in that very reasonable voice that was so totally at odds with his white nails. "Max is highly manipulative and a compulsive liar. He's probably told you all kinds of nonsense to make you sympathetic to him. Don't believe any of it. I'm sorry to say that my son is an irredeemably violent person. You should stay far, far away from him."

I nodded stiffly. "Okay. I'll remember that."

"Good. You do that. Now, if you'll excuse me, I've got some work to catch up on. I'll be in my office if anyone needs me." He left the kitchen for the same back area he'd emerged from on Thursday afternoon.

I doctored my coffee with generous amounts of milk and sugar and brought my prizes to the kitchen table to devour them. His words pressed down on my heart, giving me that drowning sensation again. Max hadn't tried to make me sympathetic to him. If anything, he'd encouraged me to think the worst of him, saying that every word Trent had spoken about him was true.

So what was going on with his dad? Why would he say that about Max? Trent had said the same thing; he was a master manipulator. At the time, I'd believed him. Yeah, maybe I'd thought he was exaggerating a little bit, but essentially I'd assumed what he told me was true. Now, I wondered.

Max had been only ten years old at the time of the accident. How many ten year olds are so calculating they'd deliberately murder anyone, let alone their own siblings? It was possible, sure. But it didn't seem very likely and it didn't fit with the way Max came across in person.

I'd told both Trent and Paige that Max gave me the creeps, but that had been a lie. I'd said it to cover up the humiliating fact that he could arouse me just by being in the same room with me. He'd never given me the creeps at all.

I didn't know what to think. I looked down at my plate and realized I'd eaten the whole slice of pie without really tasting it. My coffee mug had been drained, too, but I didn't remember drinking the coffee.

If I asked Max about his past, would he tell me the truth or would he put me off with a bunch of lies the way Trent and Mr. Kincaid had?

Chapter 8

Max: Monday evening became catch-up time for my design business. I was falling behind because of all my school work, and it was beginning to worry me. Education was important, but I didn't want my business to falter just when it was getting off the ground. I'd lose important momentum that way and it might take a while to recover.

I was working on a logo for a local brew-house, and I had two proposed designs to show them, with a third still in the beginning phase. When I had the third one down, I'd e-mail them the designs and with luck they'd approve one of them. Then I had several book covers, both nonfiction and fiction, and two newsletters, among other things.

The problem I had was my mind kept wandering to Caroline. My cock was half hard virtually all the time, and the minute I allowed my attention to waver, it returned to fantasies of all the things I'd like to do to her. School wasn't the only reason my work was getting backed up.

My phone rang and I answered without looking at the caller I.D. "Kincaid Design Group."

"Is this Max Kincaid?" said a familiar female voice.

"Selene?"

"That's me."

Selene was a member of my circle and a former lover. I hadn't seen her in a few months. The last time had been when the circle helped me move down here. For them, it had really been more about visiting with Brad and Marie—who'd preceded me in the move—because I didn't have a lot of stuff to haul. I hadn't actually needed help. But they'd come down with me and we'd all hung out for a while. Selene had spent the night in my bed.

"How are you?" I said. Why was she calling? We weren't a couple anymore, not that we'd ever really been together in the first place. Our relationship had been more fuck buddies than boyfriend and girlfriend.

"I'm fine," she said. "How are you? Are you surviving small town life?"

"Yeah. Actually, I like it here." More every day, come to think of it. Could have to do with a certain blonde.

"Really?" Her voice oozed skepticism. "I can't imagine. It looked like the kind of place that's crawling with rednecks when I visited."

"It's a college town. There are a few non-rednecks here," I said dryly.

"I guess." She must not have liked my answer, judging by her tone. "What do you do for fun around there?"

"I'm too busy for fun. Work and school take all my time." Except for when I was chasing Caroline. Somehow I didn't think Selene would want to hear about that.

"I've been working a lot, too. Overtime. I wish they'd fill that empty position so we weren't always being called in."

"Sounds like a drag."

I didn't want to talk about work. In fact, I didn't much want to talk to Selene at all. Our hook-ups had been fun at the time, but that was over. I wanted Caroline.

"I have tomorrow and Wednesday off and I was thinking about coming down to visit you," she said. "I had to work over the holiday and I could really use a fun break."

"I think you'd be bored out of your mind. All my time is taken up with work. I'm falling behind because of school."

"You can't even spare an afternoon?"

"Selene, you know it would take more than an afternoon. Besides, it's a long drive down from Seattle. Why would you want to spend all those hours on the road just to turn around and do it again on the way home?"

"Well, I thought maybe I could spend the night." Her voice became a suggestive purr.

I bit back a sigh. I didn't want to hurt her feelings. Selene was a friend, and still a member of my circle. However, I wasn't especially excited to sleep with her, fuck her, whatever you want to call it. I'd thought that part of our relationship was over.

She practiced polyamory, which for her basically meant she screwed anyone she felt like screwing. When I'd wanted exclusivity, she hadn't been interested. After I'd thought about it for a couple of days, I'd decided that was fine with me because I wasn't all that attached to her. We'd parted ways amicably and I'd given her very little thought since, except to compare her with Caroline.

"You're hesitating," she said. "That isn't good. Do you have someone else?"

"No. I don't."

A one-night stand with Selene might take my mind off Caroline. Maybe if I fucked someone else, I could get my semi-permanent state of arousal under control. My mind would clear and I'd be better able to plan my attack instead of simply reacting to the raging lust she inspired in me. Because I was close to going off the rails with her. My desire to be with Caro was getting way too close to overtaking my need to hurt Trent.

"I've got a bottle of wine to share," Selene said coaxingly.

"Okay. Let's do it."

"Awesome! I should be able to make it by early afternoon."

* * *

Selene knocked on my apartment door at noon on Wednesday. That meant she had to have been on the road at the crack of dawn. She must have been eager to see me. I wasn't sure how I felt about that.

I opened the door and she threw her arms around me. "Max! It feels like it's been forever."

"Hi, Selene."

She pulled my head down and kissed me on the mouth. Given how sexually frustrated I was, it should have sent me into instant arousal, but it was strangely unstimulating. I kissed her back, a bit dutifully, until she decided to come up for air.

"It's so good to see you," she said.

"Come in." My neighbors paid no attention to me, but I still didn't want to stand on the landing and make out with her.

She pranced into my living room and turned in a slow circle. "It's still completely bare."

"Not completely. I have a desk now."

"Ooh, a desk," she said, pretending to be impressed. "But no couch. No chairs. Don't you ever have anyone over?"

"Not really, no."

She gave me bedroom eyes. "I hope you have somewhere nice to sleep."

"I've got a mattress on the floor." The same one she'd spent the night on when she'd "helped" me move in.

"It'll do."

She dropped the overnight bag she carried on my floor and sashayed back to me, swinging her hips. The snug, black knit tunic she wore left nothing to the imagination and I could see that her nipples were hard under the tight fabric.

She twined her arms around my neck. "Why don't you show me the bedroom?"

"Aren't you hungry? You've been on the road for hours."

"I'm starving, but not for food." She rubbed herself against me, pulling my head down to hers. Her mouth tasted like cola, not one of my favorite flavors for a kiss.

I pulled back. "I'm hungry. For food. I've been working all morning without a break."

Selene pouted. "Can't you wait?"

For the first time in my life, I put food before sex. "I don't think so."

"Oh, all right. Where should we go? I don't want fast food."

"There's a cafe a couple of blocks from here that's pretty good." I stepped back from her clinging arms with a surprising sense of relief.

Selene and I had had quite a few good times in bed, so I didn't really get my own reluctance. She wasn't going to move in with me or anything like that. She was only here for one night, and then she'd return to Seattle and I wouldn't have to deal with her. This wasn't even a small commitment.

Yet I wasn't really looking forward to having her. Even the minor contact I'd had with Caroline excited me more than Selene's well-rehearsed moves. What could I make of that? I wasn't sure I wanted to know.

We had an amiable lunch at the cafe, talking shop, discussing the occult scene in Avery's Crossing—not that there was one. The town was extremely quiet, but we both agreed there were probably at least a couple of working groups here. They simply didn't advertise. We didn't either, so no surprise there.

I could have told her about Caroline's ghost, but for some reason I held back. I didn't want to share Caroline with Selene. For one thing, Selene would never approve of my plan to get revenge on my stepbrother. If she knew about it, she'd try to talk me out of it. For another, Caroline was in a completely separate category from the booty call of my former fuck buddy. I didn't know what that category was, and I didn't want to define it, even for myself. All I knew was I didn't want to mix the two.

Selene and I made our way back to my apartment and my bedroom. The sex wasn't what I remembered. It wasn't much better than if I'd taken care of matters on my own.

Chapter 9

Caroline: She wore a halter top in bright red and a pair of hip-hugger jeans that barely clung to her narrow hips. Her long, pale hair was held back by a leather headband tooled in a floral pattern and dyed red. A beaded Indian-style choker in red and blue wrapped her neck. She looked like a poster girl for Woodstock.

The air in the room felt icy cold. Outside, a songbird called in the tree by my window.

The girl leaned over me where I lay on my back in bed. My heart zoomed out of control. I couldn't move. All I could do was stare up at the young woman leaning over me, her hair slipping forward over her bare shoulders.

Her mouth opened and her lips moved. Was she trying to say something? I couldn't make out the word. I was no good at lip-reading. She made the same motions again, and again there was no noise. It was like watching TV with the sound turned off.

A look of frustration came over her. She frowned at me and repeated the word, her face contorted as she said it again. She seemed to be silently shouting at me.

Sweat trickled down my sides. I wanted to tell her I couldn't hear her, but I couldn't move my lips. I couldn't move my arms. My whole body seemed to be frozen in place.

The girl pressed her lips together, still frowning. She shook her head, her eyes traveling back and forth across the wall   next to my bed like she was trying to think of some other way to get through to me. Her hands came up to her head.

She was really upset that she couldn't make me hear. I tried to force my mouth to open, but my muscles refused to obey me. The girl turned her head to look back over her shoulder at something behind her. The only thing I could see was my dorm room, so I had no idea what she was looking at.

She turned back to me with regret and frustration in her blue eyes. Then she disappeared.

The instant she was gone, I could move again. I sat up in my bed, shivering. What the hell was that? Outside, the little bird still sang.

Had I been dreaming? That was the logical explanation, but it had seemed so real. Much more real than any dream I'd ever had. And there was no sense of awakening, of transitioning to the ordinary world. It felt all of a piece.

Could Max be right? Maybe Retro-girl wasn't a figment of my imagination or a dream character, but a real ghost. Of course, I didn't believe in ghosts...but I did believe in trusting my own experience and intuition. And my intuition told me I'd just seen a true apparition. A ghost.

Either that or I was following in Aunt Jo's footsteps. I wasn't sure which possibility was worse.

* * *

The River House was a pricey restaurant on the second floor of a nineteenth-century building downtown. A long bank of windows looked out on the Willamette River, which was bounded by trees and brush, a few leaves in varying shades of orange, brown, red and gold still clinging to mostly bare branches. My parents had taken me and Trent there for lunch, since they were on their way down to Eugene to visit my grandma. We'd taken a table right at the window.

It was the beginning of dead week, the week before finals, so I couldn't go with them to Eugene. I had to study. And study. And study.

My mom has hair like mine, except she spends what seems to me like hours every day making it so straight and smooth you can almost see your reflection in it. I guess I could do mine the same way, if I could get the hang of it, but as with high heels, I don't have the patience or motivation to master the technique. Instead I bumble along with my wild curls vining around my head like Medusa's snakes.

My siblings, Lily and Landon, chattered almost nonstop to anyone who would listen. They always got overexcited when they came to campus to visit me. Maybe it was something about the idea of a school the size of a small town that got them going. They were fascinated by all the buildings and the fact that I lived *at the school.*

"I wish I had a room like yours," Lily told me, bouncing in her seat. "I'd paint the walls pink. Or maybe purple."

"We're not allowed to paint our walls," I said.

"Oh." She pouted for an instant, then smiled. "Can you put decals on them? I'd use decals."

"You'd put a bunch of girly stuff up," Landon said with withering scorn. "Unicorns. Gag. I'd have Superman decals." Superman was his current obsession.

My mom smiled at me as we picked up our menus. "I could swear your hair is getting curlier every day."

"Not really, Mom. It's pretty much the same."

She looked at her menu instead of answering.

"How are your classes this term, Trent?" my dad said in the hearty tone that meant he was trying to keep things pleasant.

"Good so far," Trent said in a neutral voice.

"Getting ready for the day you take over Kincaid Construction?"

That was the construction company owned by Trent's stepdad. Max's father. It hit me suddenly that Trent was going to inherit the business that should have gone to Max, if he'd stayed with his family. How did Max feel about that? Not that I cared.

"I'm not looking forward to my stepdad retiring," Trent said. "But I am anticipating being able to work for the company full time."

"I'll bet," my dad said.

"I haven't heard anything about your career plans lately, Caroline," my mom added.

I stifled a sigh. "That's because I don't know what I want to do yet."

"You know, now is the time to get in all those extra-curricular activities that can help you get a job after you graduate."

"I know, Mom."

"Employers look for young people who are involved in things besides their studies and partying."

Another sigh attempted to escape me. "I know that. I'm not a partier."

"You're not a joiner, either."

I looked at Trent, hoping for a bit of support, but he just smiled at me. Maybe he agreed with my mom.

"I'll look into it, okay?" I said, hoping to placate her enough to get her to leave me alone.

"I hope you do," she countered. "You'll meet new people, too."

"I met someone new this morning," I said. "She was standing over my bed."

What on earth had made me blab that all over the lunch table? Now everyone was staring at me and I had to explain.

I laughed nervously. "I saw a ghost this morning. She was in my dorm room."

My mom laughed too. "Was she carrying her severed head by the hair?"

"No. It was a real ghost. She looked like a regular person."

My dad pursed his lips. "How do you know she wasn't one of your dorm mates?"

"Because she disappeared right in front of me."

Trent looked at me with a puzzled and disbelieving expression. "You never said anything to me about it."

"That's because I was in a hurry to get ready." And because the stupid urge to confide hadn't hit me yet.

"I'm sure you were just dreaming, honey." My mom patted my hand.

In the past, my parents' skepticism had always kept me quiet on matters like these. In fact, I'd mostly agreed with them. After all, being like Aunt Jo was my worst nightmare and I would have done anything to deny my connection with my former favorite. This time, some stubborn part of me refused to let go of my ghost. I knew what I'd seen.

"It wasn't a dream. I was awake the whole time."

Both my parents raised their eyebrows.

"Don't tell me you actually believe in that stuff," Mom said.

"I don't know. I just know what I saw."

"Caroline, you're starting to worry me."

And I was beginning to get upset. "You know, there are intelligent people who believe in ghosts. Intelligent, non-alcoholic, non-drug addicted people."

"Well, I haven't met any of them," Mom said.

My dad chuckled.

"I have a friend who goes here and he believes in them." Referring to Max as a friend was stretching things quite a bit, but they didn't know that.

Trent looked at me sharply, while my mom and dad just continued to chuckle indulgently.

"Are you talking about Max?" he said.

I shrugged. "I know several people who believe in ghosts. The point is, believing in them doesn't make you an idiot or crazy."

"You made fun of me at Halloween once because I was worried about them," Landon said.

I gave my little brother an apologetic smile. "I know and I'm sorry about that."

"So ghosts are real?" Lily said.

"No, honey, ghosts are not real," my mom told her.

I gritted my teeth. She was undermining me. I didn't want Lily and Landon to feel unsafe, but it wasn't exactly fair to make me look like I was delusional.

"If you're talking about Max," Trent said, "you should know he thinks he's some kind of magician."

I frowned at him. "Magician?"

"Yeah. Not a stage magician. I mean a real magician. He thinks he can do real magic." Trent snorted at this idea.

Max practiced magic. Why hadn't he told me? Probably because he was afraid I'd react just like my parents were, with contemptuous laughter. Plus he didn't know me all that well. To be honest, I didn't know what to think about this revelation. Magic wasn't real, right? It was make-believe, something you saw in movies or read about in books. It was Disneyland stuff.

I thought about all those drawings in his sketchbooks, all the dragons, demons, and skulls. He'd sure been fixated on that stuff. God, maybe he was crazy. Delusional, like Jo. Maybe I should make sure to stay far, far away from him from now on.

But then there was my ghost. If she was real, maybe magic was real, too.

"Who is this Max guy?" my dad said. "He sounds like quite a character."

Trent rolled his eyes. "He's my crazy stepbrother."

"I had no idea you have a stepbrother."

I glanced at my mom, who raised her eyebrows. That probably meant she'd told my dad about Max but he'd forgotten the conversation.

My dad was now studying Trent as if he'd never seen him before. "How does he feel about the business going to you instead of him?"

"I have no idea," Trent said. "But he ran away when he was sixteen and he's rejected every offer to come back to the family, so I assume he doesn't care."

"Max isn't crazy," I said. I didn't know why I felt compelled to defend him. Maybe it was the broken ribs picture. Even if he was crazy, he couldn't have deserved that. Could he?

"You barely know him," Trent said. "Unless there's something you're not telling me."

"I talked to him long enough to know he's not insane."

"He's unbalanced. He believes in magic, Caroline. I mean, come on. Magic? He thinks he can cast spells and talk to spirits."

Maybe he really could. "That doesn't necessarily mean he's nuts."

Now Trent was looking at *me* like he'd never seen me before. "I can't believe you just said that."

"Why not?"

"You've never told me you believe in that crap and why are you defending Max? You know how I feel about him. Is this about the box you found?"

This wasn't what I wanted for our lunch out together. I should have known better than to try talking to either Trent or my parents about anything paranormal. They'd never understand. They wouldn't even make an effort to understand.

Max would. He'd get it immediately. But Max wasn't here, and Trent was looking at me with the same combination of concern and bafflement as my parents.

"It's not about the box," I said. "It's about a real experience I had."

"But you don't believe in ghosts. You know better than that. At least, I always thought you did."

"I'm not sure what I believe. I only know Max isn't crazy."

"He worships the devil," Trent said.

My eyes must have bugged out, I was so shocked. "He what?"

"You heard me. He worships the devil. He's a Satanist, a witch, a whatever they call themselves nowadays."

"No."

Trent smiled grimly. "Oh, yeah. You've seen that pendant he's got around his neck? It's a pentagram. He wears it all the time."

"I think you'd better stay away from Max," my dad said.

"I can't believe it," I said.

"It's true. He's been messing around with that sh—uh, stuff since high school, maybe even earlier."

"Okay. Forget it," I said. "I'm sure you're right. It was just a dream, ghosts aren't real, and Max is crazy. Can we eat now?"

They could think what they wanted, and I didn't care if they believed I'd capitulated the same way I always had. In my heart, the knowledge that I'd seen something not easily explained away remained intact. If Max was really a devil worshipper, though...that put my attraction to him on a whole new level of stupid.

Chapter 10

$\mathcal{M}ax$: Trent and his fellow bullies were between me and my science class and the bell was about to ring. The hallway boomed with the loud voices of kids laughing and shouting as they dashed into their classes at the last minute. I'd been late three times this semester already. If it happened again, Mr. Brown had promised me detention. But in order to get in the class, I had to make it around the knot of football players and wrestlers that had congregated near the door of my class.

Trent was at the center.

I was small for my age; I hadn't hit my growth spurt yet. That gave Trent and company a major advantage over me, not to mention all the social clout they had as athletes. But they couldn't keep me from getting into my class—not really. They could only make it difficult and embarrassing. I lifted my chin and squared my shoulders, my hand tightening on the strap of my backpack. Striding forward as if they didn't intimidate me, I pretended I hadn't even seen them.

One of the bigger boys stepped directly in front of me. "Where do you think you're going?"

I stepped to the right to get around him, but he mirrored my actions.

"My class is right there," I said with a movement of my head to indicate the room.

"My class is right there," he mocked in a high voice.

Was that the best he could do? Idiot. Still, he was bigger than me and he had back-up. I glanced at Trent. He was watching with a grin, arms crossed, legs spread, obviously enjoying my discomfort.

I tried again to pass, but the bully wouldn't let me. Like I said, I was small for my age. A lot smaller than Trent and his buddies.

"Let me by." I tried to make my voice strong. Unfortunately, it cracked in the middle of the sentence.

They laughed. One of them shoved me.

"Don't be in such a hurry, Maxi-pad," Trent said.

"Yeah. What're you in such a hurry for?" someone echoed.

"Maxi-pad," another guy said. "Good one."

Other students began to gather around the spectacle we were creating, their faces alert with interest. I was burning all over, my neck and face hot with shame. Would Mr. Brown take this incident into account when he decided *whether or not to punish me? Probably not. He hadn't any of the other times it had happened.*

"You're going to be late for your classes," I said.

"Oooh, we're shaking in our shoes," the first guy retorted. They could probably get away with lateness. Their type always seemed to get away with shit that would get a kid like me in huge trouble.

The bell rang. Their audience melted away as kids scurried to make their classes before they were officially late. I heard a few of them repeating "Maxipad" to each other and laughing. Great. That would be my new nickname from today onward.

Mr. Brown came out of his class, frowning. "What are you boys doing out here?"

"We're just helping Max get to class," Trent said.

Mr. Brown fixed me with a stern glower. "Late again, Max? I warned you what would happen, didn't I?"

"But they're late, too. Why don't they get detention?"

"This isn't about them. It's about you. Now get in the classroom and take your seat."

I obeyed with a sullen clench of my jaw as my stepbrother and his friends stood in the hall, chortling.

* * *

Caroline was avoiding me. She wouldn't even look at me. In the essay class, she kept coming in late and choosing the seat farthest from me, her gaze carefully turned away from me.

It hurt. It shouldn't have, but it did. She was supposed to be nothing more than a means to an end, yet here I was moping because she wasn't friendly to me anymore.

I needed to get my head back in the game.

There were more important things to think about than whether or not Trent's sorority chick girlfriend liked me or not. Fred's warning, for example. I hadn't heard anything more about this ghost who was trying to contact me and I'd been too busy to do any ritual work designed to bring the spirit closer.

On Saturday morning, I drove out to Brad and Marie's farm. I found them in the garden in back of the house, working at some gardening activity I couldn't identify. Marie's hair was braided and coiled on her head like an old-fashioned milkmaid. They both wore ragged jeans and ratty old sweat shirts and were dragging around a plastic tarp covered in some kind of brown chunky stuff.

Brad looked up at me and waved. "Max! You're here just in time to help."

"I don't know what you're doing," I said.

"That's okay." Brad grinned. "I'll teach you everything you need to know."

"That's just what I was afraid you were going to say."

"We're spreading mulch over the beds. When we finish that, we'll set some cold frames over our winter crops."

"Okay, sure. Mulch. Cold frames." What the heck was a cold frame?

Although I'd grown up in Billings, I'd really been a town kid. I'd had little exposure to the country, and when I ran away I ended up on the streets in Seattle with no way out to the countryside that bordered it. My parents hadn't been gardeners. So I hadn't experienced the deep-down inner quiet that came along with clean country air and the wind-rustled murmur of tall grass and trees until I'd followed Brad and Marie down to Avery's Crossing.

I'd been here a few months, and it still surprised me how quickly I'd adapted to small town life and how much I liked being out here on the farm. It was almost like an instant meditation, where all I had to do was get out of my car and a light trance state came over me.

When Brad and Marie had told me they were moving down here, I'd dreaded it. I wanted to go with them, but live in Avery's Crossing? I figured there would be absolutely nothing to do here, and that was sort of true but I loved it anyway.

"What brings you out here today?" Marie said after a while.

"Can't I just come out and visit my family?" I said.

"Of course you can. But I can tell there's something else."

I glanced at her, then at Brad. He had a baseball cap pulled low over his eyes, so it was hard to see his expression.

"Fred told me something recently," I said. "I wanted to run it by you guys."

Brad sat back on his heels. "What was it?"

"He said..." I chewed on the inside of my lower lip as I thought about how to approach the subject. Direct was probably best. "He said there's a spirit trying to get in touch with me."

"Did he have a name?" Marie said.

"No. He couldn't even tell if it was male or female."

They exchanged a glance. Did they already know something about this?

"What?" I said.

"Huh?" Brad replied.

"You two looked at each other like you were having a silent conversation."

He still looked puzzled. "I don't think we were."

Maybe it was just the effect of being married to the same person for so many years. What would that be like? My dad had lost my mom when I was five, and they'd only been married about six years at the time. Of course, he'd been with my stepmom for a long time, but that wasn't a marriage I'd use as a role model. My stepmom followed his orders...to the letter.

"We don't know anything about your spirit," Marie said. "But we can find out for you if you want."

Did I? I'd driven out here for the express reason of talking to them about the situation, yet now I was here I wasn't sure I wanted to investigate. Something about this particular spirit...I could sense it would change me in a way I couldn't imagine and wasn't sure I wanted.

"I don't know," I said finally.

"It's probably better to find out than to wonder," Marie said.

"Whatever this entity wants, you know you have free will, right?" Brad added. "You don't have to cooperate with it. If you don't like what it's telling you, send it away and ignore it."

I bowed my head with a sigh and pulled another dandelion from the ground. Something told me ignoring this spirit wouldn't be so easy. "I know."

"Let's get washed up and have lunch," Marie said. "Then you can decide if you want us to go further with it."

I followed them back to the house, thinking how lucky I'd gotten when I'd found them. Or when they'd found me. Most kids on the street weren't so fortunate. They never found any significant help, or they ended up with adults who only wanted to use them. Sometimes worse than they'd been used in their families of origin.

It was thanks to Fred, of course. He'd nudged me in their direction, the same way he'd protected me from the worst effects of living on the streets. Fred had been a guardian angel of sorts for me ever since I'd been eleven. If it weren't for him, I might not have survived my adolescence.

* * *

For lunch, we had turkey sandwiches around Brad and Marie's kitchen table. After we'd cleaned our dishes and put them away, we reconvened at the table and Marie pulled out her Tarot cards. She hadn't done a reading for me in a long time.

Brad lit the pillar candle in the center of the table and Marie closed her eyes, whispering the invocation she always used before a reading. The atmosphere in the room settled and deepened as Brad and I also focused our energies on the cards and the question. I wondered which

78

spread Marie would use. The particular spread chosen would shape the reading and affect the kind of answer we received.

She opened her eyes and began to shuffle the cards. After a few repetitions, she sorted through the deck and pulled out a card. Then she handed the deck to me to shuffle.

"Celtic Cross," she said. "Using the Knight of Cups as significator." The significator represented the querent—that was me—while we took turns shuffling the rest of the cards.

"The Knight of Cups?" I looked at her with a quirk in my brows.

"A young man with powerful psychic abilities and a deeply emotional nature."

"Deeply emotional. That's me," I said dryly.

"Just keep shuffling."

Brad winked at me. I finished shuffling and handed her the cards. She gave them another few rounds of shuffling and then laid them out in the traditional Celtic Cross design. A Tarot reader usually lays the cards face down and turns them up during the course of the reading. The Knight of Cups remained at the bottom, face up, to represent me.

Marie turned up the first card. "Seven of Swords. This represents the situation you're in and what you're doing at the present time." She took a breath. "Seven of Swords indicates sneaking around, deviousness. You're hiding something from those around you and hoping you don't get caught. You're either spying on someone or carrying out some kind of plot against another."

Although she didn't look at me, I flushed. This was not what I'd expected to come through in the reading. It was supposed to be about the spirit who was trying to contact me, not my plan to take revenge on Trent.

She overturned the next card. "What crosses you is the Two of Cups. A new love affair opposes your sneaky plans. You have a new chance here, a chance to change your direction. Will you take it?" She glanced up at me, her gaze full of meaning. I said nothing.

The next card was the Six of Cups, reversed. "This card indicates a bad childhood. No surprise there. You have memories of evil being done to you and this is what's at the bottom of all the sneaking around you've been doing. Now, behind you is the Seven of Swords. There is much strife in your past, but you didn't fight well. Or you were unable to fight. Unable to defend yourself."

I nodded. I'd been too small to fight Trent then. Too small to fight my dad.

She moved on to the next card. "Above you—this is the best that can be expected in the circumstances. The Reversed Hanged Man. In the past, you acted as a sacrifice, a scapegoat. Your days as a sacrifice are soon to be over, but only if you can conquer your perceived need to be devious."

That couldn't be right. Only deviousness would allow me to get back at my stepbrother.

"In the future," Marie said as she turned over another card, "you have The Hermit, which indicates you will soon be looking for truth. A solitary search. Only you can say what is right and what is wrong for you in this situation. But you surely have a search for truth in your immediate future. Maybe a reckoning with it. A great truth is going to be revealed.

"Here we have the way you see yourself. The card in this place is Queen of Cups."

"I don't see myself as a queen of any kind," I said dryly.

Marie frowned at me. "It's metaphorical, as you know perfectly well. You are in an emotional place. There is an emotional woman who is very close to you. A woman who is having powerful psychic experiences of her own. She can look into your soul and divine your true nature. She can make or break you."

This immediately made me think of Caroline. Even the hair on the woman in the picture was blond like hers. But why did the Queen of Cups appear in my place? Shouldn't she be in another position, like friends and family or the future?

"Friends and family," Marie said. "The Page of Cups. A young child, perhaps? Someone very close to you, with a powerful emotional connection to you." She closed her eyes. I could see them fluttering back and forth beneath the lids, as if she followed an inner vision. "This person is...this is the person, or spirit, who is trying to reach you. I feel it very strongly. It's a boy and he's trying to reach you because he has some very important information for you. It's personal. He knows you. I think it's Carter."

Her eyes popped open and she stared at me. My throat closed up and my mouth went dry. Carter was trying to reach me? But why? What could we possibly have to say to each other?

"It's Carter, Max. Your brother is trying to talk to you."

I licked bone-dry lips. "Why?"

She studied the cards. "I'm not sure. But I think it has something to do with the reversed Six of Cups and maybe the Hanged Man. It's something in your past."

"It would have to be in my past, because Carter is from my past."

Marie shook her head. "Not necessarily. He could be like Fred, trying to help you in your current life. But, judging by the other cards in the spread, I'm convinced it has to do with the past. Let's see what the final two cards have to say."

My palms were slick with sweat. I'd never been nervous during a reading before and it was a strange feeling. Because I wasn't sure I wanted to know what the other cards were going to tell me. The gist of the reading so far...well, I wasn't sure what it was trying to say. Stop looking for revenge? Go for Caroline? Give her up? What did Carter want from me?

"Hopes and fears," Marie said, turning over the next-to-last card. "Justice. You long for justice, but you fear it too. This is because you don't understand your true nature or your true place in the story. Justice is a two-edged sword and those who wish to wield it must realize it can turn on them. Those who have impure motives beware. They can be harmed as badly as those against whom they seek justice. In your case, it's surrounded by the Page of Cups and the reversed Four of Swords, so I believe this is justice in favor of you."

Still, it was a timely reminder that justice could cut both ways. Did I want to risk my revenge twisting and coming back on me? Was it worth the possible fall-out?

Hell, yes. It would be worth it. Worth anything to see Trent squirm.

"Last one," she said. "This is for all and everything, the final outcome."

She flipped over the card and I stared at the image, baffled. It was a Medieval tomb with a carved stone knight lying still and silent on top of it, a nobleman's tomb, the kind you would see if you visited an ancient European cathedral.

"Reversed Four of Swords. Your days of cold isolation are over. You are waking up, coming out of your trance. You are rejoining the living."

Marie took a deep breath and met my gaze. "You need to get in touch with Carter and find out exactly what he has to tell you. There's an important truth about your past that you need to know. Only when you find it will you have peace and freedom."

She wanted me to face the little boy I'd killed. I rubbed the back of my neck. "I don't know if I can do it, Marie."

"I know. Nobody said it would be easy." She tapped the Four of Swords. "But, Max, this is good. This is so hopeful. It's a wonderful sign of healing."

"Is it?" I wasn't so sure.

"Marie knows what she's talking about," Brad murmured.

"I'm not questioning her ability. It's just hard to look at that card and see healing."

"Well, that's why it's reversed," he said. "Instead of being a sign of unhealthy withdrawal, it's indicating that you're going to open up more."

"Get in touch with my feelings?" I tried to keep the smirk out of my voice, but it did creep in a little around the edges.

"There's nothing wrong with feelings," he said. "Everyone has them. Either you deal with them or they deal with you."

"What does that mean?"

"It means that ignoring them doesn't make them go away. They just move underground, so to speak, where they influence everything you do, only you're not aware of how they're affecting you. And if you're not aware of a problem, you can't do anything to solve it."

I blew out a huge breath full of the tension that had accumulated during the reading. "I suppose I can see that."

"Grudgingly." Brad's eyes were crinkled at the corners. His eyes were smiling, although his mouth remained serious.

I nodded. "Grudgingly."

Marie gathered her cards and put them back in her box. She wrapped the box in a scrap of indigo silk and set it on the table again. "Well," she said, "who wants oatmeal cookies?"

Chapter 11

Caroline: The music was so loud I could feel it in the soles of my feet. I could feel it in my belly. Bass notes seemed to thunder through the floorboards, making me suspect it was playing somewhere in the basement of the frat house. It was a last blowout before Dead Week began and everyone had to bury their heads in their notes. We wouldn't come up for air until after finals.

"What would you like to drink?" Trent said.

"Beer." Not my favorite, but less likely to give me a headache than the sweet garbage they were serving in those ever-present red plastic cups.

"The bar is over here." He led me toward the kitchen.

People already packed the fraternity house and the conversation alone was deafening. I'd promised to go to this party with Trent, although I wasn't much of a partier. He wanted to go. It was important, and I was his girlfriend so I had to accompany him. So, here I was.

The theme for the party was Las Vegas—don't ask me why—and I'd dressed the part in a black satin cocktail dress and skyscraper black heels that were already killing my feet. Maybe if I practiced wearing heels, they wouldn't be so difficult for me to handle, right? But that would mean I'd have to wear them, and as I said before, I hated wearing heels.

But, hey, at least tonight I didn't feel under-dressed.

They'd set up gaming tables in the living and dining rooms, so I figured the dancing was probably downstairs, where the music seemed to be located.

"Let's dance," I shouted at Trent.

"Maybe later. I want to talk to some people first."

I followed him as he wound his way between clumps of partiers, looking for whomever he wanted to meet. He paused and spoke to Greg Talbot, although I couldn't hear a word they said because of all the other noise. Then it was on to the next group, and the next.

I tipped back my beer. It was a cheap, mass-produced lager, but it was cold and wet and it helped take my mind off the boredom of tagging along after Trent.

Too bad Paige hadn't been able to come tonight, but she'd had a dinner date with some guy named Dan. While I hoped she had a good time with him, I was selfish enough to miss her company. She would have made this party bearable.

So would Max, except I couldn't picture him in this setting. Unless he were fighting with Trent, maybe.

My feet really were killing me. I tugged on Trent's sleeve. "I need to sit down."

He looked slightly annoyed. "Okay. Find a spot. I'll get back to you."

Right. I shrugged and moved off, looking for a chair. I wandered through the dining room, where all chairs were taken, and into the living room. People sprawled on the couches and the floor, and every other available surface. Everyone seemed to already know each other, whereas I was the stranger.

How had I managed to pledge a sorority while being such a sorry introvert?

I located a tiny plot of floor space under a window and lowered myself into it, moving awkwardly because of the heels. My beer was almost gone and I was starting to feel pretty buzzed. Yeah, I'm a lightweight.

I should have picked up another one before I found my resting spot, but I was here now. I didn't want to get up and lose my place.

"Hey, you."

I looked up to see Greg Talbot standing over me with a beer in one hand and a red plastic cup in the other.

"Hi, Greg."

"Looking for company?"

"Sure."

He plopped himself down in front of me and held out the cup. "You look lonely."

"Yeah." I took the cup from him. Really I was only bored. But this was his fraternity, so I wasn't going to actually say that.

I tossed back a gulp of the mixed drink. Gag. It was cheap sugary drink mix in red flavor with some kind of hard liquor—probably vodka—in it.

"I can't believe Trent left you alone," Greg said.

"He's busy, I guess." I tossed back another gulp of the drink. It didn't taste so bad on the second try.

"Dumbass. He should be with you."

That's what I thought, but I wasn't going to admit that to Greg. Instead of replying, I took another swig. Yep, it was definitely improving in flavor.

Also, my head seemed to be floating pleasantly about three inches above the end of my neck. Weird.

A warm weight settled on my upper thigh, right where my skirt had pulled up and my bare skin began. I rotated my head lazily and looked at Greg. He was staring at his own hand where it rested on my leg. His thumb began to stroke my skin, back and forth, back and forth.

"You have beautiful legs," he said.

"Greg, I'm taken."

"Yeah, but he's not here." He moved his hand a couple inches higher.

"You need to stop doing that." I would have slapped him, but I was too floaty and relaxed to care enough to lift my hand. It didn't seem especially important at the moment to stop him.

"If he doesn't want to share you, he should spend more time looking out for you," Greg continued.

That was true. But it didn't mean I wanted Greg Talbot fondling my legs.

"No, really. You need to stop."

"Aw, come on, Caroline. You know you like it." He leaned down and planted a sloppy kiss on my thigh. "There are empty rooms upstairs. Let's go find one."

The alcohol haze enveloping my brain retreated enough for me to shove his hand off me. "Knock it off. Now."

I scooted away from him and got my feet under me. He reached for me, but I stood up, swaying, and walked away from him. He didn't follow. With a glance over my shoulder, I saw him sitting against the wall and staring with unfocused gaze at the crowd of people in the room.

I guess he wasn't that serious about wanting me.

Where was Trent? It was time for me to go home.

I pushed my way through the packed rooms, craning my neck to see him and trying at the same time not to fall over and sprain my ankle. Being drunk made walking in the crazy shoes I'd chosen ten times more difficult.

I was about to give up on finding him when I caught the sound of his voice coming from somewhere to my right. I turned. And there he was, with his face buried in the cleavage of some skinny yet stacked brunette. The girl moved her head and I recognized her. My very own sorority sister, Tiffani.

Was I really seeing this? It was definitely Trent, definitely Tiffani. How cute. Their names started with the same letter. She had her hands buried in his blond hair, her head tipped back as her mouth opened. It looked like they were having foreplay in the middle of the fraternity living room.

His hands clutched her ass. He was touching Tiffani's ass. I took another step toward them, only half aware I was even moving. What should I do? Should I break it up? Tear the cow's hair out?

Maybe I should find a pair of scissors and cut off his balls.

But there were so many people here. Too many witnesses. If I made a big scene, it would be all over campus by the morning. Everyone would know.

Besides, cutting off men's balls was illegal and I didn't want to go to jail.

I'd go home without him. He'd abandoned me at this stupid party and that was bad enough, without taking into account the cheap little slut he was currently feeling up. Yeah, that's what I'd do. Go home without him.

Turning on my heel, I teetered back through the living room and into the hallway. In this part of the house was a game room, a study and bathrooms. There was also a side entrance I'd noticed on an earlier visit.

I found the door. A guy I didn't recognize had a girl up against the wall right next to the exit, his hand inside her pants. They didn't seem to notice me as I opened the door and walked outside.

A mist hung in the air and I had no jacket. My little black dress was sleeveless and the mist felt cold on my bare arms. Humidity always made my hair go crazy, so by the time I got home it was going to be completely out of control.

I didn't care. At least I was away from the party.

The bass notes of the music thumped monotonously. Pulling my phone out of my mini purse, I tried to activate it so I could call a cab. Nothing happened. After another three tries, it dawned on me that the battery was dead. Great. I never left home without my phone, yet somehow I'd forgotten to charge the battery.

Now what? I could either walk home or go back into the party and use the house phone. I really, really didn't want to face that crowd again, especially with Greg Talbot hitting on me. And I didn't want to see Trent. That left walking.

The lawn on the side of the house had no walkway leading to the sidewalk. When I stepped onto the grass, the heels of my shoes sank deep into the moist ground and trapped me. I hadn't reckoned on the wetness of the ground in fall.

"Shit." I slipped out of them and bent down to pull them from the soil.

Behind me, the house still roared with party mayhem. I straightened, my head spinning. It wasn't too far from the fraternity house to the campus, even in high heels. I could do this.

I kept my shoes in my hand and walked across the squishy lawn barefoot to keep from getting stuck again. At the sidewalk, I put them back on my feet. How long would it take Trent to notice I wasn't there anymore? Maybe he never would.

He'd never done anything like this to me before. Or maybe I'd simply never caught him at it. After all, we'd been apart for the three months of summer vacay, and he could have been cheating the whole time for all I knew. Until now, it had never occurred to me to wonder.

I ground my teeth as I pictured them together. Tiffani was the perfect sorority girl, always dressed for the occasion, always perky and friendly, even if she did seem like she was made out of plastic.

My angry thoughts plus the alcohol in my bloodstream made me unsteady as I minced carefully along the dark sidewalk. There were a lot of huge, old trees in this neighborhood, and even semi-bare their canopies blocked much of the light from the streetlights. Thick roots buckled the pavement in places, so I had to look carefully where I stepped. This slowed my progress even more. It was going to take me a lot longer to get back to the dorms than I'd thought.

The thrumming of an engine came around the corner behind me, headlights casting a blinding glare over the street. The car approached slowly. My heart rate picked up. I kept my gaze forward as I walked, pretending I didn't know the car was there.

It kept pace with me for about a block as sweat began to trickle down my sides. What did they want? I wasn't sure I wanted to know. Then a window rolled down. I glanced at it from the corner of my eye. A guy I'd never seen before was leaning out of the passenger side window.

"Hey, want a ride?" he said.

"No, thanks." I kept walking.

"We'd be happy to let you ride with us."

"I said no thanks."

The righteous anger brought on by liquor and witnessing Trent's cheating had left me, chased away by an adrenalin rush of fear. It was possible these guys were just being friendly, although in a really inappropriate way. It was also possible they were thinking of dragging me into their car if I refused to get in voluntarily. After that, anything could happen.

My toe caught on a crack in the sidewalk and I stumbled. After an awkward lurch, I caught myself in time to prevent a fall. My hands were shaking.

"You should ride with us," the guy said. "A pretty girl like you shouldn't be out here walking."

"Thank you, but I don't want a ride."

The car stopped. I picked up my pace, focusing on a giant spruce tree growing on the upcoming corner. Maybe I could lose them if I could get into the shadows under that tree. I could cut through the overgrown garden it anchored. But I could only move so fast in these abominable heels. Why, oh why had I worn such stupid shoes? The car door opened. I heard the guy's footsteps on the pavement.

He was definitely not taking no for an answer.

His hand clamped around my upper arm just as Max stepped from beneath the shadowy branches of the spruce tree. He wore a black leather jacket and in the darkness I hardly recognized him. Yet somehow I knew who it was. There was a kind of energy in him that I knew, like the jolt that had traveled up my arm the first time we'd touched.

"Let her go," he barked.

The nameless guy released my arm. I stumbled toward Max. He might be creepy, but I knew him. Trent knew him. If he did anything bad to me, my boyfriend would beat him to a pulp.

"We were just trying to help," the guy said.

Max caught me with an arm around my shoulders, and I could have kissed him with relief. "She didn't want your help."

I looked at my pursuer. He was watching us with a sneer on his face.

"How would you know?"

"I heard."

The guy gestured to his friend in the car. "There's two of us and only one of you. How do you think this is going to go down?"

Max drew himself up, and even though his arm was still around me he seemed to grow taller and broader, his form filled with menace. There was something almost eerie in the way he radiated threat without even holding a weapon. The other two men shrank back as they exchanged an uncertain glance.

"Leave," Max said. Even his voice seemed deeper and sharper. "Get in your car and drive away."

"Okay," the first guy muttered. "Yeah, sure."

They turned tail and ran back to their car. The doors slammed and the car peeled away with a screech of rubber. I slumped against Max's body.

His arm tightened around me. "Are you all right?"

"Uh huh. How did you do that? Was it a Jedi mind trick?"

"Not exactly. They didn't hurt you?"

"No. They didn't have time." I looked up at him and frowned. Why was he walking around alone at night in this neighborhood? There was almost nothing but frat and sorority houses here. "Wait a minute. What are you doing here?"

"Just good luck, I guess."

I pulled back a little. "You just happened to be walking in the neighborhood?"

"Yeah," he said in a careful tone, apparently seeing I was getting angry.

"No way. Too much of a coincidence. I don't buy it."

He pursed his lips. "I had a feeling something bad was going to happen. That's all."

"A feeling. About me?"

His eyes grew wary. "Yes."

I shoved at his chest. "You *are* following me."

"No, Caroline, I'm not."

"Yes, you are. How else would you just happen to be in the right place at the right time? You're stalking me." And now I was alone with the stalker. My confidence that he wouldn't dare hurt me evaporated. We were standing in the dark in the middle of the night and he could probably do anything he wanted. No-one would notice. Maybe he'd use that mind trick on me to keep me from yelling for help.

Who would help me, anyway? The guys in the car? I was better off on my own.

"Stalking you?" he said angrily. "What kind of person do you think I am?"

The kind who would shoot his little brother. "Do you know those guys? Is that how you were able to chase them off so easily?" I shoved him again, harder this time, and he let me go.

"I never saw them before tonight."

"When tonight?"

"Just now." He extended a hand toward me. "Caroline, you've got it wrong. I'm not stalking you. I had a hunch I needed to be out here tonight and I followed it. Why can't you believe that?"

"Because it's bullshit, that's why." God, I couldn't believe I'd almost kissed him. I'd almost thrown my arms around him and kissed him. What an idiot.

"Stay away from me, Max." I spun around and stalked away.

I'd forgotten the shoes on my feet. My ankle wobbled and twisted on the uneven pavement. A stabbing pain ripped through my lower leg. With a cry, I fell to my knees, catching the force of it on my hands.

Max leaped to my side. "Are you hurt?"

Damn. Damn, damn, damn. Now I couldn't run away from him or anyone else. I gritted my teeth against the pain and blinked back tears.

"Yeah. I'm hurt."

He crouched down beside me. "Your ankle?"

"Yes." I was so furious with myself that I snapped at him.

"Do you think you can stand up?"

Why was he being so understanding when I was being a bitch?

"I don't know."

He took me by the elbow. "Let's try."

I grabbed his arm and leaned heavily on him as I tried to stand. As soon as I put weight on my injured ankle, fresh pain shot through me and I gasped.

"I can't."

"Okay. Lean on me and let's think about this for a second."

I didn't want to lean on him. He was a stalker. My boyfriend had been kissing another girl. The only thing I wanted from men tonight was to tie all of them together and use them as one big punching bag. But my foot and ankle hurt so much I could hardly think straight, so I leaned on Max.

He felt strong and solid under my weight, and so warm I decided leaning on him wasn't so bad after all. For the first time, his presence didn't leave me feeling overwhelmed by the achy butterfly sensation. I was too overwhelmed already by pain.

"We can try to make it back to your dorm this way," Max said. "Or I can carry you."

"Carry me? Get real, Max."

"On my back."

"Piggyback? Seriously?"

He looked down at me, his mouth curling up at the corners. "Why not?"

"Because I don't trust you."

His budding smile disappeared. "I won't hurt you. Ever. Do you hear me? I'd never hurt you, Caro."

"Don't call me that. My name is Caroline."

He sighed. "You need help and I'm here. Let me help you."

"What if you drop me?"

"I won't drop you. Want to try it?"

I groaned in defeat. "I'm not sure I can. I've been drinking and I don't know how well I can hold on."

"Yeah, I thought I smelled alcohol on you. Were you at a party?"

I didn't want to discuss it. "Yes. It sucked."

He laughed. "Okay. Well, we'll try hobbling along like this until you've had enough and then we'll put you on my back. How's that?"

I shrugged ungraciously. "I guess that's okay."

"All right. Ready?"

No. "Yes."

We started forward at the pace of a speeding earthworm. My ankle screamed in agony every time I put the least amount of weight on it, and even leaning on Max, I had to touch it to the ground with each step forward. My face screwed up into a grimace as we inched our way down the street.

"We should get you to a doctor," Max said after one painful block.

I groaned again. "I can't make it that far."

"I wouldn't make you walk all the way," he said, a smile in his voice. "I'd leave you at a cafe or something and get my car."

I just grunted.

"I think that's a better idea than taking you home, just in case you've broken something." He stopped walking.

"It's not broken. Just sprained."

"How do you know?"

"I can feel it."

Max snorted. "You're just trying to get rid of me."

That was true. I wanted to be on my own. I could get help from someone in the dorm and then I wouldn't have to deal with Max.

"It's not going to work," he said. "I'm taking care of you tonight whether you want me to or not."

"Fine. Whatever. Take me to the emergency room. No, I can't afford that. Take me to the dorm. I'll put some ice on it and tomorrow it'll be fine."

"Like hell." He scowled down at me.

"Max, I really don't have the money for an emergency room visit. Do you know how much they cost?"

"How about one of those urgent care centers?"

"Maybe." They were expensive, too, but my parents did have insurance and as a dependent I was still covered under their policy. I sighed. "Okay. Urgent care."

"Good. Can you stand on one foot?"

"Huh?" I gave him a baffled stare.

"Until I get in front of you. I want you to climb on my back." He pulled away from me, leaving me to balance on one precarious foot. Then he slipped off his jacket and handed it to me. "Put this on. You look cold."

I was cold, but I hadn't noticed it until now. I'd been too keyed up, what with the party disaster and then those creepy guys. "Thanks."

The jacket smelled of leather and some kind of masculine spice I'd never smelled before. Different from Trent, muskier. Sexier. Essence of Max. It sent a shivery, aching sensation through me. God, I hated how much I wanted him.

I put on the jacket. It was still warm from his body.

Max sank to his knees. "Okay, get on."

I clambered awkwardly onto his back and wrapped my arms around his neck. This position put my face so close to his that if he turned his head, we could kiss. The achy butterflies were back. "Are you sure I'm not too heavy?"

He pulled my calves up over his arms, so that I was wrapped around him, and stood. "I've backpacked with more weight than this."

"No, you haven't." Who had a backpack that weighed over a hundred pounds?

"Yes, I have." He started walking with no apparent effort at all.

"Why would you have such a heavy pack?"

"Because it had everything I owned in it, including my food and drinking water."

Oh. That must have been when he lived on the street.

"I'm sorry."

"I don't want your pity, Caro."

Didn't I tell him not to call me that? "It's not pity. I just don't like thinking of you that way."

I shouldn't have said that. Apparently the adrenalin rush hadn't truly destroyed the alcohol in my system. It was still in there, making me blab like a fool.

Max bent his head for an instant, as if what I'd said moved him in some way. Then he straightened up and strode forward like nothing had happened.

We continued in silence for another three blocks. I have to admit I was impressed with Max's strength and endurance. My weight didn't seem to bother him in the least, and while I'm not very big, it's still a lot to carry even a petite adult on your back.

We reached the edge of campus. A string of shops and little restaurants lined this side of the street. On the opposite edge of the sidewalk sat a long, low concrete planter filled with pansies and flowering kale.

"You can put me down there," I said. "I'll sit on the edge of the planter."

He lowered me to the makeshift bench. "I'm going to get my car."

"Okay."

Max glanced around at the empty street. At one in the morning, everything was closed except the tavern in the next block. A couple of guys came out the door, whooping with laughter, and staggered down the street away from us.

He gazed down at me, glowering. "I don't like leaving you here by yourself. Especially not dressed like that."

"I'll be fine."

"Like you were earlier?"

He did have a point. "Do you have your phone? We can call a cab."

Max rolled his eyes. "I can't believe I didn't already think of that."

After he called a cab, we had nothing to do but hang around and wait. Max sat down next to me on the lip of the planter. His jacket kept me from feeling the chill in the air, but I missed the sensation of his hard, warm body clasped in my arms and legs anyway. And that was so wrong. How could I force myself to stop thinking of him that way?

"What happened at the party?" he said, staring off into the distance.

"I don't want to talk about it."

"That bad, huh?"

"Yep."

He glanced at me. "You gonna be all right?"

"I'll be fine."

"Would you tell me if you weren't?"

"No."

He bent his head and rubbed the back of his neck. "I don't know how to—I just want to help. That's all."

This was so confusing. I didn't really know who he was—the creepy brother-murderer Trent described or...someone else. Someone likable and kind who'd made a terrible mistake as a kid. My stomach ached every time I thought about that drawing he'd made, the words he'd written under it.

Maybe I was being unfair to him.

I turned my body toward his. "I'm grateful you were there tonight. I really am. And for helping me get here and call a cab and everything. But you aren't responsible for me. I can take care of myself."

Max just looked at me.

I flushed. "Okay, I wasn't doing such a great job tonight, I admit. But normally I'm fine."

"I guess you have no reason to trust me, and you probably don't even like me. But you should know that if you need anything, if there's something Paige can't help you with, I'll be here for you."

I couldn't meet his eyes. I just couldn't. The problem wasn't that I disliked him; it was that I liked him too much. A guy who'd killed his brother, a guy hated by his own family, a guy who kept trying to get me to see him even though he knew my boyfriend didn't want me talking to him. Or was he that other guy, the kind one I wanted to know better?

I studied my hands. "Okay, Max. I'll keep that in mind."

"I heard you spent Thanksgiving with my—with Trent's family."

"Yeah," I said, wondering who'd told him.

"Did you have a good time?"

A sidelong glance revealed he was carefully watching me. "Not especially."

"No? My stepmom's a great cook."

"The food was good."

He cleared his throat. "But?"

"It felt weird being there, knowing you weren't allowed."

"I told you once, don't feel sorry for me. I don't need it."

"That's not what I meant." I frowned at him. "You're putting words in my mouth."

Max just looked at me. My face burned and I knew I was blushing yet again.

"You look just like your dad," I said. "And I found your old sketchbooks."

His face and body grew still. "My sketchbooks?"

"Who broke your ribs, Max?"

He withdrew from me. Not physically. His body stayed in the same place, the same position, but emotionally he pulled back. I saw it in his eyes, the set of his mouth as he looked away from me, staring at the closed-up shop fronts.

"I'd rather not say."

"Why?"

"Because all that happened a long time ago. It's over. I don't like thinking about it." There was anger in his voice.

I pulled my arms closer to my sides. "Okay. I won't ask again."

Chapter 12

Max: The urgent care clinic took a lot longer than I expected. I kept my arm around Caroline's waist as we hobbled into the building. She felt so good against my side, smelled so good in spite of the haze of cigarette smoke and beer than clung to her hair, I felt my groin beginning to ache. Damn it. This wasn't a good time for a boner.

I glanced up and saw a row of wheelchairs next to the reception desk. "Stay here. I'll get you a wheelchair."

"I don't need one of those."

"Yes, you do. I can see you wincing every time your foot touches the floor. Just hang on a minute. Lean against the wall."

I carefully pulled away from her and left her with her hand against the wall as I snagged one of the wheelchairs. She sank into it with a sigh, letting me know without words I'd made the right choice. She had a lot of pride, but she didn't want to walk all the way up to the reception desk and then to a chair in the waiting area.

After getting her checked in, I wheeled her over and parked her next to a chair for myself. Her face looked kind of pinched, her mouth tight. She was in pain and needed some distraction.

I nudged her elbow. "Have you decided what you're going to do with that French major yet?"

"No. Why does everyone keep asking me that?"

"You don't want to be a teacher?"

"God, no. My mom's a teacher."

"Hmm." I rubbed my chin. "How about a translator?"

"Maybe. You have to go to a special school for that, though, and I've heard it's really tough."

"You could be a mime."

She rolled her eyes. "You don't have to speak French for that. Mimes don't talk."

"You could be the world's only talking mime."

That got me a smile. "I don't think so."

"You think there are other talking mimes? Maybe you're right. You should get on the Internet and find out. I'll bet the others would like to know they're not alone."

Caroline poked me, laughing a little. "There aren't any talking mimes. Besides, I don't want to be a mime."

"No? Not even when you were a little girl?"

"No. I wanted to be a ballerina."

I could see that. It was kind of a turn-on, imagining her leaping across the stage in point shoes. I grinned at her. "Sexy."

"Knock it off, Max."

No way. I'd gotten her to laugh. Score. "Maybe you could open a French shop. You could pretend to be French and impress everyone with how snooty and French you are."

"I'm not snooty. Plus, what would I sell?"

"Who cares? You could sell anything and you could be snooty with a little acting. I bet you'd have a ton of customers. Everyone would want to buy from the beautiful, snooty Frenchwoman."

She gave me a disbelieving stare. "Beautiful? I think you need glasses."

That stopped me cold. "Don't you know how beautiful you are?"

Her face turned pink. "Cut it out."

Other people in the waiting room were starting to listen in on our conversation, so I decided to have pity on her.

"Okay, I'll stop for now. But don't think this is over."

She looked at me out of the corner of her eye and smiled. Gods, she was stunning. And I'd gotten her to laugh and smile at me. Maybe all was not lost.

A nurse appeared at the doorway leading into the exam rooms called Caroline's name. She smiled at us. "Would your boyfriend like to come too?"

Caroline blushed even more brightly. "He's not—"

"Yes," I said. I got up to wheel her into the back area.

It turned out she did have a sprained ankle, which they wrapped before releasing her. She was supposed to stay off it, ice it, elevate, all that crap. I had the feeling she wasn't going to follow directions.

I called another cab to take us home. We rode without talking. Caroline leaned her head against my shoulder, thinking whatever dark thoughts were on her mind. I wanted to wrap my arm around her, but I stopped myself. That would be too much at this point. Something must have happened between her and Trent at that party. Did I dare to hope they'd broken up?

Nah. She would have said something if that were the case. They'd probably just argued. Or, hell, maybe she hadn't liked the drinks they were serving or the music they played. How did I know?

The cab pulled up to her dorm. She opened the micro-purse she was carrying and pulled out a wad of bills just as I was getting out my wallet.

"I'll pay," I said.

"You don't have to do that."

"I want to."

"But you paid for the one to the clinic."

"So?" I opened my wallet. "How much?"

"Max, I'll get it this time."

I shoved a fifty into the cabby's hand.

Caroline glared at me. "Why did you do that?"

"Because I could." I resisted the urge to kiss the tip of her nose. She might have slapped me.

The cabbie gave me my change, I gave him a tip, and then got out of the car. I held the door open for Caroline and extended my hand.

She looked up at me with a ferocious frown. "What are you doing?"

"Helping you upstairs."

"I don't need help. Go home, Max."

No way was I letting her go inside alone. What if she fell? "I'll go home when I know you're safe in your room."

She heaved an exasperated-sounding sigh. "Oh, for pity's sake. You just don't give up, do you?"

"No. Now get out of the car."

"Yes, sir, Mr. Bossy Pants."

The cabby snickered. I guess he felt safe since I'd already paid him and forked over the tip. I fought back a smile.

Caroline held out her hands and let me pull her from the car and help her stand. The brace the clinic had given her seemed to help her stand up without wanting to collapse. The narcotics they'd given her probably helped too.

Maybe they should have given her a stronger dose. She might have been easier for me to manage.

I gave her my arm and she took it without argument. She still wore my leather jacket, too. I liked the way it looked on her. Made it easy for me to imagine she was mine.

We made it all the way into the lobby of her dorm without fighting. But as soon as she'd pushed the up button on the elevator she looked up at me and I knew what was coming.

I narrowed my eyes at her. "Don't even say it. I'm taking you up to your room."

"I don't need your help. I can lean on the wall."

"Don't care. I'm taking you to your room and that's final."

"Good grief." She rolled her eyes. "Has anyone ever told you you're a pain in the ass?"

"Almost everyone I know. What's your point?"

She blew a little gold curl out of her eyes. "You've done enough for me tonight. More than enough."

I didn't agree. There was so much more I wanted to do for her. "It would ease my mind if I knew you were safe in your room."

"Max, the dorm is locked. Nobody's going to attack me here."

"It's a coed dorm. There are men living here who could hurt you."

"And you're a man."

This argument wasn't going my way. "Can't you just humor me?"

"It's not a good idea." She slid out of my jacket and gave it to me. "Thank you for everything tonight. I really mean it. You saved me."

The elevator arrived. The doors opened. She stood there looking at me. I should leave but I didn't want to. The doors closed again.

Did she have any idea how hot she was? How much I hungered for her? This wasn't only about payback for Trent and never had been. I wanted Caroline for my own.

I wanted her so fucking bad my hands started trembling. I stuck them in my pockets.

"I need to go to my room," she said softly.

"I know."

"I'm going to call the elevator again."

I leaned forward, slowly, giving her time to say no or back away. She waited for me. Her face tilted up and her lips parted and they were so damned sexy, those lips. I caught her lower one between both of mine, my heart pounding so fast I could almost hear it.

My hand made it out of my pocket and up to her face before I knew what I was doing. I palmed the side of her face. Her skin felt smooth and perfect under my hand and her lips moved beneath mine.

She sighed. Her mouth opened enough to accept my tongue. As I tasted her, she slipped her arms around my waist and my cock jumped violently behind my jeans. A moan escaped me.

Her body felt perfect against mine. I put my arm around her back, holding her to me as I explored her mouth. This was a mistake. It was too early; she didn't trust me enough yet. I should keep my hands off her, but I didn't want to stop just yet.

A little more. I'd take a little more and then I'd stop.

Her body undulated against mine as her hands slid under my jacket to stroke my back. I clasped her head, trembling, wanting, plunging my tongue into her as if I could claim her that way. She wanted me just as much as I did her, and the cold, watchful part of my mind rejoiced in that fact because it would help me take her from Trent.

The rest of me only wanted to bury myself deep inside her and never leave.

The elevator pinged and the doors began to open. I released her with a start as the doors slid back and some guy I didn't know got out.

He gave us a cursory glance before walking across the lobby. I hadn't even noticed the elevator leaving, I'd been so wrapped up in Caroline.

She stared at me, her breath fast and uneven, her lips reddened by my kiss. I couldn't look away. Her eyes looked so dark they were almost black with arousal. I leaned in for another kiss.

"No." She held up a hand. "I can't."

"Caro—"

"No, Max. It isn't right." Her eyes glistened. She looked like she was about to cry.

Damn. I never meant to make her cry.

"All right. I understand." I backed away.

She took a deep breath. "Thank you. I'm going now."

"Okay."

I watched as she got into the elevator. She didn't look at me at all, kept her eyes trained on the floor as the doors closed and shut her away from me. That kiss had been a bad idea, but I hadn't really been thinking when I did it. Apparently, neither had she.

Nothing I'd done with Selene had made me feel the way kissing Caroline did.

If I'd ruined whatever trust we'd built up between us, I was going to have to start over with her. I needed to keep better control over myself. The one thing I wouldn't do, though, was give up. I had to have her. Now that I'd tasted her, I knew I had to have her.

* * *

Fred showed up just as I left Caroline's dorm and started across the quad, a kind of courtyard on steroids that filled in the central space created by her dorm and another three which all connected in a giant square. The quad was pretty dark at this time of night, and I figured most people weren't looking out their windows, so when Fred appeared beside me I didn't scold him. He wore a denim jacket and jeans, a kind of outfit I'd rarely seen on him, since he usually wore the clothes of his own era.

"You look like a student," I said quietly.

"That's the idea."

"Can other people see you right now?"

"Maybe. I'm not sure. I think it depends on the abilities of the one who's looking." He stuck his hands in the pockets of his jacket and looked at me. "You saved her."

"Yeah, I guess."

"They didn't have good intentions, Max."

I nodded. "I know. Thanks for the heads-up."

"I was glad to help. I'd hate to think of Caroline being harmed."

"Me, too. I could have killed those bastards just for scaring her."

"You care for her."

I shot him a sidelong glance. "Maybe a little. But I wouldn't let any woman be abused."

I really didn't want to talk about my feelings for Caroline. They were private. And also incredibly stupid. If I let myself become emotionally involved with her, my plan would go sideways in a hurry. And right now, I wanted to hurt Trent more than I wanted any woman. Even her.

"I know what you're doing," Fred told me.

"Oh? What's that?"

"You think if you seduce Caroline, it'll hurt Trent."

"I can't argue with that."

"Don't you think it'll hurt her, too?"

"I'm not going to force her to do anything, Fred. She's a free agent. If she wants to be with me, who am I to say no?"

He shook his head. "You're better than this, Max."

"Apparently I'm not."

We fell into silence as we left the quad and headed toward downtown Avery's Crossing. The mist had turned into bona fide rain, yet Fred didn't seem to be getting wet. I guess the dead need their little perks, since they can't eat or dream or have sex anymore. That must really suck.

"How did you die, Fred?"

He jerked his head around. "What?"

"I was just wondering. Were you as young as you look when it happened?"

"How young do I look?"

I shrugged. "I don't know. Twenty-five, thirty maybe."

"I was thirty-five and I was shot."

"Damn. I'm sorry."

He waved that off. "It was a long time ago. I'm over it."

"Really?" It seemed hard to believe. How did you get over being murdered?

"Yes, really. And don't change the subject. You shouldn't be toying with Caroline. It isn't right. It's dishonest and dishonorable."

"I don't want to talk about it."

"Max, you could really hurt her. You could hurt yourself."

I gave a short laugh. "Myself? I'm the last person you should be worrying about in this situation."

"Actually, I think it's Trent who has the least to lose."

"Now why would you say that?"

"Figure it out for yourself," he said, gazing off into the dark distance.

"What, you're going to lecture me about honesty and then pick that one thing to go all mysterious about? That isn't right."

He spread his hands. "You don't want to listen to me. So I'm not going to talk about it anymore."

He vanished. I stalked down the sidewalk, my head bent against the rain as I fumed. He'd done that just to tease me. To make me think about what a fool I was to choose this method of getting back at my stepbrother.

Of course, Frederick the Wise would probably tell me I shouldn't be seeking revenge at all. Well, fuck that. Someone had to take my prick of a stepbrother down a few notches, and that someone was going to be me.

Chapter 13

Caroline: Max's kiss left me shaking. I ached and tingled all over, especially between my legs. It had taken all my self-control to make him stop, because what I'd really wanted was to bring him up to my room and ravish him.

I had to lean on the wall the whole way down the hall to my room, because even with the brace my ankle wouldn't hold me. All the while I was wishing I'd asked Max to come with me; instead I'd sent him away. I'd done the right thing and I knew it, so why was I feeling so regretful?

His kiss had turned me on in a way I didn't even know was possible. I ached for him, for pity's sake. My panties were wet. I'd never ached for Trent, not even a little. And that made me feel like shit.

What kind of girlfriend was I? All this time I'd thought of myself as the loyal, supportive, good girlfriend who would never cheat or even look at another guy. And here I was, head over heels in lust with someone else. Clearly I was not the person I'd always thought.

Max and I were going to have to stay far away from each other.

What about Tiffani, though? Didn't Trent deserve what I'd done, considering he'd been all over another woman that very night?

Maybe he did. Maybe my actions hadn't been quite as wrong as I'd first thought, in the context of Trent cheating. However, I could have broken up with him first and then thrown myself at another man. I paused in my snail-like progress down the hall.

Break up with Trent? Was that what I really wanted?

I should at least give him an opportunity to explain himself...although what believable explanation he could give me totally escaped me at the moment.

He knocked on my door at ten o'clock the next morning. I'd just gotten back from breakfast and was putting my hair in a French braid to keep it out of my way. I sighed, abandoning the braid, and opened the door.

Trent looked like hell. He had big, dark circles beneath his eyes and his hair stood out in a dozen different directions. Brown stubble covered his cheeks and he still wore the same clothes he'd had on last night. Stubble wasn't a good look for him.

Standing there with him in the hallway, staring down at me, I didn't know what to feel. Last night, I'd been furious. Now I was numb.

"What do you want, Trent?"

He hung his head. "To apologize."

"Oh? For what?" I wasn't going to make it easy for him.

"I know you saw me with Tiffani."

"You do? How would you know that?"

He turned his head to look both ways down the hall. "Can I come in?"

"Be my guest." Not that the cardboard dorm walls would give us much more privacy than the hall did. I shut the door behind him.

"She threw herself at me," he said. "She'd been drinking. So had I. I wasn't thinking, that's all."

"Uh huh. You do that a lot?"

He frowned at me. "No. Of course not."

"You had your hands all over her. On her ass, Trent. You had your face in her tits."

He flushed. "It was just a stupid, drunken mistake. I'm really sorry, baby. It won't happen again."

"How do I know? Why should I believe you?"

He took my hands. "I swear to you I won't touch her again. I won't even look at her. I love you."

Whoa. I felt like the breath had just been knocked out of my lungs. He was looking at me with a little smile, and there was something almost smug in his face, as if he thought he had me all wrapped up with those three little words. He hadn't even asked how I'd gotten home last night or asked me why I had a brace on my ankle. How could he claim to love me?

The smug expression drained from his eyes. "Caroline? Don't you love me too?"

"Right now I don't know how I feel about you."

His mouth opened. "I thought—but you—we have something really good here. I know you're angry, but..."

"Trent, you haven't asked me how I got home."

"Um...did you take a cab?" he said in a hopeful tone.

"No, I did not. My phone's battery was dead. I tried to walk."

"Tried?"

"It's hard to walk in five-inch heels. Some guys in a car harassed me."

His brows came down. "Who? Are you all right?"

"Yeah, I'm fine, but only because Max came along."

"What?"

"Your stepbrother happened along just in time to keep those creeps from—from doing whatever it was they were planning to do. He saved me. And you weren't even there." Until I spoke, I hadn't realized how angry I still was.

Trent's lips tightened and his eyes narrowed. "So you were with Max last night?"

"He helped me get home."

"Great. That's just great." He flung up his hand in obvious frustration. "I told you to stay away from him."

"Oh, so I should have let myself be raped so I wouldn't have to talk to Max?"

"That's not what I meant and you know it."

I put my fists on my hips. "What did you mean then?"

"I don't know! Fuck." He rubbed his forehead. "I'm glad you're safe. But Max—"

"He protected me because you weren't there. And he called a cab and got me to the urgent care clinic and wouldn't let me pay for any of it. He was really nice, Trent. I think you're being totally unfair to him."

"The urgent care clinic? I thought you didn't get hurt."

"I sprained my ankle trying to get away from your terrible, evil stepbrother."

Trent's jaw worked as he tried to digest this piece of news. He pressed his fingers against his temples. "I can't believe this."

"Believe it."

"Has it occurred to you that he might have been waiting around for you to come out of the house?" he said, glaring. "He could have even hired those guys to bother you."

"Do you know how paranoid that makes you sound? How could he have known that I would go home early and by myself?"

"I don't know. He's strange. Sometimes he knows things nobody else could know."

"Oh, please."

"No, really. He's weird and he's involved in some spooky stuff. He's a magician, remember?"

I wasn't going to give Trent any wiggle room.

"You know what? I don't care right now how weird Max is. I don't care if he can turn me into a newt. What I care about is the fact you were so busy feeling up Tiffani that you didn't notice I'd left the party. And just now you didn't ask me how I'd gotten home or even notice I have this brace on my leg. You love me, Trent? Really?"

At least he had the decency to look ashamed of himself. "You're right. I should have done a lot better and I'm really, really sorry. Please forgive me."

He sounded contrite. He looked contrite. I let out a heavy sigh. The truth was I didn't want to break up with him. The thought of being on my own again...God, I was a coward. And he was right. We did have a good thing. If I dumped him, I'd lose what we'd built, and over nothing more than a single slip-up.

But it wasn't really him I wanted. It was Max, whispered a little voice in my mind.

"Okay," I said, shoving my misgivings out of my mind. "I forgive you."

Trent broke out in a huge grin and threw his arms around him. "Thank you."

"Just make sure it doesn't happen again."

"It won't." He kissed me and somehow we ended up on the bed and half undressed before I knew it.

They always say make-up sex is the best, but for me it wasn't any different than any other time I'd been with him, except for being even more awkward due to the ankle brace. I found myself staring at the ceiling and waiting for him to finish. This wasn't how it ought to be. Why couldn't we have the same kind of fire I felt with Max? Why couldn't I stop thinking about Max?

I was more than disappointed with myself.

* * *

On Monday, Max came into the essay class we had together, his black leather jacket glistening with rain, and sat down next to me with a casual smile, as if we hadn't shared the most passionate kiss I'd ever experienced just a couple of days before. Was he going to pretend nothing had happened? I'd spent the whole weekend thinking about him, about how he'd tasted, how he'd felt, and yet trying not think about him. Now we were together and I was so embarrassed and shy I could hardly look at him, and here he was acting totally normal.

"How's your ankle?" he said.

"It's better. Thanks for asking." I buried my nose in my laptop.

"Are you icing it and keeping it elevated?"

Raising my head, I rolled my eyes. "Yes, Mom. I promise I'm being a good girl."

He grinned. "Now that's what I like to hear."

My whole body turned hot. I ducked my head again. "Don't worry about me."

"Did you tell Trent I helped you?"

"Yes, I did."

"How did he take it?"

I made myself look at him. "How do you think he took it? He didn't like it, of course."

"What I meant was did he get nasty with you?"

"No. You two sure have a low opinion of each other."

His mouth twisted wryly. "It's warranted."

"Oh both sides?"

"Yes."

I shook my head. "You are a complete mystery to me."

"I worried about you after I got home. I thought he might get mean. Because of me." He regarded me with an unwavering stare. "You didn't tell him we kissed."

It sounded almost like an accusation.

"No. Why should I?"

Max blinked. His heavy black lashes lowered, obscuring his eyes. "Okay, I guess I deserved that."

"I didn't mean it like that. I'm not going to ruin what I have with Trent just because you and I had a two-minute make-out session."

His beautifully curved lips twisted again. "Okay. Fair enough."

All my words seemed to come out wrong. The truth was, I was rethinking my whole relationship with Trent, but I couldn't admit that to Max. I was being too hard on him. But I didn't know how to behave with him anymore. Let's face it, I'd never known how to behave with him. He completely threw me.

"I don't know what you want from me, Max."

His gaze flicked up to meet mine again. "Yes, you do."

My face began to burn. "I can't talk about this right now. I need to get ready for class."

He wisely left me alone after that.

Chapter 14

Max: The familiar nightmare about Carter woke me in a tangle of sweaty sheets. The silence in my room was so thick it almost hurt my ears. I stared up at my ceiling. A different ceiling from the one in the dream, plaster instead of drywall, an old house in a small college town instead of a giant suburban log mansion built in the nineties. But my heart raced, my hands shook as if the gun had just gone off.

I covered my face. Why had I been playing with that goddamned gun? Why had I thought it was unloaded? If I'd had any common sense at all, Carter would still be here. He'd be seventeen by now, just starting his senior year of high school. Football games and homecoming and prom. Girlfriends. Instead he was rotting in the ground.

With stiff, awkward motions, I pushed myself into a sitting position on the mattress. That was when I noticed Frederick sitting on the floor next to the altar below my window. Odd. He never sat on the floor.

He wasn't wearing the sack suit, either. Instead, he had on a pair of loose denim pants, not jeans exactly but something similar, and a flannel shirt with the sleeves rolled up. He looked like a lumberjack.

His hair wasn't slicked down the way it usually was, either. Or maybe I'd just assumed he slicked it down, because he normally had that derby on and today he didn't. His head was bare. His hair looked so much like mine...his eyes were almost identical to the ones I saw in the mirror every day. It gave me a really creepy feeling all of a sudden, like I was seeing a nineteenth-century version of myself.

"Morning, Fred." My voice sounded rusty.

"You were dreaming," he said, his dark-blue Max-like eyes sad.

"Yeah." The less said about that, the better.

"It wasn't your fault, Max."

"Sure it was." I looked away from his knowing gaze. "I was the one with the loaded gun."

"You thought it wasn't loaded."

"Isn't that what they all say? I didn't know there were any bullets in it. It's a bullshit excuse and you know it."

"What was your father thinking, keeping a loaded gun in a house with three boys? Have you ever thought about that?"

I shrugged. "That doesn't relieve me of the responsibility of what I did."

"You're determined to blame yourself."

"Because I'm to blame." I threw back the comforter and crawled out of bed. Time for some coffee.

What a life I led. My closest friend was a ghost no-one else could see. I spent my time studying, working on my computer, and talking to said invisible friend. It hadn't been this way in Seattle; I'd known quite a few people up there. Here in Avery's Crossing, the only person I wanted to spend time with was my stepbrother's girlfriend, and that wasn't happening.

Dressed only in my underwear, I stumbled into the bathroom. Luckily, Fred chose not to follow me. He could have come right through the wall, but he'd learned over the years that I liked to have at least an illusion of privacy.

Now for coffee. He was waiting for me, leaning against the counter of my cramped kitchen. I measured beans into my grinder and tried to ignore him. After a dream like the one I'd had, I didn't want to talk or think. If I could have erased myself, I think I would have.

I gave my ancestor a reluctant glance. "Coffee?"

"Hah. Don't taunt me."

"You look like a farm laborer or a lumberjack. What's with the clothes?"

"My suit needed cleaning."

I laughed in spite of myself.

"How did you get hold of that gun, Max?"

My laughter died. "It was in my dad's office."

"Yes, but why did you go in there and get it?"

Thinking about that terrible day made everything in me hurt like hell. I didn't want to remember. But Fred was looking at me expectantly as I ran the coffee grinder.

"I'm not sure. I think Trent had asked me about it."

"Trent asked you to play with it?"

"No. I don't know. I'm not sure, all right?" I sighed. "It was a long time ago, and I've done everything I can to forget." Even though the image of Carter's broken body covered in blood would be engraved on my brain cells forever.

"I don't want to cause you pain," he said. "But I think it might help to remember everything you can about that afternoon."

"Why?"

"I'm not sure. Something is missing."

"Weren't you there?"

He shook his head. "No. Do you think I would have let you do something like that if I'd been around to prevent it? I wasn't aware of you until after the accident."

I tossed the freshly ground beans into my coffee maker and added water. Coffee was really the only thing I knew how to make, except stuff that could be heated up in the microwave.

"Fred, I appreciate that you're trying to help me, but I don't want to remember anything about Carter's death. Remembering won't change anything; it won't bring him back or make me any less guilty. I just want to let it go. All right?"

"I understand, but I think you're making a mistake."

To hell with the coffee. I abandoned my efforts at cooking and went back into my bedroom for my clothes. The last thing I wanted right now was a heart-to-heart with Fred about the worst moment in my life.

My jeans and t-shirt went on fast. I stuck my feet into my shoes and made for the door. He stood in the middle of my living room, watching me but not doing anything to stop me. His eyes still looked sad, and I didn't want to see that.

Outside, rain fell. I'd forgotten my jacket, but I didn't care. I wasn't going back into my apartment for it because then I'd have to talk to Fred. Out here, if he showed up I'd just ignore him. Easier to ignore him when I had the excuse of not wanting to look like a madman to the other people in the vicinity.

By the time I made it to the local coffee house, my shirt and hair were soaked and I was starting to shiver. It was Caroline's coffee house, the one she'd brought me to that day we walked by the river. I got myself a bagel and coffee and sat down in the back. Early on a Saturday morning, there weren't many people here, which left me too alone with my thoughts. I looked2 around for a newspaper or something to take my mind off my past.

A mom came in with two kids, a boy and a girl. They both had pale blond hair. My stomach cramped. They looked so much like Carter it was painful to see them, chattering and laughing just the way he always had. The boy was tugging on his mom's arm and pointing at the pastries on display in the glass cases next to the cash register.

I looked away. Damn it. I couldn't even go out for coffee without being reminded of him. When was it going to stop? Twelve years hadn't been enough—not nearly enough—to take away the pain of what I'd done.

If I could to back to that afternoon and trade places with him, I would. Except then he'd be the one with the murderous burden of guilt on his shoulders. He'd be the one wishing his life away, and I would never do that to him. To anyone.

"Max?"

I looked up to see Caroline standing next to my table. She wore a damp navy-blue pea coat and a blue hat with a down-turned brim. She had a little smile on her face, like she wasn't sure whether I would acknowledge her or whether maybe I'd pretend she wasn't there. This weird surge of yearning and annoyance came over me, a crazy desire to snap at her for being so inconveniently taken and kiss her at the same time.

"Caroline."

She had a cup of coffee in one hand and a plate with a piece of cake in the other. "Mind if I join you?"

"Um...no. Go ahead."

She sat down across from me. "I never come in here. And when I finally do, you're here."

"You want me to leave?"

"Oh, no. That's not what I meant at all. It's just kind of strange. Do you come here often?"

"I usually make my own coffee." I tilted my head, studying her. "Should you be talking to me? Trent won't like it."

Her cheeks turned pink. "I know."

"And..."

"I don't want to talk about that right now." Her gaze narrowed. "Why are you soaking wet?"

"I forgot my jacket."

"Max, are you okay?"

"I'm fine." My voice came out in a bark.

She recoiled slightly. "Maybe I should go."

"No, don't go," I said with a regretful sigh. "Sorry, it's just been a weird morning. I didn't mean to take it out on you."

"Do you want to talk about it?"

"Not especially."

She bent her head and sipped her coffee. I could tell I'd made her uncomfortable. It pissed me off that she was with Trent when I wanted her. Dumb, I know, but I wanted her so damned much it was all I could do not to reach across the table and caress her hand. The fury of my frustration made me growl low in my throat.

"I'm surprised you're here after Trent told you I'm a devil-worshipper," I said.

Her head jerked up. "How did you know he told me that?"

"It's what he says to everyone."

"I didn't believe him. Should I have?"

My grin was without real humor. "That's up to you."

"Well, is it true or not?" She frowned. "You said it wasn't."

"Did I?" I couldn't remember saying anything about it until now.

"Or...no. You said I should believe every word he said about you. So is it true?"

I shrugged. "I don't believe in the devil."

"Then what are you talking about?"

What was I talking about? Was I trying to start a fight with her?

I shook my head. "I'm a freak and you should stay away from me."

If I stayed here any longer, I would do something we'd both regret. Standing abruptly, I took my coffee and bagel and headed for the door. I could feel her gaze following me all the way out of the coffee house, but I didn't look back. I plunged out into the pounding rain.

"Max, wait!"

Gritting my teeth, I turned to see her hobbling after me through the downpour, moving as fast as she could with that brace still on her ankle. Didn't she understand? I was a killer. Not the kind of person she should be hanging around. Still, I couldn't allow her to hurt herself trying to run after me, so I waited.

"What?" I said, my voice full of all the confusion I couldn't discuss with her.

"I just—why haven't you talked to me?" Her face turned pink. "I mean, I haven't seen you at all since the party, except that one day in class."

The words "since the kiss" hung in the air between us. But I wasn't going there.

"Like I said, I'm not a good person for you to be around."

"But why?" she said, frowning.

"You know why."

Her lips pressed together, the corners turning down. "I'm pestering you. Sorry."

She rotated her body away from me. I'd hurt her feelings. I didn't want to hurt her; I'd only meant to warn her what kind of guy she was trying befriend.

What the fuck was wrong with me? I was supposed to seduce her. I should be celebrating the fact that she sought me out on her own, not trying to run her off.

"No." I caught her by the wrist as she turned to go. "You're not pestering me."

The touch of her skin sent hot shivers through my body. And it was only her wrist, nothing intimate. What would she do to me if we were to kiss again? My own face heated and I knew I was blushing.

"I'm sure you have better things to do than stand around talking to someone like me," she said.

That made no sense. "Someone like you? What are you talking about?"

"I'm boring. Not like you."

"Caroline, you're anything but boring."

The pinched look of her mouth relaxed and a tiny smile hovered around her mouth. "You don't think I'm boring?"

Had she noticed my blush? "I think you're the sexiest woman I've ever met."

Her face went blank. Shit. I'd gone too far, way too far. We'd only kissed that one time and she was already taken anyway. I should never have told her that.

"I, um, I want to know more about you," she said, shifting her weight from one foot to the other.

"You do?" Celebrating. I should be celebrating.

"Yeah. Can we maybe talk a while?"

Screw celebrating—I should be studying. It was Dead Week, after all. I couldn't bring myself to turn her down, though. She might never make the offer again.

"Okay, sure. I'd like that."

She smiled at me. "Great! But you should get a coat. You're soaked."

I glanced up at the sky and rain fell in my face. Our conversation had so absorbed my attention I hadn't even noticed the water falling on me.

"Let's go back to the coffee place. I think they'll let us in."

"Okay." She nodded, a little shy. "Yes, I'd like that."

"All right."

They didn't even seem to notice us as we came back into the restaurant and chose a table. My coffee was still hot, but Caroline's cake looked mushy with the rainwater it had absorbed. I got up and bought her another piece.

"Thanks," she said when I put it in front of her.

"No problem. The first piece didn't look edible."

"What, you don't like chocolate cake soup?"

We laughed and it sounded forced. Then we sat without talking as we took exploratory sips of our respective coffees.

"Have you seen Retro-girl lately?" I said into the awkward silence.

"No. I haven't seen her since the day at the student union."

"That's good, I guess."

Right. We stared at each other for another minute or so.

"I'm sorry Trent is so rude to you," Caroline said. "I tried to get him to go to coffee with you, but he just got mad at me."

My forehead puckered at the bizarre thought. "Coffee?"

"Yeah. I thought it would be neutral if we met here, or some other place like it. You know, so you could maybe get on better terms with each other."

I didn't want to embarrass her by smiling at the idea, but it was so unlikely, so improbable I couldn't help myself. "Um...that's sweet of you, Caroline, but I think we're good the way we are."

"That's what he said."

"I guess Trent and I agree on one thing, then."

"It just seems sad, you know?" Her dark eyes were soft with concern. "I don't like thinking of you being alone."

I could feel the heat in my face. "Why? You hardly even know me."

She blushed too. "I don't have to know you well to be worried about you, do I?"

"I don't know. Evidently not."

"People need families. That's all."

"I haven't had a family of origin since I was ten. Not one I wanted, anyway." Fred was my family now, and he wasn't even alive. And I had Brad and Marie. They were all I needed.

"Family of origin?" She sounded puzzled.

"My foster parents and my working circle are my family now."

"Oh." Her eyes were wide and watchful. "I didn't know you had a foster family."

"They helped me get off the street."

She pushed a bite of cake around her plate. "What's it like to be alone?"

I shrugged. "It is what it is. I haven't known anything else, so I can't really tell you. I hitchhiked west to Seattle and like I said, I was on the streets for a while before I met Brad and Marie. They took me in, helped me get my GED and a job. When I had enough money, I decided to go back to school." That was more than I'd told anyone about my life in a very long time. I felt like I'd taken off all my clothes and done a series of naked back-flips or something.

"You're very independent."

"Yeah. I am."

She still looked worried. "Do you miss them? Your family of origin, I mean."

"No." Kinda hard to miss people who despise you.

"Oh." Her shoulders slumped a little. "That's...too bad."

"You don't need to worry about me or try to fix me. I'm fine. Honest."

Her gaze shot to mine. "I'm not trying to fix you."

"Good." I hated it when women thought they could change me, make me into some domesticated animal who would fetch their slippers for them. That wasn't me. I'd been on my own too long for that kind of shit. Even before I'd run away, I'd been essentially on my own.

"So, um, you believe in ghosts." She gave me an embarrassed-looking smile.

"Yeah. Why?"

"I've just never met anyone who was open about it. It's...unusual."

How much could I tell her without freaking her out? I didn't want her running away and screaming, or more likely since this was her room, kicking me out. Some people got extremely worked up when they found out what I did.

"I'm interested in paranormal phenomena," I said after a pause. It was the most neutral way I could think of to describe it.

"Do you believe all that stuff they do on those ghost TV shows?"

"I think they exaggerate a lot of stuff on those shows. But that doesn't mean ghosts aren't real."

She seemed to ponder that for a minute. "Okay. I guess that makes sense. It's just...in my family, nobody believes in that stuff. They make fun of it."

"People tend to make fun of things they don't understand. Especially if they're afraid."

Her brown eyes met mine. "Yeah. That sounds reasonable."

"I usually don't talk to people about it if I know they won't understand. It's easier that way."

Caroline smiled. "I know exactly what you mean. I tried to tell my parents about Retro-girl and they laughed at me."

She kept smiling at me and I wanted, more than anything, to go to her and tilt her face up and kiss her. The only thing that stopped me was Trent. It's not that I didn't want to hurt my stepbrother. Frankly, after everything he'd done to me, he had it coming. But I wouldn't do that to her—make her choose between us.

Something in her expression told me she might be having similar thoughts. She twined her fingers together, her hands moving nervously against each other, blond curls sliding down over her face. She had delicate hands, slender fingers, the nails unpainted. Suddenly I wanted so badly to feel them on my skin that I started to shake.

I should leave.

Instead, I got out of the booth and went around to her side, sliding in next to her. "I'm glad I was there to help you out the night of the party," I said in a low voice.

"You are?"

"When I saw you out there with those guys, I was scared for you." I reached out and took her top hand.

She didn't pull away like I expected her to. My thumb stroked across the smooth, tender skin of her hand, the fine bones beneath. She felt warm.

Her body inclined toward me. I eased a little closer, keeping her hand in mine. All I could think about was that kiss we'd had and how much I wanted another.

"I'm glad you were there," she said. "I was terrified."

"I would have killed them if they'd hurt you." That probably wasn't the best thing to say, considering my background, but she didn't seem to think less of me for it.

She bit her lip. "Whenever I ask Trent to take me home, he thinks I'm being stupid. He doesn't like having to do it."

"If you were mine," I said, hardly believing the words coming out of my mouth, "I would always protect you."

Caroline glanced up at me through thick blond lashes. "That's sweet of you to say."

I leaned closer, all the while screaming silently at myself to stop. Leave. Like an idiot, I didn't listen to myself. Her lips were so perfect, so soft-looking as they parted on an in-breath. My hand came up to cradle the side of her face as I bent down. Touched my mouth to hers.

Part of me thought she might slap me. Or push me away. Instead, she softly kissed me back. Her free hand came up to clasp the back of my neck, under my hair.

By now, my heart pounded so hard I felt lightheaded. My cock shoved at the inside of my jeans like it wanted to climb out and take care of matters on its own. I stroked my thumb over the silky skin of her cheek and sighed against her mouth. Her lips opened beneath mine and I pushed my tongue into her mouth.

Caroline gave a little moan as I tasted her. She angled her head, sweeping her tongue across mine. She tasted of the mocha she'd been drinking.

I let go of her hand so I could pet her back. Somehow my hand found its way along her rib cage to her hip, the soft flare that I found so enticing.

Her hands shoved at my chest. She wanted me to stop? The shoving continued as she pulled away from me. Panting, I let her go. It hurt. My whole body was focused on one thing only, and she wasn't going to let me have it. Not that we could have done anything real in a booth in the coffee house, but still.

She scooted away from me on the bench seat. "I'm sorry. I can't do this."

I hung my head. Damn. "I understand."

"I like you, Max. I really do. But Trent and I—well, I'm not the kind of girl—"

"I said I understand. You don't have to explain." I stood up, unable to look at her. "I'd better go. I'll see you around."

"Yeah. Okay." Her voice was just above a whisper.

I don't know what she looked like as I left the restaurant. Kissing her again had been a dumbass thing to do, but I hadn't been able to stop myself. I wanted to do it over and over.

Chapter 15

Caroline: Paige and I met at our usual spot in the cafe on the second floor of the student union. She had her black hair up in a messy French twist; she wore a pink twin set over skinny jeans and a pair of hot pink ballet flats. In that outfit, she put my sloppy ponytail, jeans and hoodie to shame. I sat down across from her and gave her the once-over.

"You look different," I said.

"I'm meeting Dan later. We're going to dinner and some other stuff." She giggled. "He's awesome. I really like him."

Paige had broken up with her long-time boyfriend last winter after he'd cheated on her, so it had been a while since she'd dated.

"I'm happy for you. What's he like?"

"Super hot. He's an engineering major and he likes camping." She wrinkled her nose. "Not my thing, obviously, but maybe I can learn to like it."

I'd never been much for camping, either, although to be fair my family had done very little of it. I hadn't had much opportunity to experience it.

"You never know until you try," I said.

"So true. How are you and Trent doing?"

I took a long swig of my coffee and gave a noncommittal shrug. "We're okay, I guess."

"Now that's enthusiasm."

"I saw him kissing Tiffani."

Her eyes almost popped out of her head. "What? Tiffani? Oh my God, tell me you're kidding."

"Nope. Not kidding. He apologized and said it'll never happen again."

Paige groaned. "That's what they always say."

"Yeah. Well, it pissed me off so much I went home early and met Max on the way."

"Yum."

I blushed and tried not to show it. Unfortunately, I have no clue how to control blushes so my efforts were useless. "He was really nice."

"Yeah, I'll bet." Paige laughed. "You should see your face."

Leaning across the table toward her, I whispered, "We kissed."

This time, her eyes popped and her mouth fell open. "Say that again."

"We kissed. Twice. It was...really good. Incredibly good. I didn't know kissing could be like that." I kept my voice low in case one of Trent's spies might be listening. Which was totally, utterly ridiculous. Trent didn't have spies and the fact I was so paranoid about him finding out was probably just an indication of how guilty I felt.

"Wow." There was reverence in Paige's voice. "You finally found one."

"One what?"

"A guy who can turn you on."

Yeah. Yay, me. "And it's the absolutely wrong guy. The wrongest guy in the world, Paige. Why did it have to be Max?"

"I don't know. These things are a mystery."

"Do you feel the same way about Dan?"

"I think so. It's been pretty incredible so far." She smiled with a secretive glint in her eye. "I'm spending the night with him tonight. At his place. He has his own apartment."

"Ooh. Big step," I said.

"Yes, it is. I don't think we're going to get much sleep." She tilted her head. "What are you doing tonight?"

"I'm on my own. Trent is going out with some friends. Girls not allowed."

* * *

My delivery pizza was cold. I'd only eaten two slices, so I stacked the rest and crammed it into my tiny dorm-size fridge for the next day. With Paige at Dan's and Trent out with his buddies, I was on my own tonight. It was just me, cold pizza, and a book.

Instead of studying, I went for a romance novel on my tablet. Curled up on my bed, book in hand, I escaped into someone else's problems and tried to forget my own.

I'd been reading for a couple of hours when the temperature in my room dropped suddenly. It was like the normal, warm air had been completely exchanged with the air from a walk-in refrigerator. Shivering, I pulled my throw blanket around my shoulders. This building didn't have air conditioning, so the sudden drop in temperature didn't make any sense.

The atmosphere in the room grew heavy. There was an odd feeling, almost like a pressure all over my body, and a faint buzzing sensation in my head. The hair on the back of my neck stood on end. I suddenly had the idea someone was with me. Watching me.

My pulse raced and my palms began to sweat. I didn't want to turn my head. I didn't want to see whoever or whatever it was. The intruder couldn't be human, could it? Because I'd been in here for hours with the door locked and there really weren't any hiding places big enough to conceal a grown human being.

As the feeling persisted, grew stronger, I forced myself to turn my head. To look.

She sat in my desk chair, watching me. This time, she wore a plain, off-white cable-knit sweater with her bell-bottoms. Her perfectly straight hair hung loose around her shoulders. Her face was a sickening bluish-white color and her lips were blue.

I screeched. She smiled and it was ghastly, grotesque, with those blue lips. God, if this was the kind of thing Aunt Jo saw, then it was no wonder she started drinking.

The girl mouthed a word. It looked like the same word she'd tried to say before, and I still couldn't make it out.

"I'm sorry," I gasped. "I can't understand what you're saying."

She repeated herself.

I shook my head, my whole body shaking. "I don't read lips."

The girl lifted a hand and pointed at me. Her lips moved again, in a different pattern this time. It looked like...

"Max?" I said.

She nodded and repeated his name again.

"You w-want Max?"

Another nod.

"O-okay. I'll—um—tell him f-for you."

The girl vanished. I didn't even blink this time. She just disappeared. The air temperature immediately returned to normal. I could feel the warmth of it on my skin, but I was still so cold I kept the blanket around me.

My hands shook as I got off the bed. That had been real. Either it was real or I needed some major psychiatric intervention, and for now I was going with real.

She wanted Max. Max, the supposed magician and conjurer of spirits. After that kiss we'd had in the coffee house, I was nervous about talking to him. I'd pushed him away, told him no. How was I going to call him up and ask him for help? The thought made me cringe inside.

I didn't have to go right to Max, though. Maybe Trent would come and help me figure out what to do. I speed-dialed him.

"Yeah?" he said, sounding annoyed. "What's up?" In the background, loud music played and male voices laughed.

"You'll never guess what happened to me just now," I said, pacing as I talked to him.

"You know I'm busy. Can't this wait?"

"No. I saw the ghost again. In my room."

Trent snorted.

"No, really. I did. It scared the hell out of me."

He sighed audibly. "Baby, get real."

"Don't you even want to know what happened?"

"Not really. I'd like to go back to my pool game."

I laughed a little, even though it didn't seem especially funny to me. "It was pretty freaky."

"I'm sure it was."

"I'm kind of still scared. Can you come over and keep me company?"

"No. No way. I'm not cutting my night short because you have an overactive imagination." The hostility in his voice took me aback.

"Aren't you at least concerned?"

"No. You're fine. Call Paige if you can't stop worrying."

"Paige is spending the night with her boyfriend," I said.

"Well, I'm busy. Find someone else."

"There isn't anyone else." My hand tightened convulsively on the phone. "I can't believe you're being so uncaring. What if someone tried to break into my room? Would you worry then?"

"No offense, Caroline, but doesn't that aunt of yours see ghosts and shit? What was her name? Janine? Jerri?"

"Jo," I said, feeling like I was shrinking inside.

"Maybe you should stay away from that kind of thing. You know? You don't want to end up like her."

That was pretty much the same thing my parents had told me ever since I'd been a little girl and Aunt Jo had gone off the deep end.

"I'm not like Jo," I said. "She's crazy and an alcoholic."

"I'm just saying you don't know how it started with her. It's probably not a good idea to encourage it."

"I'm surprised you want to be with me if you think I'm on the edge of losing my mind," I snapped. "And I wasn't encouraging it. It happened on its own, without any encouragement from me."

"I'm just saying—"

"That even thinking about ghosts could push me over the edge."

Trent gave a long-suffering sigh. "That's not what I meant. At all."

"Then what did you mean?"

"I don't know. I didn't think you believed in that spooky crap anyway."

"I don't. Didn't." I rolled my eyes. "I'm not sure what I believe in anymore."

"Well, ghosts aren't real. They're just people imagining things and wishing they were real. That's all. So don't worry about it."

"Okay." Whatever. Clearly, he didn't understand and wasn't about to try.

"I'm going back to my game now. You'll be fine." He ended the call.

My head hurt. My boyfriend, who claimed to love me, couldn't be bothered to cut short a pool game and a night of drinking with his buds to help me. He was...he was...I didn't know what he was. But I was furious with him, that much was clear. He seemed to think he could do and say whatever he wanted and I'd always be here waiting for him.

Those days were over. I wasn't waiting for Trent anymore. He didn't deserve it.

I could still feel a lingering sense of presence in the air, like Retro-girl was waiting for me to keep my promise. Like she was on the other side of some invisible barrier, where she could watch me. Monitor me.

The ghost had asked specifically for Max. I had to call him, no matter how squirmy it made me feel. I turned my phone on again. My hands were shaking and moist and I almost dropped it. My fingers trembled on the screen as I called up my contact list. Max's number was listed right after Trent's. The call connected, and The Decemberists' "Rise To Me" played in my ear.

"Caroline?" Max sounded more wary than surprised.

"Can you come over tonight?" I blurted before I could lose my nerve.

There was a long pause.

"What's going on? You sound upset."

"I saw that ghost again."

"I'll be right over."

No questions asked. No mockery. Trent had given me all kinds of grief, but not Max. Instantly, I felt better, less alone.

I popped off the bed and paced, holding onto my elbows. The air still held an icy edge, although I could tell it had returned more or less to its normal temperature. That eerie sense of being watched lingered too, and I didn't know if it was real or only my imagination.

The ghost had been real. I was sure of that now. But was she really still here, lurking in some other dimension where I couldn't see her? I felt like she was, but I really didn't know for sure. Maybe Max could tell me.

I didn't like being here alone. With her. I could go down to one of the lounges to wait. The first floor, maybe, or just stand by the front door so I could catch him when he came in. That way I'd be sure not to miss him. Because if I stayed here by myself, I was going to go nuts from the tension.

There was a knock at my door. I jumped to open it. Max. I almost sagged to the floor in relief when I saw him. He wore the same leather jacket he'd had on the night of the party, and he looked way too sexy.

"How did you get here so fast?" I said, staring at him.

"I was in the area."

"That's weird. Do you know how weird that is?"

He smiled wryly. "Yeah, I do. I have pretty good intuition."

"So this is like that other night? You just had a feeling you needed to be somewhere around here?"

"Yep. Do you want me to come in?"

"Yes. Sure." I stepped back from the door. "Thank you for coming."

"No problem. So this is the third time you've seen her?"

I shut the door. "Actually, it's the fourth. She made an appearance last Sunday morning, too."

"Okay." He walked slowly through the tiny open space of my room, an odd sort of detached look on his face, as if he heard music no-one else could hear. "What was that like?"

"She tried to say something to me, but she couldn't make any sound and I couldn't read her lips."

He stopped walking to stare at me. "She actually tried to talk to you?"

"Yeah. She got really frustrated when I couldn't tell what she was saying." And now I had to deliver the big news. "Max, she asked for you tonight."

He frowned, his stare growing even more intent. "Me? She asked for me by name?"

"Yes. I even asked her if I had it right and she nodded."

"Weird."

I gave an anxious laugh. "If you think it's weird, it must be truly bizarre."

Max sat down on my bed as if his legs had given out. "Did she say why she wanted me?"

"No. Your name was the only thing I could understand out of what she said."

"Did she threaten you in any way?"

"No. But she looked really scary. She looked dead. Her face was this disgusting white color and her lips were blue."

He rubbed his stubbled chin, still frowning. "Hmm. Okay, she shows up here three times, trying to say something to you. And when she finally gets a message through, it's my name. Was she trying to talk when you saw her on the street?"

"No. That time she just stood there looking at me. If I hadn't seen her in my room, I would have thought she was a regular person." I sat down next to him, keeping plenty of room between the two of us. "She was dressed very retro. Bell-bottom jeans and embroidered tunics and headbands. She looks kind of like a flower child."

"Maybe she died during the late sixties or early seventies."

"She must have been really hip."

His face was drawn into thoughtful lines, his dark-blue eyes far away. "I might know what this is about."

"What?"

He glanced at me. "It's something I don't like to talk about."

"Okay. But it has something to do with me, or Retro-girl wouldn't keep coming to my room."

"Retro-girl?" He grinned. Oh, boy, that grin. It just about knocked me down.

"I don't know her real name." I angled my body toward him. "I can't make you tell me, but I'd really like to know. Why is she here?"

Max's grin faded. He regarded me for a minute or so, then closed his eyes and drew a deep breath in through his nose. "Carter."

"I don't understand."

"I received a message recently that he's trying to get in touch with me. Maybe Retro-girl is helping him. Maybe she finds you easier to contact than me, so she got you to alert me."

"But...how the heck do you receive a message like that? Did you get an email? A text?"

He opened his eyes again. They sparkled with humor. "A ghostly text? That would be convenient, but no. The message came through the Tarot. A friend read for me last weekend."

"What's the Tarot?"

"A deck of cards with a different scene on each card. They're used for divination." At my uncomprehending stare, he said "telling the future."

"Fortune telling? A fortune teller told you Carter is looking for you."

"No, not a fortune teller. A diviner. Marie isn't one of those fake gypsies with a crystal ball. She's very good at what she does and she takes it seriously. It's a calling."

"I see." Really, I didn't. Then I thought...Marie. Did Max have a girlfriend? I didn't like the surge of jealousy that came over me. I had no right to be jealous over Max. I glanced at him. "Um...is this Marie person some kind of witch or magician?"

"More or less."

"Is she a close friend of yours?" I said, trying to keep my voice casual.

"She's my foster mom."

"Oh. Foster mom." I nodded sagely, hoping he hadn't noticed or guessed my true reason for asking. "You told me that the other day, didn't you?"

"She and her husband Brad took me in when I was seventeen. If it weren't for them, I'd probably still be on the streets. Or dead." The reverence in his voice moved me.

"They mean a lot to you."

"Yes, they do."

"Are they the ones who taught you about ghosts and stuff?"

He smiled. "Not exactly. I started seeing a spirit named Frederick when I was thirteen. He's another one I owe a lot to. He's always looked out for me and given me good advice."

That made my eyes go wide. "You're saying you have a friend who's a ghost."

"Yeah," he said with a sidelong glance at me. "I'm not crazy."

"I didn't say you were."

"It's all over your face, though." He watched me knowingly. "I don't tell people about Fred. Only you and my circle."

"Why me?"

"Because knowing about Fred might help you be less afraid of Retro-girl. He kept me alive. When I was so down I didn't want to live another day, Fred kept me going."

I wanted to take Max's hand, to comfort away the sadness I saw on his face, but I was afraid the gesture would be misinterpreted. "I'm so sorry, Max."

He shook his head. "Don't be. It's over. I survived."

And he didn't want my pity or my sympathy. He'd made that clear before. I cast around for a change of subject.

"Trent told me you're a magician."

Max laughed. "I'll bet he did."

"He also said you were a Satanist and a witch."

He laughed. "He's just throwing every scary occult term at you that he can think of."

"What did he mean?"

"That I'm a crazy sonofabitch who thinks I can turn people into toads or some shit."

"That isn't what you think?"

"No." He shook his head, still smiling. "Real magic isn't like that."

"Oh." I'd never heard anyone use the term real magic as if it could be something almost ordinary, something regular people could do. "What is it like, then?"

"Real magic means manipulating energy. My energy, the energy of the earth, the stars, whatever is available for use. We channel and direct energy to influence events."

I frowned at him. "That sounds totally New Age."

"That's because the New Age people borrow terms and ideas from ancient magical and spiritual systems. They just kind of repackage it is all. And they charge a fortune to teach stuff that many occultists can teach you for free or only a small fee."

"And you're an occultist."

He met my gaze, square on, no flinching. "Yes, I am."

I took a deep breath. I had the feeling I was standing on the edge of something big, like maybe an enormous canyon, something I could fall into and hurt myself irreparably in the process. Something that would forever change the way I saw everything in existence. I could tumble in and break my bones on the rocks, or I could learn the terrain and move slowly and safely into this new territory. Or I could turn around and run back to my safe, ordinary, previous life.

"Not a Satanist or a witch," I said.

"I'm neither, although what I do is pretty close to witchcraft. I'm more what you'd call a wizard.

"Wow," I said after a long hesitation. "That's a lot to take in."

"I hope you're not afraid of me now," he said softly.

My gaze snapped up to his. "Not at all."

His eyes softened. "Good. I don't ever want you to be afraid of me."

"Have other girls?"

"Oh, yeah. That's why I don't tell people about Fred or any of this other stuff until I get to know them really well. And most of the time, not even then."

The urge to touch him was growing stronger with each moment that passed. "You don't know me all that well. What if I run around blabbing this stuff to everyone?"

"I'm trusting you because of Retro-girl." He reached for me. Took my hand. "Can I trust you, Caroline?"

It was only our hands touching, but it made me tremble and ache. I laced my fingers with his. "Yes."

"Okay. The first thing we need to do is try to get Retro-girl to talk to us. It sounds like she's having trouble with that, so we need a tool to help her."

"Like what?"

"I normally use a pendulum, but mine is at home. Do you have a necklace I can borrow? The best kind is a simple metal chain with a pendant."

"I might have something that will work." I got up and went to the built-in wardrobe that functioned as my closet. My small jewelry box had several necklaces in it. I pulled out a silver heart and held it up so Max could see it.

"Will this work?"

"Perfect."

I dropped it into his palm. He patted the bed beside him and I sat down. I wasn't sure what had just happened between us, but it felt like more than friendship.

Max closed his eyes, holding the pendant in the palm of his hand. I didn't know whether it was okay to look at him while he did that, so I stared at my lap instead. After a few minutes of meditation—or whatever he was doing—he held the necklace by the end of the chain, so the pendant swung gently in the air.

Once it settled down and stopped swinging, he started talking to it. The fact that he was talking to what I'd always assumed was an inanimate object gave me pause. It was just too kooky. But I'd asked him here; I'd asked for his help, and it would be extremely rude for me to show how uncomfortable this made me.

He asked it basic stuff, like what direction was yes and what was no, was his name Joe Smith—that was a no—and were we on the surface of Mars. I gave him a few sidelong glances during this process, while biting my lip to keep from nervous giggling. He seemed completely serious about it.

"I'm asking these silly questions to get the feel of this particular pendulum," he said softly. "Not because I'm an idiot."

I looked at him, wide-eyed, and said nothing.

Max grinned. "Okay, now down to business. Retro-girl, are you here?"

The pendulum remained still.

"Blond girl from the sixties—we don't know your name, so we're calling you Retro-girl. I hope you're not offended by that. We mean no offense at all. Can you tell me if you're here? If you can make this pendulum swing in the yes direction, then we'll know you're here and you want to talk to us."

Still no response. The silver heart remained motionless at the end of its chain.

"Is there someone here who would like to communicate with us?" Max said.

We waited. And waited. Still no response.

"Is there a blond girl who may have died in the late sixties or early seventies?"

The pendant simply hung there like an ordinary piece of jewelry.

Max sighed. "I don't know. It seems like she's not around anymore or maybe she just doesn't know how to get through to us."

"Is there anything else you can do? I don't want her appearing to me like that again. It scared the shit out of me."

He handed the necklace back to me. "I'd have to go home and get my kit. I came right over when you called me because you sounded so worried I didn't want to take the time to go home first."

"Okay."

"Thing is, if I prevent her from coming back, we'll never know what it is she wants to say."

I chewed my lip. "I don't know if I can sleep in here, knowing she might show up any time."

"Can you get someone to stay with you?"

"No." I shook my head. "Paige is spending the night with her boyfriend."

"What about Trent?"

I looked him in the eye. He showed no sign of jealousy or resentment of my boyfriend. "He's out with his friends tonight. I don't want to ruin his good time over this."

"Does he know about the ghost?"

"Yes. But he thinks it's my imagination."

"Well." Max looked down at his hands, clasped in his lap. "I can stay with you, if you'd like."

My heart jumped. I went hot all over. "I don't know, Max..."

"We won't do anything except sleep. You can put this extra mattress on the floor, if you don't want me in the bed with you."

The problem was I wanted him in the bed way too much. My skin burned even more hotly. I was sure he could see me blushing. Hell, they could probably see me blushing all the way on the other side of campus.

This was such a bad idea. If he stayed here, something would happen between us. I knew it. He probably knew it.

"Tell you what," he said. "You can come over to my place and sleep in my bed. I'll take the floor in the living room."

"I don't want to make you sleep on the floor," I said.

"I've got a sleeping bag."

"Still—"

"Caroline, I've slept in much worse places, believe me." He smiled. "Really, it's not a big deal."

"It is to me."

"That's because you're so sweet. But it won't hurt me to sleep on the floor once and I don't want you staying alone if you're going to be scared."

The achy butterflies were back. I wasn't sure how he could call me sweet when he was the one making all the sacrifices. And sleeping in his bed...it sounded so intimate, even if he wouldn't be there at the time.

"I don't know," I said.

"Come on. Do it for me. Otherwise, I'll be up all night worrying about you."

I gave him a skeptical glance. "You will?"

"All night long."

I closed my eyes with a sigh. This was going to change things between us, not to mention between me and Trent. There was more at stake here than the way my relationship with Max would develop.

But I didn't have to let it change anything, right? We could hold on to our friendship, and Trent would never have to know I'd spent a night at Max's place. We'd go on the way we'd been before. It was just this one time, after all.

"Okay," I said. "But just this once."

"Right. Just this once."

I gathered a few things and threw them in my backpack. We left by the back door and I didn't see anyone on the stairs or in the quad when we got outside.

* * *

It took Max and me about twenty minutes to walk to his place. He lived close to downtown, in an old house that had one of those high, curved roofs like the ones you see on traditional American barns. The house was painted yellow, not red, though, so it didn't actually look like a barn. It was cute, but there was something spooky about it too.

"Your house gives me a weird feeling," I said as we walked up the concrete walkway to the front door.

"It's in the same style as the Amityville Horror house," he said, opening the door.

"Oh. Yeah, you're right."

"It isn't haunted, though. Except by Fred, but he's only here because of me."

I swallowed. "Am I going to meet Fred?"

"I don't know. He doesn't usually show himself to visitors, but with you he might make an exception."

The foyer of the house seemed incredibly small, considering the size of the building. But I guess it had been carved up into apartments, so whoever had adapted it had probably carved up the original foyer too.

We climbed a narrow staircase to a small landing on the second floor. Max opened the flat, apartment-style door and let me into his living room.

It was a long, mostly empty space with bare wooden floorboards, a metal filing cabinet, old wooden desk, and one chair. On the desk was the biggest computer monitor I'd ever seen.

"That's a huge monitor," I said.

"It helps me when I'm designing. I like to be able to see what I'm doing."

Oh, right. That made sense.

Max slipped off his jacket and hung it on a nail in the wall next to the door. "You can put your coat on the back of the chair."

I followed directions. It was an office desk chair. Did he have any normal, home-type furniture at all? The place wasn't very cozy.

"Want a beer?" he said.

"Sure."

I trailed after him as he went into the kitchen. It was a pretty good size for an apartment, and it looked like it had been built in the fifties and never updated. There was a red laminate counter with a metal edging, like the kind you see on mid-century diner-style tables. There was a wooden drop-leaf table shoved under a window on the near side of the room.

Max opened the fridge and pulled out a couple of beer bottles, handing one to me.

"Do you have a bottle opener?"

He reached into a drawer. "Here you go."

"I shouldn't be here," I said as he handed me the bottle opener.

He gave me a wary look. "Why not?"

"Because of Trent. I feel like I'm cheating on him."

"We're not doing anything like that. We're just talking. Hanging out."

"Yeah. I guess." I opened my beer and gave the opener back to him. "Why does he hate you so much, anyway?"

Max opened his own beer and took a swig. Was he trying to avoid my question? He kept the bottle in his hand, staring down at the brown glass, his brows crimped together.

"He always hated me, from the day we met. I think he resented my dad, too. He didn't like the fact his mom was remarrying."

"That's too bad. Are his folks divorced?"

"Yeah. And his dad almost never sees him. My dad is more of a father to him."

"And he still hates you even though he's so close to your dad?"

"Obviously."

I tasted my beer. It was good. Not what I was used to, because I usually drank the cheap, mass-produced stuff. This was better.

"I think that's incredibly unfair."

He shrugged. "People can't help how they feel, I guess."

"He doesn't have to be so mean to you."

His lips curled up. "Taking my side, Caroline?"

Someone had to. Although I was still a little skeevy about the whole murder thing...but it had happened when Max was only ten and nothing he'd done since I'd met him had given me the impression he'd ever enjoy hurting another person.

"I hate it when people are cruel to others, especially to my friends," I said.

"Am I your friend?"

"I hope so."

His smile turned a bit bashful. "I'll be as much of a friend to you as you'll let me."

Wow. I wasn't sure how to take that.

"I still don't get why Trent hates you and not your dad," I said. "Your dad is the one who married your mom. Not you."

"I was an easy target. Small for my age. Trent got a kick out of picking on me." He said it matter-of-factly, like it wasn't a big deal.

"Right now I don't like him very much."

Max leaned back against his kitchen counter. "I don't want to get between the two of you."

"You're not."

"Are you sure?"

"Yeah." I lifted my shoulders. "You know, sometimes lately I've been wondering where I belong, though. The people I usually spend time with...they don't understand about the ghost thing. They either laugh at me or tell me I'm being stupid. And those are the ones I've been dumb enough to talk to. Most of my friends I wouldn't even try to say anything about it because I know how they'd react."

He listened with sympathetic eyes. "Yeah, I know what you mean."

"But you have friends who understand. You have your circle. Isn't that a group of people who do magic together?"

"Yes. Where did you hear that?"

"I'm not sure. Maybe I read it somewhere."

"I do have my circle," he said. "But most people don't understand and I'm careful how I talk about it in public. I made the mistake of telling some people about Fred when I was young, and the fallout was ugly."

I nodded. A feeling of weight and tension in my shoulders that I hadn't even been aware of fell away, and I seemed to breathe more easily. It felt good simply to share this stuff, to talk about it to someone who didn't think I was either crazy or an idiot.

"Does Trent know about Fred?" I said with a glance at Max.

"No. At least, I've never told him." He grimaced. "I don't know what might have been said behind my back, but I think if he knew, he would have thrown it in my face."

"Probably." I was beginning to realize my boyfriend was not only *not* the great guy I'd first thought but was actually kind of an asshole. "I'm starting to wonder what I ever saw in him."

"I really don't want to talk about Trent," Max said.

Well. That was understandable, I guess. But what else could we talk about besides Trent or ghosts?

"Why don't you show me some of your designs," I said.

We went back into the living room and Max pulled up some of his work so I could see it on his monitor. I didn't know much about design, but his stuff looked really professional to me.

"I'm not much of a judge," I said, "but I think your work is really good."

"Thanks."

Was he blushing? That was awfully cute.

"I'm starting to fall behind because of school, though," he said. "My work load was really picking up before I enrolled and I can't keep up with it."

The beer was making me all warm and floaty and a lot less shy. The ghosts didn't seem quite so scary at the moment. I tilted my head, looking at him, wondering.

"What?" he said, smiling.

"Can we try talking to Retro-girl here?"

"We could, but it would probably be easier if we try making contact where she likes to appear." His fingers plucked at the fabric of his jeans. "Of course, if I got through to Carter then maybe she wouldn't need to bother you anymore."

"So are you going to do that? Talk to Carter, I mean."

His gaze dropped. He had the most beautiful eyelashes, so thick and long that I wanted to pet them.

"I don't know what I'd say to him." His voice sounded raspy all of a sudden. "I killed him. What can I say now?"

"I don't know." If I hadn't had a beer, I would have kept my hands to myself, but I was buzzed and my good judgment was shot. I reached out and laid my hand on his arm. "I'll be with you, if you'd like."

He shot me a glance and then looked down again. "You don't have to do that."

"I want to be there for you, after what you did for me."

"I didn't do anything anyone else wouldn't have done."

"Max, that's not true and you know it. Some guys would have just joined in the fun and a lot of people would have pretended they didn't see anything."

He just kept looking at the floor.

I squeezed his arm. "You're a good person."

Max snorted. "No, I'm really not, Caroline."

"Why would you say that?"

He finally lifted his gaze to mine. "You really have to ask?"

"It was an accident. Wasn't it? If it wasn't, if you did it on purpose, then tell me. Tell me you meant to shoot him."

He pinched his eyes closed. His nostrils flared and his jaw clenched, released, clenched again as his mouth briefly contorted. He opened his eyes and looked straight at me. "It was an accident."

The expression in those dark-blue eyes was so empty that it hurt me to look at them. But I couldn't look away. I had a hunch that he needed me to look at him, to hold his gaze.

"You were just a kid yourself," I said.

He passed his hand over his eyes. "I don't want to talk about this right now."

I was pressing him too hard. We barely knew each other, and here I was trying to get him to open up. Lecturing him on how it wasn't his fault. It just hurt me to see his pain.

When I'd been with Trent, it had been easy to judge Max, to think of him as someone who could kill for fun. I hadn't known him at all then. Now, everything was different.

It must be because he'd stood up for me against those guys. I'd been terrified and he'd protected me. That had changed the way I saw him. But it was too soon to expect him to bare his soul to me.

I smiled. "Okay. No Trent, no Carter. Got it."

So else what could we talk about? The weather? Maybe our respective majors. That was usually a safe subject. Boring, though.

"So," Max said. "What do you like to do in your spare time?"

"Read," I answered with a sense of relief. He'd found what ought to be a safe subject.

"You're a bookworm, huh?"

I frowned at the surprise in his voice. "Did you think I couldn't?"

He grinned. "No, I didn't think you were illiterate. It's just most of the sorority girls I've met didn't seem especially—um—intellectual."

I rolled my eyes. "I'm not sure my reading material counts as intellectual. I mostly read genre fiction."

"Which genres?"

"Fantasy, romance, sometimes mysteries."

He sank to the wooden floor. "I read a lot, too."

"Where are your books?" I followed him down to the floor and arranged myself cross-legged. It was a bit drafty down there, but I wanted to be near him.

"I don't have many," he said. "Mostly I go to libraries. I haven't had a place to keep books for the last few years."

"But I thought you lived with Brad and Marie."

He shrugged. "I did. But I didn't want to clutter up their place with a lot of my shit."

That was sad. His real family hadn't wanted him, and when he did find a place, he was afraid to impose on them by actually collecting any physical possessions. I was pretty sure he wouldn't like it if I vocalized that thought, however.

"What's your favorite book?" I said.

"The Song Of Ice And Fire series by George R.R. Martin," he said without a second's hesitation.

I made a face. "Those are so dark and depressing."

"Yeah, but they're real."

"I suppose." To him, dark and depressing must seem more real because it matched the life he'd led. It was probably wildly inappropriate, but at this moment I very much wanted to take him in my arms and comfort all the pain away.

"What's your favorite book?" he said.

I blushed. "I'd rather not say."

"Oh, come on. I showed you mine. It's only fair for you to show me yours."

My face got even hotter. "You'll laugh."

"No, I won't. Promise."

I shook my head.

"Come on. You can't tease me like that. You have to tell me."

I put my hands over my face, then peeked out from between my fingers. "Fifty Shades Of Grey," I said as fast as I could.

He blinked. A slow smile spread over his face. "Isn't that a naughty book?"

"Maybe." I hid behind my fingers again. "Or trilogy. It's actually a trilogy."

"And isn't there a lot of bondage in it?"

I nodded. It had seemed strange to me that I could like a story so much when it revolved around a passionate sexual relationship, because I'd never experienced that kind of passion and wasn't convinced it existed in real life. Now, of course, I knew it did. I had it with Max.

"Wow. That is so not what I thought you'd say." He had a big smile in his voice, too, and the timber had changed, gotten deeper.

"You're laughing at me."

"No, I'm not. Really, Caro, I'm not." He leaned forward and pulled at my hands. "Don't be embarrassed. Sex is a good thing."

"Says the heathen, devil-worshipping magician guy."

He laughed. "Exactly. And I know what I'm talking about."

I let him pull my hands down. "You really don't think I'm some kind of slut?"

"No. I think you should own your sexuality. Embrace it. It's not healthy to live in denial."

"A lot of people think it's a really badly written book."

He raised his brows. "But you think..."

"The story was really fun. And that's what matters."

"Well, there you go."

Our hands were still clasped. He raised them to his lips and brushed a kiss across my skin.

"Thank you," I said.

He smiled at me, and the warmth in his eyes made me tingle all over, the achy butterflies swarming up inside me. "That makes two things we have in common. No, three. Ghosts, folk music, and fantasy fiction."

"We're two weird peas in a pod. Now that I've realized how weird I am, I can never go back to my sorority house." I was kind of kidding, but in a way it was true.

"A lot of people are gaming these days and there are all those ghost-hunting shows on TV, so I doubt they'd think you're all that weird," Max said. "It's mostly those of us who work magic who get the funny looks."

"I don't know. I've gotten a few of those looks. More than a few, actually."

"That sucks." He leaned forward, still holding onto my hand. "You know you can always talk to me about this stuff, right?"

"That's why I'm here."

My arm was stretched out in his direction because of his hold on me. I could have pulled it back, disengaged. Instead, I scooted closer.

His eyes seemed darker, heavy-lidded and hot as he gazed at me. My pulse sped up so fast I felt almost dizzy. He was going to kiss me. Was he going to kiss me?

I should leave. Technically, I still belonged to Trent. If Max and I were going to have an affair, I should first break up with my boyfriend. I should definitely leave. But I waited while Max came up on all fours and stalked me like a prowling cat.

His head tilted, slowly, as he came near. He was once again giving me a chance to back out. I didn't want to back out and I didn't want to call Trent to break up with him. I wanted to kiss Max.

My body leaned a little farther toward his and our lips met. His were soft, warm, coaxing. They clung to mine for an instant and then released.

I brought my hand up to the side of his face. His perpetual stubble felt scratchy under my palm. Our lips caught again. I opened my mouth and licked him.

He let out a sigh. We opened to each other at the same time, our tongues sliding, probing, tasting. I pushed my fingers into cool, silky black hair as he pulled me forward into his arms.

His body was as hard with muscle as I remembered. I put my arms around him, flattened my hands across his powerful back. His shirt was in the way. I slipped my hands underneath it to enjoy the smooth warmth of his skin.

He clasped the back of my head in one large hand and devoured my mouth, licking and nipping me, plunging his tongue deep. I ached so badly for him I couldn't contain myself as I wriggled against him. Strange little whimpers and moans escaped me.

Max lowered me to the floor and stretched himself out, half over me and half beside me. His leg slipped between mine and his hand crept under my t-shirt and slid upward to my breast. I arched into his touch. The ache in my core pulsed and throbbed.

His thumb brushed my nipple through the thin satin of my bra and a bright bolt of pleasure shot through me from my breast to my core. I gasped. He did it again and I cried out against his lips. My legs moved restlessly against the relentless aching pleasure inside me.

We were both panting desperately. I could feel the hard ridge of his erection pressing against my thigh. Weirdly, it excited me even more. I'd never found a guy's arousal especially exciting until now.

He pulled up my t-shirt and unclasped the hook on my bra, baring my breasts. I stared up at him in a haze of desire and found him staring back at me. The expression on his face was something I'd never seen on a guy before, awe and reverence overlaying the obvious desire in his eyes.

Bending his head, he took my nipple into the warm wet of his mouth and sucked. I grabbed onto him with a helpless whimper. It was the best thing I'd ever felt.

He tormented first one side of me and then the other until I was wildly aroused. When his hand left my breast and slipped beneath the waistband of my yoga pants, the brush of his fingers against my inner thigh brought another moan from my throat.

135

"Caroline," he said raggedly. "If you want to continue this, we should go to the bedroom."

"Okay."

"Are you sure? I want you to be sure."

I sat up, my clothes all rumpled and my bra hanging open. "I'm sure."

We got up, hand in hand, moving from the bare-bones living room to a bedroom just as sparse. There was nothing in here except a big mattress on the floor and, next to it, a desk lamp on top of a cheap plastic single drawer. Max and I sank to the bed, kissing hungrily and pulling at each other's clothing.

"Trent said your pendant is a pentacle. Is that true?" I said, reaching out to touch the beads.

"Yes and no," Max said. He pulled the necklace out from beneath his shirt collar.

The beads were some kind of silvery-black mineral interspersed with the occasional white to clear bead. There were two pendants layered over each other. On the bottom was a silver pentacle and over it a beautiful silver owl in flight.

"Ooh," I said softly. "That's so pretty. Not what I expected at all."

"Too pretty for a guy?" he said with laughter in his voice.

"No. That's not what I meant. I just thought it would be something like a skull. You know, something all scary and stuff."

"Oh, I see. Something ominous, because I'm a sinister master of the occult."

I glanced up at him to see him grinning at me. "You're making fun of me."

"Maybe a little. But only in the nicest way possible."

I shoved him playfully. "It's not my fault I don't know anything about this stuff."

"Yeah, but skulls are big fashion nowadays. I'm surprised you don't have any on your purse. Or maybe a t-shirt with a sugar skull on it. You're sadly lacking in the trend department, little girl."

I stuck my tongue out at him. "Am not. Anyway, my mom would probably kill me if I came home wearing something with skulls on it." Of course, she'd treat me to a long lecture on the mental health dangers of dabbling in the paranormal first. When she was done schooling me, I'd probably be glad to die.

"You always do what your mommy tells you?" His dark eyes sparkled, crinkling at the corners.

"Of course not. But I have to pick my battles." I pressed my fingertip gently to the owl's wing. "Why do you wear these? Do they mean something in particular to you?"

He covered my hand with his much larger one. "The pentacle was a gift from Brad and Marie. It represents a number of things, one of them being the five elements."

"Five? I thought there were only four."

"Earth, air, fire, and water, plus spirit makes five."

"Oh. That's actually kind of cool. What about the owl?"

He shrugged a little. "You might say it's my totem animal. I think of the owl as a creature that's comfortable in the realm of the dead, a creature that sees and understands the hidden parts of existence."

My eyes were round now. "Spooky."

His other hand cupped the side of my face, his thumb stroking along the line of my jaw. "I don't think of it that way. It's just another part of the world, one we don't usually pay much attention to. But it's not necessarily dangerous."

My gaze drifted to his lips. They were so beautifully cut, just full enough, and every time I looked at them I wanted to kiss them. "The only other person I ever discussed this stuff with was my Aunt Jo. And she's crazy."

"Hmmm. Well, I'm pretty sure I'm not crazy."

I'd begun to tingle again between my legs. "What about the beads? Do they have meaning too?"

He slid his hand to my neck, caressing the sensitive side of my throat. "The black ones are hematite. They're grounding and protective. The white ones are clear quartz. They have a lot of uses, especially enhancing psychic abilities."

I leaned in closer. "I had no idea."

He tasted my lips. "Did you know sex is magical too?"

"No." I took his bottom lip between my teeth. "That sounds totally wild."

"Yeah." Gently, he cupped my breast. "You can raise a lot of energy that way."

His hand found its way between my legs again and I let my thighs fall open with an eagerness I'd never thought I could feel.

He moaned. "You're so wet, baby." Coming from Max, the endearment excited me in a way it never had before. The naughty talk, too. I wished he'd say it again.

I wanted to touch him, but I was suddenly shy. Instead I let him pet me, brush his fingertips over my exquisitely swollen and sensitive flesh while I quivered and gasped. One of those fingers slid inside me, making me arch my back as my eyes rolled up.

He moved his finger rhythmically and it felt like a pleasure bomb exploded in my body. I threw my head back with a loud cry. His mouth came down on mine and I shoved my tongue deep into him, trying to take him the way he was taking me. Max groaned as I kissed him, his mouth frantic on mine, as if he wanted to utterly consume me.

He drew back, his breath coming hard. "I need you, Caro. Please."

"Yes."

He fumbled in the drawer. A moment later I heard the rip of a condom packet. He rolled it onto himself and I reached down to grasp him and help guide him into me. When my hand closed around him, he shuddered.

He slid into me. We both moaned. He felt so much better, so much *more* than any guy I'd ever been with before. Not that there had been many. Just two before him, and they were driven completely from my mind as Max began to move in and out of me.

The pleasure I'd had earlier was nothing compared to this. I bucked beneath him, my legs wrapping around his waist, my hands clutching his shoulders as he reared over me. He seemed to be hitting every pleasure point in my body, nerves I hadn't even known I possessed singing with delight.

I moaned his name. My gaze and his came together and clung. We stared at each other as we moved together, both of us moaning. It was almost too much. I never looked—I never—

He was everything in my world. The way his hair slid into his face as he moved over me, the musky scent of him, the sound of his pleasure, the hot silky weight of him on top of me, inside me...Max took me over and there was nothing else. The rhythmic push and pull of him detonated another ecstatic explosion in me; wordless cries and groans fell from my mouth and I didn't even recognize my own voice.

As the pleasure ebbed for me, Max threw back his head on a yell that sounded like pain. His face tensed in a grimace, his eyes shut tight. He shuddered, moaning and whimpering as I held him close. The vulnerable noises he made brought out a tenderness in me that was new for me. I turned my head and pressed kisses to his naked shoulder as his trembling subsided.

We lay quietly together. Our breathing slowed. I stroked his back, exploring the long ridges of muscle along his spine.

Max kissed my forehead. "I think you killed me."

I looked up at him with a quizzical smile. "I killed you?"

"With pleasure. That was...amazing. Mind-blowing. At least, for me it was." A shadow seemed to cross his face.

"For me too."

His mouth slowly turned up in a smile. "Yeah?"

"The best."

His gaze took on a searching quality as he stroked my temples with his thumbs. He opened his mouth, as if he wanted to say something, then shut it again. I smiled up at him, trying to reassure him.

His forehead creased. "I'm too heavy for you."

He withdrew from my body and rolled to the side, pulling me tightly against him. I reached for his head and drew him down for a hot kiss. Something about Max brought out a side of me I'd never really experienced before. I felt freer, like I could do and say whatever I needed to without fear of reprimand.

"I'm glad you're here tonight," he whispered against my hair.

"So am I."

My whole body glowed. I'd heard of "afterglow", but had never really experienced it. My other two sex partners had never left me feeling like this. I'd always been vaguely relieved at the end of our sexual encounters, glad it was over and I didn't have to pretend to be enthusiastic anymore. None of the boys I'd dated in high school had aroused me the way Max did, either.

This made me wonder about my prior choices in guys. Had I been going for the guys who didn't attract me, and if so, why?

The answer came to me almost instantaneously, like it had been waiting just under the surface of my consciousness for me to notice it. Guys like Trent were the safe choice. The sensible choice. They fit right in with my family, with my parents and their need for everything to come in tidy, predictable packages. My mom and dad had liked and approved of every one of the guys I'd dated.

They would not approve of Max.

I flung my arm around the taut curve of his waist and touched my lips to the hollow at the base of his throat. All of his warm, naked skin pressed up against mine and his sexy masculine smell filled my nose. He wore no cologne. He smelled of clean skin, sweat and sex. I rubbed my face against his chest.

"Are you marking me?" he said in an amused tone.

"What?"

"Like a cat. Marking me with your scent."

"I like the way you feel."

He made a rumbling sound in his chest, one big hand sliding down to clasp my butt. "I like the way you feel, too."

Was this as special, as different, for him as it was for me? I hesitated to ask. I really didn't want to get a humiliating answer, or even worse, a lie.

His fingers buried themselves in my hair. "I don't think we can go back to the way we were before."

"Neither do I." And I didn't want to.

"I want to keep seeing you."

I drew back and stared at him in complete surprise.

His face fell. "Uh...I guess that's not what you want, so forget I said it."

I'd never seen him look so unsure of himself. Usually he was so self-assured it was almost obnoxious.

I put my fingers over his mouth. "No, I do want it. You just surprised me."

"Really?" He smiled. "You want to keep seeing me?"

I smiled back. "Yes."

"Good." He gave me a lingering kiss. "Because I don't think I can stay away from you."

That admission made me feel ridiculously happy.

"I feel the same way."

We dozed for a while. I'm not sure how long we lay together like that, listening to the rain pattering against the windows and the creaking of the old house. At some point, I remembered Fred and how Max said he popped in for unexpected visits. Was he watching us right now? I hoped he had more courtesy than to peep at us while we were making love.

Wait. Was I seriously thinking about the existence of a ghost, taking his reality for granted the same way I did living people? I wasn't in danger of ending up in Jo-ville; I'd already arrived. After all my determination to be nothing like her, I was turning out to be her younger copy.

"My Aunt Jo believes in ghosts," I said softly.

"Mmm?" Max sounded only half-awake.

"My family thinks she's crazy."

His lids opened slowly and he blinked at me with sleepy eyes. "You have a psychic in your family?"

"No, I have a lunatic alcoholic. She used to live with us, but then she started drinking and talking to invisible friends and my parents kicked her out."

"They just tossed her on the street?" he said with disapproval in his voice.

"Pretty much, yeah. I guess they tried to get her to see a psychiatrist or something, but she refused. They were afraid she'd influence me, or maybe that she'd hurt me or the twins. I'm not really sure. Anyway, they kicked her out and I haven't seen her since."

"What happened to her?"

I looked away from him as I toyed with a lock of his hair. "I don't know. I haven't seen or heard from her since."

"I hope she's okay."

"Me, too." I felt suddenly guilty for not checking on her or even asking about her in all these years.

That suffocating guilt was something I hadn't experienced in a long time, but it was familiar from the days after she left. I'd blamed myself.

"Sometimes I worry that I'm like her."

"You're not crazy, Caro."

"I know." Or at least I hoped.

He used his free hand to tip up my chin. Then he kissed me. "I can tell you're worried. You're not crazy. Lots of people see ghosts and they're not crazy either."

I clutched his arm. "But how do we know? What if I'm just sort of standing on the edge of crazy and one day soon I tip over into completely nuts?"

"All I can say is if you're crazy then I must be too. I've been seeing and talking to Fred since I was thirteen. And I'm still functional. I don't have a single foil hat, for example."

I smiled weakly. "That's true."

"There's no sense in worrying about it. Worrying doesn't increase your hold on sanity. It just makes you anxious."

"Jo drank a lot. I remember how she used to smell sometimes. She was one of those drunks who gets mellow, so I wasn't afraid of her at all." Memories flooded back to me, memories of Jo playing with me, taking me to movies, reading and discussing my kids' books with me as if they were just as interesting as adult fiction. She'd been a wonderful aunt, except for the drinking part.

"I thought it was my fault they kicked her out," I whispered.

"Why? How old were you?"

"Eleven."

"I don't see how it could have been your fault," he said.

"Well, it was because of me. I guess I was imitating her, pretending I could see ghosts too. It really freaked out my parents. They didn't want me taking after her."

"Yeah, but it was their decision to make her leave. Not yours. Did you want her to go?"

"No. Not at all. I loved her." There was no-one else in my family like Aunt Jo, except maybe for me.

"Are you afraid you take after her?" Max said.

"Yeah, a little. Okay, a lot."

He played with my hair, and the gentle stroking seeped relaxation through my scalp and into my whole body. I sighed, nestling into his embrace.

"If you are like her," he said, "I think it's in a good way."

"Sometimes I worry I'll end up on the streets, talking to people no-one else can see." I bit my lip. "God, I'm sorry. That was incredibly tactless. I didn't mean it the way it came out."

He kept petting me. "It's all right. I know what you mean. There are people on the streets who are completely delusional, who've really lost their grip on reality."

"Yeah," I said, relieved he hadn't taken offense.

"There are also a lot of people who believe in ghosts and who aren't insane. I like to think I'm one of them."

I moved my head so I could meet his eyes. He was smiling. "I know you are."

"And you can be, too. Besides, how do you know your Aunt Jo is crazy? Maybe your parents were mistaken."

I'd never thought of that before. "Maybe you're right. I was never afraid of her, I know that."

"She might have started drinking because of the spirits. Some people find alcohol dulls their psychic abilities. Maybe she drank to shut them off because she didn't know any other way."

That was so close to what I'd thought when I saw Retro-girl in her corpse guise that it almost stole my breath. "That could be."

"And it won't happen to you, because I'm going to teach you how to manage it."

"You can do that?"

"Yep. And if I can't for some reason, you can find someone else to help you. We can ask Brad and Marie for recommendations."

"You'd do that for me?"

"Of course I would." His eyes looked soft with an emotion I could only describe as tenderness, which surprised me. I'd never expected to see that on his face. "I'd like to do a lot more for you, if you'll let me."

"Oh, yeah? Like what?"

"Hmm. Like maybe this." He kissed my mouth. "Or this." Sliding down my body, he took my breast in his mouth. I clutched his head to me, gasping.

"Or this." Another slide brought his face right between my legs.

Giggling, I tried to close my thighs, but he wouldn't let me. He kept my legs open with his hands. Although the light in the room was dim, I knew he had a complete view of a part of my body I wasn't in the habit of displaying.

"Max, don't."

He laughed softly. "Why not?" He trailed kisses across my inner thighs.

"It's just—it's too—"

"Unbelievably sexy." He kissed the center of me.

"No-one's ever—I've never—" Apparently, I'd lost the power of speech.

"You mean, no guy's ever done this for you before?" He sounded astonished.

"No. Yes. No-one ever has."

"Well, just because they're idiots doesn't mean I have to be."

And he proceeded to completely shatter my universe.

Chapter 16

Max: My dad had already gotten home and picked up the mail when I arrived. I opened our mailbox, just in case I could intercept my report card, but it was empty. My dad's car sat in the driveway like a silent rebuke.

I trudged up the front steps of the monstrous house he'd built for himself and my stepmom and opened the door. He was waiting for me in the foyer. His fists were clenched, his eyes cold as Antarctica.

He waved a crumpled piece of paper at me. My report card, no doubt. "Care to explain this?"

I stared him, keeping all expression off my face. "I didn't do so well this semester."

"Is that all you have to say for yourself?"

My mouth tightened down until my lips almost went numb. "I was late a lot in science."

"I know. Mr. Brown just called me." He took a step toward me, one arm bending, drawing back, like he was already getting ready to hit me. "What the fuck is wrong with you? Huh? Can't you do anything right?"

I'd been late because of Trent and his friends stopping me in the halls. But if I said so, he wouldn't believe me. No-one did.

"I tried," I said. My voice came out in an undignified croak.

He sneered. "You tried. You obviously didn't try very hard. Or are you stupid? Is that it? You're too goddamn stupid to pass tenth grade biology?"

I just stared back at him. What could I say? No matter which words came out of my mouth, they'd be the wrong ones. Ever since I—ever since Carter had died, he'd screamed at me and beat me for the smallest things.

"What are you looking at?" he yelled, just like the boys at school.

"Nothing."

"Nothing? Are you calling me nothing?"

"No. That's not what I meant."

"You little good for nothing shit. You can't get the simplest things right, can you? You're worthless. Why can't you be more like Trent? He got an A in that class. I'm prouder of my stepson than my real son."

Yeah. No surprise there. Trent had science at a different period than I did, so we didn't share that class. Plus, for some reason he got away with being late, whereas I got blamed no matter what my excuse.

My dad's fist slammed into my jaw without warning. I staggered backward and hit the door, my skull slamming back into the wood. Pain burst inside my head and my vision blurred.

I slumped against the door. He loomed over me, a bear of a man, and smacked me again on the other side. The pain in my face was already so extreme the second blow seemed almost negligible compared to the first.

Then he punched me in the ribs. I felt something break. My arms wrapped around to protect my midsection.

"You're worthless. You think you're such a tough guy? You're nothing but a sick murderer. I should have shot you that day. You hear me?"

I couldn't move, let alone nod my head. The best I could do was keep from falling to my knees, and with the way the room was spinning, I was going to lose that fight any second. I groaned.

"Fucking loser," my dad growled. "Look at you. Pathetic. Get out of my sight before I decide to put a bullet in your head."

I stumbled toward the stairs that led to our bedrooms, my hand on the wall to keep from falling.

"The next time you come home with a report card like that, you won't eat for a week. Got that?" my dad said.

I didn't answer. All my energy and concentration was focused on climbing the stairs, one step at a time, without passing out.

* * *

I dreamed that a magical talisman lived inside her body. It glowed with its own warmth and light, and its power kept me alive. As long as I had her with me, I was safe from any danger. Invincible. Never lonely. I wrapped my body around her, keeping the talisman close to me, protecting it the way it protected me.

When I opened my eyes, I had my arms and legs around Caroline, her back to my front, hugging her to me as if I'd never let her go. The sense of safety and peace lingered, even after I recognized who we really were. Her hair smelled like vanilla. It tickled my nose, but I didn't want to move my head because I needed more of her.

I rarely slept with women. Normally, we had our fun and parted ways. Even my semi-longterm relationships had included few sleepovers, yet here I was cradling Caroline like I'd never let her go.

If I'd been smart, I wouldn't have gone so far with her. Sex had been a mistake. We'd created a much deeper bond than I'd expected. Looking at her now, I knew I couldn't continue to think of her as a way to hurt Trent. That, in fact, I'd stopped thinking of her that way a while ago.

145

I'd gone into this relationship in complete cynicism, thinking I could damage my stepbrother. Knowing I might hurt Caro in the process hadn't seemed important at the time. Now, I cringed inside to think of how much pain I could cause her by coming between her and Trent. Especially if she ever suspected why I'd gone after her.

From this moment—no, from the moment we'd first joined our bodies—I left any revenge attempts behind. Whatever we had here was no longer about me and Trent. It was about me and Caroline.

She sighed and shifted her position. I might be making her uncomfortable, twining all four of my limbs through hers, so I loosened my grip a little. She laid her hand over mine.

"Are you awake?" I murmured, softly in case she was really still sleeping.

"Uh huh." She turned her head a little. "How are you?"

"I'm good. Great, actually. You?"

Her body wiggled against mine, causing my morning hard-on to pulse with sudden excitement. "I'm good too. I slept really well. Usually I can't sleep in a strange place."

I brushed her curls back, nuzzling her cheek. "You smell good."

"No, I don't," she said, turning her face toward the pillow. "Morning breath. No shower."

"Then let's brush our teeth." I didn't want to waste any time with her, just in case.

She sat up, gloriously naked, the sheet slipping to her waist. Her nipples were the most beautiful shade of pink I'd ever seen, and erect in the chilly morning air. I swallowed hard and cupped her right breast, savoring the warm, soft weight of it.

"You're supposed to wait until I brush my teeth," she said.

"I can't."

Caroline hopped to her feet, bouncing in all the right places. "Back in a sec."

I watched her dash to the bathroom and sighed. Okay. We'd brush teeth first.

A few minutes later, I had her backed against the bathroom door, my hands on her sweet little ass.

"Shower," she said between peppermint flavored kisses.

"You cleaned up last night."

"But—"

I grabbed her hips and lifted her until she wrapped her arms and legs around me. "No shower. I can't wait."

She giggled as I carried her back to the bed, her laughter turning to soft moans under more kisses. Gods, the noises she made. They drove me crazy with want.

Afterward, we lay with our arms around each other and dozed for a while. I could hear her soft breathing, feel the gentle movement of her ribs as she pulled air in and out of her body. Her hair tickled my nose. It still smelled like vanilla.

I couldn't remember ever being this happy, and it made me nervous. Something was going to come along and rob me of it, rob me of her. And I didn't deserve her. I'd gotten her by lying and cheating, and that never ends well.

Maybe I should come clean. Maybe if I confessed, explained myself, let her know how much she meant to me already, she would forgive me. My conscience would be clear and we could move forward with no bullshit between us.

"Caro," I whispered. "I need to tell you something."

"What is it?" she said in a sleepy murmur.

I seduced you to hurt my brother. Everything in me tightened up in preparation for the rejection I was about to get. "I—it's just—" I let out all my breath. "Nothing."

She lifted her head and peered at me. "Nothing?"

"Well...I'm starving. You want breakfast?" I was a fucking coward.

She looked at me for another moment, a puzzled frown between her brows. "Sure. I'm hungry too."

* * *

The coffee house was almost deserted so early on a Saturday. It smelled like coffee and that particular, yeasty smell of bread baking, which always makes me think of home even though no-one in my family baked. Coffee and baking bread has to be one of the best scent combinations in the world. We sat in the pale gray light of the window, side by side, and I put my arm around her shoulders. She looked great in the morning—no smeared mascara or weird hair. Just Caroline.

I couldn't keep her. It was going to bite both of us if I tried. She would eventually find out what I'd done and despise me for it, and I didn't think I could bear to look into her beautiful eyes and know that she hated me. Damn. I didn't want to let her go. Not yet.

But sometimes we have to do painful things.

"Caro." I withdrew my arm. I felt sick inside. "We shouldn't have slept together." Gods, it hurt to say that.

She looked at me with alarm in her chocolate eyes. "What?"

"You're still with Trent." I had to force the words out. "It wasn't right for me to come on to you. I feel like crap about it."

"Don't. I'm going to break up with him." She said it seriously, like she really meant it.

147

"Not because of me."

Caroline rotated her body in the booth, so she faced me. "What is going on with you? I thought you hated him."

"That's beside the point. I don't want anything between the two of us to be...tainted."

"Tainted? What do you mean?"

What I meant was I didn't want my stupid, ugly actions to get between us. To make her hate me. I blew some hair out of my eyes. "I don't want you to—to hate me for breaking you and Trent up."

Her lips parted. She put her hand over mine. "I would never blame you for that. What happens between me and Trent has nothing to do with you."

"Yes, it does, because Trent and I are linked. We'll always be linked."

"Max, don't do this."

"I'm sorry. I just don't think you and I can work." I started to slide out of the booth.

She grabbed my arm hard. "No. Don't you dare run out on me. If you're really worried about hurting me, then don't leave."

How was I going to argue with that? I paused and looked at her. I'd definitely ruined her morning. She almost looked like she wanted to cry. Did I mean that much to her?

What an unbelievable idea. No woman had ever been deeply attached to me, even after weeks of being together. And Caro and I had only had one night. One intensely moving night.

"I'm sorry," she said, a tremor in her voice. "I don't mean to be all clingy or anything weird."

"I don't want to go," I said. "But I think it's a bad idea to stay."

"I don't care. I want you. Please. Stay with me. It's not like we're getting married, Max. Can't we just have fun for a while?"

"Is that what we're having?" It was more than fun to me. A lot more. But maybe for her, I was just some amusement in between study sessions.

She leaned closer to me and whispered. "I've never felt anything like I felt last night. Not with any guy except you. If you—I can't go back to Trent. Please don't make me do that."

My attempt to be noble died. I relaxed back into the booth with a half-relieved, half-resigned sigh. "Okay. I'll stay."

Caroline wrapped her arm around my neck and kissed me. "Thank you. You're doing me a great service."

"Is that so? I'll be happy to service you later."

She smiled a little sadly. "You scared me there."

"I'm sorry." I kissed her forehead. "I was trying to be good."

"I think I like you bad better."

"I'll keep that in mind."

It was raining as we left the coffee house. I pulled up my hood and Caroline tugged her hat down over her eyes. The air smelled like wet earth, except for the scent of coffee that hung on our clothing. I put an arm around her waist. She felt too good there, as if she belonged right where she was forever. I never thought about forever with women. What was happening to me?

She leaned against me. "I have a lot of studying to do this week."

It was Dead Week, the week before finals, and everyone would be living with their noses in their books. "Me too."

"I guess we won't be seeing that much of each other for a while."

I glanced down at her. After the conversation we'd just had, I didn't think she was trying to get rid of me, but I might be wrong. "Are you saying we should avoid each other?" I tried to put a teasing note into my voice, but the thought made me nervous. I didn't want to lose her.

"No, of course not. It's just that I'll miss you."

I tightened my hold on her waist. "Why don't we study together?"

"Okay. Yeah, that sounds good."

Chapter 17

Caroline: "I have a sorority dinner tonight," I said regretfully as Max closed his apartment door. We'd just returned from the coffee house.

He glanced at me. "Oh? Can you get out of it?"

"Not really. I hardly do anything with them anymore as it is."

"Okay. I'll see you afterward?"

"Yes. Absolutely." I looked around his living room. "Um...I need to get my study materials from my room. You want to come with me?"

He broke into a big smile. "Sure."

We locked up again and started walking toward campus, hands entwined. I liked that he wanted to touch me. Trent didn't like public affection, and we'd never really held hands much even when we were alone. It felt good to walk that way with Max, like he was proud to be with me.

My dorm was still quiet when we got there. A few people were up, yawning on their way to the dining hall. The rest were still in bed, probably sleeping off hangovers.

"We should have brought your kit," I said as I unlocked my door. "Then maybe we could have talked to Retro-girl while we were here."

"It completely slipped my mind," Max said.

"Mine too." I'd been too busy thinking about him to remember the details of my ghost problem. Okay, the truth was I'd been too busy wrapping his naked body with mine to think about anything but how good he felt.

"Let's get some studying in and then we'll come back with my stuff," he said.

"Okay. Sounds good." I went to my desk to get my books and notebooks and stuff them in my backpack.

There was a knock at the door. I set down the book I'd been holding and went to answer it.

Trent stood in the hallway, looking as if he hadn't gotten much sleep. He frowned at me. "Where were you last night?"

"Out," I said, hoping I didn't look as nervous as I felt.

"Out where?" He peered around my shoulders, trying to get a view into my room.

"Just out. Where were you?"

"With the guys. I already told you that."

"So, you were out and I was out. What's the big deal?" I said.

I was going to have to break up with him and I knew it, but now that an opportunity presented itself I wanted to put it off. Not because I wanted to stay with him, but because I hated conflict. I didn't want to stand here and tell him, face to face, that I didn't want to see him anymore.

"I came by here and you didn't answer your door," he said with a belligerent note in his voice.

"Like I said, I was out."

Trent shoved the door open. His gaze penetrated all the way into the room and settled on Max. Fury descended on his features. "What the fuck is he doing here?"

I glanced over my shoulder at Max. He was leaning against my windowsill, his arms crossed casually and a look of detached amusement on his face.

"He's visiting. We're going to study together."

"No, you're not," Trent growled.

"Yeah, we are."

"You're *my* girlfriend."

"I called you last night with a problem and you refused to help me."

He scowled at me, his mouth hanging open in apparent outrage. "So you invited him over? To what, spend the night?"

I took a breath. "No. I spent the night at his place."

Trent blinked, looking as stunned as if I'd shot him. "Caroline?"

"I was afraid to sleep here with a ghost hanging around, so I spend the night at Max's place."

"I can't believe this shit." He raked his fingers through his hair. "After everything I've told you, I can't believe you'd go to him."

"Would you like to finish this inside?" I gestured toward the interior of my room. "More privacy."

"No. I—what are you doing, babe? Why?"

"I'm not your babe, Trent, and I think it's time for us to—to see other people."

"See other people," he repeated slowly. "You mean break up."

"Yeah," I said with a sigh. "We should break up."

"You're leaving me for him." He glared at Max.

"I'm leaving you, period."

"What does he have that I don't?"

Did he really want to have this conversation in the hallway? "He's been there for me twice now. Three times if you count the ankle separately from the guys in the car. Times you couldn't be bothered with me."

"Look, I'm sorry, babe. Don't give up on us just because of that."

"Oh, I'm not. I'm also thinking of you kissing Tiffani."

He scowled. "That's over. I told you."

"I don't care. It happened."

"But my stepbrother. Why him?"

"Because you were right. I like him. A lot."

He almost looked sick. His head dropped. "This is wrong. There's something wrong here."

"Everything's fine."

Trent lifted his head. "He's put a spell on you. Hasn't he? Haven't you, Max?"

"Trent, I think you should leave now," I said evenly.

"Why? So he can have you all to himself? Don't you care that he's used his magic bullshit against you?"

I couldn't help sighing. "He hasn't used magic on me. And I asked you to leave."

"No! You belong to me." He tried to push his way past me.

I shoved him. "Get out."

He took a step back, into the center of the hallway. His jaw stuck out belligerently as he glared at me. "You know, it's fine. You're frigid anyway. I can get someone hotter than you in five minutes flat."

If I hadn't just spent the night and part of the morning in nonstop ecstatic sex with Max, I might have been hurt by Trent's accusation. As it was, I sort of wanted to laugh.

"I'm sure you can. Good-bye, Trent."

His shoulders slumped. He turned away and I shut the door and leaned against it, blowing out all my breath. That had been fucking awful. I was trembling.

Max came over. He palmed the side of my face. "You all right?"

"Yeah. That just felt really bad. I feel like a bitch for breaking up with him like that."

"You know he's full of shit, right? You're not frigid."

I gave him a wobbly smile. "I know."

"He just said that to hurt you. Bastard."

"I was frigid with him."

"Did you fake orgasm?" Max said, frowning a little.

"No, I never pretended to come, but I did fake enthusiasm."

"And he never asked you about it?"

"He didn't seem to notice."

His frown deepened. "He never noticed you weren't having orgasms?"

I shrugged. "It didn't seem like a big deal. I knew sex was important to him and even though I could take it or leave it, I did it because he liked it so much. I faked because I didn't want to hurt his feelings."

Max leaned in and kissed me softly. "Never pretend with me. I need to know how you're feeling."

"With you, I don't have to pretend."

He slid an arm around my back and brought me up against him, capturing my mouth as he held my head in place with his other hand.

It was our annual Christmas dinner, and the outside of the sorority house was covered in strings of blue and green twinkle lights. Personally, I hated blue and green twinkle lights, but that was what they'd voted on a few years back so that was what we had. An enormous fresh Noble fir covered in shiny blue and green Christmas balls and more blue and green twinkle lights had eaten our living room. A somewhat skinnier tree stood in the corner of the dining room, just barely leaving enough space for the table and chairs.

I didn't want to be here in my little black dress and heels. I wanted to be with Max, but I had obligations to my house, so here I was.

Tiffani had her dark hair up in some kind of strange bouffant do that looked like she'd dipped it in shellac. Gigantic, sparkly chandelier earrings dangled from her ears. She had on a bright red sheath dress with a neckline so low I was pretty sure she wasn't wearing a bra. I wasn't sure what the point of the outfit was since we didn't have any guys here tonight.

Tiffani gave me one of her super-sweet fake smiles. "Caroline, could you please get the salt and pepper from the kitchen and put it on the table?"

"Sure, Tiff." I turned to leave the room.

A slim blonde walked past the dining-room archway. Retro-girl. She wore an A-line miniskirt with knee-high fringed boots and green and red paisley tunic so psychedelic it almost hurt my eyes. I bolted from the dining room into the hall, but when I got there she was gone.

"Caroline?" Tiffani called. "What are you doing?"

I poked my head back into the dining room. "Did you see that girl?"

Her forehead puckered. "What girl?"

"The blonde. She walked right past the doorway. She was wearing a miniskirt and fringed boots. Weird paisley top."

Tiffani's brows rose. "Um, I didn't see anyone."

"She was right here. Long, straight hair down to her butt."

153

Tiffani shook her head, staring at me with wide eyes. "There's no-one like that in the house. Unless someone bought herself a wig. Nobody here has hair that long."

So now Retro-girl was following me off campus. I closed my eyes for a frustrated instant. "I know I saw her."

"Are you okay, Caroline?"

"Max thinks she's a ghost."

Tiffani took a hesitant step toward me. "A ghost? And who's Max?"

"He's a—a friend of mine."

"How does he know about this girl?"

"Because I've seen her before. In my dorm room and once at the student union."

Tiffani rolled her eyes. "You and that dorm. I don't know why you can't live here like all the other girls."

Because I wanted privacy. I wanted to control my own personal space and not have all these other girls all over me all the time. Telling me my clothes weren't right and I couldn't possibly drive that car or take that derpy folk dance class.

"She disappeared in front of my eyes," I said.

Tiffani's manicured hand flew to her throat as she took a step backward. "Oh, my God. You really saw a ghost?"

Wasn't that what I'd just said?

"I think so."

She backed another step away from me. "Ew. That's so...creepy. Yuck."

"Why would she come here? Could she have been a member?"

The brunette gave a theatrical shudder. "God, I hope not."

"Can I look through our old photo albums?"

"They're in the library." She took another step back. "Just don't involve me. I don't want to have anything to do with it."

"It's not my fault."

"You probably brought her here. Either that or you're high." Her eyes narrowed suspiciously. "Are you on drugs?"

"No! Jeez, Tiffani, you know me better than that."

"Well, whatever you're doing, it's giving me a serious case of the creeps. And don't talk about it in front of the pledges. They'll think they've joined a house full of weirdos."

Great. So now I was the house weirdo. Maybe I really had inherited the same freak genes as Aunt Jo. Except Max seemed to think it was all right, and he knew more about this stuff than anyone else in my life.

"Anyway," Tiffani said, "we still have to get ready for dinner, so go get those salt and pepper shakers."

When I got back from the kitchen, the dining room had already filled up with girls. Everyone seemed to be in a good mood. They were all chattering at once, laughing about finals and the upcoming winter break. Paige sat down next to me with a wink. She, too, had on a red dress in honor of the holiday. I seemed to be the only one in black.

"Where have you been all weekend?" she whispered.

"I'll tell you later."

"You haven't been around much, Caroline," Tiffani said as she took her seat.

"I've been busy."

"Too busy for your sisters?" she chirped. A snotty tone underlay her surface perkiness. Guess she didn't appreciate my fetching the salt and pepper for her.

"Yeah, Tiffani. I've had a lot of studying to do."

"I guess that's why you haven't been paying much attention to your boyfriend either."

My eyes narrowed and my lips flattened. "That's none of your business."

She gave a little shrug. "Trent's my friend. He's been complaining to me."

"Really?"

She laughed. "No, not really. He hasn't even mentioned you, actually."

This was interesting. Here I'd been feeling miserably guilty over cheating on Trent and breaking up with him, and it was starting to sound like he'd been cheating on me. All-out cheating, not just a single instance of kissing. And groping.

"I saw you kissing him at the Vegas party," I said.

She didn't even blush. "So?"

"He was still my boyfriend, Tiff."

"It's kind of hard to tell. You haven't been spending much time with him, like I said."

Apparently, she hadn't picked up on my use of the past tense. I leaned across the table. "Are you trying to tell me something?"

The other girls were watching us with wide eyes. Paige nudged me with her elbow, but I ignored her. I'd never liked Tiffani. She was catty and mean. Trent was welcome to her.

"I'm not telling you anything you don't already know," she said with a smirk.

"Whatever." I glowered at her across the table.

"That's how to keep a boyfriend. Whatever."

"Are you trying to save my relationship with Trent or break it up?"

She smirked again, tapping her long acrylic nail against her bottom lip. "I haven't decided yet."

I smiled at her. "The fact is, I broke up with him today."

Tiffani gaped at me.

"You know, I'm just not hungry tonight," I said, shoving my chair back and standing up.

"You can't keep avoiding us and expect to remain in good standing with the chapter," Tiffani said, sounding like she was reaching for any excuse to fight with me.

"Tiff—" one of the other girls said.

"No," Tiffani said. "Seriously. She never comes around anymore. She won't live here. She hardly shows up for any of our functions. You think you're too good for us, don't you, Caroline?"

"No. I just don't think I fit in."

"Well," she sniffed. "You got that right."

I sighed. "Merry Christmas, everyone. Happy Hanukkah, Holidays, Yule, whatever. I'm going home."

I turned around and left the dining room. My coat was in the hall coat closet, so that was where I headed. In the living room, I heard the tap of heels behind me and spun to see who was following me.

"Paige. You don't have to leave because of me."

"I'm not. Well, I am, but that's okay. Let's go somewhere for dinner together."

*　*　*

We went to The River House and had sirloin steaks. The restaurant, too, was decked out for the holidays with a large tree on one side of the room and lighted garland hung up everywhere. The lights were white, instead of blue and green. I liked that a lot better, although I could have done without the canned Christmas music.

I have to confess I was glad to get away from the sorority house. What I'd said to Tiffani—I hadn't meant for it to slip out, but it was true. I'd made a big mistake in pledging and I just hadn't wanted to admit it. Plus now the news about my break-up with Trent was out and everyone would want to talk about it. I could live without that particular discussion.

Paige buttered her bread with short, nervous strokes. She kept going over the same area, smearing the butter around repeatedly even though it already had enough on it for three slices.

"Paige, what are you doing?"

"Buttering my bread," she muttered, head down. "What does it look like?"

"What's wrong? Are you mad at me for arguing with Tiffani?"

"No. Not at all. But...I have something to tell you that you're not going to like." Paige glanced at me hesitantly.

"Okay."

She shook her head, put down her slice of bread and picked up another one. "You'll hate me."

"Don't be silly."

"Okay." She took a deep breath. "Just don't shoot the messenger."

"Will you tell me already?"

"Trent has been seeing Tiffani." She winced. "There. Please don't kill me."

I leaned back in my chair and smiled. "Well, that explains her behavior tonight. Sort of."

"You're not mad?"

Actually, I felt relieved. "Not really. I already broke up with him."

"So that was true? Wow. I really didn't see that one coming. I thought maybe you'd said it just to throw Tiffani. Why didn't you say anything to me about it?"

"I don't know. I've been kind of distracted lately."

She leaned forward. "I noticed. What's going on?"

It was only fair that Paige should know first. She was my best friend, after all. Only I'd kept my feelings for Max secret for so long that it was hard to open my mouth and talk about him.

"Well..." I hesitated. "Max and I—"

Paige grinned triumphantly. "I knew it! I knew you'd hook up with him sooner or later."

It was way more than that. "I'm not sure I'd call it a hook up."

"Oh? What is it, then? True love?"

"I don't know what it is. I don't think I'm in love with him." I couldn't help smiling broadly. "But I like him an awful lot."

"Ha. Tiffani can take her attitude and stuff it."

I smiled even more broadly. "Yep."

"So...wow, I still can hardly believe you broke up with him."

"Me, too."

"I was starting to think you guys were going to get married." She glanced at me. "The other thing is, I think Trent's been seeing Tiffani for a while. The other day I heard they hooked up over the summer."

I frowned. "He told me he loved me. What BS."

"Men." Paige made a face. "Except for Max and Dan, of course."

Chapter 18

Max: Since Caroline was having dinner with her sorority sisters, I drove out to Brad and Marie's farm. Several cars occupied the space near the house because the members of our circle had decided to drive down for a visit. The lights glowed from the house windows and as I got out of my car I could hear laughter.

Too bad I couldn't bring Caroline tonight. I would have loved for her to meet everyone. We'd have to do it some other time.

They were gathered in the living room when I came in. There were only six of us total, but we crowded the small front room of Brad and Marie's house. Brad handed me a beer as I came into the room.

"Thanks."

"How's that search for truth going?" he said in a low voice.

I glanced at him sidelong. "It's going well, actually. I've made major progress."

His brows climbed into his hairline, but I didn't linger to talk. Instead, I hovered on the edge of the living room wondering where to sit. Selene was on the couch and if I sat near her, she'd see it as encouragement. I hadn't spoken to her since that booty call and I didn't want her thinking I was open to another one. The problem was, the only other option was sitting on the floor, and if I did that it would be obvious I was avoiding her.

In the end, I took the seat next to Selene, who turned on the couch and gave me a lingering hug. "How are you?"

"I'm doing well. You?"

"I'm fine." She let go of me and examined me. She wore a smile, but there was something not so happy lurking in her eyes. "I heard you've got a new girlfriend."

I leaned back against the couch with studied carelessness. "Marie told you?"

"Brad, actually."

"They have big mouths," I said lightly.

"Isn't it true?" Her dark eyes searched my face.

"Yeah," I said. "It's true. Her name is Caroline."

"How come she isn't with you tonight?"

"She had a prior commitment."

Selene was wearing a thick, tunic-length sweater with a V-neck so deep I could see almost all of her cleavage. Nestled between her breasts was a silver pentacle on a long chain. Her black hair was decorated with a scattering of multiple skinny braids decorated with silver beads.

"I've missed you," she said in a sultry voice.

"Uh, yeah. Me too."

"Seattle isn't the same without you."

Really? She'd never had any trouble finding lovers, and I'd been only one of a string.

"I like it here," I said.

"It's cute," she allowed with a slightly dismissive movement of her head.

"Yeah."

"I might be able to get used to it myself."

I gave her a skeptical look. "I thought you said it was full of rednecks."

Selene shrugged artfully, the gesture briefly enhancing her display of curves. "You convinced me the last time I was here that it's more interesting than it looks at first."

I made a noncommittal noise. She probably wasn't serious. There wasn't a single compelling reason I could think of for Selene to move to Avery's Crossing.

She inched closer. "Are you still doing ritual work?"

"Not as much as I used to. I've been busy with other things."

She pushed out her lower lip. "That's too bad. You're so talented."

"I've got a lot on my plate right now. The business, school..."

"And this girl you're seeing. Caroline? She's not into magic, is she?"

I frowned at the note of regret in her voice. "No. She's new to it."

"I see." She smiled flirtatiously. "Well, if you ever need a partner, let me know. I'd be happy to drive down and help you out."

"That's really nice of you, but I don't think it'll be necessary."

Another artful shrug sent her tunic sliding off her shoulder on one side. "You never know." Her smiled deepened. "Does she know about you?"

"What do you mean?"

"Your polyamorous nature."

I gave her a dry look. "That was your thing, not mine. If I recall, you didn't want to give up any of your other partners to be with me."

"Oh, come on, Max. You know you liked the threesomes."

I didn't answer. If I'd known she was going to behave this way, I'd have taken a spot on the floor instead of the couch.

Marie came over and knelt on the floor next to the couch. "Have you gotten in touch with Carter yet?"

In most circumstances, I would have been severely annoyed by anyone bringing up Carter. In my circle, though, it was okay. Everyone knew about him already and, as far as I could tell, they didn't judge me for what had happened. I thought they should, but they didn't.

"No," I said. "Not yet."

She scowled. "Why not? You shouldn't wait."

"It's Dead Week. Once finals are over, I'll do it."

Marie shook her head at me. "It isn't wise to make him wait."

"Why not? It's not like he's going anywhere."

"Because he might have something timely to tell you. What if he can't get the information to you until it's too late?"

"Marie, I really doubt that's the case. And it's only two weeks."

"What's this about Carter?" Selene asked.

The others perked up their ears, too. If I didn't watch out, this would turn into a project involving the entire circle.

"He's been trying to contact Max," Marie said. "But he's having trouble getting through."

"I've had other things going on," I said.

"Such as Caroline?" Marie gazed at me knowingly.

"Maybe."

"I don't blame you for wanting to spend time with her, but you need to deal with Carter too. Especially since Caroline is involved."

Selene's eyes turned round as saucers. "Wait. Caroline is involved? How's that?"

"It's nothing." I gestured dismissively. "She's only peripherally involved because we've been seeing each other." I sent Marie a warning glance.

"It sounds like you could use some help with this," Selene said.

"Nope. I don't need help."

"But—"

"I'll take care of it myself." The words came out a lot more harshly than I'd intended them.

Selene gave me a hurt look. "Okay. I don't mean to intrude."

Good. I didn't want the involvement of my circle in any of this. It was too private. It was something only I could deal with, and I had to do it alone.

* * *

The next morning, Caroline showed up at my door with her overnight bag. She smiled at me and there was both hope and uncertainty in her face. "Hi. I brought my stuff."

I let her in. "Good. I missed you last night."

"Me too." She twined her arms around my neck and we kissed for so long I forgot what we were going to do.

I pulled back to nibble on the delicate skin of her neck.

"I found out last night that Trent was cheating on me," she said.

"What a fucker."

Caroline laughed. "It's no worse than what we're doing."

"I think it is, because I can't imagine wanting to cheat on you. What's wrong with him, anyway?"

"What a nice thing to say." She caught my lower lip between her teeth.

I scooped her into my arms, still kissing her, and carried her into the bedroom. She was addictive. I couldn't get enough, no matter how many times we came together.

Chapter 19

Caroline: "Mom, I broke up with Trent," I said into my phone. I was sitting on Max's bed while he worked on some graphic design project in the living room.

"You did?" Mom sounded shocked. "Oh, honey, I'm so sorry."

"Don't be. I'm not. He was cheating on me."

"How could that be? He seemed so devoted to you."

I bit back the snort of derision that wanted to escape. "Um, no, he really wasn't. He just put on a good show for you guys. Anyway, I have a new boyfriend."

There came a disapproving silence. At least, I thought it was disapproving.

"That was sure fast," Mom said. "Can you tell me his name?"

"No, I'm afraid I don't know it," I said without missing a beat.

Another silence. Sometimes my mom has no sense of humor.

I snickered. "I'm just kidding, Mom, Jeez. It's Max. Max Kincaid."

"Max? Isn't that Trent's stepbrother?" Now I could hear the disapproval dripping from her voice.

"Yeah, it is."

"I don't think that's a good idea, honey."

"I was hoping I could invite him to visit us over winter break." Otherwise, I was going to do a lot of driving, because there was no way I was waiting three weeks to see him again.

"Visit us how? You know I don't approve of sleepovers."

Had she missed the part where I'd turned twenty-one? Well, it was her house and she could make the rules however she liked. But I didn't have to like them, either, did I?

"No, I wasn't talking about a sleepover. I just thought maybe he could have dinner with us a couple of times. Maybe we could spend a day here and there together."

"Well." I could almost see the pursed lips and disapproving frown. "I suppose we could do that."

"You'll like him, Mom." And even if she didn't, it wouldn't stop me from seeing him. I'd just have to sneak around, which I hated.

"I'm sure I will," she said, but she sounded unconvinced. "What's he like?"

"Nothing like Trent. He's an artist. He has his own company and supports himself."

"Really."

There's nothing like having your parent disbelieve everything that comes out of your mouth. "Yeah, Mom. Really. He's very mature for his age."

"But isn't this the guy who thinks he can do magic?"

I sighed. "It's not what you think. He's not like Jo."

"Hmm. Well, I'll withhold judgment until I meet him."

I guessed that was the best I could hope for at the moment, so it would have to do. "By the way, have you heard from Jo lately?" I said, making my voice all casual, like I didn't much care one way or the other.

"No. She doesn't have our number. We changed it, remember?"

"So she couldn't find us?" The thought still made me angry.

"Yes. So she couldn't find us."

"That was a long time ago," I said.

"Well, that's kind of my point. It's been so long I have no idea where she is now."

"I wish you—I mean, we—could have kept in touch with her."

"She was dangerous," my mom said defensively.

"Really? How?"

"She was drinking. You know that. Drinking a lot. And talking to people who weren't even there. I wasn't sure what she would do next, but I knew I didn't want you and the twins involved."

How did my mom know those people who weren't even there were really not there? Maybe Jo had seen ghosts, like I did.

Or maybe she was really nuts. Maybe I was, too. Insanity ran in families, after all.

"Look, I know Jo was your favorite," my mom said. "But she wasn't well, honey."

"Then why did you kick her out?"

"She refused to get treatment. What else could we have done?"

"I don't know. It just makes me sad."

"I know. Me too." My mom sighed. "It wasn't an easy decision to make, believe me. She's my sister and I loved her, too."

I found it disturbing that my mom used the past tense. Did she think Jo was dead?

"Why do you ask, anyway?" she said. "Have you heard from her?"

"No, I've just been thinking of her lately." Because I'd been seeing spirits, like she did. If there was one thing that still scared the hell out of me, it was ending up like Aunt Jo.

"It must be the holidays," my mom said. "We tend to think of the people we've lost at this time of year. I wish she could still share Christmas with us."

"Me too. I miss her."

* * *

Sunday of finals week, Max took me out to Brad and Marie's farm to meet his circle. He drove an old beater of a subcompact, and it wasn't especially comfortable to drive. It was a far cry from Trent's luxury sedan, that's for sure, but I didn't mind at all because I was with Max.

The farmhouse was painted classic white and looked like it dated from sometime in the early twentieth century. It had a cute, storybook quality that I instantly liked, with a steeply pitched roof and gables on the second floor. A huge tree that looked like it was at least as old as the house loomed over the structure. Max parked in a wide, graveled drive near the house and led me to the front door.

We didn't have to wait. The door opened and a slightly plump middle-aged woman with thick brown hair streaked in gray came out smiling. She had a pretty face with large, intelligent hazel eyes behind wire-framed glasses.

"Marie, this is Caroline," Max said. "Caroline, this is my foster mom, Marie Bradford."

Marie smiled at me, but her eyes were keenly appraising. It made me wonder what Max had told her about me, because I was definitely being looked up and down and evaluated to see if I was good enough for her boy. I started to bristle and then it occurred to me that here was a person who actually cared about him. Deeply, judging by the expression on her face.

I stuck out my hand. "Hi, Marie. I'm so glad to meet you."

"Max has told us all about you," she said, taking my hand.

"I'm glad he has people on his side."

"Caro—" Max said.

Marie grinned at me. "I think I like her."

I glanced up at Max. He was blushing. I put my arm around his waist, wishing I could reassure him without embarrassing him further. He just slung his arm around my shoulders and brought me into the house.

The small kitchen, which looked even more vintage than Max's, had an old-fashioned diner-style table crowded with five people who were all looking at me. A middle-aged guy with nondescript brown hair who I guessed was Brad, a pretty young woman with black hair in a long braid, an older woman with a short gray bob, a young man whose brown hair hung past his shoulders. He sported piercings in his nose and eyebrows. Like Marie, they seemed to be summing me up.

Max introduced each one in turn. The middle-aged guy was Brad, the black-haired girl Selene, the gray-haired woman Nancy and the pierced guy was named Wolf. I couldn't help wondering if that was his real name or some kind of alias.

"Pull up a seat," Brad said, smiling at me.

Marie handed each of us a folding chair, which we wedged into a narrow space made by the others scooting over. Now everyone's elbows touched.

"There really isn't enough room here," Marie said. "Let's go to the living room."

Everyone got up and trooped through a curved archway into the house's small living room. There weren't enough seats for all of us, and Wolf and Selene plopped themselves down on the floor. Max and I sat on the couch, where I curled up against his side. When I glanced around the room, I noticed Selene watching me with a resentful narrowing of her eyes. What was her problem?

"I don't know how much Max has told you about us," Marie said. "We're his working circle. We do magical work together."

"So...you're kind of like a coven?" I said, hoping I wasn't insulting anyone.

She smiled. "It's basically the same thing, but only some of us consider ourselves witches, so we use the term circle."

"Ah." So which of them were witches? And what did the others consider themselves? "I've never, um, met anyone who did magic before Max."

"We promise not to sacrifice any goats while you're here," Wolf said solemnly.

Was he serious? Everyone laughed except me. I looked up at Max with wide eyes.

"He's just kidding," he said. "We'd never harm any animals. Or humans."

"Whew," I said, jokingly wiping imaginary sweat from my brow. "I was scared for a second there."

They laughed again.

"I brought my drums and stuff," Wolf said. "If anyone's in the mood for some drumming."

I looked at Max again.

"I don't know," he said. "Caroline's never done that."

"Is it a ritual or something?" My palms began to sweat.

"No, not really," Max told me. "Tonight it'll be just drumming, maybe some chanting. Singing. It's really informal."

"Oh. Okay."

"Are you game?" Wolf looked at me with a challenge in his eyes.

He was pushing me to see how far I'd go. I could see it on his face. What would happen if I turned him down? I wasn't afraid they'd do anything mean to me, but it crossed my mind that they might think less of me. It could damage my relationship with Max.

"Sure," I said. I hoped I wasn't getting into something sticky.

Max squeezed my shoulders and kissed me on the cheek. "Thank you," he whispered, softly so only I could hear.

Selene looked like she wanted to roll her eyes and was only barely restraining herself. She was jealous of me.

"First," Marie said, "let's say our names and tell Caroline a little bit about ourselves."

I felt like I was at a church fellowship group I'd attended for a few months as a teen. Or maybe a support group. There wasn't much I knew about support groups, since I'd only seen them in movies, but this introduction routine felt like the kind of thing that would happen there.

Marie went first. "I'm Marie and I spent a lot of my childhood on this farm. It belonged to my mom's parents, and they basically raised me because my mom was addicted to crack cocaine. They were great parents and they left the farm to me, so here I am."

Wow. Her grandparents raised a cocaine addict...but then they raised her, too. How did that happen?

Brad smiled. "I'm Brad, and I just follow Marie around wherever she goes."

Marie slapped playfully at his arm. "That's not true."

"Isn't it?" He winked at me. "Marie and I had been talking about moving to the country for years before she inherited the farm. I'm a rad tech—an x-ray technician—at the hospital in town."

Selene was next. She repeatedly wrapped and unwrapped the end of her braid around her wrist while slanting sneaky glances at Max. "I'm Selene. I'm an x-ray tech also. That's how I met Brad and Marie. I grew up on the east coast, but I went to school in Portland so that's where I am now."

"I'm Wolf and I run a chop shop in the slums of Portland." The pierced guy looked at me blandly, waiting for my reaction.

Max snorted. "You're so full of shit, dude."

Wolf shrugged. "Also, I raise sacrificial goats on the side."

I fought against the smile that threatened to break out. "What do you really do?"

He made a dismissive movement of his head. "I'm still in school."

"What's your major?"

Max gave me a sneaky sidelong glance. Was he jealous too? Ridiculous. Wolf did nothing for me, although he was pretty hot in a pierced, long-hair and weirdness kind of way.

"Botany," Wolf said.

"Nice. I'm doing French."

He nodded in acknowledgment. I turned my attention to the oldest person in the group, Nancy.

"I'm a yoga instructor," she said. "And a retired teacher."

"My mom is a teacher," I said. "High school English."

"Is that what you plan to do with your French?"

Hell, no. "I haven't made up my mind yet."

"Well, you still have time. And you can always change your mind," Nancy said. "No sense in rushing into things."

That was the polar opposite of what everyone else always told me...except for Mrs. Kincaid, who seemed to think I should become wife to Trent and mom to his kids. Or, she had thought that, before I'd broken up with him. I wondered what she thought now, not that I cared.

"Go get your drums, Wolf," Brad said. "We'll have some fun and then eat."

Wolf jumped up and made for the door. He seemed friendly enough, even if he was testing me. Selene, though...the way she kept looking at me and Max made me tense and wary. She kept glancing at him, making me wonder if they'd ever been together. She was quite beautiful with her long, black hair and dark eyes, her slender figure, the funky clothing that reminded me vaguely of something Medieval. Leggings, tunic, ankle-high flat boots, a scarf draped in an artistic cowl around her neck and shoulders. Pentacle earrings dangled from her ears. Maybe she was one of the witches.

I snuggled more deeply against Max's side. Selene's gaze faltered and slipped away to study something else. Wolf came back in carrying several Native American-style drums and a sack slung on his back. He set down his burdens, opening the sack and withdrawing a couple of tambourines.

"I've got a doumbek, if anyone wants it," he said.

"What's a doumbek?" I said.

"A Middle-Eastern drum shaped like an hourglass." He reached into the sack again and pulled out another drum. The body looked like it was made of metal, with intricate designs chased into the surface.

"I'll play it if no-one else wants to," Wolf said.

"No-one else can do it as impressively as you," Max remarked.

"Very true." Wolf grinned at me. "What do you want to play?"

"Uh...I have no idea. I've never done this before."

He tossed me a tambourine. "These are pretty easy."

I'd never been that close to one before. It was like a small, shallow drum. It had a skin head and little cymbal-like things set in the rim. I shook it experimentally and it gave a satisfying rattle.

"Cool," I said.

Max took one of the drums. Everyone else grabbed an instrument and Wolf sat down cross-legged on the floor. He set his doumbek on his lap so the head faced forward and the bottom of the drum faced outward behind him. Weird. I'd never seen a drum played that way before, but then what did I know about percussion? Nothing, really.

He immediately launched into a complex rhythm, which the others picked up after a few bars. My hands were still sweating. I tapped carefully on the head of the tambourine, trying to follow along without making too much noise in case I screwed up. I didn't want to ruin it for the others.

The truth was that I didn't really understand the point of all this. I mean, they weren't in a band, were they? Not that there's anything wrong with friends getting together and playing music, but there was no melody. Just the beat, which went on and on and on, seemingly forever.

Sometimes it slowed down for a while and sometimes it sped up. People offered variations that acted as percussive grace notes, for lack of a better term, but the rhythm itself just kept on. And on. And on.

I found myself relaxing into it, my tapping on the tambourine growing more confident. I even swayed a little to the beat. Max glanced at me and smiled. Apparently, I was doing all right. I smiled back.

After a while, it began to seem like the rhythm was all there was in the world. Very strange, I know, but it was like a kind of trance came over me and I just flowed with the sound. I can't explain it any other way. I could feel waves of energy moving around the room. Sound energy, sure, but there was something else, too, that I didn't know how to name.

Maybe that energy was the point?

Eventually, the drumming slowed, growing quieter, and finally stopped.

Wolf grinned at me. "You did well."

"I hardly did anything."

"Not true," Max said. "You participated. That's more than a lot of people would have done."

"Really?"

"Oh, yeah," Selene said. "We've had girls go running out of here screaming their heads off."

I studied her, wondering if she was kidding. She didn't seem to be, but there was a hint of sarcasm in her voice so I wasn't sure.

"Some people are afraid to try," Marie said. "And you tried. That speaks well of you."

I didn't know what to say to that, so I didn't say anything.

Brad set his drum down on the floor. "I'm starving. Let's eat."

I leaned into Max. "What just happened?" I whispered.

"What do you mean?" he whispered back.

"What was the drumming about?"

"I'll explain later. For now, just think of it as a way to relax."

"Hmm. Okay." It had been relaxing, so I guess it worked.

Dinner was spaghetti with meatballs. The food was good and the company was...okay. They were friendlier now that I'd participated in the drumming, but I felt awkward and out of place. They talked about things I couldn't relate to and sometimes didn't even understand. I'd have to ask Max for a translation later. Would I ever fit in with his friends?

* * *

Trent's fraternity house looked oddly sad in the rain. The garden surrounding it was in bad shape, something I hadn't really noticed before. The shrubs were all massively overgrown and the lawn was full of weeds. The siding on the house needed painting. None of it had anything to do with me, though, so why was I standing on the sidewalk studying it like I was responsible for fixing it up?

Boy, I really did not want to carry through on the reason I'd come here. I hadn't been back since the night of that awful party, and it was pretty much the last place on earth I wanted to be. Plus, I was by myself.

I couldn't tell Max I was coming here. He'd pitch a fit. Okay, probably not; he was reasonable to a fault. But it would hurt his feelings, even if he knew why I'd come.

I marched up the concrete walk to the front door, stomach churning, and rang the bell. There was no portico or other shelter from the rain, so while I waited, water dripped continually on my head. Inside, male voices shouted with laughter. They were apparently not studying at the moment.

Greg Talbot opened the door. He blinked at me and then broke out in a huge grin. "Caroline."

"Hi, Greg. I need to see Trent."

Greg glanced over his shoulder with a nervous jerk of his head. "Ah. Um, he's sort of busy at the moment."

"Well, I have something of his to return. Can he take a minute to talk to me?"

"Um...I can find out for you."

"I'd appreciate that."

Greg turned away from the door.

"Greg? I'd like to come inside. It's raining out here."

"Oh, yeah." He turned red as he opened the door enough for me to enter. "Sorry about that."

I could have asked him what was wrong, but I wasn't real eager to find out, considering he'd groped me the last time I'd seen him. Instead, I came into the foyer and stood near the door with my hands clasped, dripping. This was as far as I wanted to go. They had a visitor's room, and I wasn't setting foot in it.

Greg stuck his head into the living room. "Chambers!" he bellowed. "You're wanted downstairs."

"Busy," yelled a deep, familiar voice from upstairs.

"You have a visitor. Get your ass down here." Greg turned to me with an apologetic shrug. "He's been real busy lately."

"Yeah, I'll bet." With Tiffani, no doubt.

The thundering sound of a six-foot male tearing down the stairs preceded Trent skidding around the corner in stocking feet. He wore no shirt. He slid across the smooth wooden floor of the hall and came to a halt with a surprised stare at me.

"Caroline."

"I have something to give you," I said, and held out the paper bag I carried. Inside were the garnet and pearl earrings he'd given me.

He accepted the bag with a puzzled frown. "I don't remember leaving anything at your place."

"Yeah. There's only this one thing."

He opened the bag and peered inside. Then he looked at me with a scowl. "You don't have to give these back to me. They're for you."

"I can't keep them. They're too expensive."

"Well, I don't want them." He tried to give them back to me.

I refused to take the bag. "I'm with someone else now. I can't wear your earrings. Just—I don't care what you do with them. Give them to your mom. Whatever. But I'm not keeping them."

I turned to walk out the door.

"What's taking so long, babe?" said a sugary female voice. Tiffani. "Oh. It's her." The voice had a distinctly acid note to it now.

I suppressed a smile as I walked out the door. I'd divested myself of the earrings, my last physical tie to him, and it made me feel much lighter. Knowing they were together, possibly doing something sexual right before I'd arrived, hadn't bothered me at all. As far as I was concerned, Trent and Tiffani deserved each other.

Chapter 20

Caroline: Finals Week was over. Fall term was over, and we were all off to our various families for the break. That meant I was in Portland and Max was still in Avery's Crossing. I hated it. I'd never missed a guy this way before, with a gut-wrenching sense of loss. Even three months away from Trent hadn't bothered me as much.

Today I was putting ornaments on the tree, not with any enthusiasm, but it had to be done and it was my traditional job. I'm not sure how I came to be the family tree-trimmer, just that by the age of twelve or so it was established as my special chore. The best thing about it was I could control the lights. There were no strings of single colors on my tree, except for white. Everything else was multi-color, because that's the way I like it.

The doorbell rang.

"Lily, can you get that?" I called. "I'm all tangled up in Christmas lights."

I heard my sister's little footsteps thundering into the foyer and smiled. She never walked anywhere if she could run instead. A few seconds later, she came pounding into the living room.

"There's someone at the door for you," she said breathlessly.

"Who?"

"Some guy named Mac."

My belly began fluttering wildly. "You mean Max?"

"Mac, Max, whatever," she said, and thundered out of the room.

I disentangled myself from the lights and went to the door. He was leaning against the doorjamb, hands in his pockets, looking as nonchalant as usual, a lock of his thick black hair sliding into his eyes. Then he saw me and smiled and there was nothing nonchalant about that at all.

"Hi," I said, sounding more breathless than Lily. "I didn't expect to see you."

"I couldn't wait." He took my hands and stood looking down at me.

Awkwardness stole my words and made it impossible for me to meet his gaze. We'd spent such an intense time together, and then been parted for days. Seeing him again, especially here, was almost like having a dream figure come to life. I'd missed him so much, and now he was here I didn't know what to say to him or how to behave.

"Can I kiss you?" he murmured.

I tilted my face up. "Yes."

He cupped my jaw in his warm palm and bent his head to mine. God, his kiss, so warm and wet and tasting so exactly like Max. It melted every bit of awkwardness. I put my arms around his shoulders and kissed him back with a little moan of excitement.

"Ew," said a ten year old voice behind us.

Max released me slowly. I turned to see Lily watching us, her nose wrinkled up as tightly as it would go.

"This is my sister, Lily," I said. "Lily, this is my boyfriend, Max."

She just stared at him with her nose still wrinkled. "I thought Trent was your boyfriend."

"He was. I broke up with him."

"Oh. That's okay. I didn't like him anyway." She spun on her heel and dashed out of the room.

Max and I smiled at each other.

"Have you had lunch?" I said. "We could go somewhere."

"That would be good. What were you doing before I got here?"

"Putting up the Christmas tree. I was all tied up in the lights."

He leered at me. "Sounds like a kinky Christmas tree."

I slapped his arm and he laughed.

"We don't talk like that around here."

"Sorry." His face went sober so quickly and in such an exaggerated way that I laughed, too.

"Let me get my things," I said.

I turned to let my mom know where I was going. Max stayed at the door. I paused and looked over my shoulder at him. He seemed tense, his attitude of nonchalance gone, his hands tight at his sides.

When I realized he wasn't coming with me, I stopped and held out my hand. "Come in. Meet my mom."

"Are you sure you want that?" he said, looking doubtful.

"Don't be ridiculous. Of course I do." I grabbed his hand and tugged. "Come on."

He let me pull him through the living room with its strong scent of fir tree and into the kitchen, where my mom was deep into a batch of sugar cookies. She looked up from her work at the island; her eyes opened wider as she noticed Max and her hands stilled on her rolling pin.

"Mom, this is Max. We're going out to lunch together."

"It's nice to meet you, Mrs. Winters," Max said in a completely conventional, respectful tone. Until then, I hadn't known he could do conventional.

"Yes, um, it's good to meet you, too," Mom said. "Caroline has told us all about you."

"Has she?" His dark eyes twinkled with amusement.

"Yes. She—" Mom's gaze slid to mine, then back to Max. "She said you were Trent's stepbrother."

"Yes, that's true," Max said. He looked like he wanted to add something else, but wisely kept it to himself.

"Where are you going?" Mom said.

"I don't know," I said. "Probably Twenty-third Avenue or something like that. Maybe the Pearl District." I wanted to show Max one of Portland's funky shopping areas. I looked up at him. "Want Chinese food? There are some good places in our little Chinatown. Plus we can see the Chinese Garden."

"Sure. Sounds good," he said easily.

"Well, you kids have fun," Mom said, eyeing him. "Drive carefully. You know how crazy Portland drivers are."

I'd always heard Portland driving was excessively polite for a mid-sized city, but what did I know?

"I'm used to Seattle, Mrs. Winters, so I can probably handle Portland," Max said.

"Oh. Right. Well, like I said, have fun."

I could tell she wasn't especially happy about Max showing up. A few months ago, that would have stopped me. I would have made some excuse to Max and called the whole thing off. Now, I was sorry my mom didn't immediately like him, but I wasn't going to let that interfere with our relationship.

I linked my arm through his. "Let's go."

"I don't think your mom likes me," he said as we got into his car.

"She'll get over it. She doesn't even know you yet, and once she does, she'll like you."

He gave me a doubtful look. "I wouldn't be so sure about that."

"Well, even if she doesn't, it won't make a difference to me." I leaned across the gear shift and kissed him. "I like you."

His face slowly warmed into a smile. "I like you too."

For a moment, we just stared at each other, goofy smiles on our faces. Then Max straightened and turned the ignition.

"We can take your car if it would make you more comfortable," he said. "I don't mind being the passenger."

"That's very twenty-first century of you, but I'm fine with you driving."

Max pulled out of our driveway. "You know, that's the first time I've met the parents. Or one of them, anyway."

I stared at him, startled. "You've never met any of your girlfriends' parents?"

"No. I never had a real girlfriend before. Not like you." He sent me a smile and a sidelong glance. "You're different."

"Wow." I settled back against the seat and tried to collect my thoughts.

What did it mean that I was the first girl who'd ever taken him to meet the parents?

"I didn't have any girls in high school," he said.

"Oh? Why not? You're so hot; I'd think all the girls would be crawling over each other to get to you."

He snorted a disbelieving laugh. "Not exactly. Besides, Trent and his friends saw to it no girl would get close to me."

"What a jackass." Why had I dated that guy?

Max shrugged. "I got really good at dealing with bullies because of him."

"What about Brad and Marie? Didn't you take any girls home to them? Or go to the girls' homes?"

"I never really dated in the usual sense," he said. "And the one girl I was with for more than a couple of weeks was someone they already knew."

"What about her family?"

"They live back east." He slanted another glance at me. "I really don't want to talk about them, anyway. They're in the past. You're here with me now."

He picked up my hand and lifted it to his lips. The sweetness of the gesture made my heart clench. When I'd met him, all I'd seen was the rebel. A hot rebel, sure, but still all bad-boy attitude. That was a part of him and probably always would be, but now I could see a gentle, sweet side that I loved.

Loved?

That word stopped me cold. I stared out the window at the rain, our hands still clasped, and wondered if I'd fallen in love with him. For a while, I'd thought I was in love with Trent, yet the way I'd felt about him was like the flame on a birthday candle compared to the bonfire that was my feeling for Max.

How would he react if I said I loved him? It was probably too soon. I didn't want to scare him away or make him think I expected anything from him. Like a ring, for example.

"What are you thinking about?" he said.

"Nothing. Just letting my mind wander."

Chapter 21

Max: Caroline dragged me home for dinner. I was pussy enough that I really didn't want to go—not because I didn't want to spend more time with her, but because I could tell her mom was none too enthused about me. I couldn't run away from this encounter for long, though; not if I wanted to be part of Caroline's life. I'd taken off when I was sixteen. Since then, I'd learned that life isn't about running away; it's about facing your fears and pushing past them. That's the only way we grow.

So I manned up and went anyway, to make Caro happy. And because the thought of leaving her to drive back down to Avery's Crossing caused me physical pain. I wanted to put it off as long as possible.

We hadn't found any time to be alone, except in the car, so we hadn't done anything but kiss. As I pulled into her parents' driveway, the force of my craving for her struck me hard. It wasn't so much arousal as it was a bone-deep need.

I put the car in park and looked at her. "I don't know if I can wait until winter term starts."

She gazed at me with longing. "I know what you mean."

"You need to drive down to see me."

"I'll do that. In the meantime, I'll try to think of a way to get some privacy."

I leaned across to kiss her. "You taste so good," I whispered.

"Don't get too excited. I think my dad's watching."

Reluctantly I pulled back. "I'm getting too desperate to care."

She gave me a naughty smile that turned me on as much as anything we'd done that day. "Maybe if you're very good, I'll reward you later."

"Promises, promises."

Giggling, she opened her door. "Let's go and get this over with."

Her dad was in fact standing on their front stoop, watching us. I got out and advanced on him, extending my hand.

"Mr. Winters, I'm Max Kincaid."

He held my gaze for an instant before taking my hand. "Good to meet you, Max," he said in a tone that suggested he was reserving judgment on how good it really was.

Caroline slipped her arm through mine. "Is dinner ready or do you and Mom need some help?"

"It's already on the table." He looked at me like it was my fault we'd gotten here late.

I gave him my blandest smile, the one I used when I wanted to finesse some authority figure. His hawk-like gaze didn't soften one iota. Yep, this was going to be an enjoyable dinner.

As I'd noticed before when I'd picked her up, their house was surprisingly shabby. I'd expected Caroline to live in some Lake Oswego McMansion, kind of like the one my dad had built for my stepmom, except maybe not made of logs. Instead, they had a modest—very modest—seventies ranch that looked like it might have all the original stuff. There was even a vintage vinyl floor in the kitchen, in a pseudo-Spanish olive green and russet color scheme. I kind of liked it.

Their dining room table was crammed into a small dining nook off the kitchen. A cheap, brass chandelier hung above it. The room smelled like Italian food—not surprising, with the huge blue and white bowl of spaghetti and meat sauce in the middle of the table. Mrs. Winters smiled politely at me.

"Hi, Max. I thought you might join us."

"Thank you for having me." Contrary to the opinion of many, I did have manners and could haul them out when they were needed.

Caroline took a seat in the middle of the table and pulled out a chair. "Sit by me."

I sat down as Lily and a blond boy of the same age galloped into the room and skidded to a full stop across from us. Both of them stared at me.

"Are you Caroline's new boyfriend?" the boy said.

Out of the corner of my eye, I saw Caroline turn red and start playing nervously with her silverware. Was she ashamed of me?

My chin rose as I extended my hand across the table to the kid. "Yeah, I am. My name's Max."

He took my hand with round eyes. "I'm Landon. I'm her brother."

"It's good to meet you, Landon."

"You look really different from Trent."

"Landon," Caroline admonished in a stage whisper.

"Well, he does."

I smiled at him, hoping I looked reassuring. "That's because I am different."

Lily had taken the time I'd talked to Landon to seat herself and place three tiny fairy dolls next to her plate. She looked up from her play. "I like him better than Trent."

Landon grimaced. "You don't even know him."

"So?"

"Lily, Landon, hush up and leave Max alone," Mrs. Winters said. "You're making him uncomfortable."

The kids subsided. I winked at them and Lily started giggling. They weren't really bothering me at all. It was Mr. Winters' icy glare that was making me think accepting Caroline's dinner invitation had been a bad idea. He was certainly living up to his surname.

We ate in silence for a few minutes before Winters cleared his throat. "So, Max, what are you planning to do when you graduate?"

I looked at him with another bland smile. "I'm going to put all my time into my business."

His brown eyebrows climbed up his forehead. "Business? And what business is that?" I think he suspected I was a drug trafficker or something along those lines.

"I'm a graphic designer. I have my own company."

The brows rose another centimeter. "You have your own business."

"Yes. Graphic design."

"And what's the name of this business?" he said, sounding as if he thought I was bullshitting him.

"Kincaid Design Group."

"Group? Do you have others working with you?"

I flushed. "No. I thought it would make the business sound more prosperous if I named it something like that instead of going with Max Kincaid Designs."

"I see."

His dry tone made me bristle. I fought down my resentment; getting angry with Caroline's father wouldn't do anyone any good.

"He's really talented, Dad," she said.

"Is he? Well, that's good to hear. So what's your major? Art?"

"No. Business."

I hadn't thought his brows could get any higher, but they did.

"You're a business major?"

"Yes, I am."

He put a bite of spaghetti in his mouth. His chewing gave me a reprieve. I glanced surreptitiously at Caroline, who didn't seem nervous at all. She smiled at me and touched my wrist under the table. Across from us, Lily and Landon were giggling and poking each other, apparently oblivious to the tension in the room.

"Trent tells me you're an occultist," Mr. Winters said.

Great. Here we go.

I cleared my throat. "That's true."

"Do you conjure demons?" he said, his tone faintly mocking.

"That would be stupid, so no."

"Stupid? How's that?" He eyed me with his fork halfway to his mouth.

"Well, if by demons you mean evil spirits, it doesn't seem very wise to call up something that wants to eat me for lunch. Sir."

"But you believe these demons exist."

If I said yes, he'd use it against me and if I said no, well, he'd use that against me too. I went for honesty.

"Yes, I do. I've experienced them."

He stared unwaveringly at me. "Caroline has an aunt who believes in that crap. She's an alcoholic junkie who lives under a bridge somewhere."

"Yeah, Caroline told me all about Jo."

I flicked another glance at her. She was staring at her plate, her face red, her fork frozen in the act of twirling spaghetti.

"I don't know if I like the idea of my daughter dating someone who does magic."

I could hear the implied quotation marks around the word magic.

"Dad!" Caroline gasped. "Don't be like that."

"I understand," I said. "It's not something you're used to dealing with."

"You one of these wackos we read about on Halloween, the ones who believe in some goddess or other and dance naked around bonfires?"

I smiled, and this time it wasn't so bland. "That depends on which goddess you're talking about. There are so many."

"You're kind of a smartass, aren't you? Answer the question."

"Bob, please," Mrs. Winters said.

I put down my fork and gave Caroline's dad my full attention. "I believe a wide variety of spirit beings exists. My religious beliefs are private. I think everyone has to decide for him or herself what to believe and I have no interest in converting other people to my ways. Does that answer your question?"

Caroline looked like she wanted to cry. I wasn't sure if she was more upset with me or her dad. I reached over beneath the table and took her hand. She gave me a squeeze and I relaxed a degree. It seemed she wasn't angry with me for standing up to her old man.

Mr. Winters gave me a grudging nod. "I can respect that."

"Thank you."

"Understand, I'm only trying to protect my daughter."

"I want to protect her, too," I said.

"He saved me, Dad," she said. "Some guys were harassing me and there was no-one else around. I was really scared. Max showed up and made them run off. If he hadn't come along, I don't know what would have happened."

"What do you mean, he made them run off? How'd you do it?" The last was directed at me.

I shrugged. "Just a trick of posture and voice projection to make myself seem more dangerous than I really am." Also energy manipulation, but I wasn't going to tell him that. I was pretty sure he wouldn't get it and would think his impression of me as a nutcase had been confirmed.

"I'm glad you were there," Mrs. Winters said.

Bob Winters repeated his unwilling nod of acknowledgment. "Yes. Thank you for that. I appreciate you standing up for her."

"It was no problem at all. I was glad to do it." And that was the truth. It would have destroyed me if Caroline had gotten hurt, especially if I could have done something to prevent it and hadn't.

"Let's have some pleasant conversation now," Mrs. Winters said.

I caught her eyes. "I care for Caroline a lot." It struck me just how inadequate those words really were. I didn't simply care for her.

"You don't have to say that," Caroline whispered.

"Why not? It's true. I'd never let anything bad happen to you if I could help it."

She looked at me, her eyes shining, and I felt some barrier in my heart crumple and give way. I was falling for her, fast and hard. No, that wasn't true. I'd already fallen. I loved her.

Chapter 22

Caroline: That year's winter break was the longest one I could remember—not just in chronological time but in subjective time. It felt like Max and I were apart forever instead of only three weeks. Even though we saw each other once or twice a week, it wasn't enough and too much of that time was taken up with driving back and forth between Portland and Avery's Crossing.

On the day I got back to campus, I didn't even bother unpacking my stuff into my dorm room. Instead I went straight to Max's apartment with my suitcase.

I parked my car in the driveway behind his and got out, popping the trunk so I could get to my suitcase. He came out of the house just as I was lifting my bag. He wore a dark blue Henley with the long sleeves pushed up and snug faded jeans.

I dropped the bag and ran to him. Laughing, he caught me and lifted me in his arms as I threw my arms and legs around him. We kissed, a long and hot caress of our mouths, and it left me starving for more.

"I'll get your bag and we'll go upstairs," he said, his voice husky.

"Does that mean I have to get down?"

"Yes. Although right now I wish I had four arms so I could keep holding you and carry the bag at the same time."

I released him. My knees were wobbly from the hotness of our kiss. "Let's hurry."

He grinned at me, blue eyes sparkling. "Yes, ma'am."

We went upstairs and into his apartment as fast as we could move. Max set my case down on the floor at the foot of his bed and grabbed me, pulling me against him with one arm while he clasped my head in his other hand.

His mouth crashed down on mine. I clutched him to me, moaning into his kiss, my body undulating against him. It had only been a few days since my last visit and I felt like if I didn't have him naked against me, inside of me, within the next few minutes, I would expire of sexual frustration.

We sank to the bed, Max tugging impatiently at my coat. I shrugged out of it, my mouth still fused with his. The coat ended up somewhere on the floor, my shoes, sweater and jeans following rapidly.

He cupped my breasts through my bra and I arched into his touch, whimpering at the pleasure of it. "You're so beautiful," he said.

I was too far gone to argue with him. He unclasped the bra and then the slightly roughened heat of his bare palms met my flesh.

"This isn't fair," I said. "You still have all your clothes on."

He let go of me to yank his shirt over his head. I set my hands at his waist and kissed him right between his collarbones. He sighed. With my hands still at his waist, I continued kissing him down and across his chest, through the thin sprinkling of black curls over his pecs. I pushed him backward until he stretched out on the bed and then I bent to press more kisses to his ribs.

These bones had been broken once. If I could have kissed away all the pain he'd suffered, all the ugly memories, I would have done it right then. But memories don't erase so easily.

I wished there were words, something I could say that would heal the wounds of the past.

Lifting my head, I looked into his drowsy eyes. "I love you."

His lips parted. He studied my face with an air of shock, as if those were the last words he'd ever expected me to say.

"You don't have to answer," I said. "I just wanted you to know."

He lifted a hand to caress my face. "Caro, you're so sweet. You're the sweetest girl I've ever known."

But he didn't love me. I could live with that. Couldn't I?

Maybe I shouldn't have said anything. I didn't want the mood ruined, so I returned to kissing him, this time along the length of his belly.

I fumbled with the button on the fly of his jeans. He took over for me, lifting his narrow hips and skinning out of the pants so fast I laughed. Max grinned at me and rolled me under him.

"Don't laugh at an aroused man."

"Or what?"

"He might eat you." He buried his face against my neck and growled.

I shrieked, giggling as I writhed underneath his weight. The playful wrestling turned to passion in an instant and soon we were moving together, our moans and cries driving us to greater and greater ecstasy.

When his orgasm hit, he bent his head, black hair falling forward to hide his face. "Caro—" he gasped. "Love you. Love—"

He broke off into a wordless groan, his body shuddering in my arms. My eyes stung. He didn't really love me; he'd only said that to make me feel good. A false declaration of love was worse than none at all, and I hated the way some guys would say those three words when they didn't mean it. I should definitely have kept my mouth shut.

Afterward, he held me against his body, his hand stroking tenderly along the length of my back. His touch felt loving. It had since the first time we'd been together, the first time we'd kissed. Maybe I'd been wrong. Maybe he wasn't lying when he'd said the L-word.

It was wrong to ask. Too clingy, too pushy. But I needed to know or I'd drive myself crazy wondering.

I tilted my head back to see his face. "Did you mean it?"

"Hmm?" he said sleepily, eyes closed.

"What you said...did you mean it?"

His eyes opened. He brushed a curl from my face. "Yes, I did. I love you."

"You didn't have to say it just because I did. I wasn't trying to push you into anything."

"I said it because it's true. I love you."

I couldn't answer. All I could manage was a shaky little smile.

"Hey," he said, tracing my cheekbone with his thumb. "What's going on?"

"I just don't know what you see in me."

His eyebrows lowered. "What?"

"I'm not beautiful or sexy. I'm not witchy and cool like Selene. I'm boring. Ordinary."

"Caro, you're not ordinary. Trust me on this. And you are beautiful and sexy. How could you think you're not?" He sounded genuinely puzzled.

I flicked one of my curls. "This stupid hair of mine, for one."

"I love your hair."

I snorted. "You do not."

He lifted himself up on one elbow. "Yes, I do. Why don't you like it?"

Was he for real? "It's all fuzzy and it never does what I want it to do. It looks like a mess of snakes on my head."

"But it's interesting. It's not like anyone else's hair."

I rolled my eyes. "Exactly. That's the problem. Maybe I should get it straightened."

"Don't you dare."

I frowned at him. "You really like it?"

"Yes. I love it. I love how unpredictable it is." He pulled a curl out until it straightened, then released it and watched it spring back into its usual corkscrew shape.

"My mom's hair is exactly the same, except she works really hard to make it straight. I think she uses, like, fifty different products to make it look all smooth and shiny."

"Yours is better. It's wild and sexy, like you."

I gave him a skeptical look and he grinned.

"You were sexy the minute I met you and the wild...well, you're getting there."

"You're crazy, Max," I said, poking him gently in the belly.

"I'm glad I met you. I'm glad you're here." He kissed my neck. "I love you, Caroline Winters."

* * *

I woke suddenly. My heart was racing and I didn't know why. The light in the room had faded and there was nothing left of it but a weak gray glow. It looked cold and unfriendly, and a chilly draft blew across the bare wood of Max's floor. I shivered.

Max was sitting up in bed next to me, staring at the wall. His faded blue comforter had fallen around his waist, so he was bare on top in the cold room. His shoulders were slumped, his back curved in apparent defeat. Although he said nothing and didn't move, I could sense the despair radiating off him.

I placed my hand lightly on his back. "What's wrong?"

He turned his head and looked at me with bleak eyes. "I'm going to lose you."

I sat up, pulling the comforter around our shoulders. "What are you talking about?"

"I don't deserve you," he said, his voice rough and low.

"Of course you do, Max." I moved so we faced each other, the comforter wrapped around us, and put my arms around his shoulders. "I love you. Do you hear me?"

He buried his face in my hair. "You're too good for me."

"That's bullshit. No-one's too good for you."

"I wish that were true." His lips moved against my hair. "I really do."

"You're a good person. You saved me from those guys the night of the party; you helped me with Retro-girl; you listen to me and you never make fun."

"Do other people make fun of you?"

"Sometimes."

"Assholes," he said.

"You never do. You're so good to me."

His shoulders slumped even more. "It's not enough. I didn't really do anything with those guys and I sure didn't help you with Retro-girl. All I did was talk to her and let you sleep over here. Which was to my advantage, I might add."

"If it wasn't for you, I would have ended up raped that night, so I have no idea how you can say you didn't do anything. And you did help me with Retro-girl. You listened without laughing; you gave advice. No-one else would have done that for me."

"Caro—"

I took his face between my hands and stared into his beautiful eyes. "You are a wonderful, strong person, Max. How many people do you think manage to get themselves off the streets, get a GED and go into business for themselves? Not very many, I'll bet."

"I had help. I didn't do it by myself."

"So what? That's not the point."

He sighed, shaking his head inside the cage of my hands. "You don't get it."

"Yes, I do. You're determined to hate yourself because of your past. Don't let it control you."

"You don't know what really happened."

"Then tell me."

"I can't." His voice cracked. "I just can't."

My whole body ached in sympathy for his pain. I pulled his head down and kissed him. He needed forgetfulness, and physical intimacy was the only thing I could think of that might give it to him.

The sex this time was slow and sweet. I tried to show him how I felt with caresses instead of words, but I couldn't tell if he got the message. Every movement of his body seemed filled with sadness that I couldn't touch or soothe away.

"Never forget I love you," he murmured to me as he entered my body.

"Yes," I said.

He began to move. "No matter what happens, remember I love you."

I stared up at his troubled eyes. "Max, you're scaring me."

What had happened while I slept to disturb him so deeply?

"I love you," he said, sliding deep into me.

The burst of pleasure that came with his movement drove the worry out of my mind. But only temporarily. When we were finished, I held myself over him and fixed him with a determined stare. "Tell me what's wrong. What happened to you?"

He gave me what I think was supposed to be a carefree smile. "It's nothing. I just had a bad dream. Sorry I scared you."

"Max—"

"Really, it's nothing. Don't worry about it."

Chapter 23

Caroline: Six weeks after I broke up with Trent, he caught me when I was on my way from my French literature class to the dining hall for lunch. Max and I didn't have any classes together this term, so I typically didn't see him until the afternoon, thus giving Trent an opportunity to catch me unawares.

He caught up with me right after I left the foreign language building. My French lit class had ended and I was on my way through the January drizzle to the dining hall. I had my hat pulled down so far the brim narrowed my field of vision, so I didn't see him dashing toward me. I just heard his voice.

"Caroline!"

I turned before I realized who it was. He had a baseball cap pulled low over his eyes and a blue running jacket that I didn't recognize. But I knew him instantly.

I paused, dreading the encounter. "Hi, Trent."

"How've you been?"

"Fine. Good." I smiled politely. "How are you?"

"I'm okay. Are you on the way to a class?"

"Um...no." Why did I have to be so honest? I should have lied.

People were walking around us like we were rocks in the center of a fast-moving stream. They paid no attention to us, but I still didn't want to have any kind of conversation with Trent in such a public place.

"I'd like to talk to you for a few," he said. "Catch up."

"There's really nothing to catch up."

"Just as friends?"

That was exactly what Max used to say to me, before we became romantically involved. I lifted my brows. "Friends?"

"Look, I know things didn't end so well between us, but I'd like to think we're still friends," Trent said earnestly.

I pursed my lips. "Okay. I guess we can be friends. But you should know I'm seeing Max."

He gave a solemn nod. "Yeah. I know."

"Okay. Well, I'd better go." I took a step forward.

"Can I buy you lunch?" he said, matching me.

Oh, boy. "Trent, I don't think that's a good idea."

"Aw, come on. I just need to talk to you for a few minutes."

"You're talking to me now."

"Yeah, but there's no privacy here."

That was exactly what I'd been thinking. However, I didn't like where he seemed to be going with it.

"I don't see why we need privacy," I said. "We're just friends. Besides, Tiffani wouldn't be happy if you went off alone with me."

"Yeah, about that. Things aren't going so well with her."

I glanced at him. He wasn't looking at me and the expression on his face was neutral, giving nothing away.

"I hadn't heard," I said.

"I thought maybe Paige had told you."

"No. She's been busy with Dan, so I haven't seen much of her. And because of Tiff, I haven't been to my house, so I'm out of the loop."

Trent grabbed my hand and pulled me off the sidewalk and under the prickly canopy of a massive Douglas fir tree. "Actually, she broke up with me," he said, gazing watchfully into my face.

"I'm sorry."

"Don't you want to know why?"

I pulled my hand from his grasp. "Not really."

"She said I wasn't over you."

I took a deep breath. "Trent—"

"We were good together, Caroline."

"No, we weren't. You said I was frigid, remember?"

He rolled his head to the side, his eyes closing briefly. I wasn't sure if the gesture was supposed to convey sorrow or irritation. "I didn't mean it. I was just angry."

"But it was true. I didn't respond to you."

His eyes snapped to mine. "What does that mean?"

"It means we're not very well matched."

"That's not true." He reached out and recaptured my hand. "I miss you. All the time."

"I'm with Max. And I'm happy."

He scowled at me. "You can't be happy with him. Not possible."

I struggled not to laugh in his face. "It's totally possible. Max is a great guy. I'm not interested in leaving him, if that's what you're implying."

"But—"

"Trent, it didn't work with us. Let it go."

"I can't let it go. I need you. Please, Caroline, give me another chance."

He seemed genuinely sincere and it hurt me to disappoint him. But I couldn't go back to the loveless, sexless existence I'd had before Max came into my life.

"I care about you," I said. "But I can't be your girlfriend. I'm sorry Tiffani wasn't the one for you, but I'm sure there will be others. Just not me."

I tugged at my hand until he released me. Before he could resume his campaign to get me back, I strode from under the tree and into the foot traffic headed toward the student union. I didn't look back. I didn't want to give him the idea I regretted my decision or that there was any wiggle room.

* * *

When I got to the student union, I noticed my hands were trembling a little. I got in line at the sub shop and hauled out my phone to send a text to Max.

Hey. Saw Trent just now.

He answered immediately. *R u ok?*

Fine. No. Upset.

At the student Union?

Yes. The commons.

Be right there

I'd just reached the front of the line when Max slid an arm around my waist and kissed me on the temple. "You okay, baby?"

I leaned into him and lifted my face for a kiss on the mouth. "I'll be fine."

"He didn't threaten you, did he?"

"No. I'll tell you in a minute."

We ordered sandwiches and took them to a booth at the edge of the commons, where we had at least a smidgen of privacy. The place hummed with the voices of all the students who came here for lunch or snacks between classes, not to mention the people who conducted their study groups here. In a way, the noise level was a good thing, because it made it difficult to pick out any single conversation, so it was unlikely anyone would be listening to what we said.

We sat down next to each other, shoulders touching, and ate quietly for a few minutes. Then Max put his sandwich down and took my hand. "So what did he say?"

"Tiffani broke up with him. He wants me to come back."

"Are you going to do it?" he said quietly.

I turned to him as my mouth fell open. "Of course not. How could you think that?"

He studied me soberly. "You went out with him for a whole year. I figured you might still be attached."

"No. Not like that."

"So you are attached in some way?"

I shook my head. "No. I'm not attached to him. I'm attached to you."

He lifted my hand to his lips and kissed it. "I'm glad to hear you say that."

"Max, I have no romantic interest in Trent. I'm not sure I ever did."

His black brows descended. "Why did you go out with him, then?"

"I don't know. I've asked myself that question over and over. I guess he just seemed like the kind of guy I *should* be dating, you know? The kind of guy my parents would approve of."

"And I'm not," he said dryly.

"They don't know you very well yet. Once they do, they'll love you just like I do."

He leaned close, a smile beginning to light his eyes. "I hope not *just* like you do," he murmured in my ear before biting my earlobe.

I yelped, then laughed. "Stop that."

"I can't help myself. Every time I see you, I want to take a bite."

People were looking at us because of the noise I'd made. I felt my whole body heating with embarrassment as Max continued to nuzzle me behind my ear and along the length of my neck.

"I love it when you wear your hair up like this," he murmured. "With all the little curls escaping."

He really did seem to like my hair, a concept I found amazing. His lips made a warm, erotic trail along my neck and I found myself beginning to ache and sigh in spite of our audience. Everything he did, every touch, felt like heaven to me. I lifted my hand and buried my fingers in the silk of his hair.

My gaze lifted and met Trent's as he stalked through the commons toward us. His blue eyes were narrowed and even from several yards away, I could see his jaw clenching rhythmically. My fingers tensed in Max's hair.

"Ow," he said, lifting his head.

He saw Trent and went still, his hand tightening around mine. The blond slid into the booth across from us and leaned back, folding his hands on the table top as if it belonged to him. He smiled unpleasantly.

"What do you want, Trent?" I said.

"It just occurred to me that you probably don't know," he said.

"Know what?"

"Why Max went after you."

"Don't do this," I said.

"He did it to get to me."

"Knock it off, Trent," I said uneasily. "You know that isn't true."

My stomach churned and my head began to ache. This was the same story he'd told me when he'd first explained Max's relationship to him and it pissed me off he was dragging it out again.

"Tell her, Max." Trent's smile turned mocking. "I know it's true, so you might as well confess."

"Tell him he's full of shit," I said, turning to Max.

Something in his face made me pause. It looked like...guilt. My mouth opened as my body flushed hot, and then icy cold.

"Max?"

He gazed at me, his beautiful ocean-dark eyes full of regret. "I wanted you, Caro. From the first minute I saw you."

"But...why are you looking at me like that?"

Trent snorted, an ugly sound. "Because he doesn't want to admit the truth. That he pursued you to get revenge on me."

I was staring at Max and I knew my face was full of doubt and mistrust, because that's how I felt. The morning after our first night together came back to me, the way he'd tried to break things off before they'd really gotten started. He'd sounded kind of guilty then and I hadn't been able to make sense of it. In light of Trent's accusation and the expression currently on Max's face, it was beginning to make sense after all.

"It's true, isn't it?" I said in a choked voice. I felt sick.

Max closed his eyes briefly. When he opened them again, I knew Trent was right.

"I wanted to be near you," he said. "No matter what it took."

"But you wanted to hurt Trent, didn't you?" I edged away from him until I was sitting on the very limit of the bench seat.

Max swallowed. His eyes were so sad. I don't think I'd ever seen him sadder. "Yes."

I stood up, hoisting my backpack to my shoulder. My hands shook. "You lied to me. All that garbage about love. It was a lie."

"No. That was never a lie." His voice sounded dead. "I love you."

Even now, he wouldn't admit the truth. How could he look at me and say those words after what he'd done?

"Bullshit, Max."

Out of the corner of my eye, I could see Trent smirking. I hated him as much as I now despised his stepbrother.

"It's true," Max said. "I love you. I'll always love you."

"Don't. Say. That." I took a step backward. "I don't want to see you again. I don't want to speak to you or hear your voice. Don't come near me." I spun on my heel and walked away.

My throat hurt. My heart hurt. My eyes stung, but for some reason I wasn't crying. That seemed wrong. I should be crying. I'd just lost the love of my life.

It had all been an elaborate game to him, a game he was apparently still playing. All of the tenderness, the passion, the declarations of love, all lies. The knowledge tore me apart inside. I moved blindly through the commons, bumping my hip into a table without stopping, slamming through the door and into the rain outside.

Cold water fell relentlessly on my bare head. I ignored it. The icy pinpricks of the raindrops perfectly matched my mood, although I wasn't even sure how to define that mood.

Anger. Rage. Grief. Despair. I seemed to be drowning in so many emotions I couldn't make sense of any of them. Razor-like claws were ripping a hole inside me. I couldn't imagine anything ever filling that hole, ever making me well again. It was like my world had been destroyed in one little conversation.

"Caroline, wait!"

God, not Trent. I kept on walking.

"Wait a minute. Are you all right?"

"Leave me the hell alone."

"I didn't do that to hurt you." He caught my arm.

"Don't touch me," I snarled at him. "You hear me? Never touch me again."

He recoiled, dropping my arm. "Caroline, I just thought you should know."

"You did it for revenge. Well, you got what you wanted. I hope you're happy now."

"No. I want to help you."

"I don't need your help." I sped up, hoping he'd get the message.

"I need to make sure you're all right."

"If you think this will make me go back to you, you're deeply confused."

"I know you," he said in a reasonable tone that reminded me of his stepfather. "You need a guy in your life. You hate to be alone."

"Fuck off, Trent."

"What did you say to me?"

"You heard me. I don't want you, now or ever. Leave me alone or I'll call campus security."

"Jesus." He stopped walking to gape at me.

I just kept on going. At the moment, I didn't know who to despise more, him or Max. They were both bastards. Lying, cheating bastards.

Max had manipulated me after all. He'd cozied up to me, pretended to be my friend, pretended to care about me, all so he could steal me away from Trent. All so he could hurt his stepbrother's ego, embarrass him, humiliate him. He'd used me and I couldn't forgive that.

I was better off alone than with one of them.

I made it to my room without breaking down. As I inserted the key in my lock, a terrible feeling came over me, worse even than the despair that had hit me in the commons. This was like a weighted blanket settling over me, hopelessness woven into its fabric and sealed in with every stitch.

My hand hesitated on the knob. I was trembling. The key didn't want to go into the lock. My legs didn't want to hold me up. Somehow I managed to get the door open. I went inside and shut it behind me and sank to the floor, staring at the contents of my room without seeing.

The sadness felt so big I couldn't wrap my mind around it. Max and I hadn't even been together that long. Six weeks? Not long at all, yet it felt like forever. It had felt eternal.

What a sick joke that was. We hadn't even made it two months.

I'd told him I loved him. And it was true. I had loved him. I still loved him. My body craved him.

Slowly, I curled up on my side. The hole in my insides kept widening, deepening, yet tears refused to come. All I could do was stare at my carpet, my mind a blank desert of pain.

Chapter 24

Max: The brewpub had sent me a sharply worded email asking me why I hadn't submitted the final on their logo design yet, and I couldn't focus. If I didn't get my act together, I was going to lose their business. Yet I sat at my desk and stared blankly at my monitor, which was the same thing I'd been doing all afternoon.

It had been two weeks since Caroline had left me. I hadn't seen her at all in that time. I'd gone to her dorm room and knocked, but either she wasn't home or she refused to answer. I'd called. Texted. No response.

I couldn't sleep or eat. I'd lost her. From the beginning, I'd known it would happen sooner or later, but stupidly I'd hoped for later. Much later.

I hadn't talked to Brad and Marie. If I went there or even called, they'd know instantly something was wrong. And I didn't want to tell them. How could I explain what I'd done? How could I look in their eyes and admit how I'd used Caroline and how I was now paying?

It served me right, of course. What I'd done was indefensible. That fact did nothing to ease the pain of her loss.

Someone knocked on my door. Caroline? I jumped up so fast my chair went zooming across the floor, my heart pounding in sudden, stupid hope.

I opened the door and it was only Paige. My shoulders fell about a foot.

"I'm here for her things," she said, giving me an appraising glance. "Wow, you look terrible."

"Thank you. Come in and I'll get them." I felt like howling.

Not only had Caroline not come, she was taking away her things. She'd sent Paige for them so she wouldn't have to speak to me or look at me. I felt like a piece of shit she'd scraped off her shoe.

Paige stood tensely in the center of my living room while I went into the bedroom to get Caro's stuff. She'd left a tote bag with some overnight things in my room.

The bag was on my mattress, where it had been when she'd gotten up that morning. I hadn't moved it. I picked it up and looked inside.

A small cosmetic bag with some make-up, a toothbrush and toothpaste, her panties, a camisole, a pair of socks. I pulled out the camisole and held it to my nose, inhaling her scent with closed eyes. It made me ache.

I threw the camisole onto my pillow and carried the bag out to Paige. She was standing in front of my computer and staring at my monitor. As I came near, she looked up at me.

"Is this your design?" She pointed at the logo.

"Yes."

"You're really good," she said in a somewhat grudging tone, like she hated to admit it.

"Thank you."

She held out her hand for the bag.

"How is she?" I said, almost fearing the answer.

"How do you think? She's terrible. You broke her heart." Paige glared at me as she took the bag from me.

"I—tell her I miss her. And I love her."

"No way. I'm not telling her anything."

"She won't talk to me."

"Hm. I guess you have a problem, then." She gave me her back as she walked to my door.

"I want to explain. I need to explain," I said, following her.

"She doesn't want to see you."

"Is she—" My throat closed down painfully. "Is she seeing Trent?"

Paige shot me a disbelieving glance. "No, she is not. She won't talk to him either."

That gave me a spurious sense of relief. At least she hadn't gone back to my prick of a stepbrother.

"Please tell her I need to see her."

Paige opened my door, shaking her head. "I'm not getting involved in this. Picking up her stuff is as far as I go. If you want to talk to her, you make it happen."

She walked through my door and shut it behind her. I shouldn't have asked her to be my go-between. She was Caroline's friend, not mine, so of course she'd be loyal to Caroline. And that was good. I was glad Caroline had a friend on her side. I just wished I had someone on mine, but everyone had deserted me. Even Fred hadn't come around.

I went back to my computer and emailed the logo to my client. It was good enough, and if they didn't like it they'd let me know. Better to send them something imperfect than nothing at all.

That chore done, I went to my refrigerator and got myself a beer. Gods, I'd sunk low, drinking by myself. I hadn't done anything like this in years, but what the hell? I flopped onto the hard wood floor, perversely enjoying my own discomfort, and downed the contents of the bottle as quickly as I could.

"You need to fight for her." Fred's voice came from behind me.

I turned my head lazily. "Surprised to see you. Thought you'd lost my address."

"I had some matters to attend to."

"Oh. I see." I got up and went back to the fridge for a second beer.

Fred waited for me in the living room. He was back to wearing the sack suit and derby, but the moustache was still missing. Without it, he looked like me in historical costume. I settled back on the floor and swallowed a good slug of beer.

"She doesn't want me to fight for her," I said.

Fred scoffed. "Of course she does."

"She said she didn't want to see my face or hear my voice." Another slug of beer.

"Spoken in the heat of the moment," he said.

"Yeah, well, she seemed pretty sincere at that moment."

"Max, she loves you."

I tilted the beer again and let it run down my throat. This shit wasn't doing the job. I wished I had some whiskey or vodka.

"She tell you that?" I said without looking at him.

"I haven't spoken to her, but I have observed. She seems as miserable as you are."

"Then why won't she answer my calls or texts?"

"Pride, I suppose." He sighed. "Women are very proud creatures in their way."

"Fight for her," I said, and took another swallow of beer.

"She wants you to."

"That's an assumption, Fred. Never assume."

"She's not eating."

I set the bottle on the floor and looked at him. "Not at all?"

He shook his head. His eyes were serious, almost mournful. He was worried about her. "Not as far as I could see. She just drinks coffee."

My stomach gave a nauseous lurch. "She'll make herself sick."

"She very well might."

"I'm going over there." I got up, leaving the beer on the floor.

"Good." Fred disappeared.

* * *

I ran almost all the way to Caroline's dorm. My hair and jacket and shoes were soaked with rain by the time I got there, but I barely felt the cold wet of my clothes. Fred's words had fired me up, given me a reason to move beyond my work desk and bed. They'd given me a reason to hope.

I can't explain why the knowledge that Caroline wasn't eating gave me hope. Except maybe that she was suffering, too. Maybe she missed me. Maybe she still needed me.

The gods knew I needed her.

As usual, I got no answer when I knocked on her door. She could be anywhere—out with Paige, at a class, at the student union, the library, a movie. And if I called or texted her, she'd know I was trying to find her and then she'd go out of her way to avoid me.

Instead, I sat down on the floor next to her room and settled in to wait as long as it took. In mid-afternoon, the hall was lively with students going to and from their rooms. They all gave me curious looks, but no-one said anything.

I don't know how long I sat there. My bladder filled because of all the beer I'd had. It was starting to hurt. Damn it. I didn't want to leave, not even to go take a piss, in case she showed up while I was gone.

Eventually, though, I had to give in or wet my pants. I hustled down the hall to the male side of the floor and used their bathroom. It reminded me of the locker room in my high school—not a place filled with good memories. Finishing up as quickly as possible, I hurried back to Caroline's side in time to see her putting her key in her lock.

I strode toward her, determined to catch her before she could lock me out. I'd almost reached her when she glanced up and saw me. Her face lost what little color it had.

She looked ill. Dark smudges shadowed her eyes. There were hollows beneath her cheekbones and her hair was dull and tangled-looking. She stared at me with a mixture of dread and fascination—at least, that's what her expression looked like to me.

"Caro," I said, my voice coming out all hoarse and stupid-sounding.

"Max, go away. Please."

I shook my head. "I have to talk to you."

"No. It's over." She struggled with her key, the metal rattling against the doorknob.

"It's not over. Not for me."

Her chocolate eyes glistened with unshed tears. "Paige brought me my things. Thank you. Now please, just go."

"Why won't you let me explain?"

She shook her head, biting her lip. "There's nothing to say."

"Yes, there is. You haven't heard my side."

Finally she got the door open. She held onto the knob and twisted her body to face me. "Don't you get it? I don't want explanations. I just want to be left alone."

My face crumpled. Damn it, I was going to lose it any second. Going to break down and cry right here in front of everyone on her floor.

She eased into her room. "Good-bye, Max. Don't come here again."

Her door shut in my face. I leaned my forehead against it, struggling for control. I couldn't give up and go away. If I did, I might never see her again. It seemed pretty clear that she'd never come looking for me.

The only strategy I could think of at the moment was to wait her out, so I slid back to the floor.

I'd never missed anyone like this. Never needed anyone before. She was like some nutrient my body needed to function correctly and now she was gone and I was slowly falling apart. If this was love, I wasn't sure it was worth the agony.

A girl with mouse-brown hair in a high ponytail came up to me, her head tilted to the side, her eyes full of worry. "Are you okay?" she said softly.

"I'm fine."

"You don't look so good."

"I'm waiting for my girlfriend."

She looked over her shoulder like she was hoping for some support, but no-one was there. "I overheard her tell you to leave. I'm sorry to bother you, but I was just wondering if I could help."

I stared up at her, knowing my desolation was painted all over me and that there was nothing I could do to hide it. "I'm waiting so we can talk it out."

"Okay." She offered a tentative smile. "Good luck."

"Thanks."

The girl turned and disappeared into the room across the hall. Had Caroline heard any of our conversation? Did she know I was still here, waiting pathetically for her to come out and acknowledge me?

Never, in all my dreaming about girls, had I imagined myself in a position like this.

A long time later, she opened her door again. She came out and stopped short when she saw me. Then she heaved a gigantic sigh.

"Max, go home."

"Hear me out."

"There's nothing you can say that will change my mind."

I thought I saw pity in her eyes, and that pissed me off.

"You need to leave," she said. "Don't make me call campus security."

My mouth opened. And closed. And opened again. "You'd do that to me?"

"I don't want to, but if you won't go on your own, I will."

"Jesus, Caro." I climbed to my feet. "What happened to us?"

"You happened. You lied to me. Used me." Her chin trembled and her voice broke. It hurt me to see that. "You have no idea how bad that feels."

"I know how bad it feels to have thought of doing it, for even one second. I'm so sorry, Caro."

Her lip was trembling now as well. "So am I."

"Please, let's talk about this."

She reached into her purse and pulled out her phone. "It's too late for that. If you don't leave, I'm going to call security."

I'd thought I'd already hit bottom. I'd been wrong. This was much further down than I'd been before.

She turned on her phone and started to hit the number buttons. There was nothing left for me to do except leave, so I started walking. The only other option was to kidnap her and make her listen to me, but that was not only illegal, it would definitely make her hate me even more than she already did.

I was beaten.

* * *

I walked home. Normally, a walk will calm me and take me to a place where things look less hopeless, but not tonight. When I got to my house, I stared up at the second floor and couldn't bring myself to walk up to my apartment. The thought of one more night alone in that place was too much.

I got into my car and drove out to Brad and Marie's place. The lights were on in the living room. They were home and I was going to tell them what I'd done and they were going to be so fucking mad at me. But it was the only place I had to go.

"Hi, Max!" Marie's welcoming smile faded when she got a better look at me. "Damn, you look like crap."

"That's what everyone says these days."

"Come in. Brad's in the living room watching TV."

I followed her into the living room. Brad took one look at me and turned the TV off, motioning me to sit with him on the couch. They flanked me, like they were trying to prevent me from escaping. I sat down and stared at the blank TV screen, my hands loose on my lap.

"What happened, hon?" Marie said.

"You look like someone died," Brad added.

"Caroline left me."

Marie's small hand covered one of mine. "I'm so sorry to hear that."

"It was my fault. I drove her away."

She squeezed my hand, but said nothing. Both of them sat silently with me, waiting. I stared at the TV. The only other time I could remember feeling pain like this was that day, that long ago day, when my brother had died because of me.

"I used her to hurt Trent and she found out," I said.

"Oh, Max." Marie sounded so disappointed in me.

"I didn't mean—I thought we could move on, that it didn't matter—"

"But it did," Brad said. "Didn't it?"

"Yeah." It did.

"You love her," Marie said.

"Yeah."

She patted my hand. I just kept staring at that blank TV. I didn't know where else to look or what to do. It seemed that nothing I said or did would get Caroline to even listen to what I had to say, let alone think about coming back to me. So I sat and stared and tried not to think about anything.

"You look like you haven't been eating," Marie said.

I shrugged.

"Come on." She tugged at my arm. "We just finished dinner. I'll get you something."

"Not hungry."

"Take a few bites for me."

"Leave the boy alone," Brad said.

"He needs to eat or he'll make himself sick."

Getting sick sounded good right now. It would almost be a relief to sink into illness, something that would blank out my mind even more than it already was.

"Get up, Max." She tugged me again. "Come on. Just a few bites. Then I'll stop bugging you."

I gave in because I knew it would make her feel better to take care of me. The kitchen still smelled like pan-fried chicken. She bustled around in between the fridge and the cupboards while Brad pulled out a chair and sat down next to me.

"You want a beer?" he said.

"Sure."

Marie set a bottle of ale in front of me. I took my key chain out and used the miniature bottle opener to open it. Even though this house was new to me, the sight and sound of my foster parents and the smell of Marie's cooking was familiar and comforting.

Brad laid a heavy hand on my shoulder. "You're not alone, Max. You have us. You'll always have us to come home to."

My eyes stung. "Thanks," I said hoarsely.

Marie set a plate in front of me. Just a few bites, she'd said. She'd given me a large piece of the chicken, plus a giant helping of homemade mashed potatoes and gravy and some kind of carrot dish.

"Thanks." There was no way I could finish this.

I stuck my fork listlessly into the mashed potatoes and put it in my mouth. They were buttery and perfect. I took another bite.

"We love you," Marie said, taking the remaining chair.

"I love you, too," I said, sticking a piece of chicken in my mouth.

She smiled at me. She wasn't going to lecture me on my shameful behavior toward Caroline, apparently, and for that I was grateful. I didn't think I could handle a scolding at the moment.

When I'd put away about half the food, I pushed the plate across the table. It was probably more than I'd eaten in the whole two weeks Caroline had been gone. "Sorry, but I can't eat anymore."

"That's okay. You did good." She took the plate and put it in the sink. "Would you like to stay here for the night?"

I looked at her and then Brad and slowly nodded. "Yeah." They were babying me and I really didn't care. I didn't want to be alone right now.

Chapter 25

Caroline: I'd never felt more alone than when I watched Max walking away from me. Leaving me. Clearly I'd lost my mind, because I was the one who'd made him go. But, God, it tore me apart to see him do it.

I'd been on my way to meet Paige for dinner. I probably wouldn't have eaten more than a bite or two, but she wanted to see me and I owed her for getting my stuff for me. Now I didn't think I could face her or anyone else. I turned around and went back in my room, texting her that I was canceling.

Then I lay down on my bed and stared at the ceiling. Maybe I should withdraw from this term and go home for a few months. I could always come back in the spring, when I'd had a chance to get over him. It would be running away, but so what? At least I wouldn't have to worry about running into him or having him come to my room and wait in the hall. How long had he been waiting out there? An hour at least.

I rubbed my eyes. They were dry of tears, but my throat was thick and tight with the need to cry. Love sucked. It sucked big time.

I heard a rustle and a sigh from the other side of the room. My heart paused and I went cold. Slowly, I turned my head, expecting Retro-girl, but it wasn't her. It was a man.

He sat in my desk chair, watching me. He had dark hair and wore an odd, old-fashioned looking brown suit. His face, especially the eyes, reminded me of Max.

"W-who are you?" I whispered, clutching my comforter in my fists.

"I apologize if I startled you," he said. "My name is Frederick Marchand."

"You're F-fred? Max's Fred?"

"The same." He smiled and it was Max's smile. "I'm very pleased to meet you, Miss Caroline Winters."

"Um...it's nice to meet you, too." What a bizarre thing to say to a ghost. Slowly I sat up. "I don't mean to be rude, but why are you here?"

"To plead Max's case."

I closed my eyes. "Look, Fred, there's nothing to plead. Max and I are finished."

"He loves you."

"No, he doesn't. He only said that to get me away from Trent."

"Is that so? Then why didn't he drop you as soon as you broke up with his stepbrother? Why say he loved you? There was no need, if his only purpose was to hurt Trent."

I shook my head. "I don't know. And I don't care. I can't take him back. I could never trust him again."

"I urge you to reconsider."

God, how I wanted to give in. How I wanted to call Max and tell him to come over, that I forgave him, that everything was all right. But it wasn't all right. He'd lied to me.

"I'm better off without a man," I said.

"Are you?"

"Yes. They're overwhelming and dictatorial and untruthful and I—" *Miss him so damn much I can't stand it.* I blinked rapidly to hold back the tears.

"Please think about giving him another chance," Fred said. "You won't regret it."

I couldn't speak. If I opened my mouth, I'd start sobbing and I really didn't want to cry in front of a stranger. Even if he was a ghost.

My hands came up to cover my eyes. He made no sound and when I lowered my hands a few minutes later, he was gone.

* * *

On Saturday morning, I was getting ready to go to breakfast when I got a knock on my door. My whole body tensed. Could it be Max? My heart raced as I went to answer it. I ought to be furious with him for ignoring my rejection, and part of me was, but most of me rejoiced that he'd come back. Most of me wanted to throw my arms around him and kiss him.

I opened the door. It wasn't Max. A petite, brown-haired woman stood there, staring at me in obvious apprehension.

Her hair was cut in a chic bob and she wore skinny jeans and kitten heels with a loosely-knitted, artistic looking gray tunic with a long, narrow red scarf. Interesting outfit.

Then I took a better look at her face and my breath stopped. I recognized her. I knew her.

"I'm looking for Caroline Winters," she said, looking unsure of herself.

"Aunt Jo?"

She broke into a huge smile. "Caroline! Oh, my God, it is you! You're all grown up."

"I can't believe it's you. How did you find me?"

"A friend let me know where you were," she said.

That sounded mysterious.

"I was about to get some breakfast. Want to come with me?" I said.

"Yes. I'd love to."

I locked up and we started down the hall. "I asked Mom where you were but she didn't know."

"Yeah, she hasn't talked to me since they kicked me out."

"I'm so sorry about that. I never meant to get you in trouble."

Jo frowned at me. "What are you talking about?"

"They kicked you out because of me. Because I—well, you know—I was talking to an invisible friend."

"Sweetheart, it had nothing to do with you. Your parents wanted me to get treatment and I refused. It wasn't your fault."

I bit my lip as I pushed the elevator call button. "Are you sure?"

"Of course I'm sure." She looked at me with wide eyes. "Have you blamed yourself all these years?"

I shrugged. "Yeah. Kind of."

She made a pained sound. "I'm so sorry. It's my fault, all of it. If I hadn't started drinking, they wouldn't have kicked me out."

I couldn't argue with that, so I didn't say anything.

We went to a nearby family-style restaurant that served pancakes and eggs. Jo kept staring at me in what looked like wonder. I didn't know why, or what was so wonderful about me, but I guess it was because she hadn't seen me in so long. I'd been a little girl of eleven when she'd left.

"You look so much like your mom," she said after we'd ordered.

"Do I?" I'd never thought that.

"Oh, yeah. Your hair is exactly the same, and your eyes are really similar, too."

My mom did have brown eyes. But the hair...

"She makes her hair straight," I said.

"Does she? She used to have it curly."

"Not anymore. It's so shiny and smooth it looks like a mirror. She's always ironing it and covering it in some kind of gloss stuff."

"I like the way you have yours better," Jo said. "It's natural."

That's what Max had said. "Thanks. You look good, too."

She smiled. "I'm doing pretty well. I'm sober and I have a decent job as an office manager in Portland."

"I'm so glad."

It was good to see her looking healthy and happy. That was something I'd thought would never happen. I'd always imagined her dying alone and cold under a freeway overpass or something like that. I'd had nightmares about it for years.

"I worried about you," I said.

"I worried about you, too." She studied me thoughtfully. "Do you still see them?"

I blinked. "See them? You mean ghosts?"

"Yes."

I took a sip of my coffee in order to gather my thoughts. "For a long time, I didn't see anything. Recently, though, I've been having...experiences." I glanced at her. "Do you see them too?"

"Oh, yes. I started drinking to get rid of them, but that didn't work. It only made me an alcoholic and a drug addict."

Wow. That was just what Max had said. Suddenly the yearning for him came back full force, hitting me with a choking wave of sadness.

Jo leaned over the table, looking concerned. "What's wrong?"

"Nothing." I waved my hand vaguely. "What you said just reminded me of my ex-boyfriend."

"Oh. A recent break-up?"

"Two weeks ago," I said through the lump in my throat. "I l-loved him."

"That's always so hard."

I nodded, unable to speak.

"Hang in there. Things will get better eventually."

I nodded again.

"Is that why you look so thin? I didn't want to say anything earlier, but you look like you don't eat enough."

"I don't have much of an appetite."

"That happens to me, too, when I'm sad. You've got to force down a few bites, though, or you'll hurt yourself."

"Yeah, I guess." I lifted my coffee cup so I'd have an excuse not to say anything more.

Paige was always pestering me to eat. She kept bringing me treats like cookies and ice cream sandwiches, ordering pizzas and waving them under my nose in an effort to make me hungry. It never worked. I had no appetite at all and I didn't care enough to force myself. The only time I put food in my mouth was basically when Paige held something to my lips and refused to take it away.

"So, how are your parents and the twins?" Jo said brightly.

"They're good. Lily and Landon are in fourth grade this year."

My aunt shook her head in amazement. "I can hardly believe it."

I pulled out my phone and called up my pictures of them to show her. She pored over them, not even looking up when the waitress brought our food. I could see lines around her eyes and mouth that I didn't remember from before, and there were silver streaks in her hair, but she still looked beautiful. My strange and lovely aunt.

"Max believes in ghosts," I said.

She looked up from my phone. "Is he the ex?"

"Yeah. He's an occultist."

"Really? What tradition does he practice?"

"I have no idea. He took me to this drumming thing once, though."

"Hmm." Her eyes sparkled. "He sounds interesting."

"He is." And charming. And sexy. Very sexy.

"I think you're still in love with him," she said. There was no judgment in her eyes, only acceptance.

"Yeah," I said. "But he lied to me."

I told her our story, right up to him pleading with me to hear him out. The whole time I was talking, I kept moving my fork across my plate, cutting my scrambled eggs and pancakes into tiny pieces. But I didn't eat any of it.

"It sounds to me like you should hear him out," Jo said. "Give him a chance to explain."

"I can't. What if he lies to me again?"

"There's always a chance your partner will hold something back from you, but Max wants you. He obviously didn't only pursue you to get back at Trent, or he would have dropped you right away."

That was what Fred had told me.

"I don't know. I'll think about it."

"Good. Now eat your food like a good girl."

I sighed. "Okay, I'll try."

I forked up a bite of pancake and put it in my mouth, chewing gingerly. Part of me tasted it and knew it was good. That was the part of me that thought and felt the way I'd always—normally—thought and felt. But the me who was mourning the loss of Max couldn't tell the difference between fluffy pancakes with maple syrup and sawdust. Mushy sawdust.

I stuck another bite in my face to pacify Aunt Jo. She was right anyhow. I couldn't continue taking in nothing but coffee or I'd make myself sick.

Should I forgive Max? Should I call him and tell him I wanted him back? It seemed I'd be sending the message it was okay to lie to me. That I could be manipulated and used and I'd still hang around hoping for some affection. I'd known girls—even grown women—like that, and I didn't want to be one of them.

But it hurt so badly. I would never find another man like Max, never find anyone else I wanted as deeply, as hotly, as I wanted him. I feared was consigning myself to a sexless life if I didn't take him back.

A sexless but dignified life versus a passionate life lived at the mercy of a man who couldn't be trusted. What a choice.

I covered my sigh with a gulp of hot coffee. Dignity was better—I was reasonably sure of it. At least I wouldn't be jerked around. Right?

I'd lost the only man I'd ever met who understood my budding psychic abilities, the only man who'd never make a disparaging remark about them. But there had to be more men like him out there somewhere. Wolf, for example—not that I was romantically interested in him. It was the fact of his existence from which I had to take courage.

Where Wolf and Max existed, there had to be more like them.

Looking at Jo sitting across from me, I didn't worry anymore about going off the deep end because of my abilities. Seeing her, well-dressed, well-spoken and sane, was a complete reassurance to me that my ghost sightings did not mean I'd lost my mind, and that knowledge lifted a burden from me I hadn't been fully aware I carried. The weight of my fear of insanity melted away and with it, some of my pain.

The grief was still there, but it was bearable now. I could move forward with my life. I would survive.

Chapter 26

Max: I spent the night in Brad and Marie's little guest room under the eaves. It still sported the same worn, little-girl quilt that had probably covered its bed for the past thirty or forty years. The thing was covered in a pattern of girls in giant, flowered bonnets and long, ruffled aprons, circa 1975.

I didn't mind the decor. The room was chilly and rain pattered fitfully against the window glass, but through the open door came the rich, dark smell of coffee. I could hear movement and voices downstairs. Brad and Marie were already awake.

I got up and pulled on my jeans and shoes. I'd take a shower later. Right now, I needed some of that coffee.

Caroline, and pain, lurked at the back of my mind, but I ignored them. My mental reprieve would only last a short while and I intended to make the most of them.

The old, bare wood stairs creaked as I walked downstairs. I went into the kitchen and stopped short. Selene was there, sitting at the table and chatting with Marie while Brad cooked scrambled eggs on the stove top.

Selene looked up at me with a huge smile. "Good morning, sleepy-head."

I grimaced. "'Lo."

"Grumpy in the morning, huh?"

Marie indicated the coffee-maker with a movement of her head. "Pour yourself a cup."

"I'm surprised to see you here, Selene," I said as I opened a cupboard in search of a mug for my coffee.

"Didn't I tell you? I'm moving down here."

I turned to stare at her. "I thought you hated it here."

Selene shrugged, giving me a flirtatious look. "I decided to give it another try. Since Brad and Marie are here, and you, too. It's gotten lonely up in Seattle."

"Hmm." I turned back to the coffee.

"Selene got here not long after you went to bed," Marie told me. "I had to put her on the couch."

"Sorry about that."

"Oh, don't apologize," Selene said. "I heard about what happened."

Great. Now she'd renew her campaign to get me in bed.

I brought my coffee to the table and sat down across from Selene. Next to her would be way too close; she'd probably try to grope me under the table or something. Brad finished with the eggs and started setting plates in front of us. There were home-made muffins to go with them.

"You two get up really damn early," I said. "But thanks. These look good."

"It's farm life," Marie said with a smile. "You know, roosters and all."

"I see."

"I heard the rooster this morning," Selene said. "I could hardly believe it. A real rooster."

Marie laughed. "You're not a country girl, huh, Selene?"

"No." Selene made a face. "I thought Seattle was a small town when I got there."

"Avery's Crossing is going to be an adjustment for you, then," Marie said.

"Thank the gods for the Internet," I remarked.

They laughed.

After breakfast was over and we'd cleaned up, Brad and Marie got to work on their endless farm tasks. I went back upstairs to put on one of Brad's sweatshirts so I could help out. Selene shadowed me, grabbing my elbow on the upstairs landing and stopping me from going back into my room.

"Max, I'm sorry about Caroline."

"Me too." I turned toward the bedroom.

"I'd be glad to, you know, keep you company. Help ease the pain."

"Thanks, but I'm fine." I pulled out of her hold.

She pouted. "You're no fun these days."

"I love her, Selene. I'm not going to get over it in a day or two." Probably not in a decade or two, either.

She tossed her long, black hair. "She doesn't deserve you. She's not good enough for you and you're better off without her."

I turned my face away from her. "You're not helping."

"I'm just trying—"

"I know what you're doing and I appreciate your concern, but I don't want a fuck buddy."

Her quick intake of breath told me I'd hit a nerve. And hurt her feelings.

"Damn," I said. "I'm sorry. But I can't be your friend with benefits or one of your string or whatever it is you call your sex partners."

She laid a manicured hand on my arm. "Max, that's not what this is about. I really care for you. And I don't have a string anymore, especially since I just moved here. I don't know anyone but you."

"I give you two weeks before you have a crowd of men following you around with their tongues hanging out."

She looked hurt. "You don't think very highly of me, do you?"

"I like and respect you. But you and I want completely different things out of a relationship. It would never work."

"No." She shook her head. "I've changed. Honestly. I want to be exclusive. With you, Max." She took both my hands as she stared soulfully into my eyes.

Gods. The last thing I wanted to do right now was hurt Selene. She was a good, kind person whom I'd always liked, whether or not we were sexually involved.

I squeezed her hands. "Thank you for being my friend. But that's all I have to offer. I'm sorry."

Her dark eyes glistened as if she wanted to cry. She nodded, biting her bottom lip. "Okay. That's okay. I understand. I—I'll see you later."

Selene turned and ran downstairs. I seemed to do nothing but hurt the women in my life lately. My feet turned toward the stairs to bring me back to Selene and tell her I'd been wrong. That I wanted her. But I stopped at the edge of the staircase, knowing I couldn't do it, that I couldn't be with any woman but Caroline.

The woman I loved wanted nothing to do with me. Fuck.

Chapter 27

Caroline: Aunt Jo left in the afternoon to drive back up to Salem. I went back to my room to study. I'd been doing a lot of that lately, since there was nothing else to take up my time. Being boyfriend-free was going to be great for my GPA.

I put on some classical music and curled up on my bed with the novel I was reading for French lit. Frankly, the story didn't interest me much and even my beloved French language couldn't make up for a dull tale, so it was slow going.

By dinnertime, I was nodding off repeatedly. The book slid out of my hands and onto my comforter as I leaned my head back against my stacked-up pillows and closed my eyes. My decision about Max nagged at me every time my mind wandered, and it was wandering mercilessly at the moment.

I shouldn't call him. I shouldn't even want him. But I did want him, with everything in me. That's how weak and silly I was. The thought of a whole life without him was like preparing myself to live without my hands. Or my eyes. He felt that essential to me.

God, what was I doing? I didn't even know who I was anymore. No-one had ever been essential to me until him, so obviously I could get by on my own. I had to.

A slight tremor in my bed made my eyes pop open. What was that? I'd been lying still, so I hadn't caused the sensation. It felt like someone had shaken the frame. I braced my hands against the mattress, glancing nervously around the room for a sign of Retro-girl. I was alone.

The bed vibrated again. I gasped. I'd actually been able to see it moving that time.

"Who's there? What do you want?" I said in a low voice.

Naturally, there was no answer. At least, not one I could hear. Sweat trickled down my sides.

The bed rattled and bounced in a frenzy of shaking. I let out a cry and jumped off the thing. It jogged back and forth like it was trying to get up and walk from the room.

"Stop it!" I said.

My coffee mug lifted off my desk and sailed toward my head. I ducked. It smashed against the wall next to the door, broken shards raining down on the carpet.

"Holy crap." Whatever this was, it seemed to be trying to hurt me.

The textbooks I had stacked on my desk lifted, one by one, and hurled themselves at me. I dodged the first one, but the second slammed me squarely in the middle of my back.

"Ow!" I grabbed my purse and ran from the room, panting.

In the hall, I could hear banging coming from inside. The ghost, or creature, or entity—I didn't know what to call it—was evidently still in there having its little temper tantrum. With shaking hands, I yanked out my phone and punched in Jo's number. She'd probably know what to do.

All I got was her voice mail.

I leaned against the wall. Now what? Paige would be no help, and I sure didn't want her getting hurt by a flying book or my extra coffee mug.

The door across from mine opened and Ivy stuck her mousy brown head out to stare at me. "What's going on in there?" she said, her eyes wide behind her glasses.

"Oh, uh, well, it's a ghost. I think." I smiled lamely.

Her eyes got even wider. "A ghost? You're kidding, right?"

"No, Ivy, I'm not." My hand was still shaking as I lifted it to push my hair from my eyes. "It's a poltergeist or something."

"Holy shit. That's...that's awesome!"

My eyebrows shot up. "You think so?"

"Yeah." She sounded genuinely excited. "Can I look?"

"If you want, but it threw a cup and a pile of books at me, so be careful. One of the books hit me in the back."

"Wow." She edged out of her room and put her hand on my doorknob. "You sure it's okay if I look?"

Inside the banging continued.

"Sure. Please yourself."

She opened the door a crack and peeped inside. "Oh. My. God. That's incredible. I—" Words seemed to fail her as she stared at the wild show going on in my room.

"Shit." She recoiled and slammed the door. Something thumped hard against the closed portal. "It threw another book at me. A big one." Ivy turned her head to look at me. "What should we do?"

"I don't know," I said. "I guess...I'm going to have to call my boyfriend. I mean, my ex-boyfriend. He might know."

"Is that the guy who was sitting out here in the hall the other day?"

She'd seen him? "Yeah, that's the one."

"He's hot. I can't believe you broke up with him."

"Neither can I," I muttered.

I so didn't want to call Max. Except I did. God, how I wanted to hear his voice, see his face, touch him. But that couldn't happen—the touching. We had to keep this on the level of friendship only.

I hit his number.

"Kincaid," he said in an impersonal tone, as if he hadn't noticed my number on his phone.

"Max, it's Caroline."

Dead silence. Oh, hell, I'd done the wrong thing. He didn't want to hear from me after all, and who could blame him after the way I'd talked to him.

"I'm sorry, I shouldn't have bothered you," I said quickly.

"I'm just surprised. I didn't expect to ever hear from you again," he said.

"Yeah. I didn't think I'd call you."

Another uncomfortable silence followed.

"So..." He finally broke the quiet. "What's up?"

"I seem to have another ghost problem. A poltergeist. Isn't that what you call them when they throw stuff?"

"That's it."

"Something's been rattling my bed and throwing books around in my room. It hit me with one of them."

"That sounds dangerous." He sounded carefully neutral. There was no joy in his voice, nothing to show he was glad I'd called.

"Yeah. I thought so." I fidgeted nervously, trying not to glance at Ivy, who was standing there openly listening.

"Is there something you want me to do about it?" Max said. "Because I can help if you want, but you're going to have to ask for it."

"You want to humble me, is that it?"

"No. I just want to be clear about exactly what you want."

I drew a deep breath in through my nose. Fine. "Please help me, Max. I'd really appreciate it if you could come over and see if you can do anything to make it go away."

"I'll be there in a few." He cut the connection.

I glanced at Ivy. "He'll be here soon."

"This is so cool. Can I hang around while he does his thing?"

It was hard not to laugh. Ivy really didn't fit my preconceptions about what people interested in paranormal phenomena looked like. "Sure, why not?"

"Awesome sauce." She grinned at me.

Awesome sauce? I hadn't heard that expression since about fifth grade.

"So, are you a freshman?" I said.

"Nope. I'm a sophomore, actually."

"An independent?"

"Yeah. You?"

"No, I'm in a sorority."

Her eyes widened again. "Oh. I didn't know you sorority girls lived in the dorms past the freshman year."

"We don't, usually. I just wanted to be on my own."

She cocked her head. "How does your sorority feel about that?"

"They hate it."

We chatted for a while about the difference between being an independent and a Greek. Ivy seemed smart and likable, and I wondered why she hadn't pledged. From the way she talked, I'd guess she hadn't been interested. Some of my sorority sisters—Tiffani, for example— would never believe that anyone could be completely uninterested in pledging. They always assumed independents had tried to pledge but had failed to be invited. They were losers, in other words. Talking to Ivy, I was suddenly sure that wasn't true.

And anyway, was it right to label someone a loser just because they didn't fit into sorority life? Even if they had tried to pledge and been rejected, that didn't make them losers.

Ivy's gaze moved to the end of the hall behind me, lingering on whatever she saw there. Probably Max. My heart sped up again and my achy butterflies made a grand entrance, fluttering so furiously I thought I might be sick. What was I going to say to him? How could I look at him without giving myself away?

I turned. He was wearing his black leather jacket and carrying a messenger bag slung over one shoulder. His eyes were sad. Distant. His gaze collided with mine and broke away, as if he couldn't bear to look at me.

I pressed my lips together and stared at the floor. His feet, in worn black skate shoes, came closer and closer until they stopped in front of me. A tremendous bang sounded inside my room.

"Sounds like they're having a party in there," Max said.

"It's incredible," Ivy said.

He glanced at her. "You saw it too?"

"She let me peek."

"Are you okay, Caroline?" he said. "You said it hit you in the back."

"I'm a little sore, but I'll be fine. I just can't go in my room." I glanced up at him. And caught him staring at me.

There was so much undisguised yearning in his eyes that I couldn't look away. We stared helplessly at each other for an endless minute.

Max cleared his throat. "I'd better get started. You two stay out in the hall."

"Can't I watch?" Ivy said. "I was really hoping to watch."

He gave her a faint smile. "I guess, but don't blame me if you get smacked with something."

"I won't."

He didn't ask me if I wanted to watch. He just opened my door and stood in the opening, watching whatever was going on in my room.

"Are you the one who's been throwing things around?" he said.

Ivy and I exchanged a wide-eyed glance. I couldn't hear the answer he received. He took a step over the threshold.

"We'd like to come in and talk to you."

Whatever it was must have given him the okay because he gestured to us to follow him before entering the room entirely. Ivy happily tromped after Max, but I hung back. I really didn't want to be winged with another book.

I peered around the door and saw Retro-girl standing in the center of my room. Wait. *She* was the one who'd smacked me? I hadn't perceived her as violent before, and it bothered me now to think she'd attacked me.

The air in the room felt refrigerator-cold again. She wore the same outfit she'd had on when I saw her at the sorority house—mini-skirt, high fringed boots, long red and green paisley tunic. Her hair was loose and ultra-straight. She had her arms crossed and was staring at Max.

I sneaked into my room and closed the door. Retro-girl glanced at me before going back to staring at my ex-boyfriend. She looked annoyed. Well, screw her. What did she have to be annoyed about? She wasn't the one who'd been hit by a big-ass textbook and had her favorite mug broken into a million pieces.

I sat on my bed and glared at her. "Why are you messing up my room?"

"I'm here to talk to Max, not you," she said in a perfectly clear voice.

"Well, la-di-da," I said. "You broke my cup. You hurt me. I don't like it, Retro-girl."

The blonde frowned at me. "My name is Sharon, not Retro-girl."

"Fine. Sharon. Whatever."

"Caroline, stay out of this," Max said.

"It's my room and my stuff. I want to know why she attacked me."

"You weren't talking to Max," she said. "I had to make you."

"That's why you hit me? Couldn't you have just said something? You know, like with words?"

"I didn't think you'd listen. You didn't listen to Fred, so why would you pay any attention to me?"

Max turned his attention to me. "Fred came here?"

"Um...yeah," I said, flushing.

"He wanted her to listen to what you had to say," Sharon told him. "But she refused. I didn't think she'd listen to me and I had to do something. Carter is desperate."

Max sat down on my bed next to me as if his legs had been cut out from beneath him. "Carter."

"He needs to talk to you. He has something to tell you, but he's having trouble getting through. He needs you to reach out from your side."

"Why didn't you tell me this before?" he said. "Why haven't you spoken until now?"

"I was afraid. It takes a great deal of energy to do what I'm doing right now. I'll be weakened for a long time afterward."

"Would an offering help? Max said.

She tipped her head to the side, making her hair hang down like a golden curtain. "Maybe."

"What would you like?"

"Flowers." Sharon smiled. "Lots of flowers."

"Okay. We'll have flowers here for you by tomorrow afternoon."

"Thank you." Her smile turned flirtatious. "You're cute, you know."

He blushed. "Um...thanks."

"I haven't kissed a guy in forty years."

What the hell? She couldn't find a ghostly boyfriend somewhere? Why did she have to go after mine? Except he wasn't mine anymore. I'd thrown him away.

Max dropped his head. "Look, Sharon, you're very pretty, but..."

"Please? Just a little kiss?"

He glanced at me. I had no right to tell him not to do it, so I tried to keep my jealousy off my face. Max turned back to Sharon.

"Okay. Just a little one."

She beamed at him. "Cool."

He muttered something that sounded like "yeah, right."

Sharon walked over to him and bent down. Max lifted his head. I couldn't watch. It pissed me off to even think of him kissing someone else, let alone to watch it happen. Luckily, they didn't make that lip-smacking noise that sometimes goes along with a kiss. If they had, I might have smacked Sharon in her ghostly jaw.

She sighed dreamily. "Thanks. I really like you. I'll never forget you, Max."

His face got redder and redder. "I—uh—"

That was kind of cute, actually. He was so tongue-tied. Self-possessed Max didn't know what to say.

"Get in touch with Carter as soon as you can," Sharon said.

Max's face resumed its normal color. "Do we need to perform the ritual here or can I do it somewhere else?"

"You should be able to do it anywhere," she said. "It would be better at the place where he died, but I guess that isn't possible. Right?"

"It's in Montana and my dad won't talk to me," Max said.

"So it doesn't really matter what place you pick. Just reach out to him." She looked at me. "Sorry I hurt you. I didn't mean to hit you so hard."

I gave her a stiff nod. "Apology accepted."

"Okay. 'Bye for now." And she vanished.

"Wow. Oh, wow," Ivy said. "I can't believe I just saw that."

"When are you going to talk to Carter?" I asked Max.

"I don't know. Tonight, I guess, if I can get some supplies together that quickly."

"Can I watch that one too?" Ivy said.

"No," Max and I said simultaneously.

Her face fell.

"It's too personal," I said. "Max will want privacy. It's not you, Ivy."

"Okay," she said in a small voice.

"Caroline's right," Max said. "Carter was my little brother. I don't think I can handle having anyone I don't know really well there."

"Okay. I get it." She backed toward my door. "Well, I'd better go. Thanks for letting me come into your room and everything."

"No problem," I said. "I'll see you later."

She left and I started picking up the stuff Sharon had tossed around. The coffee mug was a lost cause, but I picked up as many of the pieces as I could find. I needed to borrow the hall vacuum cleaner to get the rest of it.

"I'd like you to come with me," Max said quietly. "When I reach out to Carter."

I stopped in the act of picking up a piece of mug. "I don't know."

"Please."

I sighed. He had come right away to help me, after I'd turned him away in a truly insulting manner. I owed him one. Maybe more than one, now that I thought about it.

"Okay," I said.

He gave me a smile so faint I wasn't sure I really saw it. "Thank you."

"Can we have dinner first? I'm starving. I was about to get food when Retro-girl—I mean, Sharon—started lobbing coffee mugs and textbooks at me."

He nodded. "Sure. What would you like?"

"Pizza?"

"Primo's okay?"

"Yeah, that would be great."

We took his car. It was the height of dinnertime on Saturday and Primo's was packed with mostly students. I felt so strange standing next to Max and waiting to be seated. It was just like we were together again, except different. Because everything had changed and there was this invisible wall between us, a barrier that kept me from reaching out and touching him the way I wanted to.

Max said something to me, but I couldn't hear him over the roar of voices. "What?" I yelled.

He bent near me and I tingled all over. "We might be up really late tonight."

"That's okay."

The hostess came to seat us. She gave us a window booth. Max slid in on one side and after a moment's hesitation, I slid in after him. He looked at me with surprise on his face.

"It's too loud to sit across from each other," I said.

He nodded. "Okay."

She handed us our menus and left. I already knew what I wanted, so I didn't bother to open mine.

"Thank you for helping me today," I said as he scanned his menu.

He gave me a sidelong glance. "You're welcome."

"I wasn't sure you'd be willing."

"Why not?"

"After the way I kicked you out of the dorm? I wouldn't blame you if you never talked to me again."

Max's mouth flattened. "I didn't blame you. What I did to you was wrong. It's my fault we broke up."

"Well, I—I felt bad about it afterward. Actually, I felt bad about it at the time."

"Don't worry about it." He kept his nose in the menu, studying it as if it held the secret of eternal youth or something.

He didn't want to discuss this at the moment. Okay. I could take a hint. I took a sip of my water. This wasn't the best location for an intimate discussion anyway.

"I miss you," he said in a voice so low I almost didn't catch it.

I swallowed. "I miss you, too."

Max set his menu on the table and looked at me. His eyes were desolate. "I'm so sorry I hurt you. I wish I could take it back."

"It's over."

He bent his head. "I know. But I want you to understand that the revenge thing, that was only in the beginning. When I didn't know you. As I started to see what kind of person you were, I dropped the idea of revenge." He looked straight at me. "When we made love, it was real. All of it was real."

Tears were threatening me again. How I wanted to believe him. I nodded without speaking, afraid my voice would break if I tried to talk.

He folded my hand in his. "I still love you. I'll always love you, no matter what happens."

Slowly, my fingers curled around his. "I love you, too."

His eyes widened. "You do?"

"I've been so miserable without you."

He lifted my hand to his lips. "Come back to me, Caro. Please. I'll make it up to you a thousand times, just come back."

Any second now, I was going to cry. "I—"

My denial died before I could verbalize it. The words refused to leave my throat. I closed my eyes and pinched my lips together to keep from crying.

Max took my upper arms and gently urged me against him, and I let him do it. I let him fold his arms around me and kiss the top of my head.

"Don't cry, baby," he murmured.

I didn't want to give in. No, that's not true. I believed that I shouldn't give in. But his body felt so hard and hot against mine, he smelled like pure sex, and resting my face against the familiar soft knit of his navy-blue Henley felt like coming home. I put my arms around his waist and clung to him.

"Say you'll come back," he murmured.

I lifted my head and looked into his eyes. "Yes."

For a moment, he just stared at me as if he couldn't quite believe his ears. Then he took my face in his hands and kissed me in a hot and leisurely union of mouths. Lust overtook me with so much force I moaned against his lips.

He pulled back to cover my face with kisses. "I love you. I need you. If we hadn't already ordered, I'd take you home right now and make love to you."

"I love you, too. But I'm also starving. I don't know if I can summon the dead on an empty stomach."

He laughed. "All right. We'll eat first." His lips traced a path from my chin to my ear. "I'm so glad. So glad you said yes."

When the waitress brought our pizza, we were in the middle of another scorching kiss. She set the food on the table without comment, but I saw her glance over her shoulder at us and smile when she got halfway across the restaurant. Great. We were providing a floor show.

"No-one is paying attention to us," Max said. "They're too busy with their own drama."

"I'm not embarrassed," I said, surprised to find it was true. "I'm proud to be with you."

His eyes took on a soft glow. "Thank you. I'm proud to be with you, too."

We leaned against each other in silence, eating and just basking in each other's presence. I was so happy to be with him again that part of me wanted to laugh out loud with joy. But another part was already thinking about what we had to do later that evening. I was trying to picture how it would work, what would happen. How a ghostly preschooler was going to communicate with us in any meaningful way. Wouldn't he just want us to play with him?

"Max, wasn't Carter only three when he died?" I said, glancing at him in apprehension. I knew he hated talking about his brother.

"Yeah." He took a bite of pizza and I wondered if he did it for the reason I sometimes took big bites of food during a conversation I found uncomfortable—so he wouldn't have to talk while he chewed.

"I don't understand how he's going to have anything meaningful to tell us. I mean, he's just a little kid, right? A ghostly preschooler."

Max swallowed. "People change when they cross over. Sometimes, not always. It's possible that Carter is more mature on the other side than you think. Spirits are eternal and all that."

"Oh. I hadn't thought of it that way."

He put his slice of pizza back on the plate and pushed it across the table. "I'm really not hungry right now."

I shouldn't have said anything. Damn it, now I'd made him nervous again and he needed to eat. He looked so thin and pale it worried me.

"He doesn't blame you," I said.

He slanted a look at me. "Of course he does."

"No. He doesn't. He doesn't blame you because it wasn't your fault."

Max's breath gusted out of him. "Caroline, I appreciate what you're doing, but you don't understand. I fired the shot. It was my fault."

I took him by the arm. "You were a ten year old boy. You didn't know there were bullets in the gun."

He shook his head, refusing to look at me.

"You need to eat. You look awful."

"Gee, thanks."

I kissed his jaw. "I'm only worried about your health."

"If you don't mind, I'd like to wrap up the rest of this and take it home."

I blinked. "Okay. Sure."

I flung my arm in the air and waved it wildly until I attracted the waitress. Max sat and stared moodily at his plate during this exchange. I hoped he wasn't going to back out of contacting Carter, because it seemed like something he needed to do. Not only because of whatever message it was that Carter wanted to convey, but for the sake of his own peace of mind.

Carter would forgive him. He'd probably already forgiven him, but Max didn't believe that and probably never would until he heard it from Carter himself. He would carry the crushing weight of his guilt and shame around for the rest of his life unless he faced his brother.

I slipped my hand into his. "I'll be there with you, no matter what happens."

He said nothing, but his hand tightened around mine.

Chapter 28

Max: I felt hollowed out and empty as I parked my car in the driveway of my house. Beside me, Caroline was quiet. The sun had set. My street was dark, the streetlights blocked by the dense canopies of the big-leaf maples whose bare branches arched over the pavement all along its length.

Caroline and I walked quietly to the front door. Her presence gave me strength to keep moving forward in spite of the dread that had overtaken me in the restaurant. The last goddamn thing I wanted in the whole world was to look into Carter's innocent blue eyes and see hatred reflected back at me. But it was overdue. I owed him much more than an apology; unfortunately, that was all I had to offer.

We put the pizza box on my little kitchen table and Caroline sat down to finish her dinner. I couldn't put a bite in my mouth. The thought of food made me want to puke right now. But I sat with her and stared at the black window glass while she ate her food.

I needed some mugwort to help open the way between this world and the spirit world. I probably still had a little in my herb stash, but I wasn't sure what was in there after the move. It had been a while since I'd done any work with the dead, other than talking to Fred, that is.

I shot a covert glance at Caroline. She seemed so calm, so easy, sitting here with me and eating pizza as if I'd never killed anyone. It always amazed me that she'd have anything to do with me, knowing the terrible thing I'd done. What exactly had Trent told her about that night? He might have lied or exaggerated.

No, make that he definitely lied and exaggerated. She deserved to hear the truth from me, even if it hurt to talk about it.

"I took the gun from a drawer in my dad's desk," I said, still gazing out at the darkness beyond the window. "His office. He usually kept the door locked, but that night it was open for some reason."

"And you tried the door?"

"It...I think it was open. Just partly, a crack. Enough to tell me I could get in there and look at stuff I wasn't supposed to touch."

She made an encouraging sound.

My apartment felt so cold we both still wore our jackets. I hadn't turned the heat on since she'd left me, and the only heat I got was what arose from the apartment downstairs.

"My dad's office was always cold," I said. "He liked to leave the window open all the time, even in the winter."

"Was it winter when you went in there?" Her voice was soft, unobtrusive.

"Yeah," I said. "There was snow all over the ground."

Carter had died in January. I hadn't even observed his death day this year; I'd been too wrapped up in my love affair with Caroline to remember. That was the first time that had happened.

"I took the gun up to my room because I knew I wasn't supposed to have it. I wanted to hide while I played with it. But I didn't shut my door. I don't know why." I looked at Caroline. She was watching me with no expression on her face. "Why wouldn't I shut my door if I wanted to hide?"

"I don't know," she said softly. "You were only ten. Maybe you forgot."

"Yeah. Maybe." I swallowed past what felt like a rock lodged in my throat. "I was pointing the gun, pretending I was aiming it at some bad guys, and Carter ran into my room and I swung around and the—the gun—it just went off."

"What kind of gun was it?"

I didn't understand how she could sound so calm.

"I don't know. A handgun. A pistol. It seemed huge to me, but my hands were small back then. And it was so loud. So fucking loud. I couldn't really hear for a while after it went off. I could see, though. I could see him, and the blood—there was so much blood—all over him—" My voice failed.

I couldn't look at her. I couldn't look at the window, either, because I could see my reflection in it and I didn't want to look at myself. And because it reminded me of that other night, when I pointed a gun at a dark window and then accidentally shot my little brother.

I bent my head and covered my face with my hands. In the resulting darkness, I could see Carter's little body sprawled across my bedroom floor, blood soaking my carpet. His eyes were open. They looked so surprised.

My edges were dissolving. My body started to shake and I didn't know why. I was losing it. Losing control, losing composure, losing sanity. I could feel it crumbling away, like a suit of armor I'd always worn without knowing it. The thing turned to dust and I only understood that I'd had it at all when it crumbled and blew away.

He'd been so small. So damn small. Dead before I could throw down the fucking gun and run to him and put my arms around him and try to hold him.

"He was so small," I said. "And broken. There was blood all over the place. It made the carpet wet and it got on my clothes and my hands because I tried to pick him up. He fell down and I ran to him and he was already dead. I killed my little brother." My voice broke. "I'm so sorry, Carter."

Caroline's hand found its way to my back. She began to stroke me and she didn't say anything and I didn't—really didn't—want to break down and cry. I didn't want her to see me like that.

I took a shaky breath, trying to hold onto my last thread of composure.

Chapter 29

Caroline: Max's apartment was so cold it felt like winter. We'd both kept our jackets on. But as I stroked his back, trying to bring him a little comfort, the air became even icier.

My breath appeared in a little white cloud in front of my face. Max still had his hands over his eyes, so he couldn't see it. He trembled all over, seemingly fighting not to cry, his big body shaking beneath my hand.

He'd been made to bear something too heavy for him. Too heavy for any child. My guilt over Aunt Jo's departure had haunted me, and that was trivial compared to the burden Max had borne for so long. I suddenly wanted to rage at Peter Kincaid for leaving his son alone with his guilt and grief. What kind of father would do that to his child?

If Peter Kincaid had been here in the room, I would have told him exactly what I thought of him. The awful things he'd said about Max when I'd visited the house in Billings...had he ever loved his son? Had anyone ever really loved Max?

"Max."

It was a high-pitched child's voice, and it came from behind us, from the direction of the living room.

Both of us jumped several inches. We turned simultaneously toward the sound. A little boy with tousled blond hair stood in the archway between the kitchen and living room. He wore a pair of jeans and a small sweatshirt with a picture of a truck on it. He was smiling at Max, his round, blue eyes full of happy innocence.

"Carter?" Max said in a rough whisper.

"It's me." Carter came closer. "I've been trying to talk to you for a long time."

"I know." Max's voice broke. "I heard."

"You're not easy to get hold of." He really didn't sound like a three year old.

"Sharon told us to contact you, but we haven't even started the ritual yet," I said. "How can you be here?"

"You were talking about me and thinking about me. It was enough of a connection to let me pass through the veil." He looked from me to Max. "Why did you ignore me for so long?"

"I'm sorry," Max said. "I was...I was afraid, Carter."

The little-boy ghost cocked his head. "Why were you afraid? I'd never hurt you."

"Because of what I did. I didn't think I could stand it, seeing you again and knowing...knowing you'll never forgive me."

Carter frowned. "Of course I forgive you. That's why I came. Because you thought there weren't any bullets in the gun."

"Yeah. But I was wrong."

"Trent told you the gun wasn't loaded," Carter said.

Max stilled, his gaze becoming hazy and far-away. Then he frowned. "Yeah, that's right. I remember that."

"But it was. It was loaded." Carter took another step forward, coming right up to Max. He looked so real, so alive. "It was loaded because he put the bullets in it."

Max and I both stared at him blankly. He stood looking at Max with an expectant expression, but Max just stared, like he couldn't make sense of what Carter had said.

"Are you telling us that Trent loaded the gun?" I said. "That he lied to Max about it not being loaded?"

Carter looked at me soberly. "Yes, that's what I'm telling you. He wanted to hurt Max."

I closed my eyes. "Oh, my God."

"I can't...I don't..." Max said. "Why? I don't understand. Did he want me to shoot you?"

"I don't know," Carter said. "But I saw him put the bullets in the gun. I didn't really know what he was doing or how dangerous it was. Until after. You know. When I got to the other side, it all became clear to me."

Max rubbed his eyes with a trembling hand. I wanted to take him in my arms and make all the pain and confusion disappear, but it wasn't the right time. Not yet.

"I wanted you to know, Max," Carter said. "It wasn't your fault. You didn't know. You were only a kid when it happened and you need to stop blaming yourself. I don't blame you. I never did."

Max covered his face again. His shoulders began to shake and a wheezing sound escaped him. I glanced at Carter, who looked back at me sadly. I put my arms around Max.

"Thank you," I said to the ghost.

"Thank you," he said. "I'm glad you came back to him. He deserves someone to love him."

Now my eyes were stinging. "Yes, he does."

"I loved you, Max," Carter said. "I still do. Please remember that. I don't know if I'll see you again, so I need you to remember that I love you."

A strangled sound came from Max's throat. His face was hidden against my shoulder. I smiled tremulously at Carter.

"He loves you, too," I said hoarsely.

"I know," Carter said. "I have to go now. I'll always remember you, Max."

He winked out, like a snuffed candle flame. I blinked rapidly at the startling sight, but he was gone. We were alone again, and the kitchen was merely chilly instead of arctic-cold.

I kept my arms around Max for a long time, long after he'd stopped sobbing and his body had calmed. He clung to me with a desperation I never thought I'd see in him. I wasn't sure what to say, so I stayed quiet and simply kept petting him, stroking his back and playing with his hair, hoping that touch would give him the comfort he needed.

Maybe he could stop hating himself now. I wouldn't expect him to get over all the blame instantly, but at least he'd had Carter's assurance he was forgiven. I hoped it was enough for him to start over.

He lifted his head. "I'm a fucking mess," he muttered.

"That's all right."

Max reached for a cloth napkin left on the table and used it to wipe his eyes. "Sorry about all this."

"You don't need to apologize. I don't mind."

He couldn't seem to look at me. "I can't understand why not."

"Oh, Max." I caressed the side of his face. He looked so tired. "It's normal to feel sad and cry when someone you love dies. Or comes back from the grave."

His mouth quirked upward at one corner. "Is it?"

"Yes. So don't feel bad about it. Plus, I love you. If you can't cry in front of me, who can you cry in front of?"

He gave me a dry glance. "I'm not going to answer that."

I just smiled at him. After a moment, he took my face in his hands and bent his head to mine. His kiss began with infinite tenderness, an expression of love and gratitude that turned hot and demanding as I wrapped my arms around him. He pulled me against him until I had to straddle him so I could get close enough.

"I need you," he murmured before tugging on my earlobe with his teeth.

"Yes," I whimpered. "Please."

Max grabbed my butt and stood up with me wrapped around him. He carried me that way into the bedroom and sank to the bed.

Chapter 30

Max: **I** must have dozed off after we finished making love. The next thing I knew, someone was pounding on my door so loud I thought they were trying to break it down. Caro lifted her head from my chest and frowned in the general direction of my living room.

"What's going on out there?"

"I dunno," I muttered. "But it's pissing me off."

She sat up and reached for her clothes. "We'd better get dressed."

"You stay here, in case it's something bad. I'll answer." I grabbed my jeans and yanked them on.

"Be careful."

I smiled at her. "It's probably nothing."

The pounding continued as I walked barefoot and shirtless into my living room. Whoever it was needed to chill out. And I couldn't imagine who it could be. I'd paid all my bills, on time and in full, and I didn't have any enemies.

Except Trent.

I opened the door and there he was, glaring at me with more venom than I'd ever seen in his eyes before. He reeked of hard liquor. And my dad was with him.

Seeing my dad after so many years was like taking a baseball bat to my solar plexus. I almost lost the ability to breathe for a second. He looked pretty much the way I remembered, except a little thinner and grayer.

My hand tightened on the edge of the door. "What do you want?"

"I want my woman back."

I snorted. "Your woman? She broke up with you. Move on."

"She only did it because of you."

"Dude, I believe she told you it was over."

Trent growled, lunging toward me. My dad grabbed his arm to prevent him from jumping on me. "She told you it was over, too. But she's back with you now. What the fuck did you do to her, you creepy piece of shit?"

I leaned against the doorjamb and crossed my arms over my chest, knowing my nonchalant pose would drive him insane. "We made up. Did you come all the way here just to hear me say that? And you had to bring Stepdaddy, too, I see." There was no way I was going to acknowledge my father as mine. We'd gone beyond that years and years ago.

"What's going on, Max?" Caroline said softly behind him.

"It's nothing, baby. You don't need to be part of this."

"He's put a spell on you, Caroline," Trent shouted. "You need help."

I laughed. "I thought you didn't believe in magic."

Throughout this whole exchange, my dad had been staring at me like he couldn't believe his eyes. I looked right at him and smirked. "Trent's lucky to have such a supportive stepfather."

"You were always jealous of him," my dad said.

I laughed again. "Jealous. Right."

Caroline inserted herself between me and the space on the other side of the doorjamb. Damn it, she was supposed to stay in the bedroom. I glared at her, but she ignored me.

"I'm not coming back to you," she said to Trent.

"Caroline—" he said.

She pointed at him. "We know what you did."

I stared at her. So did the other two. What the hell was she doing? This wasn't the time for a confrontation, not when Trent was drunk. He might do anything in this state. What if I couldn't protect her from him? After all, there were two of them and only one of me.

I grounded my inner energy, centering myself in case I needed to take action.

Trent shook his head. "I have no idea what you're talking about."

"The bullets," she said. "We know you put them in the gun."

"What gun? I'm telling you, Caroline, he's put some kind of spell on you. You know he's capable of it."

She put her arm around my bare waist in a show of support that made me want to kiss her. "The gun that killed Carter."

He went so pale, his eyes so round, I knew instantly it was true. "No! I'd never do that."

"Carter told us," Caroline said.

"A ghost? Give me a break." Trent gave a painfully artificial laugh.

"Trent, is this true?" my dad said, staring at him.

"No! It's not true...I didn't...I thought Max would play with it by himself."

My dad's eyes narrowed. "You thought he'd play with it by himself? So you did have something to do with the gun being loaded?"

"Yeah. No!" Trent glared at me with an expression of loathing. "You were supposed to shoot yourself, not Carter."

My jaw dropped. My dad's mouth opened, but no sound came out.

Trent's eyes bugged out even further as he realized what he'd said. "That's not what I meant. I just—I didn't understand what I was doing. I was just a kid! I didn't mean anything by it."

"You were trying to kill me," I said softly. "Weren't you?"

He shook his head with an air of utter desperation. "No. I wasn't. I didn't mean for anyone to die. I only wanted you to get hurt."

I snorted again. "You'll forgive me if I have a hard time believing that."

"Trent," my dad said hoarsely. "Why didn't you ever tell me this?"

Trent just stared at him blankly. In his eyes, I could see his world falling apart. He'd always been the good brother, the one I was supposed to emulate. Oops. Guess that position had just been vacated.

"Why are you here, anyway?" I said to my dad.

He glowered at me. "I came for Dad's weekend, obviously."

"Obviously." 'Cause I would know that, seeing as how I had such a great dad and all.

His lip curled in a sneer. "You drove him to it, you know. He wouldn't have wanted you to shoot yourself if you weren't such a complete fucking failure."

My jaw went rigid and so did my spine. "Excuse me?"

Caroline took a step toward him, her eyes narrow with rage. I snagged her waist and tried to pull her back.

"You have no business talking to him that way," she said. "He's your son. What is wrong with you?"

He looked at her like she'd grown a second head. Then he laughed. "I think Trent has it right. He really has put a spell on you."

With her free hand, she made a slashing gesture. "He doesn't need a spell. He's lovable the way he is."

"Caro—" I said, embarrassed. She didn't have to fight for me like this. It—I—wasn't worth it.

"You do know he dabbles in the occult?" my dad continued, contempt in his voice and his eyes, fury in the clenching of his fists. "My *son* is a freak. He was always weird, always making trouble, especially after his mother died."

"He was only five at the time," Caroline said. "How can you say he was always making trouble when he was just a little kid? Didn't it occur to you he was in pain?"

"You know, when you visited us," my dad said, "I thought you were a nice girl. Just right for our Trent. Now I'm looking at you differently, Caroline. I don't like what I see."

"I hope you don't expect me to give a damn," she said.

"Baby, don't bother fighting him," I said, tugging on her waist. "He's not worth it."

She glanced up at me, pain in her big, brown eyes. She was hurting on my behalf. I didn't want that, didn't want her to hurt because of me, but at the same time it warmed me beyond measure that she would continue to stick up for me. Especially to my dad. Grown men were intimidated by him.

I tucked her into my side, her body warm against my bare skin, and faced down my father and stepbrother. "You two need to leave now."

"Not without Caroline," Trent said, swaying where he stood.

"I'm not going anywhere with you," she said. "I'm in love with Max. I love him. Can you get that through your thick skull?"

Trent swallowed hard. "How can you love him and not me?"

"He doesn't make fun of me. He doesn't cheat on me. He doesn't put bullets in a gun hoping his brother will shoot himself. Would you like me to continue?"

Trent's mouth opened and closed over and over, like a fish gasping in the air and begging for someone to throw it back in the water.

"You—" he finally said. "You're a fucking bitch."

"Thank you. Now get out."

I smiled at him. "You heard the lady, Trent. Get out."

Trent broke away from my dad and lunged at me, his beefy hands outstretched for my throat. My fist shot out so fast I didn't realize I was punching him until I'd already clobbered him in the jaw. He staggered to the side, knocking into my dad and forcing him against the wall of the landing. Both of them let out grunts as they hit.

Trent slipped to the floor. My dad bent over him and shook him. "Trent? Are you okay?"

Stepbro's eyes were closed. A huge bruise already spread across his jaw where I'd clocked him.

My dad looked at me. "Jesus. What did you do to him?"

"KO'd him, obviously. You want to fight me too?"

My dad just shook his head. "I didn't know you could do that."

"There's a lot you don't know about me." I'd had endless fights in middle and high school, courtesy of Trent and his buddies and all the people they influenced. And then there was life on the streets. I'd learned, eventually, how to handle myself.

"Always thought of you as a gutless wonder," my dad said.

"Because I wouldn't fight you."

He nodded slowly. "Yeah."

"You were my dad. I couldn't fight you."

My father's gaze traveled over me. "Maybe you're not quite as worthless as I thought."

Caroline was staring at him with an expression I couldn't read. I wasn't sure if she was amazed, horrified, furious...I just couldn't tell.

My dad bent and picked up Trent by his armpits. "Help me get him downstairs, will you?"

I sighed.

"Don't do it," Caroline said. "He doesn't deserve it."

My dad shot her a glare. "Trent was right about you, when he said you were a b—"

"Don't," I snapped. "Don't even say it."

He gave me another one of those looks that said he wasn't sure who I was anymore. "Son—"

"No. You lost the right to call me that years ago. Caroline's right. You can take care of him yourself. If you need help, call an ambulance."

Caroline and I retreated back into the apartment. I shut the door and locked it, throwing the deadbolt for good measure. My hands were shaking and so were hers. She put her hands up to her face.

"Are you okay?" I murmured, bending down in an attempt to see her better.

"Yeah, I'm fine. No. I'm not fine. I can't believe I said those things. I never fight with parents. Never."

I took her into my arms. "You were incredible. A warrior woman."

Caroline gave a shaky laugh against my chest. I could feel her breath gusting warm and damp against my skin. She pressed her lips to the valley between my pecs as her arms came around my waist.

"I'm awfully shaken up for a warrior woman."

"It was your first battle. Everyone's shaken up after their first battle."

She tilted her head up and smiled at me, her eyes glistening. "You know he's full of shit, right? You're not a failure or a freak. You're smart, talented, determined, sexy—"

I put my fingers across her sweet lips. "Yeah, I'm a paragon."

She kissed my fingers. "You are." Her voice was muffled behind my hand.

I laughed. "You only think that because you're infatuated with me. Just wait until you learn the truth."

Caroline shook her head. "No, I'm not infatuated. Maybe I was before, but I know you're not all sweetness and light. Or darkness and spooky sexuality, either. You're you, Max, and you almost used me to hurt your stepbrother."

I hung my head, suddenly ashamed for real. There was a serious possibility I'd spend the rest of my life apologizing for that one stupid fucking mistake.

"Hey, I'm not saying it to make you feel bad," she said. "I just mean I know you're not perfect. I love you anyway. God knows I'm not perfect either."

I scooped her up in my arms. "Yes, you are. In fact, from now on, you shall be known as Caroline the Perfect. Or should it be Caroline the Peerless?"

She giggled. "Caroline the Magnificent."

"I like that." I carried her back into the bedroom. "Caroline the Magnificent."

We collapsed onto the bed together and her fingers found the smooth, raised welt of scar tissue from the time my ribs had been broken. She caressed the mark.

"What's this?"

"Just an old scar. I broke my ribs a long time ago."

"Yeah," she murmured. "I remember that drawing you made."

Ah, that was right. She'd asked me about it after snooping around in my sketchbooks. The truth was, I'd been secretly flattered she was interested enough in me to bother snooping. I stretched out next to her on the bed and looked into her beautiful eyes.

"It doesn't matter anymore," I said. "Doesn't even bother me. It's like it never happened."

"Max." She looked sad all of a sudden. "That can't be true. Nobody gets their ribs broken and then forgets about it."

"Well, I didn't say I'd forgotten."

Her fingers found the mark again and lingered there. "Who did this to you?"

For some reason, I couldn't meet her eyes so I looked down. I could see into the gap of her blouse and the utterly hot view of her cleavage. She had a sprinkling of light-brown freckles across the curves of her breasts and I wished I could kiss them instead of answering her question.

"Max?"

I forced myself to swallow. Closed my eyes. Bent my head to hers and kissed her hair.

"My dad," I whispered.

"Oh, baby." She put her arms around me and drew me close to her.

It was strange. No-one had ever comforted me over this before. I hadn't told anyone what had happened. When my dad had taken me to the emergency room, I'd said I tripped and fell down the stairs. Even Brad and Marie didn't know.

"I think I hate your dad right now," Caroline said.

"He was mad because I'd failed my science class. He started hitting me and...he hits pretty hard. He had this ring, too, a really big one."

"Is it a signet ring with a huge letter "K" on it?"

"Yeah."

"I've seen it. When I went up to Billings for Thanksgiving."

"I think it made his fist extra hard or something. I know it tore up my skin. I think the emergency room people suspected someone had beaten me up, but I wouldn't say anything. I just kept repeating that I'd fallen down the stairs."

"Did he tell you to say that?"

Had he? "I'm not sure. I don't remember that part."

"You know what?" Her arms clamped fiercely around me. "I'm glad you ran away. I'm glad you got away from him. You might have been killed if you'd stayed."

"I know. I thought the same thing."

"I don't understand how he can not love you. How can he love Trent and not you?"

I shook my head against her and forced the words out through the vise that seemed to have clamped around my vocal cords. "My mom died because of me."

"What?" She pulled back, trying to look into my face. "How could that be? You were only five."

"I was playing in the front yard and I ran out into the street. A car was coming. Mom ran after me, tried to grab me. And the car hit her. She died later in the hospital, of internal injuries."

"And he blamed you."

"Yeah." I rolled onto my back and stared at the ceiling. "He blamed me. If I hadn't run into the road—and I knew better; I'd gotten in trouble for it before—she wouldn't have died."

"Max." She propped herself on an elbow. "You were five. You didn't really know any better and how many five year olds have good self-control? It's not your fault that your mom died."

"I know that," I said to the ceiling.

"I don't think you do. I think you blame yourself just like your dad does."

I shook my head. "No. I don't."

She trailed her fingers over my bare chest and belly. "Max, you blamed yourself for Carter. Did you ever stop to wonder why your dad had a handgun in a house with three boys? Even with the door to his office locked, it wasn't safe. He must have had the bullets nearby. If Trent could find the bullets and load the gun, you could have done it too. Maybe even Carter could have done it. What was he thinking?"

"I don't know," I said in a low voice.

"And why was Trent so mean to you? Why did he think it was okay to pick on you all the time? Did your dad set an example for him?"

I turned my head to look at her. She stared back at me with taut lips and troubled eyes. She was ready to go to battle again for me. "Maybe he did. I've never thought of it that way before."

"Because you were too busy blaming yourself for stuff that wasn't your fault at all."

I sighed. "Baby, it was so long ago. I want to let it rest. I want to forget it all. It's been a long goddamn day."

She brushed the hair from my eyes. "It sure has."

"I love you. I want you to move in with me. I want to be with you all the time, forever." The words fell from my mouth, words I'd never spoken to any woman before, and they felt absolutely right.

She smiled at me, her face lighting up as the tension evaporated. "I want that too. I love you, Max."

I bent over her and captured her mouth in a hot, wet merging of our bodies, and we fell into the sweet forgetfulness of the two of us. Forever.

The End

Don't miss these exciting love stories from Tori Minard

Temple Of The Heart, Book 1, Legends Of A Dark Empire
As a vampire in ancient Atlantis, Niko is part of a despised minority and must wear a visible mark to identify his nature. When he pulls Atlantean priestess Laila from a horrific temple fire, he breaks so many taboos they must flee those who will not tolerate contact between his kind and hers. At first frightened of the handsome vampire, Laila can't resist his dark charisma. She will risk any danger to be with Niko. But there is more to the Atlantean pursuit than fear of blood drinkers. A powerful enemy wants Laila dead and will destroy any who aid her.

Bad Company, An Avery's Crossing Novel (Gage and Nova, Book 1)
Gage:
When you owe all your fame and fortune as an actor to a deal with the devil, your self-respect takes a beating. And when the devil threatens to murder anyone close to you, well, you take measures to ensure there aren't any people like that in your life. I've existed this way so long I can't remember anything else. But Nova, the hottest and most infuriating chick I've ever met, makes me want to change. Everything.

Nova:
Getting snowed in with a cocky and demanding Hollywood star basically sucks. Except Gage surprises me. He's more than just a gorgeous face and body, more than an actor and musician, even more than a man I could love. A terrible secret haunts him, and I'm determined to find out what it is.

To sign up for Tori's mailing list: Get news of Tori's new releases before anyone else! http://www.toriminard.com/mailing-list/

About the author

Tori Minard has published fourteen romance and erotic romance novels and three novellas, in addition to a handful of short stories, both under her own name and as Tessa Tremaine. Her series include The Amaki, Legends Of A Dark Empire, Avery's Crossing, Fortunata: The Jhidris Conspiracy, and Tales Of The Demon Kin.

Tori wrote her first story in elementary school, with a lamentable lack of punctuation. In high school, she spent more time writing fiction than doing homework. Her early stories featured demonic dogs, dolls possessed by evil spirits—no, she'd never heard of Chucky—and politically incorrect post-apocalyptic romance.

She discovered science fiction in the sixth grade, with her dad's recommendation of Edgar Rice Burroughs' *At the Earth's Core,* the first book in his Pellucidar series. Prior to that, her reading had included ghost stories, animal stories and adventure tales. Around the same time, she was discovering the joys of erotica by sneaking her mom's books and reading all the naughty bits. Her mom claims to have skipped those parts.

After a long detour for such grown-up pursuits as working boring full-time jobs (State of Alaska, U.S. Postal Service), getting married and having a child, she returned to her first love—storytelling. She was born and raised in Alaska, and now lives in the Pacific Northwest with her husband, son, and micro-dog

Discover other titles by Tori Minard

Tales Of The Demon Kin:
Novellas:
Malefica
Fury Enchained
The Devil You Know
Taken By Storm

Novels:
Lucifer's Castle
Mastered By Love

Short Stories:
Stainless Steel Vampire, story number one in the Skye Donovan series
Love Potion Number Ninety, Skye Donovan story number two
If I Should Die; a Legends Of The Dark Empire story
Price of a Rose, a sexy fairy tale (novelette)
Lemon Drop, a sweet erotic toy possessed by a sex spirit

Amaki Novels:
The Heart Moon
Dragon Moon
Blood Moon

Avery's Crossing Novels:
Rush
Bad Company

Fortunata Novels:
Dirty Magic

Legends Of A Dark Empire Novels:
Temple Of The Heart
Darkness Awakened
Darkness Forbidden
Darkness Beloved
Darkness Embraced

Connect with Tori online
To learn more about Tori, visit her blog at http://www.toriminard.com
Twitter: http://twitter.com/#!/ToriMinard
Facebook: http://www.facebook.com/toriminard.paranormalromance
Pinterest: http://www.pinterest.com/toriminard/

www.ingramcontent.com/pod-product-compliance
Lightning Source LLC
Chambersburg PA
CBHW022135240626
47153CB00007B/2369